# Sha'Daa
# FACETS

CREATED BY:
**MICHAEL H. HANSON**

EDITED BY:
**EDWARD F. MCKEOWN**

FOREWORD BY: **ERIC S. BROWN**
AUTHOR OF THE BIGFOOT WARS SERIES

**MoonDream**
PRESS
AN IMPRINT OF COPPER DOG PUBLISHING, LLC

# The Sha'Daa Series

Sha'Daa: Tales of The Apocalypse

Sha'Daa: Last Call

Sha'Daa: Pawns

Sha'Daa: Facets

# Upcoming Volumes:

Sha'Daa: Inked

Sha'Daa: Toys

# Contents

# Dedication

To CJ Henderson,
writer, friend and mentor to many.
He will be missed.

*—The members of Team Sha'Daa*

# ACKNOWLEDGEMENTS

*No man is an island, entire of itself. — John Donne*


I'd like to take this opportunity to thank the small army of individuals who are responsible for this shared-world series making it into print:

All of the many wonderful and talented authors who have come on board this exciting and ongoing project.

The late **John Manning,** for writing an excellent chapter for this volume before passing away this year.

The late **C.J. Henderson,** who generously spent a good portion of the last year of his life mentoring me in the ways of writing, editing, and running a small press, as well as co-writing the final chapter of this anthology.

**Edward F. McKeown,** Sha'Daa Editor/Co-Writer, whose fierce drive and professionalism have kept this project on track through some very tough times.

Author **Eric S. Brown** for writing the Foreword to *FACETS*.

Author **Leona Wisoker** for proofreading the final galley.

Graphic Artist **Helen Harrison** for creating another one of her awesome Sha'Daa covers.

From the depth of my heart, I thank you all.

*Michael H. Hanson*
*Sha'Daa Creator/Co-Author*
*Piscataway, NJ*
*2015*

by Eric S. Brown

# The Ever Growing Reach of The Sha'Daa

**W**HEN ONE THINKS OF SHARED UNIVERSES, H.P. Lovecraft's Cthulhu Mythos is usually the first that comes to mind. Lovecraft's creation of Great Old Ones and Elder Gods, who were so far above mankind that to merely encounter them tested the limits of human sanity, have spanned across the depths of time and literature since their creation. Lovecraft's Mythos is but one example of this type of fiction. There have been many others, such as the *Thieves' World* books and to an extent, series like *The Fleet*, David Weber's Honorverse with its *Worlds of Honor* anthology series, and even Eric Flint's *Ring of Fire* series, which has expanded outward to include numerous other writers than merely Flint himself. But it is Lovecraft's Mythos that remains the best example of a shared world. Lovecraft openly encouraged others to take his creations and add to his universe, not merely in anthologies but also for full scale novels featuring the timeless entities he wrote of.

Michael H. Hanson's Sha'Daa is similar to Lovecraft's mythos in many ways and is certainly the same sort of shared universe. Since its birth, the world of Sha'Daa has called upon many authors to add to its darkness and charm, and they have been welcomed with open pages and open arms. What began as a simple themed anthology with *Sha'Daa: Tales of The Apocalypse* has now grown into an ongoing series with three sequel anthologies and two more in the planning/development stages.

I have been an outsider to the world of the Sha'Daa, never more a part of it than lending a blurb of praise to that first and now infamous anthology. As such, I have truly been able to watch the universe of Sha'Daa grow into the fan loved series it has become over the years, and grow it has. Never would I have believed, regardless of how well written and edited that first anthology was, that Sha'Daa would capture the audience that its shared-world has.

This latest anthology, *Sha'Daa: Facets*, is again everything a fan of the Sha'Daa series could hope for, further expanding the series reach into the world of popular literature. I look forward to the next two planned anthologies as well and have no doubt that the Sha'Daa will continue to grow and become a force to be reckoned with in the world of speculative fiction.

# TOP SECRET | FBI-EYES ONLY

**DATE: MONDAY, JANUARY 2, 2017**

From: Deputy Director FBI, James B. Comey

To: Barack Obama, President, United States of America

Presidential Transition Concordat #3 (aka the "Charles Bonaparte" Protocol enacted in 1908, Theodore Roosevelt administration) for ongoing compilation and threat assessment of confidential/secret accounts of supernatural, miraculous, occult, and paranormal dangers, hazards, and menaces to the safety and welfare of the people of the United States.

[Ongoing FBI Investigative Report on Project Black Stone]

Classified Documents, Forms, Transcripts, Audio, and Video files have been copied and transferred to digital format, encrypted, and stored on this flash drive, edited and noted, whenever possible, in estimated and/or approximate chronological order.

# The Night Jaunt of F.P. Willenby

by Allison Chrysler Smith

*"All life is only a set of pictures in the brain, among which there is no difference betwixt those born of real things and those born of inward dreamings."*

— *H. P. Lovecraft*

**M**ADNESS, MY MIND SCREAMS. I CAN barely hold this pen in my shaking hand as I struggle to put ink to paper. In the past I have always found transcribing entries into my personal diary a calming and meditative activity at the end of each day. I now feel it to be a lifeline to my very sanity. This fire in my mind, it is a combustion of multiple sensations, damning visions, and dare I say it, an experience beyond the comprehension of the average human mind?

Before we begin I must beg your indulgence. The events of this past evening have branded themselves indelibly into my gray matter. I am in a state of shock and suffering from a hopefully temporary case of the palsy. Hence, my cursive script is not quite up to its legible best.

I have procured a carafe of chilled sherry from my landlady and am already feeling the soporific medicinals seeping into my bloodstream and calming my shaken nerves. Perhaps now I can tell you my story. Please bear with me.

What I find most disturbing, for surely this fact attacks the very foundations of my own sanity, is that these recent events all took place whilst I was figuratively wrapped within the arms of Morpheus.

I gulp down another glass of this fine beverage. Yes, I am aware of how this must all seem to you, my earnest reader. Hallucinatory conditions induced and aggravated by large amounts of alcohol. Please, as a practicing physician I am more than aware of the altered states of consciousness brought about by the ingestion of fermented fruit juice. I ask that you trust me in my own self-assessment of my lucidity as I pen this strange account.

What happened to me last night was no mere dream. It was no hallucination.

And I, Dr. Franklin Pythagoras Willenby, graduate of Harvard Medical School (Class of 1890) and board certified internist for the State of New Jersey, have no history of dementia in either my father's or mother's bloodlines. With this said, let us be about my fantastic tale.

My journey began, simply enough, after a typical day attending my patients at my clinic in Brick, NJ. I took supper at one of my favorite establishments. It was a meal of no import, so you need not trouble yourself on that matter. There was no gastronomic etiology to my coming trek.

As per my usual mid-week itinerary, I took a long stroll on the boardwalk to help temper my digestion. With my walk finished, I spent two hours reading through the day's newspapers in the men's suite of my boarding house. I find the thick oak paneling, red leather furniture, well-stocked bookshelves, and 18th century oil paintings of this lounge most refreshing after a long day of examinations and prescriptions.

Adding to this welcoming environment is the fact that it offered a fine, rich tobacco grown and procured from a small plantation located within this state's cranberry bogs. Over the past few years I have become accustomed to a well-stocked meerschaum pipe when studying the latest physicians' publications.

I finished my reading at 8:15 pm and headed back to my room where I disrobed to commence with my evening toilet. By 9:00 pm I was comfortably ensconced between soft layers of cool white cotton. I closed my eyes and quickly fell asleep.

I break from my tale to take a final drink of the remaining sherry and to tell you once again that my story is not one of mere fabrication. The events I am about to account here are suffused with a detail and tactile nature only associated with factual quantifiable experience. I now resume my account without further interruption.

Terror, sheer unadulterated terror, this was the very first feeling to suffuse my physiology as I awoke. I opened my eyes and found myself looking down upon the surrounding countryside of my rural hometown from an extreme height of at least 300 feet.

"*I'm falling*," I thought in panic, "*but from where?*" There were no mountains, towers, or any object of man-made construction above three stories in this entire county. Was I suspended from some circus balloon's gondola?

I looked all around but could see nothing supporting me. It was at this time I realized I could not even see myself. I could sense my body, sense that I had hands clenching and unclenching, but I could not actually feel my torso and extremities. It was as if I were invisible, with a nervous system that had been rendered insensate.

"*I must be dreaming*," I thought. But it was unlike any previous experience; my mind possessed a keen clarity I could only associate with wakefulness. Never before had any of my somnolent adventures yielded such detail. Perspectives were not skewed, textures were well defined, and I slowly found that my senses of smell and hearing were also functioning at peak capacity.

Whatever had laid its narcotic effect on my body from the neck down did not seem to affect the four sense organs within my skull. Also, though it was clearly night, I found myself able to discern the finest detail in my surroundings, as if the few rays of moonlight in the air had suddenly been promoted to the full radiance of that mighty engine we call the sun.

As a thousand thoughts raced through my mind, I realized that I was moving. I felt the slightest of breezes upon my face, which prompted me to look down. I gasped. The countryside was passing underneath me at an alarming pace. Soon it became a blur.

"*Surely no railway locomotive, clipper ship, or even bird of prey moved at this speed*," I thought.

A never before known joy suddenly filled my heart. Perhaps this was the natural order of the human unconscious, that with age and experience, the timeless experience of dreams become more pronounced and detailed as a reward for the overtaxed mind. Mayhap sleep itself is of an order of complexity that balances a man's cognitive abilities as the years pass us by. Such a wonderful gift to be realized within the middle years of existence!

Within seconds I had left Brick, NJ miles behind me. Based on the relative position of the stars, I reasoned that my heading was roughly west to southwest. I could not tell precisely how long I flew over abandoned dirt roads and endless forest, for I did not have my timepiece on my person. The path of the North Star led me to believe two hours had passed.

The inexplicably aroused incandescence of the Sun's pale sister soon allowed me to see that I was traveling over a veritable sea of sand and pine trees. It suddenly struck my mind that I was now levitating directly above that large desolate corner of my state known as the Pine Barrens.

It was a stark and seemingly uninhabitable wilderness that would surely prove undesirable to even the most avid readers and youthful followers of

Robert Baden-Powell's recently published and alarmingly popular "Scouting For Boys" tome.

In moments I found myself approaching a small, unnatural clearing amidst this skeletal forest. I say unnatural because the sand in this rough circle appeared to emit a faint greenish glow. Recent articles about Madame Marie Curie's experiments with pitchblende rushed through my mind. Something in the way this light wavered led me to believe its luminosity was other than radioactive in origin. Its otherworldly glow felt, somehow, wrong. Without notice the Moon shook itself free of the clouds to shine its full brilliance directly upon this miniature desolation.

I instantly suspected that this gift of soporific night-time adventure might be the face of a far more complex set of events. A deep chill permeated me from within.

The area beneath me flashed into blinding blue incandescence. A great suction occurred and I found myself pushed among torrential winds into the heart of a gigantic, nightmarish tornado. Unconsciousness struck me like a wave.

Time passed in some oddly nonsensical way. Then I was spit back out into the air. It was still nighttime, but a night I think no human eyes had ever seen. The sky above me was a marvel of brilliant green and red stars; stars far brighter than any seen from the surface of Earth.

A powerful rush of exhilaration flooded me, and I wondered for a moment if this was how Philibert Jacques Melotte felt when he discovered Jupiter's satellite Pasiphae earlier this year.

I looked downward and gasped. Spread out beneath me was a vista most terrible and wonderful to behold. I found myself once again moving rapidly through the air and covering great distances in a short amount of time.

I flew over a storm-tossed red ocean teeming with giant, multi-tentacled predators, terrifying creatures that could grapple and engulf a large warship with ease.

At one point I was detected by a monster. It flung a gray-speckled tentacle up out of the red depths, reaching nearly fifty yards! It came within a few feet of me before falling back into the hellish ocean.

A short while later I was speeding over a wondrous and ancient jungle. Huge black monoliths, remnants of an ancient culture long extinct, stubbornly protruded up through lush foliage, barely seen within the thousands of mile-high, cyclopean trees.

And sliding, crawling, leaping, running, and gliding throughout this fantastic alien landscape were thousands of otherworldly animals, creatures which I knew had never walked the Earth.

Then it struck me. Many were intelligent, sentient even. Soon I could see the patina of decadent civilization, for easily a third of these beings were covered in the tanned and patterned hides of the lower life forms.

I left the nightmarish jungle behind me, only to be even more overwhelmed by the endless expanse of blue-green desert dunes. Large, multi-hued arachnid horrors, each one easily the size of a locomotive, warred upon one another in great numbers, spilling lakes of purple and yellow bodily fluids.

As with the jungle earlier, the gargantuan ruins of an ancient and mighty civilization were evident everywhere. Towering black monoliths and cracked crystalline domes dotted the surreal landscape like so many drops of a dying god's ichor.

Soon I reached the foothills of a range of immeasurably high mountains, each one disappearing into the clouds overhead.

My mind's eye opened wide. Beneath me, endless caravans of beasts, creatures, and monstrosities marched forward toward the base of the largest of mountains. This jagged fang of the mountain ridge appeared to be the lodestone for the surrounding multitude of approaching creatures. Living horrors were converging on this place from every direction. Thousands. Hundreds of thousands. Millions. My mind boggled at the sheer numbers. I then became cognizant of the fact that these hordes were the combined armies of this entire planet, and that they were being readied for an all out assault upon the virgin world known as Urath.

For the life of me I could not understand how this knowledge flooded into my mind. Perhaps the height at which I was levitating had placed me within the ether itself, which, acting as some kind of ectoplasmic conduit, had imbued me with prognosticative abilities. I still don't know the answer to this riddle. Suffice it to say that information poured into me as from a waterfall.

As I moved closer to the towering dagger of granite, a mountain I now knew was at least a dozen miles in height, the outline of a glowing green structure came into view.

At the very base of the mountain was an entranceway, a portal fully a mile in circumference. Its limits were clearly defined in dark marble and ebonite. Holding up the mountain overhang above this portal were two massive diamond columns roughly half a mile tall.

Standing at the base of each temple support was a cyclopean demon vaguely humanoid in disposition. I say vaguely because though they were bilateral in symmetry, each one had three Atlas-like arms on either side of their mountainous torsos. Their heads were most horrific of all, not because they displayed unnaturally harsh angles, scar tissue, and horns, but because they wore the brand of intelligence, a hideously diseased and warped intelligence.

The skies themselves split open and a torrential rain fell upon all that approached the mountain.

Without notice I found myself plunging downward directly toward the closer of the two demon bodyguards and felt my consciousness sift into its gigantic skull.

My own mind was suddenly awash with knowledge both arcane and sickening. This demon was Abraxas, a minor sexless deity in its own right, and dark guardian of the mountain's mouth, for such was this portal at the base of the giant peak, a mouth that could swallow armies and regurgitate them whole onto other planes of existence. This entire planet was responsible for the ruin and devastation of hundreds of other worlds.

I heard Abraxas conversing in some dark, unspoken manner with the mountain itself. Yes. The mountain was a living, nameless being, the malignant stationary ruler of this entire dimension. They were planning the disposition of the many armies forming nearby.

Why I was here and how I was able to escape the notice of such godlike beings was beyond me. The unimaginable strain of my journey was taking its toll and I slumped back within my mind to gain some manner of momentary rest.

And so my consciousness resided in the hindbrain of this fantastic beast Abraxas, unnoticed. Hours passed and the first horde of monstrosities approached the portal. I heard Abraxas say that the attack on Urath was now to begin. And then it struck me. It was my own home, Earth, that was to be the destination of this invasion. The beginning of an attack on all that I held dear. This very structure was a theurgic archway to the Earth itself, not unlike the rainbow bridge Bifrost of Norse mythology.

And then one last final thought sliped from the sickening, evil consciousness that was the mountain.

This was not its first attempt to conquer Earth, but the second! Less than two months ago a nearly successful breach in the fabric of reality had occurred above a sparsely populated region of my planet's largest northern land mass.

And the truth of it swelled in my mind.

The rumors and buried newspaper accounts of a bizarre aerial cataclysm that had occurred near the Tunguska River in Russian Siberia. It had purportedly taken place the morning of June 30. Whispers continued to abound that the unexplained explosion felled millions of trees over more than two thousand square kilometers.

Recently invented barographs in Britain had recorded the most unusual of fluctuations in atmospheric pressure the day of the event. Over the next few weeks, night skies over Europe and western Russia glowed brightly enough for people to read by. In the United States, the Smithsonian Astrophysical Observatory and the Mount Wilson Observatory observed a decrease in atmospheric transparency that had lasted for weeks.

I suddenly understood that had this horror occurred over a populated area of Western Eurpe, or England, or one of the great cities of the American East Coast, instead of the sparsely populated Tunguska region, it could have produced a massive loss of human life. Strangest of all, however, was an implied temporal paradox. Though this terrible event had occurred many weeks distant, it had been mere minutes ago within my host's mind. Time seemed to pass much more slowly in this arcane locale.

I knew what I had to do.

Without further thought I thrust my consciousness forward and throughout the mind of the giant who was my co-tenant. Immediately there was great resistance, but I would not desist.

The memory of a recent microscopic study I had done on the sputum one of my tuberculosis patients flashed before me. I took heart. Mimicking the insidious progress of a tubercle bacillus, I invaded the behemoth's mind with the bacterium of my consciousness. The infection that was my psyche spread forward and in moments I was in control. I sensed that this was but a temporary condition and immediately carried out my desperate plan.

A thunderstorm ripped through the heavens above, and the earlier rainfall turned into a hurricane of fierce proportions. Rain fell like bullets, hampering the approaching horde.

Just before the first of the armies reached the mouth of the portal, I raised all six of my massive arms and clutched the closest supporting column roughly. I grimaced. Perspiration ran off me in rivers. Tendons and muscles as long and thick as a battleship's anchor line stretched and tightened all across my massive body.

The mountain itself started shaking in sudden realization of what was to befall it. With a final, extreme effort, I cracked the gigantic support, breaking it off its base. Hundreds of tons of rock rained down all about me. I lunged across the front of the portal towards the other diamond column.

Massive lightning bolts split the sky and struck the sides of the mountain. Thunder deafened me. Rain filled the air, obscuring much of my sight.

My cyclopean brother-in-arms, Typhon, instantly sensed my possession and braced against attack.

Knowing I had but one slim chance to overcome this fearsome monster I rushed forward, awkwardly feinting with my upper two hands. Clutching my leading forearms, Typhon immediately grappled with me. One twist of a massive hand and one of my forearms cracked in twain like a felled redwood tree.

The rainstorm had turned the ground to a treacherous quicksand and we two titans struggled to stay upright.

Another twist and the opposing elbow popped out of its socket. I bellowed in pain. Deep in my mind I could hear the echo of Abraxas's rage. The indignity of this abuse was overwhelming. Typhon smiled and pulled me closer, assuming that with only four working arms out of six, I would soon fall.

I had him.

With a fury born of anger, fear, and desperation, and doing my best to mimic the fighting acumen of earth's heavyweight boxing champion Tommy Burns, I struck Typhon's abdomen repeatedly with my lowest pair of fists, shattering his rib cage in a dozen places.

Typhon, no boxer, quickly found my unfamiliar martial style overwhelming and tried to block his midsection. I immediately laid about his boulder-like head with earthquake-like jabs and punches from my remaining fists. After two right crosses that struck his skull like twin meteors, Typhon toppled lifeless to the ground, his forehead caved in.

The mountain shook in wild fury and several more tons of rock rained down. Two massive boulders struck me upon my shoulders, nearly knocking me off my feet. I struggled to stay upright. My vision quickly grew red and I knew that Abraxas was slowly regaining a foothold in his mind.

A massive bolt of lightning flew downward and struck my left side. Acid pain ripped through me and I released a deafening howl of pain. I stumbled forward in agony, then leaped upon the remaining diamond column and struggled with it mightily. Just as I felt Abraxas flood back into his forebrain the giant column cracked and broke within my arms.

The entire lower outcropping of the mountain collapsed onto and utterly destroyed the portal. Rocky debris buried and crushed Abraxas and I felt my consciousness sink into a heart of darkness. Right before the blackness engulfed my mind, the nameless mountain itself shouted out a parting message.

"Come The Sha'Daa," it said, "the portal will reopen, and my revenge will be merciless."

It seemed but a moment before my eyes opened again. I was lying in my bed. I sat up hurriedly and looked all about myself. My night clothes and bed were drenched. At first I thought it was an excess of perspiration, but quick examination showed my clothing and bed sheets to be soaked with foul, evil-smelling water. Had I sleepwalked and fallen into a puddle, stream, or lake last night?

I looked down. The floor was dry all about me. No wet footprints led to or from my bed!

My eyes then grew wide as I realized I was holding something in my right hand, which I quickly lifted: a large black chunk of crystalline stone!

I stripped out of my wet attire, slid my feet into soft beaver-skin slippers, and wrapped my velvet night robe about my shaking person. A sudden chill seemed to permeate the apartment. I looked out the one window to my domicile to view the waking sun cresting the ocean's horizon.

I cupped a double handful of water from the basin on my night table and splashed it into my face. The effect was unsatisfying.

A sudden panic overtook me and I frantically dug out my diary and pen and fresh ink. I needed to chronicle this just-finished journey as an anchor to my wallowing and drowning mind.

As I raised pen above paper I noticed my writing hand shaking dramatically.

"This will not do." And I quickly went about contacting my landlady to inform her of my needs. The sherry arrived shortly thereafter.

And so I sit here now at the small oak desk in my room, fondling an empty glass in my left hand and penning this disturbing epistle with my right.

This had to have been a dream. Or so I keep telling myself… My rational nature returns to the facts. I was drenched with water, but had left no sign of ever leaving the boarding house. I spend minutes considering the skull-sized chunk of black crystal that I had awoken with in my hand. How could this be? My door remained locked all night, and the window partially braced to prevent anything larger than a squirrel from entering.

Can I make this leap of intuition? That somehow, some way, I actually transported this strange stone between worlds? It sits like a huge spider upon my desktop, perhaps waiting for the unwary fly. I sense it has a purpose... and that I should keep its existence a secret.

I know not what to do or whom to tell. Surely I will be branded a madman if I share this tale with colleague, family, or friend.

If I accept this madness, momentarily embrace this utterly fantastic experience as a fact, than I can only hope that the inevitable repercussions of my actions against the nameless mountain deity, and this strange event called The Sha'Daa, are many years, if not centuries, from occurring.

I struggle as my mind plays with the quandaries it now confronts. What of the impetus of this entire dark adventure, which had flung my consciousness across distances dwarfing even Gugleilmo Marconi's transmission of the first wireless telegraph message across the Atlantic Ocean? What fantastic power or force interceded on mankind's behalf by placing me in the mind of the Gateway Guardian Abraxas at such a crucial moment?

God, you reply?

As an avowed atheist and enthusiastic promoter of the scientific method for many years, I now find myself drawn inexorably to the conclusion that cosmic forces beyond the comprehension and experimentation of mankind do indeed exist. I now know that much of my remaining life will be spent reading and studying translations of the Bible, the Koran, the Torah, and other renowned holy books which have guided mankind throughout the ages. I must explore this concept of faith…

For the moment I have decided to take a brief sojourn from my medical duties and spend time with my widowed childhood friend Sarah Susan Philips. Recent mismanagement of her property and affairs has plunged her family into severe monetary circumstances and her letters reek of despair. In comforting her I hope to take my mind off my recent thaumaturgical journey. I will leave in the morning for her apartment in Providence, Rhode Island. As if Sarah's recent financial difficulties were not harsh enough, her son Howard (my Godson) has suffered a severe nervous breakdown. Perhaps in ministering to both the fine lad and his mother I can come to terms with my own demons… I am back… a series of overwhelming convulsions suffused me for this past half of an hour… a simultaneous bout of laughter and tears. Am I mad, or all too sane?

I end this passage with the hope that mankind has now been allotted the time necessary to end its internecine conflicts and evolve into a civilization which will be more than a match for the horrors threatened not only by the nameless mountain and The Sha'Daa, but also the hundreds, if not thousands, of inimical races which populate the known universe.

May God take mercy on us all.

Franklin Pythagoras Willenby, M.D.

Brick, New Jersey

August 15, 1908

# 1909 WORLD EVENTS

British explorer Ernest Shackleton
finds the magnetic south pole

National Association for the Advancement
of Colored People (NAACP) forms

President Taft inaugurated as 27th U.S. president

Mary Pickford makes her screen debut
at the age of sixteen

Crazed physician self immolates in New Jersey
boarding house. City center destroyed,
eight hundred dead or missing

First Lincoln head pennies minted

Workers start pouring concrete for Panama Canal

Construction of US Navy base at
Pearl Harbor, Hawaii, begins

First Israeli kibbutz founded, Deganya Alef

Ghost ship mysteriously docks at St. Petersburg.
150-man crew all dead. Unknown plague suspected.

# The Commission

## by Arthur Sanchez


My dearest Sofie, I send you these diary pages so that you may understand, and forgive.

**JUNE 1, 1910**
It began with the arrival of Duke Navaro.

"Signore!" he shouted, using that vulgar tone of familiarity many aristocrats mistake for good fellowship. "You must help me." He slammed the front door to my store shut and barred it with his prodigious backside.

I must admit that upon seeing him my first thoughts were not… charitable. The Duke is not a tall man, nor handsome, nor known for his wit. But he is one of my few supporters and for that I must be grateful. The Duke thinks of us as brothers in arms, expatriate Neapolitans, languishing on the fringes of the royal court in St. Petersburg. But a jeweler is nothing more than a talented servant and I know my place. I have learned that lesson.

I guided him into the room and offered him one of the few chairs suitable for a nobleman. My shop once belonged to a cobbler and has the feel of such a rough establishment. It was poorly lit and everything, from the counters to the exposed rafters, is made of the same dark coarse wood. I hate it and would burn it to the ground if I could. I asked what I could do for him and he tells me that he has secured for me an opportunity, a very important opportunity. "Please," I told him, "rest assured I will do all I can to help."

"Good," the Duke said, "because he will be here any second."

As if on cue, a dark shadow crossed my doorstep and tried the locked door. "Quickly," the Duke instructed, "let him in."

I rose from my chair and approached the door. Surprisingly, I was gripped with an intense dread, as if Death himself stood on my doorstep.

I dismissed the thought as a foolish notion spawned by the Duke's erratic behavior. I opened the door to find a holy man (I could tell he was a holy man from his coarse cassock and mad-eyed expression) glowering at me. He had long, unkempt hair and a beard so wild it resembled a bramble bush. Despite the cold, he wore no coat but carried a rough burlap sack over his shoulder. I hesitated. This could not be the important person the Duke had been expecting.

"My dear Rasputin," the Duke called from behind me. "Welcome."

The monk pushed past me and whispered, "Lock the door." If ever there were a voice that could call to you from beyond the grave, it would be his.

The Duke made an attempt at introductions but Rasputin silenced him with an imperious wave of his hand. "Your reputation precedes you," he said, addressing me directly. "Your abilities are well known. I have need of some jewelry, some very special jewelry."

"For a man or a woman?" I asked politely.

"Both," he declared. "I want you to make as many pieces of jewelry as you can from this stone." He patted his bag. "Every shard is to be utilized. Not a single bit can be wasted. You will make these baubles for both men and women, young and old. You will make simple, modest pieces suitable for a maid and large grandiose pieces destined for the head of a household. And you need not limit yourself to just jewelry. Set the stones in anything you find useful. Do you understand?"

I didn't, but that was unimportant. "What stone shall I be cutting?"

In response he opened his sack and brought out a jewelry box, a fair-sized wooden case about twelve inches square. I felt a momentary pang of concern since a country monk with a jewelry box is unusual. If word of this were to reach the police, they would have questions.

But Rasputin read my mind. "Don't be alarmed," he told me. "The box and the stone were given to me by a housemaid, a devout woman, who, knowing my acquaintance with certain noble households, had come to me seeking guidance in finding employment. She was newly returned from America where her former employer had tragically died in a fire. As you can imagine, this left her in a very awkward position—being without references, her opportunities were quite limited. I was able," Rasputin said, with only the hint of a smile, "to exert some influence on her behalf and procure her a position. In gratitude she gave me the stone, which the doctor had bequeathed to her in his will. She thought that I, better than she, would know what to do with it." Then, taking my hand and staring me straight in the eye, he softly said: "Every aspect of this story can be verified but, perhaps, you would care to examine the stone before making any judgments." Intrigued, I signaled that he should open the box.

Inside the box was a stone the likes of which I'd never seen. It was the size and proportions of a man's skull. In fact, my first thoughts were that it was a skull. I could see clearly the depressions for the eye sockets, the nose, and the jaw. The teeth were clearly outlined. It was perfect in every way except that one tooth, a fang actually, had been chipped off.

"What is it?" I wondered aloud.

"A diamond," Rasputin offered, "a black diamond."

I shook my head. "Impossible. No diamond so large has ever been found and black diamonds are of such poor quality they shatter at the slightest touch. This thing has been carved."

But he swore that it was a diamond and of nature's own design. I could not believe it and turned to the Duke for support only to find the man staring fixedly upon the stone, spittle running down the side of his mouth. "Duke!" I cried. But the man neither saw nor heard me. "What's wrong with him?" I asked.

Rasputin stared at me intently, studying my every reaction. "The stone has that effect upon the weak-minded, but men of a stronger character," he stared pointedly at me, "are not so affected. The Duke will be all right. Won't you, my dear Navaro?" The Duke nodded. Rasputin then suggested the Duke step out for a breath of fresh air and the Duke rose and left without uttering a word.

A cold chill swept across my body. "I, I am not sure I want any part of this."

"Any part of what?" the monk asked. "This is a simple commission. Divide the stone and set the pieces. What is so difficult?"

In truth, I did not know.

"For your efforts," he continued, "you will be well compensated, gaining fame for your art, and be acknowledged as one of the greatest jewelers of history."

"That is a lot to be derived from one commission," I joked.

Rasputin did not laugh. Instead he pushed the stone towards me. "And only the beginning. He who possesses this stone will wield great influence in the royal court of Russia and from there, the world."

Again, I felt dread creep into my bones. I placed my hand upon the stone to push it back, but there was a flash of green and suddenly I could see myself standing before the Czar of Russia receiving an appointment as the royal jeweler. The assembled nobility was bedecked with my creations and they all gazed upon me as an equal. This dazzling vision nearly brought me to tears. When I finally looked up, Rasputin was gone and I was alone with the stone.

## JUNE 2, 1910

My dear child, Sofia, found me today, staring at the stone. It was late in the afternoon and I had not heard her enter the shop. She said I was in a stupor and it took several tries to rouse me. I apologized and explained that I was trying to figure out how to cut the stone. Its size and shape made it an unusual challenge.

"Ugh, it's horrible," she said, pointing at the black stone. "Where did it come from?"

I told her all that had transpired. I've come to rely on Sofia's opinion. Though still a young woman, she has a sharp mind and fierce determination. She has been my strength in my exile and I do not know what I will do once she is married.

"Really?" she said, one eyebrow cocked. "A mad monk, fresh from the country, presents you with this oddity and wants you to make jewelry from it? I hope you got half the fee up front."

I had to admit that I hadn't. In fact, I had to admit there had been no discussion of compensation at all.

"Papa!"

I told her not to worry, the Duke had vouched for the man, but that was to no avail. Her opinion of the Duke was lower than mine. Were it not for the fact that she was meeting her fiancé for dinner to plan their trip to America, she probably would have had a great deal to say about it. Instead all she said was: "Cut it up fast and be done with it. I do not like this commission and will be happy when all of this," she indicated the stone, "is gone."

I had to admit that those were my thoughts exactly.

## JUNE 3, 1910

After having locked the door I placed the stone on my workbench. I was determined to begin upon my task without interruptions. With the stone being so large, I needed to split the stone again and again until I had workable pieces. I found a ridge running down along the length of the skull. There appeared to be evidence that someone else had begun scoring the stone along this very line. I could only speculate as to why the man stopped. I placed my chisel along this cleavage line and steeled myself to strike.

I have to admit that the first blow was anemic. A flash of green from some reflected bit of sunlight made me miss my mark. Yet, it was enough to shear the stone in half. Two perfect pieces now lay on my workbench and it was as if two heads now lay there grinning at me. Their cold unblinking eyes stared at me as if I'd murdered them.

## JUNE 5, 1910

A stranger has been watching the shop. At first I thought I was just being paranoid. I have not slept well in days and have been growing increasingly concerned about thieves, but Sofia noticed the man too.

"Papa," she said as she peered out the window, "that man is watching us."

"Come away from the window," I said, as I pulled her back. I then peered out and spotted the man across the street, beneath the awning of a ladies' hat store.

Tall and lanky, he had a short-brimmed hat pulled down over his eyes. It obscured his face but did nothing to hide the wispy blond hair that hung down to his shoulders. He also wore a leather overcoat that reached down below his knees and gave the impression that he'd been traveling for a very long time. He resembled an American cowboy but somehow that didn't seem right. Perhaps he was English? He was definitely not Russian.

As I watched, the man became aware of my observation. He stood up straight, adjusted the fit of his coat, and then crossed the street towards us.

"Quickly," I told Sofia, "lock the door."

Sofia, being the child she is, chose instead to meet the stranger at the door. She opened before the man could even knock. "Yes, how can I help you?"

His voice was surprisingly soft and measured. "I wish to speak to the owner."

"What about?" she demanded.

"About a commission," he answered, "a very important one."

I could tell that Sofia did not like the man. Ice crept into her voice. "I'm sorry. My father has already been engaged and has no time for any new projects."

Now, it was the man who became firm. "I'm not speaking of a NEW project."

I stepped in to intervene. If left to her own devices Sofia would only antagonize him. "Yes, how can I help you?"

The man in the doorway looked past Sofia to me. His face appeared tired and worn, adding to the impression that he'd traveled a great distance.

"May we see some papers of identification?" Sofia demanded.

"Sofia!" I interjected. "That is not how we treat customers."

Sofia grimaced. "This tradesman is not here to buy anything, Papa. And there is something odd about him. I do not trust him."

Despite the insult, the man smiled a dazzling smile marred only by his missing a tooth. Not unusual but somehow oddly inappropriate for his face.

"Your daughter is quite right," he chuckled. "I am not trustworthy. And I never buy. I always trade." He stepped forward.

"I'm sorry," I said, "but I have nothing to trade. I am a very poor jeweler."

The man peered about the room as if my bare shelves and empty cases were not enough evidence of my misfortune. "Not to worry," he answered. "I'm sure we can find something to trade. How do you protect your eyes?"

I did not understand the question.

"Your eyes," he repeated, "how do you protect them? How do you prevent an errant splinter from a gemstone you've just cut from stealing your sight? I have here," he said, reaching into the pocket of his coat, "a pair of glasses designed to protect your vision." He produced a pair of leather goggles with green lens in them. Large and clunky, they appeared to be more suitable to an ironworker than a gem cutter. "Guaranteed to save your sight."

I was about to protest when he unfolded the ear wires and slipped them on my face. He caught me by surprise and the sudden change in perspective gave me an attack of vertigo. I clutched at the wall for support.

"Papa?" Sophia said with concern. "Are you alright?"

I turned to reassure her but my voice caught in my throat. She was radiant. Through the prism of the lenses I saw Sophia as I had always known her, as an angel of grace and beauty. Stunned, I turned only to discover that my shop did not fare as well with this new vision. The bare room spoke of shattered hopes and I could almost see the desperation that clung to the walls. There was a palpable sadness to the place. "These glasses," I said as I turned to the tradesman, "are quite..."

A blur of movement and the glasses were scooped off my face.

"Yes," he said, as he held them before me, "they are. So, what would you trade for them?"

I should have known what he was after but I did not understand the full context of my dilemma. "Well," I said, "I have a few coins."

"I never sell," he corrected me. "I trade. What do you have to trade? A small gemstone," he suggested, "or perhaps the shard of a larger gemstone?"

I suddenly felt like a cornered animal. "I have nothing."

"You can give him a piece of that ugly black rock you have," Sofia offered.

The tradesman's eyes brightened. "Ugly black rock? I like ugly black rocks."

"Sofia," I corrected her, "that is not my stone to trade."

The tradesman was like a hound upon a scent. "Of course, you must respect the rights of your client, but surely he would not miss a shard. I need only a splinter– something the size and shape of a needle, of no practical use to anyone."

"It would be unethical of me to trade in something I do not own." I wanted this tradesman gone. I did not know why, but I just did.

"Tell me," he pressed, "is it not common for the gem cutter to keep the odd pieces of a stone once it has been cut?"

"It depends on the commission," I told him. "I was given specific instructions to use every piece of the stone. I may find a use for a sliver as you have described, however unlikely."

The salesman grinned. "These glasses," he said, holding the goggles up again, "will help you see more clearly the work in front of you. Wouldn't that be a good trade for a tiny sliver of stone? Wouldn't your patron want you to have such a tool?"

Sofia stepped between us. "And why do you want this sliver of stone so badly?"

The salesman retreated a bit before her glare. "I have a use for it."

"Then why not approach the monk yourself and offer HIM the trade?" The salesman was about to protest, but Sofia wasn't having it. "Oh, please, you're not a very good actor. It's obvious you know all about the stone. I'd wager you know more about than we do. Well, for all I care, you can have the entire ugly rock. It isn't fit for sandpaper let alone pendants. And my father, despite what you might have heard, is a man of honor. He won't..."

"I'll trade you." I have no idea what made me say it.

"You will?" He made no attempt to hide his surprise.

"Yes. I don't know why, but I suspect that I will need your glasses."

For a moment the salesman stood there staring at me, as if uncertain whether or not to believe me. Then, he extended his hand and offered the glasses to me. "It takes fortitude to resist the stone. I can see why Rasputin chose you."

I did not understand him and part of me did not want to understand him. "Rasputin chose me because I am inexpensive," I answered, trying to redirect the conversation. I took the glasses and then went behind the counter and brought out the box. I opened it quickly and peered at the growing mound of cut gemstones. They were ugly but they were also rare and precious. I felt a twinge of guilt parting with any of them. The salesman, I decided, was definitely getting the better of the deal. As my mind argued my decision, my hand reached out and began to sift through the stones. I retrieved a splinter three inches long and barely thicker than a piece of straw. It had broken off after I'd made my second or third cut and I'd toyed with the idea of making it the base of a stickpin. Only, I didn't know if it would be strong enough for such use and had put it aside. I held it out to the salesman.

He smiled and then produced a silk handkerchief, unfolded it, and held the square of material out to me. I placed the shard in the center of the handkerchief. With the same speed that he'd snatched the glasses off my face, he folded up the handkerchief and placed it in his pocket. "Thank you," he said softly.

"What is it?" Sofia demanded. For a brief moment we'd forgotten she was with us. "This stone, you know what it is. Where did it come from? Don't pretend that you don't. What value does it really have? What power?" Those were the questions I should have been asking.

The salesman hesitated. Then, in the unrelenting heat of Sofia's stare, he conceded. "The stone has no value. It's an ugly piece of rock from an even uglier place. Its power?" He shrugged. "Like most things it only has the power you give it. A strong..." he stared at Sofia for a moment, "woman gives it nothing. A flawed man," he said, graciously avoiding my eyes, "gives it an opportunity. And a weak man," the Duke immediately came to mind, "gives it his soul." Then he had the door open and he was standing on the doorstep. He turned to face me one last time. "I'm sorry," he said.

"For what?" I asked.

"For what's to come," he replied. "But I think Rasputin has underestimated your strength." He looked at Sofia. "In fact, I'm certain of it." Then he was gone. Like a shadow at twilight he stepped out into the street and faded into the darkness.

## JUNE 15, 1910

The Salesman was right. With these new glasses I have been able to double my production time. I have made dozens of trinkets, some of them quite good. It pains me to use cheap settings but doing so has freed me to focus on subdividing the stone. That is what truly matters, making the most of the stone. To date I have set gems in:

A music box. (really quite pretty.)

A gentleman's gold pocket watch. (a good use of the smaller pieces.)

A gentleman's cigar humidor. (a special request from Rasputin. Odd, since he did not strike me as a smoker.)

A tiara.

The handle of one dagger-shaped key (also a special request from Rasputin. The key part is blank. Presumably a locksmith will carve it to fit the appropriate, if giant, lock.)

A gentleman's walking stick with hidden rapier.

A diamond Set comprising of earrings, necklace, and tiara. (my crowning achievement, fit for the Tsarina.)

And a host of necklaces, bracelets, rings, earrings, brooches, tie-pins, cufflinks and ankle bracelets.

My fingers ache from the work.

## JUNE 16, 1910

Today Rasputin angered me nearly to the point of murder. He came to claim whatever pieces I'd completed. I told him that he was welcome to take many of the smaller pieces but I had work to do yet on the larger, more impressive gems. He did not care and demanded them all. He said that he intended to give them to that pretender Peter Carl Fabergé. I was dumbstruck. "Not for one of those god-awful eggs," I cried.

Rasputin took an evil pleasure in my reaction and responded: "More than one, I hope."

I could have killed him. I could have picked up one of my hammers and brained him. He must have sensed my rage for he swept up what was on hand and departed without another word. The wonder is that I could have done it. I could have killed him. And for what? A few pieces of crystal? I must be losing my mind.

## JUNE 20, 1910

Given our last encounter Rasputin has taken to sending Duke Navaro to check my progress. The pompous fool now acts as if he is Rasputin's trusted advisor and not simply a messenger boy. The man disgusts me. I share this opinion with Sophia and she suggests that I quit this ridiculous commission and join her and Peter on their honeymoon trip to America. San Francisco, she assures me, is a civilized city with the wealth to support talented artisans. I challenge her assertions by telling her that I happen to know that Peter has been teaching her to shoot pistols in preparation for their "civilized" trip. She laughs this off and assures me that in America ALL women carry guns and know how to shoot. In America women are considered equals. I have my doubts regarding these modern women but I turn her down for reasons of my own. I have fled far enough from those who would control my destiny. With these stones I will be able to control my own destiny. I know they work. I have seen their influence. I may yet achieve the success I so crave.

## AUGUST 30, 1910

I have seen the face of evil and it belongs to Rasputin.

After weeks of absence the monk has returned. Only, he did not return alone. I was working and about to make a difficult cut when I heard the door to the shop open. It surprised me since I'd taken to locking the door and could swear that I'd done so today. I was wearing my goggles and, startled, looked up quickly to see a young boy entering the shop. He was no older than eight, pale-skinned, and thin-lipped. He looked like a schoolchild on a field trip. He walked primly on the balls of his feet as if afraid to make an impression on the world by letting his heels dig in. I was about to speak to him when from behind him rose a dark and menacing cloud. A roiling mass of darkness, it was completely black except for where it was shot through with tongues of fire and brief flashes of lightning. Like a demon from Hell it rose up to consume the boy.

I tore off my goggles and prepared to scream a warning only to find myself confronted not by a boy and a demon but by a young man and Rasputin. I was speechless. My mind went numb. For several seconds I did not hear a single word that was spoken to me and it wasn't until Rasputin shook me by the shoulder that I regained my senses.

Rasputin, ignoring my distress, introduced me to his companion. The young man was an attaché to the French Ambassador and an amateur naturalist. Rasputin had told him of the diamond and he much desired to see it. Rasputin then asked me to produce some of my work. Still dazed from my vision I complied by handing Rasputin the box. The monk opened it with a flourish and presented it to the man.

The change was instantaneous. In the first minute, an innocent fool of a man stood before me. He knew nothing of the world's dangers. He trusted in Rasputin as a guide and spiritual friend. In the next minute, a rapacious glee came over him as he reached out and grasped an ugly pinky ring as if it were a crown jewel. Rasputin stood at the man's elbow and stared at him with an intensity I'd never seen in any other living soul. He seemed prepared to devour the man. Then he noticed me standing there and an angry shadow crossed his face for having been so transparent. "Out," he commanded. "Leave us."

I opened my mouth to protest but no words came. A servant does not talk back to his master and despite all my grand illusions I knew my place. Ashamed, I turned and headed for the street. From behind me I heard Rasputin whisper softly to the man that this was the first of many gifts, that an *ambassador* would naturally receive many gifts. All that was required was a sign of good faith, an indication that he was one of us.

Not another word was spoken until I had stepped out into the darkness. But as soon as I crossed the threshold they dismissed me from their thoughts. So confident were they of their dominion that they never noticed me, standing there beyond the half-closed door, watching through a narrow gap. That is when I saw the young man turn and hand Rasputin his briefcase. It had the seal of France and even an uneducated clod such as myself knew that this was a violation of both oath and honor. But the moment of purest horror came after Rasputin tucked the briefcase beneath his arm and said: "Now, all that is needed is for the ambassador to vacate his position. I think a riding accident will do." And the attaché nodded his head! By all that is holy, he nodded his head!

## SEPTEMBER 1, 1910

Today I took it upon myself to learn the identities of Rasputin's victims. Yes, I call them victims for though they might be fools, I could not believe that they were evil. Surprisingly, it was quite easy to learn their names. Duke Navaro took great pride in revealing how far Rasputin's hand reached. He named members of the clergy, the nobility, and the government. I went out and attempted to warn several of them of the danger they were in, but to no avail. Once they learned who I was, they turned aside my warnings in favor of securing pieces of the black diamond for themselves. It seems there are many whom, given the opportunity, would take the devil's place.

Did I say I viewed them as victims? Can a man be a victim if he, with eyes wide open, marches willingly into the abyss? I am forced to examine my own countenance in this mirror and I am dismayed at what I see.

## SEPTEMBER 4, 1910

Rasputin was livid. He appeared at my shop frothing at the mouth and speaking such curses that I would dare not write them down here. He was not angry that I had attempted to warn off his dupes, but rather that I had revealed my existence. He demanded that I return what was left of the stone. I refused. He charged me like a wild animal, his hands clawing at my throat. I'd prepared for such a possibility. Having learned the true nature of the man, I had hidden on my person a long delicate knife with a blade as thin and as sharp as a razor. My intent was to ward off any such attacks.

To my amazement, the sight of the blade did not deter him. He charged me as if I held a feather and in my panic I drove the knife into his chest. I heard him grunt in surprise as the knife pierced his heart and as he stepped back I was horrified to see the handle protruding from his chest. Like an obscene metronome it quivered with the beating of his heart as it kept time with the last moments of his life.

But Rasputin did not die. In fact, he did not even bleed. Despite the mortal injury I'd inflicted upon him he simply reared back his head and laughed. "Fool!" he called me. "Did you think me unprotected?" With his great hands he tore open his cassock to reveal, not only the knife protruding from his chest, but a black stone, shaped like a fang, hanging around his neck.

It glowed with an unholy light and was without question the piece that had been missing when I received the stone.

"A weak man surrenders his soul to it," he declared, oblivious to my dismay. "A firm man can direct its influence. But a strong man, a strong man can command its power!" He roared with laughter again.

All I could think was: and what does a madman gain?

At that moment, as I was convinced all was lost, Sofia entered the shop. She was dressed for the theater and was in mid-conversation with her fiancé Peter when she came upon us. She stared at the scene before her and her eyes went wide with surprise. Rasputin glowered at them and to their credit neither faltered. Instead, both of them drew out their guns. I had no idea they now traveled so armed. Rasputin, faced with such an arsenal and with my knife still planted firmly in his chest, dove past them and out the open door. His howls of frustration filled the night air.

## SEPTEMBER 6, 1910

*My dearest child, it is with the greatest regret that I now leave you this burden. I know your mind must be filled with confusion but understand that this was necessary. Despite your entreaties that I join you in America and escape the madman, I know that to be impossible. So long as I have the second half of the skull, Rasputin will hunt me and I cannot let him gain possession of what's left. He can already cause incalculable harm. What would he do with twice the power? And I cannot keep the stone for I am not strong enough to resist its evil. In time I would become like Rasputin. There is only one solution, I must give the stone to one whose will cannot be corrupted. I must give it to one who cannot be found.*

*I know I told you that I would meet you on the ship. Forgive me. I lied. I can only pray that when you receive this package that you will be far from the coming insanity. I fear for the world, Sofia. I fear for humanity. But most of all I fear for you. Do not come back for me. I will be gone before you do. I will be cleansed of my sins by fire and Rasputin will learn nothing of you or of your new life. All I ask is that you keep the stone hidden. Do not speak of it. Do not contemplate it. It must be hidden from the world. Perhaps in time it will be forgotten. And if not forgotten, may God have mercy on those who will be called to fight its evil. For this evil must be fought. Of that I am certain.*

# 1918 WORLD EVENTS

**TARZAN OF THE APES premieres
at Broadway Theater**

**Collier USS Cyclops disappears in Bermuda Triangle**

**German ace Manfred von Richthofen, known as
THE RED BARON, is shot down and killed over
Vaux-sur-Somme in France**

**Thousands succumb to Spanish flu epidemic**

**Sgt Alvin York single-handedly kills 25,
captures 132 Germans**

**Robert Ripley begins BELIEVE IT OR NOT column
(NY Globe)**

**Russian Imperial Romanov family executed
by Ural Soviet. Bolsheviks loot jewelry hidden
in women's dresses**

# The Redeemed

## by Edward F. McKeown

**THE STAR—LONDON, U.K.**
Friday, June 18, 1920

Evening Edition

Personal Ads

Lazarus Club Membership:

Most urgent: emergency meeting at 8:00 PM, Monday night. Attend only if you have not found a reason to remain in this world and still believe in the cause. Otherwise, keep to your homes and loved ones, and God bless you. If you are among the faithful, prepare to voyage far and hard, with no prospect of return. Sell all of your personal belongings for gold and silver coinage and rendezvous as indicated. The time we have longed for has arrived. Bring weapons.

**LAZARUS CLUB NIGHTBOOK AND OFFICIAL RECORD**
8:00 PM, Monday, June 21, 1920

J.Q. Higgins II, Club Scribe

Pre-meeting civilities composed as the norm. Cognac and Cuban cigars were shared by the membership in the public dayroom. The fireplace was lit as an unusual chill had settled upon London this evening.

I bade my club brethren both a "good resurrection," pressing right palms in the sacred handshake, before our steward escorted the three of us into the club's oak wood, stone, and leather inner sanctum.

Upon the hour and the striking of the chimes, the membership sat before the small ebony podium with its curtained recesses. A rainy London sky showed through the green-tinted octagonal skylight. Fresh brandy was taken by all, at which time the steward locked the doors from outside, sealing us within until meeting's adjournment.

*Attending: Fifty-four gentlemen of war and fortune.

*Nightwatch Notes: A collection of five hundred pounds sterling taken for future expedition to find and retrieve the remains of Lt. John Kipling, lost in the Battle of Loos in 1915.

*Meteorological Notes: At meeting's start the external temperature was an unusual ten degrees Celsius with a barometric pressure of 850 millibars.

*Club Treasury Notes: accepted donations of William Wallace dagger, Alexander Hamilton's dueling pistol, and an American M1918 Browning Automatic Rifle, all to be stored in the club vaults.

*Previous Meeting's Minutes: Cop-canned for later review.

Club President Matthew McQuinn walked briskly from behind the curtain, trailed by a tall, lean stranger dressed in worn clothing, tan boots, and believe it or not, a long, dull-yellow duster jacket and a ten gallon American Stetson hat. I wondered if this circus cowboy with his thick, ebon hair and well-shaved face was an entertainment for the evening. All eyes went back to McQuinn, who placed his large hands upon the African blackwood lectern.

Calling the meeting to order, McQuinn spoke earnestly.

[Noted for the record and remarked on by several that McQuinn hadn't been this visibly excited at Passchendaele.] All eyes rested upon the saturnine buckaroo standing in the shadows behind him. The odd Yank sensed this Scribe's regard, caught my eye, and favored me with a chilly smile, revealing a small gap where his left lateral incisor once was in an otherwise perfect set of teeth.

McQuinn pronounced the most extraordinary news, composing himself with an effort. He displayed a letter brought from the depths of Africa by the tall gentleman behind him, whose dark eyes gleamed as they tracked across the room. We were told the letter was from our good friend and Christian gentleman, Hans Seyderlitz.

Major Dougherty quickly reminded us of our colleague's nickname, Hans the Bear, and that we should thank God that all of the Kaiser's men weren't like him, as we would have lost the bloody war.

This generated a laugh. Hans is a six foot six inch giant with arms bigger than most men's legs, and ferocious blue eyes.

McQuinn demanded we quickly compose ourselves. He spoke of how we were bonded in that terrible brotherhood borne of Great War and its suffering. Each of us is the survivor of some event which should have taken our lives: the shell that landed in one's trench, but did not explode, the machine gun that chattered, taking all but one of us, the gas that a provident wind swept away.

McQuinn continued, telling us that we were spared for some purpose, redeemed from death to serve humanity in some cause, that we had been so altered by the Great War we could not fit back into the world. And so, many of us had journeyed seeking the metaphorical grail for our second lives. The room fell silent.

McQuinn then said the grail had been found. He raised a thick sheaf of paper and told us the letter from Hans was a clarion call to such action as we have longed and prepared for. We were to take up our brandies as he read this dread correspondence and he charged us not to interrupt until he came to the end of this amazing letter. He swore every word of this letter to be the absolute and dire truth and that God should strike him dead if he be a liar. Afterwards, those of us intent on fulfilling our sworn purpose were to repair to the RMS Albion and immediately embark on a deadly adventure.

## THURSDAY, JUNE 17, 1920
Personal Communiqué

In care of Matthew McQuinn, Acting President

Hans Seyderlitz to the attention of The Lazarus Club

My faithful and fellow Lazarans:

That this letter reaches you at all is the first of many miracles I must relate to you. The tale that follows will defy your understanding my brothers, but every word is true. I swear this on my honor and those of you who know me well, know that I do not do so lightly.

When I left you last, it was for an expedition down the Nile into Central Africa to rescue the American reporter Samuel Woods. Alas, the poor fellow is beyond any help now, done in by the slavers he sought to destroy with his reporting.

With this failure I planned to make my way to the land of the Maasai and the home of Dr. Kempler, that fine gentleman missionary and my childhood divinity teacher. I spent a joyful time at his mission, making friends among the Maasai and participating in their hunts with my trusty Gewehr 98.

It came to pass one day that I gave my old Solingen hunting knife to a young Maasai, named Masigonde, who spied a lion stalking me in the underbrush and flung his spear at it, buying me the time to dispatch it with my Gewehr. The knife was a small reward for saving my life, but he would have no more, insisting it was nothing more than he would have done for any fellow warrior, but he was delighted with the knife.

The bush is no place for a man to be without a knife and I recalled that the day I left England and your fine company, a package arrived for me from my homeland. A cousin had sent me a dagger, said to be of the Romanoff family, distant relations of mine, to get it away from the damned Bolsheviks. The letter even said it was reputed to have been used to slay the mad monk Rasputin.

As I was leaving that day, I added the dagger to my kit. It was a serviceable weapon I thought, with fifteen inches of broad blade atop a haft in the shape of a key; the cross hilt was also in the form of keys. The dagger was set with black stones that had an oily look to them but were smooth and dry to the touch. I had not thought about the weapon from the date of my sailing, but now looked for it in the bottom of my trunk, believing it would do until I found a proper hunting knife

And so for the first time since I set out, I belted on the dagger, my Mauser C96 pistol and stepped out into the African moonlight, for that night I was restless and moody. I decided to go for a walk alone; as long as I was armed and near the village I felt I should be safe.

Truth be told, my friends, I was lonely. My Maria was gone these last five years, taken by the Spanish Flu; as with all of us I had lost so much and so many to the Great War.

The full moon was as bright as lamplight to my eyes. I wandered to the edge of the village at the limit of the campfires, passing Masigonde and three late-returning hunters. They supported a limping fellow between them, accounting for their untimely return. They did not seem to need my help and because of my mood, I did not stop. They nodded as they passed me, each man almost my own height though I was as broad as any two of them.

I drew out my pipe and lit a smoke. The Maasai always said the smell of it would keep any night-hunter away, so I was condemned to smoke by myself and far from their huts.

I soon found myself at a small hillock north of the village. The veldt was all about me and I could see the mud huts of the village and the white walls of the church dimly lit by firelight. I turned away from these few signs of civilization and stared up at the sky.

It was then that I saw her atop the hill. At first I wondered if I had walked into a dream as I gazed up at the shape of a young woman. She was no Maasai girl; there was something of the look of ancient Egypt about her. She wore a dress wrapped around her slender hips and a brief vest that showed she was not a girl-child for all her diminutive size. Her arms and throat were bedecked with jeweled bracelets and necklaces. More gems and precious metals winked from her hair. She seemed a princess from some fantastic land, to my eyes.

I found that I could see the stars through the slender, elegant body and the moonlight streamed through her. I said nothing, feeling that she must be a phantasm of my loneliness. I was content to gaze on her lovely visage with its huge eyes, sooty lashes and delicate features. It struck me as odd that I would dream of her, who looked like no woman I had ever known.

She beheld me a moment later and alarm overtook her features. She turned on her sandaled heel as if to flee.

I called out, foolishly in German, telling her not to be afraid. She stopped, and replying in the same language asked me what new torment was this?

Now I knew I that I dreamt, or had fallen mad. I asked her how it was that she understood German, and if Father Kempler had taught her. She demanded to know my identity and strangely enough, referred to me as an apparition. She said that I spoke her language, but that my mouth did not move with the words she heard.

I realized that this was true. For though I heard her voice with its high, sweet sound in German, her lips did not move to form the harsh guttural sounds of my native tongue.

I raised and spread my hands, telling the lady I did not know, and that we seemed to hear each other well for all that she was merely a gossamer image to me. It must be that we both dreamed and spoke the language of dreams. I laughed and said it was a pleasant form of madness.

She smiled hesitantly and told me her prison here was so grim that perhaps she had conjured up a ghost to keep her company.

I slowly walked closer and asked what prison she spoke of?

It was her turn to laugh, but there was a wild bitterness to it. She called me the phantom of her mind and that I must know she is abandoned and condemned here, a sacrifice to be made by demons and their minions who planned to invade the ancient lands her people were stolen from.

I asked her if she was a ghost then, in the land of the dead?

She stamped her foot and called me an imbecile phantom, adding that she was not the ghost, I was. She said she could see right through me to the bars and cold stone walls of her fortress prison in the Mountains of Shadarra.

I told the lady there was no prison here, no mountains, that we stood on the veldt; the little hillock that placed her above me, wouldn't merit the name *mountain* in Prussia. I said there was but a small village and one church in all sight in this sea of grass.

She protested we were in mountains and a fortress of goblins who rule over the people of the Nile.

We stared at one another. I said I was Hans Seyderlitz, of a noble Prussian house, late of the Kaiser's army, the 1st Guards Dragoons.

She replied that some of what I said was merely harsh sound, but she gathered that I was noble and a warrior. I had the look of it, that indeed no two men she had ever seen were so formidable. She repeated my name, calling me Major Hans.

I told her that Major was my rank in a defeated army and that a lady might call me Hans.

She thanked me with a shaky voice, adding that she thought her loneliness and fear had made her insane and that she spoke to the night air.

I told her that I too walked lonely in the night. My pipe had gone cold and I knocked the ashes from it and placed it in my vest. I told her that maybe I shared her madness, for I saw the stars through her body. But if this was a dream, or even if it be madness, I did not wish to wake from it. She was a dream of such loveliness as this sorry world seldom sees.

I reminded her of my earlier question.

She replied, proudly, that she was Narapok Shajeel, princess of the Ephraim. Hers were a people in the land of Egypt before her tribe was captured in the southern lands they had fled to. The goblins and the Shadalka, humans in their service, herded them through the Great Gate. For thousands of years they have labored in service of evil. Her people became a forlorn shadow of what they once were, now cringing and fearful.

I asked how she had come to her doleful fate as a prisoner.

She sighed and said it was by her own hand. Her father had raised her brother to be a warrior and a general, teaching him ancient secrets passed down from the old days. Her people prayed that he could lead a rebellion against their masters. She said a time of sacrifice was coming and one of the royal line is to be slaughtered in it. She'd offered herself in her brother's place as she could not lead her people in the coming war. Her brother must survive to do so, and in this way she could strike a blow for her people, preserving her brother's life at the cost of her own. Narapok said she wished she could but take her own life and avoid the vile, unspeakable manner of death they had planned for her, but there was not even that mercy. If she were not taken and devoured at the feast alive, the evil ones would again seek her brother.

A growl escaped me and my hand tightened on my dagger, much as it does this very moment upon this damned pen 'pon which my fingers now cramp so desperately.

Oh, my friends but it drove me to black rage to contemplate this brave princess' fate. My teeth ground in my head. But as I gripped the blade it seemed to me that I saw her more clearly. I walked close and looked into the angelic face as she struggled not to cry.

She raised her head and said she was not afraid, that she chose her fate to save her family and her people.

I told her that I would be afraid if I was a prisoner alone in the hands of enemies that knew neither God nor Mercy. Narapok asked if I was speaking truly. I nodded. Moved by her courage and her unshed tears, I said only fools and the insane do not know fear, that the hot breath of war had scourged my world for four long years and spoke of how I'd seen a whole generation fed to the furnace of war to satisfy the vanity of Kings, Queens, and Emperors. In those terrible years I saw Death itself, triumphant, walking about the world laying waste to women, children and cities and indeed to the very hope of man that rationality held any sway in our lives.

These words seemed to affect her as she drew closer to me.

I told Narapok I had known the fear an ant feels as an elephant rages above it, and had seen every form of Death. My hand, of its own accord, rose to the gorget that had ridden below my throat from the day my father gave it to me, so many years ago.

She asked me what this device was, and placed her hand on mine. Her touch felt like the wing of a butterfly.

I told her the gorget was an heirloom of my family, old when it was given to them by Queen Charlotte for their service to her. It was also the only reason I still lived. I had been stunned by a nearby explosion in battle. A poilu had seen that my eyes were open and struck down with his bayonet, which fractured on the gorget and a moment later a random bullet took him.

Narapok and I talked for hours as the moon tracked across the sky. I learned the history of her people and their miserable demon-ruled world.

Then she turned away from me as fear struck her face, whispering that one came, the goblin priest whose desires she had refused. She cried that he had come to inflict himself on her again.

I saw a shadow, a foul, ape-like shape on the other side of the hillock. This was too much for me and as she backed away in disgust and fear I threw myself upon it and my hands which have broken an ox's neck in my homeland, smote only air, causing me to fall and roll down the hillock. Then the shadow passed me and was on her, tearing at her body and clothes.

I roared, drawing the Romanoff dagger, and raced upward. My brothers, let no man tell you that God does not hear the prayers of his soldiers. For though my hands could not rend or crush the beast seeking to violate her, the dagger struck the shadowy form, meeting resistance and I felt hot blood on my hands. With the dagger in my hand, it seemed I could clutch my barely seen foe and I struck as I have never struck. I shoved the beast backward and suddenly it fell and disappeared.

Narapok cried out that I had flung the vile creature from the parapet. She raced into my arms, and great joy, I could feel her slight body. The gossamer touch of her lips and hands were on my face and I moved not, lest I somehow injure this tiny ethereal creature.

After a second she looked down at the curiously unstained dagger. I looked at my hands for though I had felt the enemy's life-blood on them I could not see it. Narapok said that she could see the dagger clearly and that it was the Key dagger! She said this dagger carried the black stones that open the gate, and asked me how I came by the weapon.

I told her it mattered not and asked if she was in danger, and if there were other enemies about?

Narapok shook her head and said his mission of rape was to be a secret; that the demons would not want her despoiled before their feast. She said he did not cry out, that my second blow all but severed his skull from his shoulders, and he was probably dead from that moment.

I growled with joy and asked this sweet princess if she could take the dagger, and let it be a weapon for her defense.

She reached for it but her hands could not close on the weapon. Narapok believed she could feel me because I held the weapon. She said that it is of her world, but in mine, and must serve as the bridge between.

I asked her where was this gate between our worlds, the one that her people were brought through.

She nodded quickly, her gold-bound hair bobbing and shimmering in the moonlight. She said that the legend placed it in a cave at the foot of a mountain in my world. The exit lay but a day's march south of where she was and that may be the case for me as well. The gate was locked from Earth's side by the Shadalka so that her people knew there would be no hope of retrieving the key and escaping.

And so, my brothers, I realized this is why I was spared in the Great War, a realization which dawned on me with a certainty only few men are granted is this life. I knew that if it was not God's purpose for me, it was now my only purpose in life.

I took her small hands as if they were the finest Austrian crystal, called her "milady," and told her I would come and free her of these demons.

She told me no, it was too dangerous, and what could just one man do?

Whatever he can, I replied.

She then whispered fearfully that she would be all alone. Oh my friends, this sight nearly broke my heart.

I told Narapok it was only for a while, and that she must bear the time apart with the courage she had shown me and that the next time she saw me, she would rest safely in my arms. I swore this by all that is holy, my brethren. I told her I knew I must have sounded like a rash boy in this, but that I loved her.

Startled, she slowly replied that she loved me also. She wondered how this was possible in such a short span of time and if we were fated for each other, or had known and loved each other in some former life. She called me "Hans, her love" and bid that I stay safe in my world and risk myself no further for her.

I told her that I would not and to end to such talk. I loved her from the instant I saw her and I would not be forestalled by man, beast or devil. I kissed her face, aware of the faint touch of her with all the care that was in my soul.

With a last look at her I turned on my heel and raced for the church, my weapons and gear.

Father Kempler had left to deliver a baby, which was just as well. I had no idea what he would think of my congress with spirits. I gathered all my weapons and ammunition and such gear as would aid my quest. I got my head down for a few hours of necessary sleep that, as you all know, every soldier requires on the eve of battle.

In the morning I found three Maasai waiting outside the church. Masigonde, the chief's youngest son, who bore my old Solingen knife, along with his friends Legeny and Sankau, the latter a loner whose only friend was Masigonde.

Masigonde told me they had stood by the hillock the night before when I had talked to the royal lady. He said he and his tribesmen guard the village and had to know if I were prey to devils or evil spirits. He said they knew what I would do and it seemed a proper job for the extra son of a chief with no prospect for a chiefdom of his own.

I said I could use his help, and was indeed desperate for any aid; but that he could not imagine what we faced.

Masigonde shrugged and said a warrior's time is brief and that it should be spent bravely. I gratefully shook his forearm and told him there must be a lonely mountain with a cave at its base. They knew of the ill-omened place, and would take me there.

We moved through the flat featureless plain, guided by Maasai sense and my compass. Though my heart bade me run until it burst, I had been at war too long to give in to it. We made the best speed practical and by the morning of the second day reached the mountain. An early morning scout uncovered a huge cave from which a poisonous, foul-smelling stream issued.

The Maasai, who fear no man, but fear devils, quailed. I did not hesitate. I had the dagger and Narapok's fate drove me forward like a whip. Into the cave I went and after a few moments the shamed Maasai followed.

The cave was wide but narrowed further in. An odd greenish glow seemed to pervade it. Natural light also seeped in from cracks above. The walls were covered in obscene glyphs and images. Bestial statues held dark pits for eyes, yet seemed to watch us come on.

The walls narrowed. I fixed bayonet and stalked forward, on guard. We came to a place barely six feet across with a raised portcullis. Our enemy struck then.

A swarm of green-skinned unmen, goblins with tusks and baleful eyes, clad in leather and mail, bearing short ugly swords, axes and clubs, charged us.

At last I faced living enemies. I, who had never known joy in the killing of the Kaiser's enemies, knew it now. I worked my Gewehr's bolt in liquid moves, never breaking the spot weld with my cheek. The flash and bang of the big rifle were overpowering in the small space and goblin after goblin fell. But I had not time to reload or draw my Mauser pistol when I fired my last shot. Ah, but my bayonet did not fail me. Butcher Blade the English call it and I used it as one. These unmen were perhaps too used to the weak and cowed Egyptians. I gave them fifteen inches of the Kaiser's steel in their guts followed with crushing strokes of my rifle's butt.

I yelled "Für Gott und Iht" with reckless joy.

In the narrow place it was hard for more than one of them to press me. When two did and one pushed me up against the cave wall, Maasai spears licked in and took them. My friends were back in the fight.

The hugest goblin dashed my rifle from my hands with a club. I returned the favor by twisting the weapon from his. He fought to grapple with me, but I am not Hans the Bear for nothing. Though the stench of his green skin revolted me, I returned his grapple. With Narapok's sweet face before me I heaved my enemy off the ground and his back cracked like a rifle shot. I flung him to the ground. Not one million of him would keep me from her.

I turned to the Maasai who stood behind me. All three had come through unharmed, through their spears were black with the blood of the unmen.

Masigonde told me I was a warrior to follow, that he had felt fear when he saw the beasts of the underworld, until I fell upon them and showed that they died as easily as men.

I thanked my friend and told him that from here I must go alone.

He shook his head and told me no. He was Maasai. These creatures had made him feel fear and now he would return the favor, teaching them respect for the Maasai spear. His companions shook their spears in agreement.

Young Legeny added that there would be lands and riches beyond, and that if only these opposed them we would all be kings.

I then heard a strange voice speak out, stating, "I hope that works out for you."

Masigonde demanded to know who it was that spoke Maasai here. Thus I knew that we faced more magic as I had heard these words in German.

A white man walked out of the back of the cave. He was strangely garbed, like a member of one of those old Wild West shows so prevalent before the war.

You are doubtless now looking at this tall, lean, gap-toothed being as this letter is read to you. He is no natural man but has acted as a friend to me since that day.

He called me Hans the Bear, and aptly named. I growled that only my close friends called me that. He claimed to be a friend, and smiled. His name was Johnny, a trader in special goods and services.

I asked if he had a thousand Gewehrs on him. He said he could acquire them easily enough, but that surely it would be a better investment to gain the assistance of men to wield such weapons first. I asked him what he meant by this.

Johnny looked past me at the Maasai. They were a good start, he admitted, brave as lions and now that they knew their enemy could die, afraid of nothing. But I needed men of science, who could make weapons where I was going and train an army to use them. Johnny added that such fellows were presently wandering about, useless, at my precious Lazarus club.

I demanded that he cease tormenting me. Oh, how I longed for the full company of you stout fellows, but my precious Lazarans were months away, if a letter could even reach them from this unknown place. How could I hope for such aid?

Johnny said I could not pass through the gate until moonrise, and I had many hours yet, so he bade me make this record for you. He promised it will be read in our main hall within days, and he would make such proofs as needed to our President, Matthew McQuinn, that this correspondence comes from me and that my need is urgent. He would also bring to Matthew the Romanoff dagger, as it would be needed to follow me where I soon go.

I swore to Johnny that if he did this, I and my house would see his hands filled with gold.

Johnny shook his shadowed head and said he had no need for yellow metal, but was interested in the gorget that my ancestors were given. He said it was old even back then and holds a great power that would be needed to battle evil in another time and place.

I took the plate off my chest; it felt odd to do so, I had so often slept with it on, and placed it in his hands, seizing them in my own. I demanded he swear before God that he would deliver my letter.

This otherworldy agent grimaced, then agreed, grasping my hand. To my shock he knew our sacred and secret handshake!

And so, my brothers, I bring to an end this fantastic message. I call on you to be faithful to the oath we all swore to make a better world. Only it will not be our world, though it strikes me that by carrying the battle into the

Devil's backyard, we may hope to help our own world. Fear not the passage of time between your reading of this letter and your arrival in Africa. Johnny has explained to me that time flows much more slowly in the other realm than it does upon our Earth. Mere hours will have occurred for me by the time you cross over and can stand at my side.

As you love honor, and fear God, I pray you, take the dagger and come with all your powers to this place. You will find me on the other side. I will rescue Lady Narapok or die in the attempt.

Done this day under the Seyderlitz family seal.

So sworn by

Hans Dietrich Seyderlitz

## LAZARUS CLUB NIGHTBOOK

Monday, June 21, 1920

J.Q. Higgins II, Club Scribe

McQuinn finished his recitation and laid the sheaf of papers upon the ebony podium. He removed his monocle and gazed levelly at the Redeemed as he drew out an ornate dagger from his coat. He turned to Johnny and realized the otherworldly gentleman was gone. We all looked about, but the saturnine cowboy was nowhere to be found.

Finnegan and Des Belges checked the main door, the only entrance to our sanctum, confirming it was still locked.

McQuinn shook himself and said he had seen the proofs and knew this entire fabulous account to be true. We had been offered a quest, in a far better cause than the one in which millions so recently and meanly perished. A friend calls to us and there is this royal lady to be considered, who seemed quite a proper sort of princess to him.

The room rumbled with agreement but fell silent as McQuinn raised the dagger high and said RMS Albion awaits; all who would undertake the quest, need stand to arms.

Every chair emptied.

# 1921 WORLD EVENTS

**Yankees purchase twenty acres in Bronx for Yankee Stadium**

**Prof Albert Einstein lectures in New York City on his new Theory of Relativity**

**Adolf Hitler elected leader of the National Socialist German Workers Party—Munich residents astonished by rare green corona full moon**

**J. Edgar Hoover assigned as Asst Director of FBI**

**In Atlantic City, New Jersey, first Miss America Pageant, a two-day event, commences**

**Virginia Rappe manslaughter trial against Roscoe Fatty Arbuckle ends in a hung jury**

# Brooches of Fire

by Wayne Joseph Borean


**SUNDAY, SEPTEMBER 24, 1922, HAILEYBURY ONTARIO**

I can't understand. Why are Ma and Pa so weird? I went into the woods near Cobalt, to hunt rabbits. I even shot a couple with my .22, and brought them home. OK. It was Sunday. I was supposed to be at church. Big deal. The minister is so damned boring that most of the time I go to sleep anyway.

Then I was supposed to be cleaning out the chicken coop. What a wonderful, stinking job. To hell with that. I went to see Helmut and Valdis.

Helmut might be a bit slow, but he's a nice guy. Valdis is, well, every guy in town is jealous of Helmut. They can't see why she married the big lunk. I can. He's not a drunk, doesn't beat her and treats her like a princess. Of course she married him.

I hope that when I grow up, I'll be like Helmut. Then I'll get a nice girl too. Maybe Helmut's daughter, Annike! Gosh, she's twelve, only a year younger than me, and she's so pretty. She's going to look a lot like her Ma, though her hair is blonde instead of red.

I won't be like my Pa. Every time he gets into the booze, he beats Ma. He beats me too. At thirteen, I'm not big enough or strong enough to fight back. Usually I can protect the younger ones by getting in his way. He beats me, and then forgets about the girls. Damn, I hate my Pa.

My parents were furious when I got home. I got yelled at so much I thought my ears were going to bust. Shit. I don't need this sort of stuff. School's bad enough. Why do they hate me so much? Well, I guess Ma doesn't. She hugged me later when Pa couldn't see.

Tomorrow I get to shovel shit out of the chicken coop before school. Wonderful.

## MONDAY, SEPTEMBER 25, 1922, HAILEYBURY ONTARIO

I got up when I heard Pa go out to milk the cows, got dressed, and started shoveling shit. What a mess. What a stinking mess. I surprised myself, got it done in only an hour. Then Ma wouldn't let me into the house. She made me wash off at the pump. Damn was it cold.

I ate breakfast, then set out for school. Or at least they thought I did. I had my .22 rifle under my red flannel jacket, and once I was out of sight of the house, I cut off the road and into the bush. To hell with school. The teacher is an idiot. Why does a farmer need to know who the King of England was a hundred years ago?

Course learning how to write was good. I can keep my diary. Valdis told me writing was important, so I've really worked on it. She's the one who suggested keeping a diary. She said the more practice I got, the better I'd get at it, just like with hockey. Valdis is smart.

There was a place I'd never been before, that I wanted to check. There's so many people around Cobalt that the game isn't really good anymore. But up the rocks, away from town there isn't so much hunting, and there's no farming like down where we live. Everyone calls our area the Clay Belt. There's rocks for hundreds of miles, and then there's really good farmland. Yeah, seasons are short, but we get good crops. Except this year. It's been damned dry.

Round about noon I found the shack. It was hidden in a cleft in the rocks, the door hanging loose. No dog, which is odd. Everyone has a dog, even if just to warn about bears. Then I saw the rusted chain. At the end of it was a skeleton, looked like a fairly big dog. I poked around, couldn't see what killed it. Of course if the owner had left it chained up without food, the poor thing would have starved.

With a dead dog chained outside, the shack was probably empty, but I looked anyway. It wasn't. A skeleton lay on a pile of blankets along the back wall, skin and rags of beard and hair still hanging on it. One leg was sticking out at a really funny angle. Then I saw the knife in its hand, and the signs of blood poured on the floor. I went back and looked at the dog again, and found a nick in one of the neck bones.

That explained it. The guy had a broken leg, and killed the dog so it wouldn't kill him. Or maybe he planned to eat it, but it ran out the door, and he couldn't follow, so they both died. I said a quick prayer for the dog. I felt really sorry for it. Why he didn't just let it off the leash so it could run free, I couldn't figure out. Then ashamed, I said a prayer for the guy.

One of his hands was on a pouch belted to his tattered night shirt. The smaller animals had been in here, fox, raccoon, maybe wolf, and they'd got some meat, but they hadn't touched his pouch. I carefully lifted the hand a bit, and used my knife to slit the strings holding the pouch to his belt. I poked the belt off his stomach so it would fall on my side, then let the skeletal arm down.

Then I sat back and studied the body. It looked like it had been here since mid-summer. Things had been really dry, and rather than rotting, the skin had turned to leather.

Now who was it, and should I tell someone. I thought about that for a while, then I remembered the crazy, bearded Finn who'd shown up in the early spring. At least that's what he said he was. Helmut and Valdis were pretty sure he wasn't a Finn. Maybe being Swedes they'd know. He was a real weird ass character, always talking about how the gods smiled on him. The one time I got close to him I knew that the gods might smile on him, but they sure as hell didn't bathe him. He stank so bad it made my eyes water.

Now I only bathe once a week. Any more than that weakens you. But this guy hadn't had a bath in months. Maybe years. And he didn't wear trousers. He wore robes like the Popish priests did on Sunday. Course their robes were clean. His were covered in food and booze stains, and looked like mud. I poked around the shack a bit more. He had a gun, a 30.06 Winchester lever action, which he'd probably used for hunting, a small iron stove, lots of dust, and yes, a money box. Make that a money and bible box. He had twenty-five dollars in the front of the Bible. I left it, and opened the pouch. Inside was a wadded up ball of fine cloth. It was really grubby. Of course he had been really grubby when I'd seen him.

I carefully untangled the messed up ball on top of the stove, and got a huge surprise. Inside were two enormous round things covered in jewels. Not rings. I knew rings. I turned them over, and on the back there was a stick pin with a roll lock. Brooches, that's what they were, brooches.

Mighty fine brooches. I wandered around a bit more: some canned goods, empty rotgut bottles, horse liniment. I found a farmer's almanac, which reminded me, now that I had some paper, I needed to shit. I carefully wrapped the brooches up, and stuck them in my pocket, then went looking for the outhouse.

Well, I wouldn't be using that outhouse. But now I knew how he broke his leg. It'd collapsed, dropping him into a pit full of shit. Must have been damned careless when he built it. I couldn't think of when an outhouse had collapsed that hadn't been a prank. This one wasn't a prank. He was probably drunk when he built it, considering all the booze bottles, and drunk when he maintained it. The wood was rotten.

Somehow he'd managed to climb out. I scouted the area. It had been at least a month, but I could still see scratch marks on the ground, since it hadn't rained. Right. He called the dog, it came, and he was able to get it to help pull him out somehow. Then he rewarded it by killing it. Bastard.

Time to leave, and let the constable know. A sudden urge hit me. I opened the Bible, and looked at the money again. The biggest bill was a two. I took fifteen dollars in ones and twos. Where was his change? Ah, in the pouch I'd cut from his belt. There was another ten dollars in change. Then I changed my mind. I took all of the paper money, and all of the change. I grabbed the rifle; it was worth at least a few dollars used, and the cartridges.

I got halfway out the door, and an urge hit me. I carefully pulled the blankets with the body out of the shack into the clearing, and laid them front of the dog's skeleton, making it look like maybe the dog and the man had fought.

Then I left that place. Why should I tell the constable? No one had found the place since summer, probably no one would find it till next summer, and no one would know anything was missing. It would be a total wreck by then. With the door hanging loose, there was nothing stopping nature from tearing it apart.

The Winchester and ammunition was a problem. Where could I hide it? I finally thought of the covered bridge. Once, when swimming, I'd found that there was a hidden spot under it. It was full of leaves, but dry. Until I could figure out a lie to cover being able to buy it with the money I had earned from doing chores, it would have to stay there. Luckily it was so dry the stream was just about gone, and if I came back and greased the gun good, it wouldn't rust. The ammo, well, brass doesn't rust.

The brooches and money I could hide under a loose floorboard in my room. There's a board I can pull up, and under it is a small hole. Good place to hide stuff, since no one else knows about it.


## TUESDAY, SEPTEMBER 26, 1922, HAILEYBURY ONTARIO

Went to school today. Wanted to hit the teacher. What a jerk. Why do I have to go to school? I'm going to end up being a farmer, or working at the Cobalt silver mines. Another year and I should be big enough.

Right now Ma and Pa won't let me quit school. I know a lot of guys who dropped out at fourteen though. Another year of this crap. Can I take it?

Kept thinking about the brooches. Prettiest stuff I've ever seen.


## WEDNESDAY, SEPTEMBER 27, 1922, HAILEYBURY ONTARIO

Another day of school. Then chores. Pa is really driving me nuts. Tomorrow he's going to sell a horse. Bastard will probably come home drunk, again.

Snuck a look at the brooches. Boy are they pretty.

**THURSDAY, SEPTEMBER 28, 1922, HAILEYBURY ONTARIO**
School. On the way home I checked. The Winchester is still safe under the bridge.

Damn, it is dry. We are lucky, we've got a stream on our farm we can use for water. Without it we would not have enough water for the animals. A couple of times our well has run dry this summer, and the stream saved us.

Pa, much to my surprise, isn't drunk. Ma is looking at him like he's strange. So am I. God, I hate living with a drunk.

Took a quick look at the brooches, and the money. Love the brooches.

**FRIDAY, SEPTEMBER 29, 1922, HAILEYBURY ONTARIO**
I don't know where to start. Pa did bring booze home. He just hid it in the barn, and after Ma, the kids and I went to bed, he went out to the barn and got stinking drunk.

I woke up before sunrise to hear him screaming at Ma. I ran out of my room in my nightshirt, past the girl's room, to Ma and Pa's room. He was hitting her with his balled up fist. I was furious. Quickly I grabbed the gazunder from beside the bed, and hit him on the head with it, spilling shit and piss all over him, Ma, the bed, and myself.

He fell off the bed, and hit the floor like a ton of bricks. Ma was screaming and crying. I helped her up, then we noticed he wasn't moving, or breathing. She noticed too, and she panicked and attacked me, clawing at my face. I hit her a couple of times really hard. Too hard. Maybe I hit her more than a couple of times. I don't know. I was crazed too.

She fell down, and she wasn't breathing either. The girls were looking in, terrified. I screamed at them, and they ran and hid in their room under the bed.

All of a sudden I wasn't furious anymore. Instead I was scared.

I checked. Both Ma and Pa were dead. Dad had a huge dent in his skull, guess I hit him too hard. If their gazunder had have been porcelain it would have probably cracked, but it was iron, and his head cracked.

Ma, well, I think I broke her neck. I don't know. I know how to skin a deer. I know how to butcher a cow or a pig. I could butcher a human, but all that would tell me maybe was how I'd killed her. It wouldn't bring her back to life.

I took off my nightshirt, washed myself clean, using Ma and Pa's pitcher and bowl, wiped myself down, and walked naked back to my room. One of the girls was looking out from under their bed, and her eyes popped wide open. I screamed at her, and she ducked back under. What was she staring at?

My dick. It was standing straight up, and I hadn't even noticed. Now I wanted to go in there and do things to the girls. I leaned against the wall for five minutes or so, and got myself under control, then went into my room and dressed. I grabbed a knapsack I used, and stuffed it full of clothes, food, then went up to the attic, and got the brooches and the money.

The girls were still under the bed.

I bent down low, and said, "There's been an accident. Ma and Pa are dead. You need to get dressed, and walk over to Widow Bishop's house, she'll know what to do."

They looked at me, terrified and didn't say a thing. I counted out six dollars, two dollars each. "Here's two dollars each. Get dressed. Go now."

I backed out of their room, and heard them sliding out from under the bed. Thinking quickly, I closed the battered door to Ma and Pa's room, and pushed a cupboard in front of it so they couldn't see. When they came out of the room, I said. "Go fast. Run."

And they did. I grabbed my diary, pen and ink, both Pa's Lee Enfield and my .22, all of our ammo, and Ma's hidden stash of money, and left.


## SATURDAY, SEPTEMBER 30, 1922, HAILEYBURY ONTARIO

I didn't light a fire last night. I was afraid someone would notice me. Instead I lay on my back, holding the brooches up against the stars so I could look at it. They're so pretty.

I snuck around the edge of the woods later. There was a real crowd at our farm. That made me mad. I was ready to try and shoot them, when I realized I only had ten cartridges for the Lee Enfield, and my .22 wouldn't carry that far. How many cartridges did I have for the Winchester? I wasn't sure, and I really couldn't go to look at the bridge. It was too close to the farm. I'd have to sneak done to get it after dark.

The entire day I was mad, sad, and confused in order. None of it made sense. Why had I hit Pa that hard? How had I hit him that hard? He was a good eight inches taller than me, and strong as an ox. Yeah, I hit him with the gazunder, but I didn't think I could have hit him that hard. And how had I managed to kill Ma? I didn't think I was that strong.


## SUNDAY, OCTOBER 1, 1922, HAILEYBURY ONTARIO

Early this morning, before the sun was up, I retrieved the Winchester. While I was doing it, I heard horses coming, so I stayed under the bridge, trying not to breathe. There were two men talking about Ma, Pa, and me. They reckoned I'd gone nuts, and it was luck I hadn't killed the girls too.

I shivered. Maybe I hadn't killed the girls, but I'd come damned close to doing something else to them, maybe something that was worse.

I'd been thinking of going to see Helmut and Valdis. That put paid to that idea. If I was tempted to do something evil like that to my little sisters, the oldest of which was only nine, what would I be tempted to do to Annike? Suddenly I knew. I was standing under that bridge, my dick hard as a rock. I knew exactly what I wanted to do.

I loaded the Winchester, and snuck out from under the bridge. Yes, only two men, both carrying guns, either shotguns or rifles, I couldn't tell in the moonlight. I took careful aim, and shot the bigger one in the back. He spun and fell off the horse. I quickly worked the lever, ejecting the spent cartridge, raised the gun, and fired again. The other rider had already hit his spurs, and was bent down low over his horse. I missed him.

Then a brilliant spark came from where the other rider had fallen, and I felt something hit my left shoulder. Suddenly I wasn't furious any more, I was scared stiff. I took off running, bent over so I'd be a harder target, reeling from the pain. There were a couple more shots, but they didn't hit me.

I heard the other horse coming back. Shit. I didn't need this. My left arm was weak, but I managed to hold the gun up and take another shot. The horse dropped. I'd hit it, and not the rider who was cursing a blue streak, as I snuck off towards town. If they tracked me, they'd see me go that way.

Then I dropped into a stream, and headed uphill into the woods.


## MONDAY, OCTOBER 2, 1922, HAILEYBURY ONTARIO

I was lucky. The shot that hit me only furrowed my shoulder. It hurts like hell, but it isn't bleeding hardly at all.

Thing is, this is October. It's still fairly warm. What will I do next month when it starts snowing?

Why am I losing my temper so often? And why do I keep getting a woody? Sure, I've played with myself, and got hard. But I've never got hard for no reason. What's going on?


## TUESDAY OCTOBER 3, 1922, HAILEYBURY ONTARIO

Now I understand. Last night I was lying in the brush, looking at the stars. I took out the brooches to look at them, and got an instant woody. Oh shit. The brooches. I wasn't like this before I found them.

I can't even throw them away. I tried. They wouldn't let me.

So what I'm going to do is finish this diary entry, and then leave my diary by Helmut's trap line, along with all the money, and the guns. Hopefully they'll be able to get the money to my sisters. It isn't much. I killed our parents. But it's better than nothing.

Helmut and Valdis can have the guns. Hear that Helmut and Valdis? I want you to make sure my sisters get the money, and you can have the guns and ammunition.

Then I'm going to kill myself. I know where I can steal some kerosene tonight, and I know where the farmers are planning to do the burn off to extend their fields. I'll go there, soak the area in kerosene, and set myself on fire.

Fire hurts. A lot. But hurting a lot is what I deserve. Yes, the brooches made me act different, but if I'd maybe listened to the minister more, and opened my heart to Jesus the way he says, I might have been able to stop myself.

I deserve to burn.


**THURSDAY OCTOBER 5, 1922, HAILEYBURY ONTARIO**
Helmut found the boy's diary and three rifles yesterday morning by our traplines. Since he couldn't read it, he brought it home to me. Just as he got home, he noticed smoke from the direction of town.

We grabbed the kids and ran. It hadn't rained hardly at all this summer, and we both knew that a fire, especially with the winds yesterday would be deadly. We made it far enough south that we were safe, and then I opened Bill's diary.

I don't know what to do with it. I can't give this to anyone. I believe what he wrote, but no one else will. Magic brooches that make you mad? I've seen stuff like this before. They haven't.

Never mind the anger. Can you imagine what they'd do to his sisters?

We don't know how many people died. We do know that Haileybury is burnt to the ground, and most of the farms to the north are gone too. We were lucky. If Helmut hadn't come back, he'd probably be dead too.

I think I know where Bill went to kill himself. As soon as the embers have cooled down enough, I'm going to look for the brooches. If they are what I think they are, the fire wouldn't have destroyed them. If they are what I think they are, I'll anchor them to a rock and dump them into the deepest part of Lake Temiskaming. And hope.

Valdis

# 1923 WORLD EVENTS

**Union of Socialist Soviet Republics established**

**Ku Klux Klan surprise attack on black residential area Rosewood Fla, eight killed—survivors described crazed KKK leader with green eyes that flashed like wildfire**

**New York State revokes Prohibition law**

**Harry Houdini frees himself from a straight-jacket while suspended upside down, 40 feet (12 m) above ground in NYC**

**First transatlantic radio broadcast of a voice, Pittsburgh-Manchester**

# A Promise Made

## by Jason Cordova

*NOTE: the following letters were found in the collection of one Lady Anne MacDowell of Scotland, which lends credence to her claims about the mysterious disappearance of her once-suitor, a gentleman by the name of Michael Shaw, of England, in the cold depths of the socialist state of Ukraine sometime in the spring of 1923. The letters, which appear to be valid in their origin (as the Lady MacDowell claimed upon her deathbed, and her family since) have been disputed by numerous noted scholars, many of whom state that they are nothing more than fanciful forgeries of a scorned woman. Despite the postage evident on the envelopes, which the estate of Lady MacDowell has provided upon request and seems to support her claims, no others at the Royal Historical Society have taken up the cause. The contentious issue lingers to this very day between the estate of Lady Anne MacDowell and scholars at the Royal Historical Society in London.*

**FEBRUARY 7, 1923—MY DEAREST ANNE,**
I arrived safely today in Constantinople and met with my Albanian guide, Ibrahim, who showed me quickly to my apartment away from the train station. I traveled light, as you suggested, and the Albanian man was grateful for my lack of luggage.

"You not need much bags where you go," he had told me in his pidgin English as he helped me with my three bags. He uttered something else in his native language but, curse my lack of preparation, I failed to understand just what he spoke. Next time, sweet Anne, please ensure that I study the proper regional dialect if I am to journey to this region once more. I feel that I am going to be ill-equipped to deal with the variety of languages I will face. It seems to me, only hours after my arrival, that every language in the region has been blended together to form a single, gibbering muck. It is very strange upon the ears.

I pray to God that as we venture into the north, the languages become more discernible. My Russian is good, much better than anything else I speak outside of Latin, French and, of course, the King's English. I was expecting this, beloved, but it still is almost overwhelming.

I did not want to tell you of the area because, quite frankly, it is an unholy mess of a city. Between the sprawling, raucous *souks* and the barks of hawkers selling their wares, and the horrid buskers seated in the roads, the overpowering *now* of this city overwhelms the more delicate senses. It is difficult for me to write this, even now, as the sounds and smells continue to assault me. The entire city seems to be in turmoil, though I cannot explain what for. The Great War has been over for five long years now; surely the ruling Turks can see that the way of the new world's order starts in Great Britain under the King?

I shall write to you regularly, as I promised before I left Sussex. In two days I shall arrive in Adrianoupolis, and from there I shall journey northwards to find the wares. I cannot ask Ibrahim about the region, because I fear he would grow suspicious of my goals and desires.

Soon, my betrothed, soon we shall be together once more. I shall acquire the objects your father has sought for his entire life and offer them as a dowry for your hand, to prove my worth to both him and you. They were thought to have been lost with the fall of the Tsars, but rumors abound, dearest Anne. Rumors drive this poor soul. I am persistent and will not give in easily to the desire to quit. I am on the trail of the items which have vexed your father for many years. I hope to have them in my possession soon.

Forever yours, Michael


**FEBRUARY 9—DEAREST ANNE,**

I know you have yet to receive my first letter, but I cannot wait to tell you just what I have discovered upon my arrival (by boat) into Romania! It turns out that there are Bolshevik agents in Constanta as well, looking for the same items which I seek. I do not trust these Bolsheviks, for it was they who ruthlessly murdered the entire Romanov family. Not these agents in particular, but the regime as a whole, I'm sure you understand. Two of the Bolsheviks, horrid men both with a decided lack of grace, class, and elegance tracked me down in my apartment and questioned me at length.

"You are Michael Shaw of England, yes?" one of them asked me when I answered the door chime. I agreed and they asked to come in. I, albeit reluctantly, agreed and they pushed past me. It seemed to me that they were seeking something, though at that very moment I had no idea just what. After a few moments of casual search, which they masked very poorly, they sat down at my small dining table. They motioned for me to sit across from them.

"How may I assist you?" I asked, sitting down. I pulled out my cigarette case and offered one to each of them. Both men partook eagerly and I lit both of their cigarettes, then my own. I leaned back in my seat and waited, my eyes flicking back and forth between the two agents. After a few moments of contemplation, the first Bolshevik spoke.

"You are seeking Faberge eggs of the cursed Romanovs." It came out as a statement, not a question. His accented English was thick, guttural and uneducated. I looked at the other, whose cold eyes stared at me like I was already dead. It was vastly unnerving, my dear, to see such emptiness in a living man. Soulless Bolsheviks, just as my father told me during their uprising.

"Those items have been lost," I reminded him, casually tipping my ash into a small ivory canister. I remained calm. It was very difficult, as I felt a growing suspicion that these two agents knew quite a bit more than I did. After a moment to steady my nerves, I continued "Or destroyed. Caught up in the fervor of revolution; some poor, thoughtless soul undoubtedly smashed them to pieces without realizing their worth. No, good sir, I am vacationing. I have never been to the land of the Turks before, and I look forward to seeing the sights, as it were."

"You're lying," the second man accused. "Do you think we are fools?"

"Of course not," I stated through gritted teeth. Only a fool would destroy something as valuable as the Faberge eggs of the Romanovs, though these Bolsheviks were no fools. Bigoted zealots, yes. Fools? Hardly.

"Which ones do you seek?" the first asked, his brown eyes burrowing into my heart. It was a pitiless stare.

I was unable to contain myself. "I hear that the Alexander III egg survived your inglorious purge. The commemorative one."

Both men shared a look. Oh Anne, if you could have seen their faces when I mentioned the precise egg that I sought. It was as though I had found a gold mine. They undoubtedly knew the egg in question, as well as just where it may have been hidden. I knew I was on the right path, so I pressed harder.

"Of course, it is not nearly as desirable to have as the angel with egg in the chariot," I said, perhaps a bit too smugly, for one of the Bolsheviks leapt to his feet and slammed his hands down upon my table. He made a sign in the air and, for an instant, I felt a disturbing presence in the room. So help me God, it was as though the entire air in the room *changed*. I recognized the forked fingers of a religious man, which I believed that the Bolsheviks were not: the agent of the Bolsheviks was warding off evil. I have never heard of such a thing from a godless heathen.

"And the egg with the hen in the basket," the seated man said with a curt nod. I said nothing, but he took that as an agreement. He shook his head slowly. "Those three eggs in particular. Why those eggs?"

I thought about it for a moment, my tongue thick and my answer sluggish. Anne, for the life of me I could not remember precisely why it was those three eggs I sought. I knew that your father had sought the precious lost eggs soon after the fall of the Romanovs, and how he was rebuffed in his every attempt. But outside of that, I did not know why I sought those eggs in particular. Was it a desire to please your father? Or did I want to simply best your former betrothed, that cowardly bastard Randall, who left you for some Romanian whore the moment he set foot in this region?

Forgive me, Anne. I know that Randall's abandonment of you is a painful subject, especially since it occurred in the lands where I tread now. I shan't speak of it again and I promise to maintain my love and loyalty to you, no matter the cost.

The Bolshevik agent said something then which made me pay close attention to him.

"Those eggs are cursed."

I was surprised. I could not believe that these Bolsheviks were as superstitious as old country bumpkins. Their Marxist beliefs demanded complete and strict loyalty to the state, and not to their religion or individualism. I felt a slight chill creep across my chest and into my heart.

"Any item which survived your purge is undoubtedly cursed," I said, my voice easy and calm despite my inner turmoil. "They carry the taint of the dead family with them. Only the Dowager Empress and her misbegotten nephew truly escaped your clutches."

"You are making a mistake, Comrade Shaw," the seated Bolshevik informed me, ignoring my jibe about the surviving Romanovs. He used my fountain pen and the writing tablet which had been laying on the table and wrote something down. He passed it across to me when he finished. "We are staying at this address. Please come to us before you start your foolish journey. These eggs *are* cursed, cursed in the ways of the old imperialists and that Satanic dog, Grigori Yefimovich Rasputin."

I thanked them and they left, leaving behind a sense of mystique in the air. Anne, how can the Bolsheviks fear these things? It is my belief that they only desire the eggs for money or, worse yet, to destroy them in another ritual. And yet...

These men fill me with doubts, sweet Anne. I wish you were here. You always were my moral guide in such times of need, when my mind became clouded with such uncertainties. My thoughts are of you, each and every day.

Please tell me how things are back in England. Is the King well? How are my parents? The weather?

I miss you so.

Forever yours, Michael

## FEBRUARY 27—DEAREST ANNE,

These past days have been rough. Ibrahim, my guide, has led me further and faster through Romania than I had thought possible. Without your replying letter, I doubt very much that I would have had the constitution for such an arduous journey. The courier somehow caught up with us as soon as we arrived at our destination, the speed of Hermes seemingly at his back.

It is troubling to hear the news you share, that of our King George and his illness. Also troubling is the news of my parents. Are you certain I shouldn't return home to tend to their needs? They might be harboring some remnant of the Spanish illness which swept the lands five years past, after all.

No, beloved. You are, and always shall remain, correct on these matters. I will heed your advice and not return home, though it pains me to do so.

I have arrived safely in Galati, where rumors abound about "mysterious events" occurring down in the old wharf area. When questioned about the events, however, many of the Romanians make the very sign that the Bolsheviks made in my apartment in Constanta. It is rather curious, something which speaks of a lurking superstition in the backwards minds of the locals. Considering that I come from an enlightened land myself, it is something of a surprise to see just how fearful these peasants are.

The port itself is mostly deserted, the ruin of war still evident in this large city on the Danube River. Though it has been a few years since the Great War, this poor city has yet to rebuild from the damage done here. It is as though something dark is holding back the healing and rebuilding process all cities must face after war. It is a cause for consternation, to say the least.

I have a feeling about this place, beloved. It speaks to me, as though this is the resting place to one of the three lost eggs which I seek. I cannot begin to explain it. It calls to me, a siren, beckoning me to a greater and brighter future. It offers much, this place, and yet I cannot shake the feeling of something much darker, something lurking in the deepest of shadows. It is a conflict far greater than that of the Great War, yet...

I shall write again soon. Ibrahim, whom I have now taken into my full confidence, believes that what I seek is within the ruined wharfs. God grant me safe journey. I love you, Anne.

Your future husband,

Michael

**FEBRUARY 29—BELOVED ANNE,**

I have found it! I have found the first of the lost Faberge eggs of the Romanovs!

My guide and I descended into the ruined wharves armed with only torches, our courage and our wits—and my Enfield revolver, that is. Ibrahim never wavered, good lad, despite the dark and disturbing surroundings. The deeper we went into the ruins, the more steadfast he became. I knew I had chosen well when I hired him to lead me into the depths of Romania!

The hen with sapphire pendant Faberge egg, which was supposed to be locked safely away in the Kremlin (at least, that's what the Bolsheviks claimed. A pox on their house, the lying, godless heathens!) is now in my hands. It is a golden hen, bejeweled with rose diamonds, and has the egg resting loosely in the mouth as it leans over the nest, which is a detailed collection of silver and gold "twigs" interwoven together. The sapphire is the clearest and deepest blue you've ever seen, with an almost ethereal glow coming from within. It is exquisite, dearest Anne, absolutely exquisite! The diamonds and rubies gleam incessantly. The skin of the hen, while gold, always seems to shine faintly, even in the utter black of night. Don't worry, I shan't spoil the surprise for you. Needless to say, I'm convinced that I am the first person since the Dowager Empress to actually see what the surprise is. It is beyond beautiful, and it will look fabulous upon your father's mantle.

Ibrahim is worried, though. He said that there was something unnatural about the entire Faberge egg, something cursed. I believe he fears the Bolsheviks more than the dangers of trespassing through the ruined wharves, which is absurd. The Russians have no claim here, in this land of seemingly perpetual darkness. Nonetheless, the next time we approach the ruins, Ibrahim will most assuredly be on guard. And armed.

Ibrahim and I both believe that the two remaining eggs are in this location as well, buried somewhere in layers of intrigue, darkness and mystery. Anne, I cannot explain how excited I am at the prospect of retrieving the remaining eggs so that I might return home to your welcoming arms. I miss your soft lips, your deep blue eyes, your touch.

Forever yours, Michael


**MARCH 3—DEAR ANNE,**

Ghastly weather has postponed our search for the moment. A wicked storm, darker than the depths of the Siberian wilderness, has descended upon the region. Harsh winds cut to the bone, and the cold... by God, the cold! Even the dreariest of English winters cannot match the sheer misery which permeates this land at times. Much snow has accumulated, blocking roads and making any traveling nigh impossible. Even the locals have barricaded them-selves indoors.

I have spent some time examining the egg. As I mentioned in my last letter, it is an exquisite work of art, one that the grand masters of the House of Faberge must be proud of. The soft glow of the egg always seems to cast a warm feeling throughout the room, though it seems to dim whenever Ibrahim comes around it. It is as if the man carries a palpable sense of gloom about him, and this carries over onto the beauty of the egg. He is very much at home in this harsh climate, let me tell you.

I feel the burning need to reunite the egg with the other two. I cannot explain why. There is something deep inside me that has been awakened by this egg, and I feel an almost kinship towards it. I can feel its pain, loneliness at being separated from its brethren. I must reunite the eggs!

Listen to me prattle on, my dearest. I believe the long days and longer nights are beginning to affect my thoughts.

Think of me tonight, Anne, when you ready yourself for bed. I hope to remain in your thoughts, prayers... and dreams.

With love, Michael

## MARCH 5—BELOVED,

Dark thoughts have unwittingly found their way into my mind, gnawing at the edges of my sanity. This new friend of yours, this Jack? I do not trust his motives or intentions, my love. I know you think me foolish for my jealousy, but he views your family and your fortune as an opportunity to advance his own agenda. You know that my family is good and proper, unlike this uncivi-lized man who seeks to tread upon claimed lands.

No matter what he promises you, my love, he can never give you what I can give. I know this because I have found the second egg.

Deep within the wharfs, in the midst of shattered bodies ruined by time and war, remains of Bolshevik soldiers were scattered about the egg. It was horrific to see how these men died. In spite of our ideological differences, I would not wish their manner of death upon any of my enemies.

But I could not tell what killed them. God help me, Anne, I could not fathom what sort of terrible men would have the ability to do such things to one another. Worst of all (and for this I fear I am damned), I did not feel any of these conflicting emotions until just now, for my soul was drawn to a dark corner of the room, where boxes were stacked atop one another. I somehow knew which box to find and, with some patience, managed to pry it open.

The egg was resting inside a chest with other rubies and gold, resplendent relics of a dead and gone nation. All of it was just part of the fabled treasures of the cursed Romanov dynasty.

The wharves are a vast network of half-sunk buildings and ruined piers, all of which I would normally be hesitant to traverse. However, the lure of the eggs is great, my dearest, and I cannot seem to stop myself in my hunt for all three. They shall be reunited. I swear this upon all that is holy!

...that was odd. A sense of determination to reunite all three eggs, for a moment, took away all reason. I have never felt that way before. I do hope that the paranoia that my guide has begun to show is not seeping its way into my mind. It would be most unbecoming if I turned into a fearful man who trembled at the slightest shadow.

The angel with the egg, the Cherub Egg, is currently resting on the shelf next to its brother, the silver gleam of the metallic angels which pull it combining with the blue hues of the first to fill the room with an unending, ethereal light. It is beautiful, Anne, though it pales in comparison to your beauty. It beckons me constantly, tugging at the very edges of my soul to find the third egg. It is beautiful, so very beautiful.

Ibrahim is not well. I fear for his health, as time in this wretched land seems to have drained him of his vitality. I feel hearty and hale, my love, better than I have felt in many years. I feel similar to the American president, that Roosevelt fellow. This sense of wonder and adventure is exhilarating! I have not felt like this since my primary school days, when fellows I cavorted with helped create the most devious of pranks upon our headmaster.

Anne, the beauty of these eggs... I cannot describe them well enough to do them justice. They make this all go away, the pain, the horror, the darkness and despair that seems to be on the verge of swallowing this wretched land whole. I cannot wait until I have all three; their luminescence will bring much joy to our lives, my love.

I shall write again before I go in search of the third and final egg. There is much studying to be done with these eggs. I wish I were more of a man of science than of the arts, dearest, so that I could try and decipher something that is... odd about the egg with the hen. The Cherub Egg, as I've taken to calling it, seems to almost—and you are going to find this silly and childish—dominate the space when the two are together, as though the egg is submissive to the other. I am certain that it is nothing, but the egg with the hen seems to be the stronger of the two.

I am certain that this is horrific reasoning, but there is a nagging suspicion which tells me that I am correct.

What say you, my beloved?

Forever,

Michael

## MARCH 16—ANNE,

I have done something that will haunt my dreams for the rest of my life. I have seen my doom. I have seen my death. I have seen my eternal torment.

I am damned, and it is all because of you.

Ibrahim and I spent a week searching fruitlessly for any sign of the commemorative egg. We traversed up and down the Danube, as far as our horses were willing to travel, but there was nothing. I was distraught, my love
–

My love? I scoff at that notion now. Perhaps I should call you something else. Perhaps... *traitor?*

I have read between the lines of your last letter, Anne, and I see that you have been smitten by this "Jack" fellow. Oh, he flatters you with poetry and sweets while I trek across barren wastes in vain search to gift to your father the eggs which would give me your hand in marriage. The man—scoundrel is a more proper term, do you not think?—this *scoundrel* seeks to usurp my place in your heart. Have you forgotten me so soon, Anne? Have you cast me off so quickly? I have two of the three eggs in my hand, with the third not too far away.

Everything I have desired in life pales in comparison to my desire to reunite the eggs. When Ibrahim told me that this was an unnatural feeling, I laughed at him. When he tried to prevent me from entering one of the many ruined buildings in Odessa, I struck him.

He was shocked that I had hit him, though no more so than I was. I am not a violent man, yet I was prepared to kill him at a moment's hesitation. He came at me so I struck him again, this time across the cheek. He reached into his belt and pulled out a long knife, one he had carried with him at all times. I cried out and somehow, before he could strike me down with his knife, had pulled my revolver out of the holster and fired two shots into his chest. His eyes were wide with shock, pain, confusion. It was strange, but I had never seen a man die before.

I wish I could say I felt sadness at his passing, Anne, but he was becoming a liability in my search for the final Faberge egg. That egg will be mine and I shall reunite it with its brethren, be it the last thing I do. Then I shall return to England and show you and your traitorous heart just how much you once meant to me and how famous I shall become, with you not by my side, as I reveal three of the lost eggs of the Romanovs.

For now, Anne, dwell upon this fact: I have bled and killed for you. In return, you have done nothing except to bring pain to a trusting and loving man. You insult me, madam, and for that I take great umbrage. The eggs shall be mine, and I spit upon your family honor.

Sincerely,

Michael

**APRIL 1—DEAREST,**

I see the sky burning, Anne, in my restless sleep and my waking moments. I see the creatures of Hell striding about, damned beasts of indescribable nature walking amongst men and women who are unawares. I see the skies explode in daylight, and at nights I watch an empty blackness cover the sky, blot out the moon, and erase the heavens. There is no hope in these visions, Anne, nor is there any reprieve for humanity.

Humanity? I should cry at its loss, but deep within I know I cannot lament the loss of my humanity, for it is I who is to blame, no other. That scattered remnant of my soul, dwelling in the depths of the lost boy I once was, seeks nothing more than to be released now. I still recall the taste of the darkness which fed upon the light of my being. This blight is slowly taking me apart.

I fear these visions and dreams are coming to me now that I have reunited the three lost eggs. Where is that rampant joy, that boundless wonder which enraptured me before?

Late last night I found it, the third egg, hidden amongst the rubble of a broken warehouse in the heart of Odessa's old district. The commemorative egg, dedicated to the memory of Alexander III, is not nearly as beautiful as the first two. It glows like the others, but it is a sickly yellow glow, like the rotting sunrise of London when the smoke clouds the skies. The glow is more powerful than the others as well, the yellow overtaking the light blue and the silver, creating a powerful green light when all three are together.

It cries out to me, Anne. Every waking moment I hear it calling me. I cannot ignore it, and I am unable to block the light from piercing my soul. It knows everything about me, Anne, down to the last secret I try to hold tightly in my breast.

I fear that I am going mad.

No, I no longer fear it. I *know* it.

This morning, before the dawn broke, the eggs began to pulse in an odd way, a steady, pulsing rhythm much like the beating of a heart. First the blue, then silver, and finally the yellow. The three eggs began to pulse wilder and wilder until it was no longer a steady rhythm but a cacophony of light. Finally, as I began to feel nauseous, the flashing culminated in the brightest flash of green I had ever seen. It startled me from my sleep, having actually pervaded upon my dreams. I sat upright hastily and tossed the blankets to the floor.

The darkness of the early morning was pushed back by the light emanating from the three eggs, the same sick green glow which I spoke of before. This time, however, it seemed to push the darkness towards the eggs, encompassing the room while containing the darkness in the vicinity of the eggs.

Things... things swam in that darkness, Anne. Things plucked from the very nightmares of children, the creature under the bed, the unmitigated horrors which that accursed American writer pens. Unimaginable horrors, yet oh so very real. So real. So...

My mind is not what it was. I remember things I should not remember. Dark things, as well as a past I did not—could not—live. They speak of demons which hunt children at night. These demons are wont to hunt grown men in the open daylight. The eggs... they are tools. They are beacons. They are evil.

I must... must remember to mail this out. Hah. The mail is quite amusing. Postage is required to send parcels across international boundaries. A pauper's ransom. Even here, in the cold depths of Ukraine... or is it the Ukrainian Soviet Socialist Republic now? It is so confusing, so very...

One last item of business, Anne, before I send this off. The eggs seem to enjoy my company, my being. I think they recognize me as a creature of its own kind. It needs me, Anne.

It? I meant *they*, dear woman. I do not know why I talked about it. It. It. That is quite amusing.

They need me. Oh God, they need me.

And I, them.

Fare thee well, Anne.

Michael

# 1926 WORLD EVENTS

First public demonstration of television, John L Baird, London

Disney Brothers Cartoon Studio becomes Walt Disney Studios

A train in Costa Rica falls into the Río Virilla, killing 248 and injuring 93—survivors report engineer tossing large black stone into the firebox before a gargantuan explosion of green flamed erupted from the boiler

Thomas Edison says Americans prefer silent movies over talkies

National Bar Association incorporates

Houdini stays in a coffin under water for 1½ hrs before escaping

# Empire Dreams

by Gustavo Bondoni

## LONDON, NOVEMBER 22nd, 1928

Dear Malcolm,

I trust this missive finds you well. From your earlier correspondence, I imagine you are preparing to winter in Bengal before pushing north into Nepal. I can only imagine what sights you will be seeing, since my own time in the Indian Territories was spent along the west coast, as adjutant to Lieutenant Governor R————. It was our duty in those days to keep a whole raft of Islamists and Maharajas from feeling we were being more benevolent towards the other group, and there was little for a soldier to do but talk. I hear things are a bit more unsettled at the moment.

Before I go on, it is my unpleasant but inescapable duty to remonstrate with you over the fact that you have not sent Alice any news for over a month. While I understand that life in the colonies is often of a hectic nature, you must make allowances for the infirmities of her sex. She is often morose, and if this continues much longer, she will be distraught. Not a day passes that the poor creature doesn't come round and ask me if I've had any news of her gallant Sir Malcolm Bester.

Having said that, please tell me all of the news of India. Captain W————— wrote recently and recounted that bit of excitement with the bandits on the road out of Berdwah. Sometimes these people drive me to despair: haven't the centuries taught them that attacking Redcoats is a quick path to Hell, no matter the true color of their uniforms? And I heard you had a company of Royal Marines along as well. Poor blighters.

As for myself, I am feeling a little out of sorts. I know it's only been three years since I took my pension, but today marks the tenth anniversary of my last active duty on a battlefield. It was on November twenty-second, nineteen hundred and eighteen that my regiment turned over the guard duty of the hospital behind the Verdun lines to the French. It was little more than a cave when we got it but, over the two years we were there, we turned it into a place where your chances of living actually improved. We even had a small rail installation. And I can still recall the night we held it against everything the Kaiser could send our way, all the way until the reinforcements managed to cross the killing field at dawn.

To you, in the prime of your life, these must sound like the ramblings of a useless old fool. Perhaps they are. But I think you, of all people, understand, even if your service is not under arms but a quest to discover new frontiers for the Empire. You well know how the spirit withers when there is no quest spurring it on.

Tell me of India, and of your preparations for Nepal. You will make this old fool enormously happy.

Yours Sincerely,

Colonel Jonathan Andrews, OBE

**BENGAL, FEBRUARY 17th, 1929**

Dear Colonel,

I was saddened to hear that my beloved Alice is pining. Despite the hardships we've suffered over the past few weeks, I've done my best to insure that my letters are more frequent than they previously had been. But, in case that is insufficient, I count on your wisdom in reassuring her that she is the light that guides me through these dark lands. I must thank you again for your intervention: it is not every man who can count on the steadfast support of his wife-to-be's father. And not every man can turn to the wisdom of the hero of a dozen battles for guidance.

As you can probably imagine from the above, I consider you anything but an old fool.

Nevertheless, I can certainly tell you about India. I doubt you will find much interest in what I write, however, as I suspect you saw much the same India as I did. Hordes of people everywhere, even in what—in other lands—should certainly be deserted wilderness. Perhaps here in the east we have fewer Moslems than what you encountered in the west, but they are quite a bit more vocal. One wonders how the peace is maintained.

We are staying at the palace of a Maharajah who calls himself the Northernmost Duke in British India. It is ridiculous, of course, as much of India is to the North, but he just smiles and says that there is no more India if one walks straight north. These Indians certainly understand the values of the Empire; in fact, I often wonder whether they aren't more British in their customs than we English. They are definitely stuffier!

The Maharajah, upon learning that an expedition headed by a member of the Royal Society was in his land, immediately ordered full court, and gave each of the men—even the simple riflemen!—a gift. My own was in the form of a cigar humidor, encrusted with black stones of what seem to be a superior caliber. It is clear that I cannot carry such a treasure with me along the road ahead, so I have sent it back with Sir William F———-, who will hand it over for safekeeping at the Trinity Club. I'm certain you will be able to enjoy it there, and trust that the lads will keep it well stocked awaiting my return.

Still, it is somewhat amusing to see how the Indians create lawns and formal gardens which require a troop of men to tend. It must not be easy to keep the grounds clear of cobras and elephants—and even when they are successful, these oriental palaces bear little resemblance to our own manor houses.

The men, of course, make light of the solemn and serious Indians. An old soldier and gentleman such as yourself would be shocked to hear how they misrepresent the Empire. But they don't seem to consider the Maharajah to be genuine royalty—even if the man has millennia backing up his claim to that particular seat—unlike most British nobles I could point at.

In any case, as you can see, my life this winter has been more about court intrigue (not much of it) and a sense of impatience. It is well warm enough to travel—but I am told the mountains in Nepal can be treacherous, so we wait.

I send you my warmest regards,
Malcolm Bester

## JANAKPUR, APRIL 31st, 1929

Dear Colonel,

I sincerely hope this letter reaches you safely, for it will likely have been entrusted to one of our bag-handlers, a man whose enthusiasm, I fear, probably exceeds his competence. But is not this type of uncertainty one of the joys of the trail?

If this does reach you safely, please send my warmest regards to dear Alice. I was worried to hear that she'd been unwell, but delighted to learn that her recovery was expected to be complete. I will be expecting news of her shortly—please send it to the 8th lancers in Bengal, as they will know how to reach our expedition.

I must say that the whole trek north was completely unlike anything I have ever seen. I know you are aware of the treaty of friendship signed with the Nepali king in 1923, but I assure you that you could never imagine the effects. Instead of heading into the unknown with a regiment of riflemen like something out of Conrad, I find myself surrounded by dandies who fancy themselves adventurers. They seem to believe that, since the Empire has tamed all the known world, the only way to make a name for themselves is to climb Everest, which they claim to be the highest peak in the world. I suspect there are probably higher in places in the rugged Andes—or even here in the Himalayas themselves. The topographical expedition can't have mapped the area completely, considering that it was closed off until relatively recently.

But these men will hear nothing of it. They insist that they will go down in history as the men who conquered the roof of the Earth. Just think: many of them haven't even done their time in the army, yet they believe they can attain honor. What is the Empire coming to?

At least, the dandies had the good sense to bring a bunch of Australians with them. Those men aren't concerned about glory or honor or anything else, they just want to see this bl**** big mountain everyone is talking about, and they reckon that, if the weather's good, they might give it a go. They make the Englishmen look positively effete. There's also a rather less boisterous group of New Zealanders with them, but I doubt whether any of those chaps will amount to much on the hills.

It is a far cry from the days when we were bringing the light of the Empire to the dark depths of Africa—now, we are on joy walks to climb hills.

Fortunately, my own expedition should prove a little more worthwhile, and possibly even more dangerous, for while the young gentlemen head for the peaks, I shall roam among the unexplored valleys. What I will find there is a mystery at the moment, but I have received permission from both the Nepali kingdom and the Tibetans to roam essentially freely among their lowlands. It is easy to keep one's gaze fixed on the sky and forget that the human side of life takes place on the ground—especially here, where no one has ever even heard of the aeroplane!

I am hoping to shed some light on the beliefs of the inhabitants, and their history, and perhaps find the basis of the legends of Shangri-La that seem to follow every explorer into these regions. Even if what comes is—as must be expected—of a considerably more pedestrian nature, it cannot be a disappointment.

Turning to more mundane considerations for a few moments, you have my sincere thanks for being the vehicle by which I confirmed that the humidor has arrived safely in London. And while I bow to Sir Thallenby's superior knowledge of jewelry, I must say that his assertion that the diamonds on the box may be worth a small fortune seems a little far-fetched. I won't even address his opinion that they might be related to some of the missing Romanov Jewelry. Pure fantasy! I personally believe that the stones are some kind of glass smoked by local Indian jewelers. They have many techniques that would surprise London artisans, and I wouldn't be the least bit surprised if this was just another case of supposed experts trying to fit everything into familiar molds.

Much more welcome was the news that the humidor is being enjoyed by all and sundry. That, after all, is why I sent it there! I'm also delighted to learn that you've been spending time at the Trinity again. The old club is never the same without you to lighten the mood with your preposterous stories of the trenches.

Well, I must be off. I hope this reaches you, and I know that my next letter will probably be even less likely to make it across the hazards. The next one will be sent from some valley deep in Nepalese territory, or perhaps even from the depths of Tibet.

We will have to trust in God and in the Royal Mail—whatever of it I can find down here, at least!—to keep us in communication.

I send you my warmest regards,
Malcolm

## GARKHA, AUGUST 17th, 1929

Dear Colonel,

We've had two miracles in our communication thus far: that my previous letter from Nepal made it all the way to England, and that your response managed to reach our support garrison, and then passed into my hands.

I won't entrust this particular missive to a third instance of Divine intervention, but will instead dispatch it with a company of Royal Marines. You will come to understand how I have such a company at my disposal as you read.

In the first place, I must tell you that the route into the depths of Nepal was much less eventful than I initially thought it would be. The King himself came to visit before we left Janakpur. That, of course, surprised us, but even more astonishing was the informality of his court and the fact that much of his finery seemed old and threadbare. He reminded me—in demeanor if not appearance—of a modern country squire: good family, but in dire need of money and of manners, and particularly desirous of any form of novelty. It seems strange to say this, but he came across as a jolly old fellow.

Informality aside, it must be said that the man's authority leaves nothing to be desired. Everywhere we went, the signet ring he gave us turned snarling packs of Sherpas into the most obsequious fellows you could imagine. Anything we wanted, we were given, and access to all the closed lands were ours.

The access was such that it quickly became apparent that our hopes of making it into Tibet itself were unrealistic. While the silly young men who are attempting to climb the mountains might be the dregs of the Empire, I must admit that the mountains themselves are daunting. I've been to the high Alps, and it must be said that they are nothing like this. These mountains are not picturesque, and they are not inspiring. The Himalayas are masses of grey rock that go on forever, and up forever, and they do not welcome anyone into their midst. To go further north would have meant adding months to the expedition—and creating the risk of never returning.

Fortunately, though, the south of Nepal would suffice to keep an expeditionary force busy for decades. It seems as though every power known to man has made its mark here, despite the difficulty of access. Apart from the purely earthly powers, I have also found evidence of all the forms of Hindu worship, of animistic cults that would seem more at home in Africa, of the followers of Mohammed and even traces of Christianity. But one temple in particular had me baffled. It was like nothing I'd ever encountered before—nor did it even incorporate the *elements* of anything familiar.

But it becomes obvious that I must backtrack or I shall lose the comprehension of my audience.

After the king allowed us to go on our way, we went towards the foot of Everest, tracing the steps of the erstwhile mountaineers—but we never actually came within sight of the famous mount because, in our way, a high mountain valley, as green as the mountains were grey, knifed off into the distance. We decided to explore it a little further, and perhaps find some people or artifacts that had been previously unknown to white man. I must also admit to visions of unlikely oriental palaces and perhaps even some approximation of Shangri-La at the end of it, but it was not something I would have willingly admitted to my men, as you can imagine.

The reason that this particular valley seemed so seductive was that the entrance was overgrown and completely hidden from casual view. Only chance made it possible for us to discover it. At one small village we were given an honorary fusillade by the Nepalese Royal Guard, who were astonished to see the King's signet on display. The sound of the gunfire—and I tell you honestly that I would have faced keelhauling rather than fire any of those antiques—caused a rockslide of considerable proportions, which fell harmlessly into what seemed like a wooded depression, empty of any true depth. You can only imagine our surprise when the dust settled to reveal that the vegetation had been concealing a thin but deep cleft between the rocks.

Although the villagers declined to guide us—in fact attempted to dissuade us from moving into the chasm—we were determined to explore, and even moreso when we found that the chasm widened into a valley that wound its way between a series of mountains in what seemed an impossible way. I honestly believe that all twenty of our party felt that we'd stumbled, quite by accident, onto something of great significance. No one raised any objections when I proposed a change of itinerary.

The valley itself was remarkable for its geography and its vegetation. I thought a place as remote as that one would have been overgrown and nearly impassable. But this one wasn't. The hiking was easy, with much of the vegetation consisting of little more than low shrubs and coarse grass. In some places, there was no vegetation at all, merely exposed and blackened stone. This last feature caused us some concern, as we immediately suspected that the cause might be lightning from the endless mountain storms—not a cheerful thought for a party with a long walk ahead of them.

In this valley, we encountered many points of interest. Abandoned villages were scattered here and there. There was even one that seemed as though it had been attacked with siege engines: the stone huts (rare in this region) had had holes opened into them that certainly seemed to have been created by a catapult rock launch or even by cannon. The evidence suggests catapults, as there were plenty of stones, but nothing that looked like cannon rounds.

We saw no sign of present human occupation until we came nearly to the upper end of the valley. There, we found traces of recently skinned animals and strange snares made of tough cord. It was impossible to locate the hunters, but we did encounter one more item of what seems to be more than passing interest.

Wedged between two mountains at the very top of the valley, we found what can only be described as a temple. It was the work of mere moments by myself and young John—surely you remember John, my irritating young cousin? Well, he has come out of Oxford after reading Oriental Studies and Archaeology, and is quite a reasonable approximation of a human being—that the temple corresponded to no creed we'd ever encountered before. While much of the imagery and iconography was more than a little disturbing, it was clearly a treasure of incalculable academic value.

So, to summarize a month of negotiations, we have obtained the Nepalese government's permission to dismantle the temple and bring it home, where I hope the British Museum will agree to display it. Even if it remains in a dismantled state in the cellars, it will certainly be of immense value to our scholars.

I must admit to having been surprised with the facility with which the king gave up the temple. The Nepalese seemed almost eager to send it away. Shows that, even if they have stuffy kings, they are not truly civilized at heart.

So, I end by asking you a favor. My team shall split into two: half of the men will supervise the transportation of the temple (and the men who will bring you this letter among them), while the other half will come with me to continue my search for other artifacts of note. Could you please supervise the delivery of the crates to the museum? I will sleep easier knowing you are there to oversee the particulars.

I have also included a letter, under separate seal, for Alice.

I send you my warmest regards,

Malcolm

## EMMA, MY LOVE,

If you can get out from under the sight of your uncle for a little while this afternoon, I'd love to show you something that will give you nightmares for weeks. I think it will have all of London society talking for some time—and you can come and see it even before the fine folk get a glimpse.

It's something a crew of my workers were hired to put together in the Museum, and the nobs have given me a copy of the key to the shed they built it in. It's not so much that they trust me, but that no one in their right mind would walk off with any piece of the thing, even if you could lift the stone blocks!

Anyhow, if you'd like to see it, try to be at the rear door at three.

Love and kisses,

Barney

## DECEMBER 22ⁿᵈ, 1929

Dear Malcolm,

I must commend you on your multiple successes. In the first place, the temple, which I have not yet seen in full illumination, is magnificent. I have never seen anything like it, nor have I ever seen the esteemed members of the Royal

Society quite so atwitter. Their behavior seemed more suited to a flock of schoolgirls than to the eminent scientists of the realm.

They are half-convinced that it is the best-preserved example in the entire world of the temple of a death-cult, although the cynic in me wonders whether that is because of the monstrous carvings or whether it is due to the fact that a young couple chose to commit suicide at the foot of the entrance. Witnesses say it was quite a gruesome scene.

The second triumph was the cigar humidor which, at midnight last night—the shortest day of the year—suddenly erupted in violent green light at the club. By what miracle of miniaturization they managed to get the battery pack inside the thin walls of the box, I do not know, but the light itself was stunning. I felt as though the wisdom of the ages passed into me through it—and I know that others among the company felt the same.

So I'm glad you're nearly back, and I wish I could persuade you to accelerate your return from Calais. It would have been fitting for you to serve as Master of Ceremonies for the unveiling tonight. I know you haven't seen your brother in over a year, but Alice is nearly beside herself with anticipation of your return—and besides, after last night's display, I wouldn't put it past any of the chaps at the club to walk off with your humidor. It was a very impressive performance.

Anyhow, I am looking forward to seeing you very soon.

Yours Sincerely,

Colonel Jonathan Andrews, OBE

## DOCUMENT OSA 0379442

British Museum Archives

Oriental Studies Archives

Oriental Religions Department

December 23rd, 1929

Report: Unveiling of Nepalese temple (stone; carvings; bas-relief)

The unveiling of the newly assembled Nepalese temple took place in a specially partitioned section facing Montague Place. Present were the curators of all collections in the Oriental Studies Department, the Museum Director, Colonel Jonathan Andrews, OBE, and several members of Parliament. Also present were certain select members of the Royal Society, by invitation only.

The event began at 7 PM sharp, and there were speeches planned in honor of Sir Malcolm Bester (by Colonel Andrews) and an explanation of the symbolic nature of the carvings on the inside of the temple, by Dr. Evans. It was then planned that the invitees could study the temple for themselves, until closure at 9:30 PM. The details of the schedule can be seen in the timetable, included under this same cover.

The proceedings were unexpectedly interrupted by Colonel Andrews himself when, after less than a minute of his speech, he proclaimed that: "The door is meant to be open," and began to strike different portions of the carvings at the front of the temple with his palms, while chanting in a language that the academics present could not decipher, but which Mr. Branniff suspected might be an ancient Cambodian dialect, possibly related to Khmer.

After about forty-five seconds of Colonel Andrews's ministrations, the doorway of the temple began to emit a faint green glow, which lasted only for a few moments before subsiding. But when it disappeared, the interior of the temple was gone, replaced by what seems to be an endless misty swamp. After a small exploratory foray, it was decided that evening dress was inappropriate attire for the terrain that had appeared within the temple, and that a mixed party of astronomers, physicists and mathematicians needed to be gathered to attempt to understand the interdimensional paradoxes that are evidently—according to Dr. Evans—at work within the temple. In addition to this, it has been decided that an experienced explorer is needed to lead any incursions.

When questioned about how he knew what to do, Colonel Andrews himself professed no memory of the incident. He seemed disoriented and a bit dizzy, and asked to sit down. When pressed, all he would say is that he remembered a light, and some knowledge. He did say that the light was green, perhaps a memory of the opening.

All individuals present at the unveiling have been sworn to secrecy so as to keep the press from learning about this. There is speculation that the knowledge gained may be useful to the War Ministry if the situation on the continent continues to deteriorate.

To be filed in confidential archives until such time as it is released by signature of the Museum Director.

Typed and filed by Catherine Tanner-Lyme
(countersigned)

## CALAIS, DECEMBER 26th, 1929

Dear Colonel,

I beg of you to forgive the scrawl, but I have just heard the news, and the excitement is almost too much. I shall leave tomorrow, and hopefully be there by evening—which means that you will receive me not long after you receive this letter!

I cannot wait to set eyes on this land of mystery that was revealed inside my temple; who could have guessed that it would contain something of such significance? My family here was extremely upset, of course. They are not the type of people who could possibly understand the call of exploration, but I have managed to ignore their pleas.

Of course, it will also be delightful to see Alice once again. I would be very grateful if you could tell her of my change of plans, and that some god must have heard her prayers for my early return! Of course, I very much doubt that there is actual divine intervention occurring, but it is a romantic thought. I cannot take the time to write another letter, as I must repack all my luggage—not a small task, considering everything I somehow managed to accumulate over these long months.

Of course, I trust that you will influence the selection of the military men who will come with me. While it is all very well and good to proceed in the name of expanding the Empire, it would probably be best to avoid selecting hotheads who might create problems with natives that would other-wise submit peacefully. I have every faith that you will be able to guide the powers that be into making the correct choice.

Best,
Malcolm

My dearest Malcolm,

I wish I had the words to tell you how I feel, but words cannot explain a love this vast, this proud, or this desperate. My heart sings when I think of you, and all my dreams hold images of our life together. I close my eyes and visualize the peaceful gardens of your country seat populated by our children: strong boys and beautiful girls frolicking in the emerald grass.

This week we've spent together has been the best of my life. I remembered why I first fell in love with you, and it also strengthened my conviction that no other man could possibly make my life worth living.

I am not writing this to convince you not to go on your journey, but to give you strength, to make certain that you know that there is a woman here in London who will love you as long as the stars shine in the sky, and as long as she lives. Perhaps that knowledge will hasten your return, or perhaps give you the strength to overcome any terrors that might threaten you on your way.

Keep this missive on your person for luck. I know that the strength of my love will ward off any danger. I know God smiles upon our union—for what is the love I feel if not the presence of the Almighty living within me?

I will love you for always, and I will await your return forever,

Alice

PS: I beseech you to ignore the stains where my tears have blotted the ink. They are just a woman's moment of weakness. I love you.

I pray that whoever finds this will not think less of me for my weakness. I hope you are not shocked, and that you will rearrange me so that I am in a dignified pose before you call the authorities. They say that hemlock causes a death that is a little less unpleasant than that of arsenic—or even wolfsbane. Still, I cannot imagine it will be a pleasant scene. I beg forgiveness.

How easily I can speak of it. But then, are you truly surprised? My life is over, and has been over since that cold January day when the portal closed, leaving my beloved Malcolm stranded where no human has likely ever gone before, and no human will ever likely reach again.

I spent my time wondering what they wanted with such a man, but the way of gods and demons is beyond my ken—and I doubt there was much of the divine in this, for what god would destroy a love such as ours.

And, friend (for who but a friend would come into my room to be able to find me?), I beg you also to ignore the swelling of my stomach. Tell the undertaker that I was promised to be married, and perhaps he will choose to forget to report my condition. There must be much human decency in such a profession. Please do not attempt to calculate the months which passed from the last time I laid eyes on my gallant, doomed Sir Malcolm. Be a friend to me in this as well.

I'm glad my father is gone, and that my brother is off in China. That way, neither of them will be the first to see me, cold and stiff.

Now I, who have stayed home while my love roamed the Earth, will be the one to take the trip—a trip no one has ever reported upon.

Perhaps it will bring me closer to my love. I can only pray.

## DOCUMENT OSA 0379475

British Museum Archives

Oriental Studies Archives

Oriental Religions Department

June 12th, 1930

Report: Disturbance near the Nepalese Temple exhibit

On the night of June 11th, 1930, Mr. Thomas Digby, a night watchman of four years' standing, with a clean and acceptable record, reported strange illuminations and sounds emanating from the sub-wing housing the reconstructed Nepalese Temple. The green lights described seem similar to those seen on the night of the temple's unveiling. The sounds, on the other hand, were described as something like "wolves howling and pigs grunting". It has been decided to avoid including the sounds in any formal description of the temple until more qualified experts can look into the issue.

He hurried along to investigate, but found the area dark and empty, with only a single sheet of some strange parchment or hide out of place. Though the watchman swears that it must have come from inside the temple, it cannot be ruled out that the sheet may have found its way—by accident or design—from some other part of the Museum. Further investigation is warranted in this case as well.

Nevertheless, it is worthy of documenting that the parchment is not blank. There is writing on it, in English, which holds words that are difficult to make out (there are dark stains on much of its surface, which, in some cases obliterate the writing nearly entirely). The best transcript this recorder could manage follows:

I am Sir Malcolm Bester, explorer and gentleman. I hope you heed my words.

Do not try to come through the portal I entered, do not send men to save us. For if you do, you send them to their doom. It is not a doom of the flesh—most of the men who entered the portal with me are still alive today. Or at least they are alive from a certain point of view.

But we will never walk in God's light, will never be welcomed back into the fold. What we have done—and what has been done to us—is different in each case, but is beyond horror, beyond perversion, beyond any trace of the human. Pillage, rape, murder most foul are just the beginning, the appetizers of our debauch.

I have known how to return. Any one of us could have returned the very moment the portal closed—from this side, its opening mechanism is nothing but a lever. But we chose not to. There was singing in our minds and temptation in our hearts and even the most virtuous of the men was lost from the start.

And now? Now it is impossible. The rot inside our souls has affected us physically. If we were to walk among you now, we would look like the most horrific of deformed creatures. And no man or woman would be strong enough to resist us. You would be nothing but food and playthings for any of our base wishes.

This is why I leave you the letter. Destroy the temple. Grind its stones to dust. I know—without knowing how I know, but that is not surprising here—that I have left behind a product of my seed. I have only enough strength in this lucid moment to leave this note, to try to save my son. For in a few more days—or perhaps weeks, or centuries, since time is so difficult and confused here—I shall be part of the invading army, and will not hesitate to eat my own child.

There is horror coming. Horror you cannot begin to imagine. There are places on the Earth through which we can influence mankind, and the wheels are already in motion.

I fear it is already too late for you.

It is certainly too late for me.

The text ends with no further explanation. The parchment is included under this same cover.

To be filed in confidential archives until such time as it is released by signature of the Museum Director.

Typed and filed by Catherine Tanner-Lyme

(countersigned)

NOTE: Document released into Museum Public Archives following House of Commons inquiry into the strange occurrences of 20__.

(countersigned)

## DOCUMENT OSA 7476661

British Museum Archives

Director's Private Archives

August 3rd, 1930

Report: Loss of exhibit, Nepalese Temple

On the night of August 2nd, 1930, the Museum was rocked by the most brutal act of vandalism in all its history. A number of artifacts from the Oriental Religions department, most notably the centerpiece of the collection, the rebuilt Nepalese temple, were destroyed in a large explosion.

Lieutenant Ernest Johnson (son of the late, lamented Colonel Johnson), a deserter from the Royal Corps of Engineers formerly stationed in East Africa, was captured on the scene, and admitted to the crime, claiming to have acted in order to revenge his father and sister—but also to be acting on the orders of mysterious voices in his head. He is clearly a madman, but that does not lessen the loss the Museum has suffered.

As maximum authority, I believe it is my responsibility, and, under separate cover, you will find enclosed my letter of resignation.

Signed,
Lord Entermas
Countersignature:
Not included


NOTE: Document released into Museum Public Archives following House of Commons inquiry into the strange occurrences of 20___.

(countersigned)

# 1929 WORLD EVENTS

BUCK ROGERS, first sci-fi comic strip, premieres

St Valentine's Day Massacre in Chicago, 7 gangsters killed, allegedly on Al Capone's orders

First Academy Awards announced

Vatican City becomes a sovereign state

US cartoonist E.C. Segar creates POPEYE

German airship Graf Zeppelin ends a round-the-world flight

Dow Jones plummets 38.33 pts (13%) to 260.64

Museum of Modern Art opens (NYC)

Salvador Dali premiere at Goeman's gallery, Paris—artist tells reporter that black diamond cufflink from girlfriend Tristan Tzara opened a green doorway to his subconscious

# A Year of Gin and Diamonds

by Jamie K. Schmidt


**JANUARY 15th 1930**

Harlem

Dear Mama,

I got a job at the Black Diamond! It's the ritziest club in Harlem. They have two doormen and you have to be dressed real nice or they won't let you in. They gave me a hard time so I stood on the curb and belted out Bell Baker's "My Man." I drew such a crowd that the owner himself, Mr. Fine, escorted me into my first speakeasy. Now, don't get all het up, Mama. It's no different from Cousin Donny's still. Yes, I know about that and the Mason jar you got under the sink. Anyway, Mr. Fine is a real swell. He got me a drink called the Bee's Knees—and Mama it was! It was so sweet and after a few swallows I wasn't even nervous anymore. I got to audition in my pretty dress that you made me. I had a full orchestra behind me and everything. It was really classy. And when he heard me sing, he hired me on the spot. I start on Saturday. I told you Mama. I told you I'm going to be a big star. When I get my first paycheck, I'll send some home. Give my love to little Eddie and Jean Marie. I miss you guys.

Love always, Eliza Jane


**JANUARY 25th 1930**

Harlem

Dear Mama,

I killed! I had men throwing roses up on the stage. I even got a few marriage proposals! But Mr. Fine kept me away from the riff-raff. He even gave me my own body guard. His brother Bennie looks out for me. Bennie's a giant. He weighs more than Grandpa's prize hog. No one crosses the line while Bennie's there. Mr. Fine says I've got to go for a makeover. He said he wants to get rid of the smell of manure and the hayseed, but I think he's just kidding. I take a bath every day. Still, maybe I should buy some perfume. You know, just in case. I'm enclosing a sawbuck. That's half my salary. It's a good job Mama. There are a lot of people here that don't have anything. I see a lot of it in my apartment. Six of us are sharing one room and someone in the building is always boiling cabbage. I sleep with my money stuffed in my sock. Last week, I came home and some hoodlums had knifed up our mattresses looking for dough. I gave some bills to a lady next door whose husband drinks their food money away. Times are tight, but Mister said if I decide to do some singing on the side for his friends, I can make some more in tips. You should see the city at night. I crawl out on the fire escape just to escape the stench and it's like Christmas with all the lights. It's another world from back home. Sometimes I feel like I'm in the middle of a movie. But sometimes, I feel like there's something watching me. Enjoying me the way I'm enjoying the scenery. That's why I have Bennie walk me home every night. I'm being careful. Maybe one day I can have enough money to send for you all to come up here. You'd like the city, Mama.

I love you all lots—Eliza Jane

## FEBRUARY 15, 1930

Harlem

Dear Mama,

How are you and the family? I'm doing great. I've got a following. Men and women are lining up to hear me—ME—sing. It's everything I've ever hoped for. Except, I'm exhausted. I barely get to bed and then it's morning. You know I can't sleep when I see the sun out. Mr. Fine wants to move me to a better neighborhood. But I don't know if I can afford it. He's offered to let me stay with him. And before you have a fit, his house is bigger than the town hall. In fact you can fit two town halls where his house is. He has a pool and there are a lot of other people living with him. Bennie lives there and I see women in and out all the time. He says he's got a room in the basement for me. It's not like I'm afraid of the dark, but it's a little spooky. I think I'd be OK though. Oh, and guess what? I'm a blond now! You wouldn't even believe it. Mister took me to this fancy salon. And they cut it real short, but pretty. I've got curls and waves around my face and I think I look a little like Mary Pickford. Mister calls me his little canary. I like him, Mama. He's super slick and handsome. But when he puts his hand on my back, I get all shivery and not in a good way. Maybe it's because he's way out of my league. And his other girls are much prettier than I am. But you know what? None of them can sing like I can. He might be able to get me on the radio, but he says I'm not quite there yet. Don't worry about me. I'll do whatever it takes. I'm sending $20 home this time. I got a big tip from one of Mister's friends. His name was Johnny. He's some kind of salesman. He liked my hair comb—the one I got at the five and dime back home. So as a lark, I put it in his hair. After my performance when I went back into my dressing room, there was a box for me. Inside I found a blue silk tie and the twenty. I knew it was from Johnny because it was the same tie he had been wearing that night. It smelled like his aftershave, all dark and mysterious. Mister wasn't too happy that his friend gave me his tie, but he didn't care about the cash. Men are so strange. Bennie wouldn't talk to me either for a few days. Do you think I did anything wrong, Mama? I suppose I can always return the tie when I see him again. Take care. Give everyone a kiss for me.

Love you—Eliza Jane

## MARCH 15, 1930

Harlem

Hi Mama,

Life is grand, ain't it? I'm making a hundred dollars a night. So Mister only has me working two nights a week, Saturday and Sunday. The rest of the time, Bennie and me get dolled up and go out and paint the town. You can't believe how big New York City really is Mama. And I think Mister might have other interests than bootlegging, but I don't have any proof except for the other night, I sang for some gangsters! I could see their bean shooters and every-thing. It was so exciting. They were good tippers too. Although one of them got a little fresh and Bennie almost broke his hand on the hood's face. The party broke up shortly after that, but I didn't care. Mister and I were drinking champagne and he's teaching me how to blow smoke rings when the band starts playing my number. I wasn't supposed to be on, but I figure what they hey a girl's gotta go what a girl's gotta do, right? And then they announce me. Only it ain't my name. Or rather it is now. Mister said that with my new hair and new clothes, I have to have a new name: Hazel. So I go up and do my thing and they start chanting my name: Hazel! Hazel! They love me. Mister said it was time. He's producing a radio show called The Black Diamond Review and I'm going to headline. My time has come. I'm going to be a star. Say hello to all the little people for me. I'm going to be on the Columbia Broadcasting System at 6 PM on April 15th.

Kisses! Love you! Hazel

## APRIL 16, 1930

Harlem

Did you hear me on the radio Mama? They're talking about giving me a part in a drama. It's just a small one. I get murdered in the first fifteen minutes. Mister says he likes it the way I scream in terror. He says I'm a natural. I didn't appreciate you scolding me in your last letter. There's no need to blow your wig. I'm a grown woman. I know what I'm doing. I will drink and smoke and kiss all the boys I want to. And there's nothing you can do about it. You didn't even thank me for the clams I sent. I hope they got to you. I will be seriously cheesed if someone filched them. You let me know. I'm going to send a C-note this time. Mister was really proud of me. He says I'm his number one girl. Don't you worry. I'm holding out for a wedding ring. But that don't mean I can't have a little fun while I'm young, right? There's this saxophone player, Mama. He's got the most beautiful eyes. He's Cuban. His name is Esteban. He watches me when no one else is looking. And when I catch his eyes, I get that fluttery feeling but in a real good way. Esteban makes my heart pound when he smiles at me. Unfortunately, he smiles at all the dolls like that. Bennie tells me that if Mister finds out Esteban is doing more than smiling with me, he'll kill him. But that ain't fair. Mister has floozies all over him night and day just because I can't party as late as the rest of them. I've got to go down to my room to get some sleep. The dark room is so quiet. Only the gin and the darkness seem to ease my headaches. I'm scared that my voice is going to go because I'm singing so much, but it never does. I don't know what I'd do if I couldn't sing no more. Bennie keeps me company sometimes. We don't do more than pet and fool around, but it helps to have company. I don't feel those eyes watching me as much when I'm not alone. I am so far from home Mama. And I don't ever want to come back. The sky here is full of stars and the darkness is like deep rich soil that I've been planted in. I'm becoming more. Sometimes when Bennie is snoring off the hooch, I take out the blue silk tie Mister's odd friend gave me and I rub it against my cheek. You don't have fine things like I do Mama. I need them. Don't ask me to come home again. I am home.

Love Hazel

## JUNE 15, 1930

Harlem

Diamonds are a girl's best friend.

No, I'm not engaged. Not yet. So many suitors. So little time.
Sorry I haven't written. Things have been crazy and a little strange.

I lost my voice for a few days. I think it was the Jamaican Ginger I was drinking. My throat just closed up. I could barely breathe. But all I could think of was my career was over. And it was OK that I was going to die. Because if I can't sing, I don't want to live. But then Esteban was there, breathing into my mouth until I caught my breath. Of course, Bennie gave him a goog for his trouble, but at least he didn't hit him in the mouth. Esteban brings in a lot of kittens with his saxophone. Can't hurt the merchandise, right Mamacita? So there I was. Alive, but can't talk. Mister tells me to lay off the cigs and wood alcohol for a few days. He swats me on the bottom and tells me to get some rest. Bennie takes me home. Only, I'm not tired and I'm not in the mood to be pawed on by Bennie, so he goes off to take a cold shower or canoodle with one of the Shebas in the pool. I hate being sober in Mister's house, so I go exploring. Mister's at the club, so he won't know if I go into his bedroom. I ain't never been. I know the farmer won't buy the cow if the milk is free. His bedroom wasn't what I was expecting. I pictured black satin sheets, wall to wall booze and a few tomatoes sleeping it off in his bed. But it's nothing like that. He's got books. Like a lot of them. And maps everywhere, posted up on all the walls. They look like treasure maps of the subway system and there are marks on them where they're constructing new lines. Names like Bobby the Deuce and Hardy John are written in red with a cross over them. I think that's where the bodies are literally buried. My throat was on fire and I would've killed for a sidecar or anything cold and alcoholic. I knew Mister wasn't a shiny penny, but I didn't think he was a thug. A bootlegger, a pimp, yeah he's got fingers in a lot of pies. But he's a gangster. All those conversations I half heard during smoky nights with my head on the bar, suddenly now make sense. There were weapons all over the bedroom too. Tommy guns and gats scattered on the floor like dirty underwear. I don't want to be a moll. I just want to sing. I went back to my own room and tried to ignore the eyes watching me in the darkness.

To make a long story short, a few days go by and my voice is still nada. Mister brings me into his office and I'm like well this is it. The jig is up. He's going to can me and I'll be on the next train back home to you and my life will be over. But it's not like that at all. Mister pulls me on his lap and I let him fondle me a bit, hoping to put him in a good mood. But I'm thinking of Esteban the whole time. Thinking that I'll never see him again. Never hear him play again. Mister is excited about something. I can tell by the way his knee is jiggling. We have a few drinks and he hands me a box that looks surprisingly like the one his friend Johnny gave me. But instead of a tie and some cash, there's something so much nicer!

Two diamond anklets, the stones are blacker than Mister's heart and I know I ought to refuse them. But I know if I do, I'll end up as one of those marks in the subway tunnel. So I hug him and cover his face with kisses. I still can't speak, but I do my best to show him how grateful I am. He puts them on my legs and if his hands get a little frisky, I'm too afraid to stop him. They are the most beautiful things I've ever seen. But they make me nauseous when I look at them. And they're heavy. They feel like prison irons. He says it ain't an engagement ring, but it's the next best thing. He tells me they're magic and I almost believe him when I look at the stones. I swear there is something looking back at me. I don't know if it was the rum I drank or maybe those anklets did have special powers, but that night in the dark of my room they glowed green. The next morning my voice was back. Better than ever.

Hazel


## AUGUST 15, 1930

Harlem

I'm in trouble.

It all started one night after the show. We were in the Black Diamond boozin' it up. I was singing for the fun of it because we had the place to ourselves. Then Mister has to go into a meeting with a bunch of trouble boys from the O'Brien gang. He takes Bennie in with him for protection. So I'm singing a song I made up and all of a sudden I hear a slow, sweet saxophone. Esteban was there. My voice, his saxophone. Well, let's just say we made beautiful music together. And from that night on, I met him every chance I got. Knowing that if we get caught it would be curtains for both of us just makes it more exciting. Mister hasn't been the same since the O'Briens came to flap their gums. We were raided twice and I know those Micks had a hand in it. Esteban got me out of there before the coppers could take me in. Mister didn't even miss me. But Bennie did. He knows something's up because I've stopped our cuddling sessions. I still get scared in the dark, but then I hear Esteban's saxophone in my head and it's all OK. Bennie tries his hardest to catch us in the act. But I'm not worried, he's a twit. Still, I don't like the idea that Mister thinks he owns me. He's got dames like he's got pocket watches. Esteban and me, we have something special. Mister made me, got me on stage, but it's my voice that's packing them in. It's my voice that's selling his bathtub gin and it's my songs that get played on the radio. I can go to the Emerald City and headline if it gets too much.

I tried to take the anklets off. There's no clasp. When Esteban tried, the green glow attacked him. It shot out like a lightning strike and knocked him off his feet. I was so scared. Then my feet started moving on their own accord and I walked out of Esteban's dressing room in my nightgown. There was nothing I could do to stop my feet from heading towards the stage. I would be a laughing stock. Not to mention what Mister would do to me. I was sobbing and crying, trying to throw myself back, but I couldn't stop moving forward. Finally, it was Esteban who hauled me over his shoulder while my anklets shot out green corrosive acid. He was badly burned. His hands are raw, red pits of agony. But he threw me into my dressing room and held the doors with his tortured hands until the green fire died. I know you're thinking it's the gin and the hop that's making me see these things. But how do you explain Esteban's ruined hands? The green mist swirls around me now, but no one else seems to see it. I think Mister does and he keeps his distance. I don't feel like me anymore when I sing. And the people who hear me sing, come away from it different. Changed. A little bit of the green mist comes out of me and into them. Don't come here. Stay far from New York City as you can. The streets are no longer safe day or night.

Hazel

## OCTOBER 31, 1930

Harlem

The shadows of the Sha'Daa are close tonight. I feel it in my legs and see them in the black diamonds. They can't break through the veil. Not yet. Not for a while yet. But there are great things stirring. We're setting the stage for them. I'm singing for them tonight at the masked ball. Herbert Hoover will be there. There's going to be more G-men in the Black Diamond tonight than gangsters. And they'll hear me croon about the great demons who will subjugate us and lead us to a new era of pain and suffering. You think the stock market crash was bad? There's always money. I'm proof of it. And if not money, then food and jewelry, fame and power. All the things that make life worth living. The Sha'Daa are coming and only the chosen will survive.

December 24, 1930
Havana
Feliz Navidad Mama,
That means Merry Christmas in Spanish. I'm hoping to be out of the hospital for New Year's Eve. But I almost died on the flight and they're really worried about me. My stumps got infected and I've been holed up here ever since trying to keep my spirits up. Trying to remember. Trying to forget.

I lost a lot of blood, but I think Esteban is more worried that the green power will come back. But it's gone. It left when the anklets fell off my legs. Esteban said he told you what happened when he called you to let you know I was all right. But I know you won't settle until you hear it from me.

Let me tell you those Secret Service swells don't fool around. I hadn't known the first lady was a geologist. Or that they had some issues with "black diamonds" ever since Black Tuesday. Well, it's too bad about Bennie. He was an OK Joe. He didn't deserve to be gunned down. He was only doing his job and protecting me. I don't remember much—certainly not breathing green fire at my attackers. I'm glad for that. I don't remember them hacking my feet off at the ankles either. I remember the screams and the smell of burning flesh. It smelled like the time we cooked Grandpa's prize hog on the spit. I'll never eat pork again.

Esteban lied to the G-men and said we were married. I asked him why Mister didn't speak up and he said that Mister was being hauled out in hand-cuffs, crying like a baby. I remember waking up in Florida when we changed planes. The agony. I thought I was in hell. I thought that the Sha . . . no—I'll never say their name again. I thought they had taken me. But it was the pain and the heat. It had been freezing in New York that night. Florida was like a sweltering fire pit. Esteban carried me to the smaller plane. His brother's a pilot and flew us to Cuba. I think the US government was glad to see me go.

I'm looking forward to singing Christmas carols in the hospital chapel tonight for midnight mass. I don't have to stand to sing and I think O Holy Night will be the last thing I need to purify my soul so I can start my life with my new husband. I hope you will come visit us soon. We're going to get married on Valentine's Day. I love you and miss you.

Your daughter, Eliza Jane.

# 1933 WORLD EVENTS

Work on Golden Gate Bridge begins, on Marin County side

German president von Hindenburg appoints Hitler chancellor

LONG RANGER premieres on ABC radio

KING KONG premieres at Radio City Music Hall & RKO Roxy NYC

Most powerful earthquake in 180 years hits Japan

Mohandas Gandhi begins a 21-day fast in protest against British oppression in India

Loch Ness Monster sighted by Aldie Mackay

Gold standard abolished

First drive-in theater opens (Camden NJ)—Police report three teenage couples missing after strange green flash of light from the main screen, suspect foul play

# Ecclesia Revenans

by Richard Groller

*"Injustice alone can shake down the pillars of the skies, and restore the reign of Chaos and Night."—Horace Mann*

## TOP SECRET–SCHUTZSTAFFEL–EYES ONLY

### CASTLE WEWELSBURG, 30.9.1936

TO: Reichsführer-SS Heinrich Himmler

FROM: Obersturmbannführer Manfred von Knobelsdorff, Burghauptmann von Wewelsburg

PROGRESS REPORT

1. As directed, your plans are proceeding apace. The architect you appointed is extremely efficient and the plans for the vault, the Totenkopfring repository and the Hall of Supreme Leaders are well along in their design.

2. Quarters have been prepared for your next visit, and the jeweler has delivered a most extraordinary walking stick that now bears the handiwork of Oberführer Weisthor. I am sure you will approve of the modifications. Otto Rahn of the Ahnenerbe was most intrigued by it.

3. On the Intelligence related matter, our agent in Rome has sent a dossier that I am including in this report. It was copied from the Vatican Archive and I attest to its authenticity. I have instituted "special measures" on the probability that this Valerius is aware that the Grail Castle is being built and might decide to turn his special attention upon it. This Catholic abomination of a vampire serving the Vatican must be stopped.

4. The Center of the New World will be protected. The power of the Sonnenrad will be restored.

Heil Hitler!


Attachments:

1–Burned Fragment from Dossier on Valerius von Geist (microfilm)

2–Vatican Classified Appendix, Catholic Encyclopedia

# TOP SECRET–SCHUTZSTAFFEL–EYES ONLY

⊕ ⊕ ⊕

# TOP SECRET–SCHUTZSTAFFEL–EYES ONLY

Attachment 1: Vatican Archives

Chronicles of the Archons: Valerius von Geist, Biographical Summary,

Brother Nicodemus Kallinikos, S.J., Historian

October 12, 1798 Fragment

…Valerius and his Archons worked tirelessly in the new regions under Hapsburg rule to eradicate the influence and power of the undead forces of the Strigoi. That was until Empress Maria Theresa enacted an edict in 1756 that prohibited all traditional processes for the destruction of vampyrs and the undead, such as impalement, beheading and burning of dead bodies, believing it to be hysteria and superstition. Their success had been their undoing. From then on, he only took his orders from Rome, whenever the Order of the Archons needed extraordinary help.

His Jesuit training and Catholicism so deeply ingrained, the theme of redemption and forgiveness pervades his thought. He believes that his life has a purpose, to find the way to salvation, even for the undead. Valerius had an epiphany when he discovered an apocryphal account of Lazarus's resurrection from the dead in some ancient scrolls. In it, Christ was so moved at Lazarus's sepulcher that he wept tears of blood over the body of Lazarus, and it was Christ's blood that brought him back from the dead. If this were true, Valerius decided, then the Blood of Christ was indeed the key to rebirth, even the salvation of those already dead. He has immersed himself in the studies of the Parsifal and the Grail Legends, the Teutonic Knights, the Arthurian Sagas, and the teachings of the Gnostics. Since then his efforts have been concentrated on the search for the Holy Grail, the key to his personal salvation and perhaps the salvation of all who bear the name of vampyr.

# TOP SECRET–SCHUTZSTAFFEL–EYES ONLY

⊕ ⊕ ⊕

# TOP SECRET–SCHUTZSTAFFEL–EYES ONLY

Attachment 2:

The Catholic Encyclopedia, Vatican Classified Appendix, Volume 10, 1913

Entry: Mystical Body of Christ

Fragment

In the history of the world, Father Valerius von Geist actually did a new thing under the sun. He created anew the Mystical Body of Christ by his will, and expanded the Communion of Saints. The Church Militant (*Ecclesia Militans*) is comprised of all living Christians, who are "Soldiers of Christ" in the struggle against sin, the devil, spiritual wickedness, and the rulers of the darkness. The Church Triumphant (*Ecclesia Triumphans*) is comprised of the Saints in Heaven. The Church Penitent (*Ecclesia Penitens*) is comprised of those Christians presently in Purgatory awaiting the Last Judgment where they can finally be united with the Saints in Heaven. And now a new Communion has been reborn, the Church Revenant (*Ecclesia Revenans*), for those members of the Church who were dead but walk again, and still do the work of God. Only two others in history to this point are known, Lazarus of Bethany, friend of Jesus and the first person the Christ resurrected, and Talitha, the daughter of Jairus. Both of these were biblical. But now there walks a new thing under the sun or more to the point, under the night sky to wage war against the foes of Holy Mother Church.

# TOP SECRET–SCHUTZSTAFFEL–EYES ONLY

⊕ ⊕ ⊕

# TOP SECRET–EYES ONLY

Intercepted HF transmission, coded manual Morse:

ZZZZ DTG 2015Z26MAR1945

For the Commander, Third US Army

From the Commander, Third Infantry Division

MG O'Daniel sends for LTG Patton: Kudos–your crossing of the Rhine on the 22nd was fortuitous. Have crossed the Rhine today. By God's grace will make Wewelsburg within the week. Hope to find the Grail and keep it safe for you. Iron Mike.

# TOP SECRET–EYES ONLY

JMJ

Vatican Archives

April 14, 1945

Chronicles of the Archons: Valerius von Geist, Biographical Summary

Update–Transcript of recorded eyewitness account.

I attest to the events of this mission, as the only survivor.

Brother Marius Palladino, S.J., Archon / Historian, Order of the Archons

We were unaware at the time that Reichsführer-SS Himmler had ordered Major Heinz Macher to come to his headquarters in Brenzlau on Good Friday, March 30, 1945. There he personally ordered Heinz to destroy the Wewelsburg to prevent its artifacts from falling into Allied hands. We knew that the Allies had broken through the Siegfried Line south of Zweibrücken on the 15th of March.

As soon as the Mass concluded, we were ushered into the sanctuary and Valerius told us we must gather our things and leave immediately for a task behind enemy lines. The task of retrieving The Holy Grail was finally at hand.

We had been staged in a monastery in Basel in anticipation of a raid into Wewelsburg, and were less than 600 kilometers away as the crow flies. Through the good graces of the Vatican, we had a small Savoia-Marchetti S.M.81 Pipistrello transport plane at our disposal. It had a 2000 kilometer range on internal fuel and a maximum speed of 340 km/h at 1000 meters, thus we could fly in safety through the Vosges Mountains in France, cruising along the Rhine, then behind Patton's forces up to Mainz. The last hour would be through enemy territory under cover of darkness.

Our five-man team planned to parachute in, do our duty and then lay low and repatriate once the Americans arrived. The flight in was remarkably uneventful. We parachuted in next to the deserted Niederhagen concentration camp. It had supplied labor for the remodeling of Wewelsburg, but was dissolved in 1943 when most of the prisoners were resettled to Buchenwald. This course would allow ingress from the North. We made our way quietly through the half mile to the Grail Castle, taking advantage of the cover of darkness and whatever masking terrain we could find.

As Valerius, I, and the rest of the Archons moved to the base of the north tower of Castle Wewelsburg, we had a dark foreboding. The circular stone guard post was manned. Our first obstacle was overcome quietly and efficiently; Valerius himself, with his vampiric speed, dispatched the guards. As we descended the steps, the tension built. Our information said that the castle complement consists of members of both the *Allgemeine SS* and the *Waffen SS*. Others working at the castle were scientists and academicians, proponents of "Germanic Applied Research," a kind of SS esoteric philosophy consisting of Germanic mysticism, ancestor worship, and the study of runes. Wewelsburg Castle was also a center for archaeological excavations in the region, and housed the Library of the Schutzstaffel.

As we entered the Vault, we saw an ornate structure resembling a Mycenaean beehive tomb. Twelve plinths were spaced around its circular walls as resting places for funereal urns, places of honor for deceased high ranking SS Leaders I assumed. The shape of the room, its acoustics and lighting, projected a solemn yet eerie atmosphere. I caught my breath as the light illuminated the center of the room, where an eternal flame burned. At the apex of the high domed ceiling stood a relief of an ornate swastika engraved in ochre stone. Our footsteps echoed though we trod lightly. When we entered the center of the vault, the sensation passed surreal. As I tried to speak to Valerius, my words seemed eaten by the crypt itself, suffocated, disappearing into the ornate swastika above on the ceiling.

We made our way to the Hall of Supreme Leaders, regarded by the SS leadership as the Center of the New World. Cut into the center of the green and black marble floor was a symbol with twelve jagged arms branching off a black circle, composed of three circles and twelve rays in the form of SS sig-runen–The Black Sun. I shuddered at the sight of this symbol of eternal darkness and we continued. We found the corridor leading to the study rooms of the castle, which were arranged to refer to characters in the legends of the

Grail: King Arthur, King Henry, Henry the Lion, Widukind, Christopher Columbus, Aryan, Course of the Seasons, Runes, Westphalia, Teutonic Order, Room of the Reichsführer-SS, Frederick II of Prussia), Christian the Younger of Brunswick, and German language. And one was named Grail.

The Grail Study Room had four suits of armor in the corners; each bore a medieval weapon, spata, morningstar, halberd and flail. Would that I had studied them more closely. Yet they were nearly concealed behind the bookcases, lighted tables, glass enclosed desks of ancient scrolls and parchment. In the center of the room stood an empty glass display case, clearly meant for a chalice.

Out from behind one of the suits of armor strode Brigadeführer Karl Maria Wiligut, known as Weisthor among the SS occultists. Wearing full uniform, he cut an imposing figure in cape and black boots, with an SS dagger and a Luger on his belt, and a jewel encrusted walking stick.

"I have been expecting you Archons for some time now," he said in his resonant voice. "So, you are the Vatican's secret weapon. It seems our plan to sack Rome after we had conquered the world must have been leaked, and did not sit well with Pope Pius XII. Or perhaps you have more personal reasons for coming to Wewelsburg?"

He looked directly at Valerius and said, "I believe you are looking for this." With his free hand he held up an ancient chalice. "Try to take it if you can, Valerius, if the dead can lay hands on it." Weisthor spun on his heel and disappeared through a door at the rear of the room, and the rest became a blur of deadly action. The four suits of armor contained undead monsters that sprang into action and immediately cut down my three companions. I would have killed too, had I not been standing closest to Valerius. He threw me across the room out of the way and captured the staff of the pole-arm meant to decapitate me in a single blow.

I was dazed as I watched Valerius, with his preternatural speed, use the point of a pole-arm to impale the armored evil in the throat, then deftly twist the blade to sever its head. He turned and the other three *draugars* were upon him. Back and forth he parried, as they engaged him, each faster than the last. The halberd was slow compared to the spata, morningstar flail and a horseman's mace in the hands of the Nazi *draugars*.

These Wiedergänger were wild and powerful. After taking a crushing blow from the flail to his left shoulder, Valerius turned, broke the halberd in half, and used it as a blocking staff and as a short weapon. He turned aside a thrust from the spata with the broken staff as he used the hook of the halberd's hook to snag the chain of the Morningstar and pull the *draugar* to him.

The third *draugar* took the opportunity to aim a killing blow at Valerius' head, but by that time I had the presence of mind to get back into the fight, unloading my sawed off shotgun with its silver shot into the creature's head. The helm went flying across the room. Valerius used the moment to disarm the *draugar* with the morningstar, throwing it bodily onto the other *draugar's* spata. While thus impaled, he beheaded the last *draugar* with the blade of the halberd, then thrust it aside as he used the morningstar to strike again and again at the helm of the pinned *draugar*, until the helm was smashed and the head was pulp.

The shotgun blast had alerted others to our presence. Valerius and I rushed to the door Weisthor had escaped through and discovered a small room with a closet/pantry. In the wall we found a large dumbwaiter. We squeezed into the small space and followed what we desperately hoped was Weisthor's trail. The dumbwaiter went down maybe five stories distance then opened out into a catacomb underneath the castle. Valerius bade me to stay back and guard our rear, in case anyone or anything followed us down the dumbwaiter.

About thirty meters into the subterranean structure, it turned to the west. Valerius made the corner and stopped, peering around it. I followed as far as the corner while he proceeded westward. I could see about twenty meters ahead in the darkness lit only by a torch in a wall sconce. Weisthor was laying the chalice into a chest filled with Totenkopfrings. Valerius had blended into the darkness as only a vampire can, and was nearly upon Weisthor.

But Weisthor, aware, turned to face Valerius. He laughed, as he lifted his cane like a staff before him and said, "Behold, the power of Sha'Daa". The jeweled eyes of the Death's Head on Weisthor's cane, two black diamond eyes, flashed a green bright light, blinding the Holy Revenant, and the force sent Valerius hurling against the wall. As he struck stone, it was as if he turned to dust. Valerius was gone, leaving no trace.

I knew I was powerless to stop the Nazi fiend, and retreated out of the cavern and back up the dumbwaiter into the Castle. There I hid in an alcove behind some crates on the ground floor, until things quieted down. Whether Weisthor noticed me or deemed me unworthy of pursuit. I know not.

Before dawn, I escaped into the nearby woods, biding my time for the arrival of the Americans. We had failed in our mission. And I fear that the Vatican has lost its only vampire.

## PERSONAL DIARY OF VALERIUS VON GEIST,

Feast of All Saints, November 1, 1945

Fragment

...As Weisthor's cane flashed its malevolent green light, I was blinded. I knew the force that held me against the wall was enormous and would crush me, so I had no choice but to retreat. When I heard the word "Sha'Daa", I knew that the fight was bigger than even I had imagined. The Vatican had heard of this, but belief in the impending event was mixed within its ranks. In my many years fighting the Strigoi, I have learned quite a few of their tricks. I decided to go with the force, and allowed myself to transform into a mist, which passed through the solid cave wall into a cavernous chamber behind it. Then all went black.

A month later I regained consciousness. In that time most of the castle had been blown up or burned. The war in Europe had ended. But a new terror was inexorably encroaching upon the world of men. And as for me now, my personal quest for the Grail must wait. There is a much more important fight for mankind that must be fought. The Grail must linger a little longer, until after the Sha'Daa...

## "DIE SALZBURGER ZEITUNG", 1.4.1946

Obituaries

Karl Maria Wiligut, 12.10.1866–1.3.1946

Karl Maria Wiligut, also known as "Weisthor" died yesterday of complications of stroke. The former resident of Salzburg and former SS Officer had moved to Arolsen in Hesse, DDR, for access to the spa, where he died on 3 January 1946. His death at 79 is ruled natural causes from complications of stroke. In an odd turn, rumors have been circulating that the death of this high ranking Nazi was under unusual circumstances due to his unhealthy pre-occupation with studies of the Occult. The rumors say he was found drained completely of blood. The coroner's office refused to comment except to say "This death was ruled via natural causes. Let the dead lie in peace."

# "L'Osservatore Romano", 12 June 1958

*(et portae inferi)* ***"non praevalebunt"***

Giuseppe Dalla Torre di Sanguinetto, Editor

"Theft Reported at the Vatican Archives"

Major Paolo Benidetti of the Corpo della Gendarmeria reported that a crude chalice and an oddly decorated walking stick were stolen by the Pontifical Swiss Guard from a vault in Vatican City where they were being inspected by a visiting researcher. The researcher was found unconscious but unharmed, and has no recollection of what occurred. Anyone with information concerning this matter should contact the Gendarmeria immediately.

# 1941 WORLD EVENTS

Joseph Kesselring's ARSENIC AND OLD LACE premieres in NYC

Blizzard in ND kills 151—survivors claim tent revival preacher raised green storm devil after feeding a live snake a black diamond wristband

Joseph Stalin becomes premier of Russia

5,000 drown in a storm at Ganges Delta region in India

Mount Rushmore Monument is completed

President Roosevelt delivers DAY OF INFAMY speech to US Congress a day after the bombing of Pearl Harbor

# The Melody Lingers On

by Rob Adams and Deborah Koren

## SEPTEMBER 10, 1946

Dear Susie –

Thank you for the loan, sis. Things were getting desperate, I'm ashamed to admit. But I'll be able to pay you back soon, I promise. I finally got a job about two weeks ago, working as a domestic for an old widow who lives up in Beverly Glen. I couldn't believe the size of the house when I first saw it. The job doesn't pay a fortune—why are the rich ones always the cheapskates?—but it's enough to cover room and board for now. The old lady's foreign, too. Russian, I think, though she's been living in the States for over twenty years, so I guess that's all right. Her name is Mrs. Olga Galvinton, but I bring in her mail, and she gets a lot of letters addressed in fancy script to Olga Naranova. I guess it's her maiden name, but it's kind of unsettling sometimes. I just hope she's not a Communist.

I met a nice fellow named Tony last week, an ex-serviceman. Oh, you should see him, sis. Tall, dark, and handsome, with wavy brown hair and nice shoulders. Kind of quiet-voiced, though. Like Glenn Ford or Gary Cooper. He was a master sergeant in the army, though he won't really talk about the war. Just a mention and he clams up faster than dad can flip a flapjack. I know he landed at Normandy on D-Day, and he was stationed in Berlin after the war, but that's all I've gotten out of him. He's been following the Nuremberg trials pretty closely. And he has a purple heart and a silver star. I think dad would approve, except for the fact that Tony doesn't have a job. He's looking, but hasn't turned up anything. We go Dutch when we go out, which bothers him, I think. He's the kind of guy who likes to treat a girl right. Nice, huh? I mentioned to him that Mrs. Galvinton was looking for a gardener, but he thinks doing physical labor is beneath him. Honestly, how do you get it through their thick heads that without money you can't pay rent?

I wish he'd change his mind, sis. Apart from anything else, I'd sure like to have him around to keep me company. That old mansion is awfully big for just one old lady and me. I wish you could come and see it. It has a genuine ballroom. Just imagine the parties and dancing you could have there on a summer evening—not that Mrs. Galvinton is the type to throw a party, so that lovely wood floor just sits there unused. What a waste! There's a pool too (of course), and more bedrooms than I can count. It really is extravagant. There's certainly nothing like it back home—and I've heard from my girlfriends that her house isn't even one of the big ones. Some of the movie stars have even bigger pads. Still, I guess that's Los Angeles for you.

Write me soon, okay? Let me know how mom and dad and Joey are doing, and how things are on the farm.

Love,
Betty

What follows is a stenographic report of the statement by Francis Anthony Carmichael to Detective Andrew Hagen on Sunday, October 13, 1946, at 18:24.

**PRESENT:** Detective Andrew L. Hagen, Officer James Reilly, Francis Anthony Carmichael.

**HAGEN:** This is the preliminary interview with Francis Anthony Carmichael regarding case **46-09/1124**, Detective Hagen presiding. Also present is Officer James Reilly. Mr. Carmichael, for the record, I'll remind you that you have the right to have an attorney present during this interview.

**[INAUDIBLE]**

**HAGEN:** Sorry, I'm going to have to ask you to speak up for the stenographer, Mr. Carmichael. Can you hear me, Mr. Carmichael? Do you want a lawyer present?

**CARMICHAEL:** Presents?

**HAGEN:** No. Present, Mr. Carmichael. Do you want a lawyer *present*?

**CARMICHAEL:** Lawyer? Why would I want a lawyer? That's a [expletive deleted] stupid present. *Lawyer.* How'd you like someone to give you a lawyer?

I want… something. Can't remember. Can't… Where is it? *Come on.* Where have you hidden it? I *want* it!

**HAGEN:** Calm down, Mr. Carmichael. What is it you think I've got?

**CARMICHAEL:** You think I don't know? You think I can't hear it? Think I can't hear it *singing* to me? It's close. It… *You've* got it. Where is it? Where the [expletive deleted] is it?

**HAGEN:** Mr. Carmichael, I don't… Jesus. Has he been like this since he was brought in?

**REILLY:** Pretty much. Medics said he was lucid when they pulled him out of the car, but he's been mumbling on like that ever since. Doc reckons it's shock.

**HAGEN:** I'm not surprised. Half the goddamn car was crushed under that bus. He's lucky he's alive.

**REILLY:** Luckier than that girl he hit, aye. Mac said they had to put her in three body bags.

**[INAUDIBLE]**

**HAGEN:** Did he just… Mr. Carmichael? Could you repeat that for me, please?

**CARMICHAEL:** [Expletive deleted] had it coming.

**REILLY:** Had it… Why you coldhearted son of—

**HAGEN:** Jim, don't. Mr. Carmichael? What happened? Why did she deserve it?

**CARMICHAEL:** *Why*? She stole my [expletive deleted] box, that's why. Told me we were partners, told me we'd split everything right down the middle. Hah! Yeah. Well, I showed her right down the middle, didn't I? Split her—

**REILLY:** That's it. He says one more word, I swear—

**CARMICHAEL:** Ooh, look. Piggy's got a temper.

**REILLY:** Oh, you're dead, mister!

**HAGEN:** *HEY*! Cut it out, both of you. Mr. Carmichael, calm down right now or I'll bring a guard in to restrain you. Jim, if you can't control yourself I'll have you tossed out of here and you can cool your heels wondering just how bad my report's going to be when I file it with Lawton. Okay? *Okay*?

**REILLY:** Yeah. Sorry, boss.

**HAGEN:** Damn straight. Okay. Mr. Carmichael. Tony. Why don't you tell me how this started? I mean, I've read your file. According to that, you spent the last three years beating the hell out of the Nazis during the war. Says your captain put you forward for a silver star. Hell, I should be saluting you, not looking to put you behind bars. How did you go from that to cutting some poor kid in half with your goddamn car?

**CARMICHAEL:** Poor. Yeah, we were both poor. You know the only difference between me and her, Detective? I was *happy*. Sure, I had nothing, but I spent three winters in freezing foxholes with nothing but my M**1** and a spit of hope to keep me going. Poor. Huh. Kid didn't know the meaning of the word. I knew. *I* knew, and I saw her eyes. She wasn't going to share. She only wanted me around so she had some muscle in case things went south when she broke into that old lady's house. I shoulda seen it. I shoulda seen it…

**REILLY:** It just me, or did some of that actually make sense?

**HAGEN:** Maybe. Okay, Tony, tell me what happened. From the beginning.

### OCTOBER 8, 1946

Dear Sis –

I had to write you immediately. The most horrible thing happened today. A man died right in front of me.

I was in the middle of dusting the shelves in Mrs. Galvinton's enormous library when the front bell rang. It was an old man. He was stooped so badly he seemed even shorter than I am, and he was shivering even though it was ninety-five degrees outside. He was carrying this little iron box. It couldn't have been more than six inches across, but the way he was struggling with it you'd have thought it weighed a ton. He whispered something in some foreign language and handed it to me, and no sooner had he let go then he staggered and fell down. I screamed and called for Mrs. Galvinton. She came running, faster than I've ever seen her move before. "Anton!" she said, and she all but fell down next to him, murmuring something in the same language he'd used, Russian, I guess. She checked his pulse, but you could see he was gone; then she looked up at me and noticed the box I was holding. I swear, sis, I never saw anybody look so spooked. Her eyes widened, and she told me to put it down on the table.

Now, I was so scared by that old guy keeling over in front of me that I hadn't even thought about the box until she asked me to set it down, but when she did, my first reaction was to refuse. I didn't want to let go of it, and I can't tell you why. It was heavy, that's for sure, but seemed almost warm, comforting, like I was holding onto a precious teddy bear, not some ugly iron box. Isn't that strange? But she snapped at me again, and I have to admit, she scares me too, so I did as she asked.

I asked her if we should call for a doctor, but she didn't answer me. She found a key in his pocket, which she fitted to the lock on the iron box. Now *her* hands were trembling. Of course, I wanted to know what was in there, so I edged closer to peek as she opened the box. I thought the metal hinges would squeal or squeak, but it was all soundless and then the box was open, and I could glimpse what was inside.

Oh, sis, it was the most beautiful thing I ever did see—a gold box, the top of it inlaid with an intricate pattern of black jewels. Faceted and sparkling, like the box had been frosted with black diamonds. Honestly, I think they were. Diamonds, I mean. It took my breath away. But when she saw I was staring at it, Mrs. Galvinton slammed the lid down right quick and locked the iron box up tight again. I asked her what it was, but she just muttered that it was a music box and not to ask any questions, and then she tucked the key into a pocket and carried the box upstairs without even looking back. That's when I realized I'd have to call the police myself about the body. Can you imagine? They showed up quickly, and I told them everything that had happened, though I didn't tell them about the music box. I don't know why, but I just figured Mrs. Galvinton could tell them that part when they talked with her.

Well, I wanted to have adventures when I came to California, so I guess I can't complain.

Write me soon.

Love,

Betty

OCTOBER 9, 1946

Dear Sis –

I know I just wrote you yesterday, but I had to write again. I heard that music box play. I made some tea for Mrs. Galvinton this morning and took it up to her room. And there it was, just sitting there on her table, as beautiful as I had remembered. No. More so! It wasn't hidden inside that ugly iron box anymore. I could see all of it, all the intricate details, and those gorgeous black diamonds on top, sparkling like some treasure out of a museum. I couldn't take my eyes off it. I'll bet just one of those diamonds would be worth thousands. I'll tell you, I can't help dreaming about all the things I could do with that kind of money.

I asked her politely if I could hear it—she'd told me it was a music box, after all—but she told me not to touch it. I didn't mean to disobey her, honest, but standing that close, I felt I couldn't leave that room until I heard it play. I know it's silly, but it was almost like it was begging me to listen to it. The little clasp was right in front of my fingers, and I flipped the lid open without even thinking. There was a flash of green, and then the music started. Oh, sis, it was so beautiful! Like Debussy or Ravel, but more beautiful than either. Mrs. Galvinton slammed the lid down almost on my fingers just seconds later. She was really mad at me, and I apologized and got back to work immediately, but I could still hear that music. I can still hear it now, even though I only heard a few bars. It plays in my head as if I'd heard all of it. I don't know if it's a symphony or a ballet or what, and I didn't have the nerve to ask her.

I wish you could hear it. You remember how we use to listen to mom's Victrola when we were little? If the music box were mine, I'd come visit, just so we could listen to it together, like the old days. Wouldn't that be lovely?

love,
Betty

**HAGEN:** Tony, do you remember what you told me before, about how Betty Garson came to you and asked you to help her? Do you remember that?

**CARMICHAEL:** Uh-huh. Spent my life… helping people. *Protecting* people. I'm a good guy.

**HAGEN:** I know you are, Tony. Tell me about Betty.

**CARMICHAEL:** She wasn't a good guy. No. She was… was… She came to see me one day. Says to me, "Tony, how'd you like to be rich?" Well, course I'd like to be rich. Here I am… here… living in some crummy apartment in the [expletive deleted] end of town. Course I want to be rich, but life… life ain't like that, I told her. Life ain't *fair*. It ain't like those romance novels, all tiaras and dancing and… and dance… dancing. I told her. Some people get to live up in the nice house in the hills. The rest of us get… get…

**REILLY:** A nice warm jail cell?

**HAGEN:** Cut it out, Jim. What did Betty say when you told her that, Tony?

**CARMICHAEL:** She said I was right. Said life… life *ain't* fair. Said we gotta *make* it fair. Told me all about this old guy… this guy turned up at their door that morning.

**HAGEN:** Anton Kalganin?

**CARMICHAEL:** Don't know. She… never told me his name, just said that he… turned up with that little box. Turned up and… and fell down. He'd lost the music, see. Lost it. When… when the music stops. When it stops, we… we all fall down. We…

**REILLY:** Christ. He's rambling again.

**HAGEN:** He's making perfect sense, Jim. You just have to listen.

**CARMICHAEL:** Yeah. Yeah, you have to listen. Always have to… The music. Listen to the music. Tells you… tells you what it needs. Tells you…

**REILLY:** Oh, yeah. Perfect sense.

**HAGEN:** Just listen, would you? Tony? Tony, tell us about the box.

**CARMICHAEL:** Beautiful. It was… That old lady took it, she said. Didn't even… didn't listen. Didn't even want to look at it, Betty said. Just locked it away. It… it ain't right, that. Ain't right. Something that… that beautiful. You don't hide it away. Can't… can't just lock the music away like that. You can't. You *can't*. Stupid [expletive deleted] dame! She… she didn't deserve something like that.

**HAGEN:** Okay, Tony. Calm down. So, Mrs. Galvinton locked the box away? What did Betty want you to do?

**CARMICHAEL:** Just… just get it for her. For us. For… She said the old battleaxe wouldn't miss it anyway. She'd locked away, out of sight. Out of… She said… said we could take it, and no one would know. Said it was worth… She said we'd share it. Fifty-fifty, she said. All we had to do was… was…

**HAGEN:** Break in.

**CARMICHAEL:** No. No. Didn't have to. She… she had a key. The old dame had given her a key. We could just… sneak in. Sneak in, find it and… and rescue it. Easy. Should have been so easy.

**HAGEN:** But it wasn't, was it?

**CARMICHAEL:** Betty… she knew the old girl's routines. Saturday she went to the theater. Saturday we could get in. We… yeah. We got in and went up… up and up. But she was *there*. They were all there, all of them. I… I thought they were singing to it. Thought they were… but no. Not singing. Trying…

They were trying to stop the music. Trying to stop it from *singing*. Couldn't… I couldn't let them. Had to do something. Had to keep it *safe*.

## OCTOBER 12, 1946

Dear Diary–

I shouldn't be writing this. There's no time. He'll be coming after me, but if I don't get this down now I won't remember later.

I've showered three times. There was no time for that either, but I couldn't help it. The smell of the fire—it wouldn't come off. I'll never forget that smell as long as I live. Not like a nice fireplace or a campfire, or even a brush fire. *They* burned, and the smell of that black fire is the worst thing I've ever…

I still have to pack, but there's not much to grab. A few dresses, my shoes, the paste jewelry. None of it matters anyway. I can buy new dresses. What matters is the box is safe. And I have it. It's sitting on the desk in front of me. I don't know how such rich music can come from so small a box. It's even more beautiful here than it was at the old lady's house. Real gold is so deep in color. And the black diamonds sparkle so fiercely. And she was trying to destroy it, her and those old cronies of hers. How could anyone even think of destroying something so expensive, so beautiful? But it's mine now. Mine! And no one is going to take it away from me. Not even Tony.

I know he's coming for it. I feel like if I close my eyes, I can almost reach out across the city and feel where he is. Or maybe it's the box. If I just open the lid… There, the melody is so achingly beautiful. I want to crawl inside the box and let it surround me. I…

I'm wasting time. I have to keep it closed. It's too easy to just listen to it. You know, I realized I've never had to wind it up. It just plays as long as the lid is open. How does it do that?

I'm not getting down what I wanted to record, and look, dawn is coming. The whole night is gone.

Tony and I went back to the house last night. Saturday night. Mrs. Galvinton always goes to the theater Saturday nights. The Santa Anas were blowing, too, which was just perfect. It would be so noisy outside from the wind, that the neighbors wouldn't hear a thing even if we made noise. I used my passkey to get us in. We were both wearing masks, and Tony had brought his pistol. It made me kind of nervous, but he said it was better to have it just in case the old lady *was* around and needed a little persuasion to part with her trinket. We snuck up the staircase to her bedroom, but she wasn't there and neither was the box. I could tell Tony was getting antsy, but I wouldn't let him go. He didn't understand. He hadn't seen the box. He hadn't *heard* it. He didn't understand that now that I was there, I was not leaving without it.

Then we heard voices coming from downstairs, from the ballroom.

Mrs. Galvinton and five of her old friends were inside. Three men and two women. The lights were off, but the room glowed with candlelight. I spotted the box then, sitting in the middle of that polished dance floor. The candles were arranged in a circle around it, and outside that circle stood the people, all of them chanting in unison. I couldn't understand a word they said. It might have been Russian, or Latin, but it might as well have been gibberish for all I cared. My eyes were on that box. I could feel it calling me. I could feel its *distress*, and it was only Tony's grip that kept me from running in there and scooping it up.

"That's it?" he whispered. "It must be worth a fortune!" I looked at him then and his eyes glittered, the same way the black diamonds on the box did. Now that he'd seen it, he couldn't take his eyes off it. I knew right then that he wasn't going to leave without that box either.

The candles flared in the room, the flames rising impossibly high. The chanting got louder and louder, and I recognized the same words being repeated over and over. The six of them joined hands, a ring around the ring of candles around the box.

Tony strode into the room then, brandishing the gun and shouting at them. He shoved one man aside, breaking their ring, and he kicked at the candles, scattering them. He was kneeling next to the box before I had even moved out of the doorway. I ran after him, not wanting to be left behind, suddenly terrified he would take the box and forget about me.

Mrs. Galvinton was yelling at him not to touch the box, but he already had the tiny clasp opened, and he raised the lid. A flash of green light surrounded it, then the music poured out. It was only the second time I'd heard it, but it was just as beautiful as I remembered. No, if anything it was more beautiful, comforting the way your mother might lullaby you to sleep, or the soft way a man might hold you and tell you he'll protect and love you forever.

One of the women in the circle jumped on Tony, but he just threw her aside. "What are you people doing?" he demanded. He pulled his mask off and flung it aside. "What are you *thinking*? This is priceless!"

Mrs. Galvinton was asking, *begging* him to close it, to please just close it, that he didn't know what he was talking about, but he ignored her. He still had the gun, but none of them seemed to care. They all yelling at him now, and some of them started toward him. I thought he'd call me to come carry the box while we beat a hasty retreat, but it was as if I didn't exist anymore. I started to get mad. That was *my* box.

Something poured out of it, then, like smoke or a black cloud. It engulfed the old people, including Mrs. Galvinton, and clung to their bodies like oil or tar. And then… whatever was covering them ignited with a loud whoosh. Black flames burned on their bodies. They swayed and pirouetted, arms waving in the air, *dancing*. It would have almost been pretty, like some strange choreographed ballet, except that they were screaming and screaming while their bodies seemed to move without their consent. The flames consumed nothing but them, not even scorching the floor beneath their burning feet.

"That waltz!" Tony yelled over the sound of their screaming. I didn't know what he was talking about. I heard no waltz, just the same beautiful melody as always, but Tony was swaying back and forth, the gun in one hand, the box in the other, as he watched the macabre dance of the five old people. A grin split his face, and his eyes glowed black and intense. He seemed to be relishing the scene before him.

I wanted to leave. The smell—it wasn't like anything I've smelled before, and not even the music could drown out the inhuman screams filling that room. All I could think was that someone would hear, someone would call the police, and the box would be taken away from me.

One of the people—it might even have been Mrs. Galvinton—started screaming words that sounded like part of the chant. She staggered toward Tony. He set the box down on the table behind him and faced her—and I saw my chance. I ran forward and snatched it up, bolting for the door. The lid slammed shut as I ran, and the music was silenced. That just made the screaming even louder. I could still hear it even as I raced into the driveway. I thought Tony was screaming too, but it sounded like he was yelling, "No, no, no, no!" It took me two tries to get the car started, but then I was driving away. I heard gunshots before I reached the street, then there was nothing but the roar of the automobile all around me, and the swoosh of trees bending in the wind.

I was shaking, but the box was safe on my lap. It's mine now, all mine. I knew from the moment Tony saw it that he would never have shared it with me. I saw it in his eyes. I was a fool to think he'd help me. A man like that? No, he wanted it for himself. And I heard those shots—he might even have shot me!

So, I've showered and washed the stench of that black fire off me. I'll leave the car here and walk to the bus stop, catch a bus down to Union Station. Cars are easy to track, I know that much from the movies, but a bus ride, and then a train… No one will ask my name, no one will know who I am. Tony will be coming for me. Not for me, for the music box. He won't get it. I'll keep it safe. I promise. It won't ever—

**CARMICHAEL:** Took it. All those people trying to… trying to destroy it, trying to kill me, and she just took it and ran. Said she'd share it. Said it was ours, but she just wanted… Had to get away so I could find her, stop her, but that crazy old dame and her friends just wouldn't let me go. Had to… Had to…

**HAGEN:** You had to stop them first.

**CARMICHAEL:** Right. I had to stop them. Had no choice. They… they were so mad. Wild. Grabbing me, hitting me, scratching. I just… just wanted them to stop so I could go after Betty.

**HAGEN:** You recognize this, Tony?

**CARMICHAEL:** Sure. Looks… looks like my **.45**.

**HAGEN:** Well, you're half right, Tony. It *was* your **.45**, but you should have handed it back in when you were discharged. You want to tell me how it is that you've still got it?

**CARMICHAEL:** I… I didn't think. There were so many. I didn't think they'd miss it.

**HAGEN:** Yeah, well, turns out they didn't. Until I ran a check on the serial number, they didn't have the first clue.

**CARMICHAEL:** Am… am I in trouble?

**REILLY:** Trouble? Are you— Is he for real?

**HAGEN:** We found this on the floor of the car you stole, Tony, under the passenger seat. There are six rounds missing. Now, I was talking to our ME, and he tells me he pulled six forty-five caliber slugs out of the bodies from Beverly Glen. That isn't a coincidence, is it, Tony?

**CARMICHAEL:** I… couldn't stop them. I tried. I tried, but they just kept coming at me. I *had* to. She was gone, it was gone, and they just kept coming at me. The music. It was… I couldn't get away. I couldn't get out. I had to…

**HAGEN:** Tony? Tony, I need you to focus. Look at me. Tell me what happened.

**CARMICHAEL:** One of them… one of them on my back. Still burning. My back, my neck. Burning. Wouldn't let go. Had to… oh, God. Had to break her fingers just to make her let go. Screaming. She was… we were all screaming. Threw her off, but… so many of them. Like fighting a wave of flames and fists and nails and noise. Tried to get out, but this one… he… he grabbed my arm. Started pulling me back into that room, and… and the music was… it was fading. Had to get him off. Had to get them all off. In my hand before I even knew it. Felt cold after those flames. After the music.

**HAGEN:** Go on.

**CARMICHAEL:** First guy was almost on me again. There was so little of him left. The black fire. Still burning, and his skin was… it was *cooked*. Like… like a burnt steak. Oh, Christ. The smell. First guy. First guy went down in the doorway. Bullet in his head, still looking up at me. I… I could still hear him screaming. The others… don't remember. Feels like… like a big black space here, right here in my head, like there's a bullet up there, too. Next thing, it's quiet. No more screaming, just me and the flames and the music. The music… fading. Still fading. I could barely hear it anymore. Just this tiny, tiny piece of it left. Had to find it. Had to get it back. Had to find it and keep it… keep it safe.

**HAGEN:** So you followed Betty back to her apartment.

**CARMICHAEL:** Yeah. Yeah… no. No. Couldn't. Not straight away. She… she'd… the car was gone.

**HAGEN:** Yeah, but that wasn't a problem, was it? Mrs. Galvinton had that nice, big '39 Maybach. All you had to do was find the keys—except you couldn't go back into the house, could you, Tony?

**CARMICHAEL:** Too late. Already… already burning.

**HAGEN:** But you said this "black fire" of yours didn't burn anything other than the people.

**CARMICHAEL:** Right. Yeah, but…

**HAGEN:** But what, Tony?

**CARMICHAEL:** They… they were still looking. All of them. Staring at me. They knew… I could feel it. I could feel them staring at me. Had to stop them staring. I… I had my matches with me. Found a few bottles of wine, vodka. Poured them… poured them over the… oh, God… I poured them over a couple of curtains, threw them over the bodies and lit them. Went up so fast, almost caught me. Had to run out the door to get away. Only… only realized about the keys when I was outside. Couldn't go back in. Couldn't. Had to… had to hotwire the thing. Hadn't done that since… since Italy. Sicily. Forty-three. Easier, though. No one… no one shooting at me.

**HAGEN:** But you still had to hurry. Betty was getting away.

**CARMICHAEL:** I… No. No, she… felt like… like she was waiting for something. I could feel it. Feel her, and… and I could hear it. I could still hear the music. Such a beautiful waltz. Wish… wish I could hear it now. Stopped. No. No, not stopped. Just… different. So different. Wish I could… wish it was the same. All I hear… it's wrong. All wrong. Sounds like, like someone else's song. Like… like my song's over. Why does it sound like that? Why… why are you making it do that? Why won't it sing to me anymore?

**REILLY:** Oh, man. He's gone again, boss. He was spouting this baloney when we brought him in. "Why can't I see it?" "Why won't it sing to me?" Jesus.

**HAGEN:** Cut it out, Jim. Tony? Tony, I'll make you a deal. You tell me what happened, tell me *everything* that happened, and I'll see if I can get you what you want. Okay?

**CARMICHAEL:** You… you can get it?

**HAGEN:** Of course I can, Tony. But you have to help me first. What happened after you left Beverly Glen? Where did you go? Betty's apartment?

**CARMICHAEL:** Yeah. Yeah, but she was gone. Window was wide open. I guess… guess she heard me coming. But I could still hear the music. Drifting. Like… like it was on the wind or something. Calling. Calling for me to follow it. Find it. Get it back. It *wanted* me to find it.

**HAGEN:** So you followed it to Union Station?

**CARMICHAEL:** Took so long. Felt like she took every side street, every alley between her apartment and the station. I… I almost lost her… lost it. Must have… must have taken a wrong turn, cause all of a sudden it just… I thought, I thought that's it. I thought that I'd lost it for sure, and when the music stops… when it stops…

**HAGEN:** All fall down.

**CARMICHAEL:** Right. *Right.* But I hadn't lost it. Just… just took a wrong turn. Found it, followed it, all the way to the station. Then I saw her… right there, not fifty yards away from me. She… she had this little bag with her. Holding it on her lap. She… she kept stroking it, like it was… I knew it had to be in there. But there were so many people. So many people, but they… they couldn't hear it. People coming and going, sitting and waiting, kissing and waving and… and no one even looked at her. This guy… this one guy, he sat down right beside her. Saw her flinch, saw her… she looked like she wanted to run away, but this guy just sat there and opened up his newspaper. Didn't even look at her, and that's when I knew. I could…

I just walked right in. Got out of the car and walked right up to her like it was no big deal. She… she looked like she'd seen a ghost, like she couldn't believe I was there. I… I reached for… and then she screamed. Oh, man, she screamed. Worst thing I ever heard. Worse than when those people were burning, worse than that, worse than anything… and no one paid her any mind. Guy beside her just sat there reading his paper like we were both invisible. Like we weren't there at all. I… she wouldn't let go. Had her fingers tight around the straps of that bag, knuckles all white like the skin was all gone and they were right down to the bone. I kept trying to pull it away from her but she wouldn't give it up.

I… I… uh… She hit her head on the bench, I saw her hit her head and then she let go and I was running. Almost ran straight out the station before I remembered the car. I… I was trying to start it when I heard her. Heard her screaming. She… she was coming straight for me. Her… her face. The look on her face, it was like… like some kind of demon, like it was Betty on the outside but behind her eyes there was something… She was there before I could get it started, pounding on the hood, on the doors, on the windows. Man, I never liked any sound more than that engine when it caught. I just wanted to get out of there. Shoved the thing into reverse and just gunned it. I… I put it into reverse. I did. I know I did, but… the car… it just… oh, Christ. She'd tried to get round to me, round to my side. She… the car just… it was so *fast*. It just leapt forward, and she was… the… the bus was just… it was just *there*. Oh, God. The blood. All that blood. And the music. All that blood, and right then I heard the music, and it was never sweeter. Never sweeter. Then… then…

**HAGEN:** Okay, Tony. Okay. I think maybe we should take a break, guys. Jim, why don't you escort Mr. Carmichael back to his cell?

**REILLY:** Sure, boss. Come on, Carmichael. You heard the Inspector. Time to go.

**CARMICHAEL:** What? But… No. No, you promised. You… you said I could have it. You said if I told what happened, you'd get it for me. I want my box. I want it! You promised!

**REILLY:** All right, now just calm down. I said— Boss, I'm going to need some help here.

**HAGEN:** Tony? Tony, calm down. Calm down right now.

**CARMICHAEL:** No. No, you promised. You promised! Where is it? Where is it? I need it. I can hear—

**HAGEN:** Hear what, Tony? Music? Singing? There's no music. No singing. We searched that car from top to bottom, searched the entire station, and you know what we found? Nothing! And you know why, don't you, Tony? Because there never was any box. It was all in your head, the whole thing. It was all you, Tony. It was all you.

**CARMICHAEL:** No! No… I… I saw it. I heard it. It… it sang to me. Ask Betty. Ask her, she'll… No! No, it was real. I had to be real. You've got to believe me. I… I can still hear it. It's nearby… I can hear it! Please…

**HAGEN:** All right, that's enough now. Come on, Jim, let's get him back to his cell. I'll set up a briefing with Captain Lawton for first thing tomorrow. He'll want to know where we're going on this.

**REILLY:** Like there's any question… Christ. If the attorney doesn't plead insanity…

**HAGEN:** Yeah. Okay. You got him? Oh, damn. Hang on. Uh, note for the record. Interview terminated at… nineteen fifty-four. Suspect to be remanded into custody pending trial.

[*End of transcript*]

## NOVEMBER 1, 1946

Dear Pop –

How are you doing? I'm so sorry I haven't been able to write you during the last three weeks. I was working on a nasty murder case. So nasty that… well, Pop, I quit the force. I know, being a detective was one of my dreams, and I worked my way up through the department for so many years, but I guess sometimes these things just don't turn out the way you expect.

I'm going to try something new for a bit. I've come into… well, it's hard to explain, so I'm coming home to show you. I need to get out of Los Angeles for a while, anyway. It's too crowded here, just like you always said. Too many people with their prying eyes and ears. They're always watching and listening, and it's driving me nuts. I can't think out here, knowing they're listening, just waiting… And nobody needs to remind me how many thieves and murderers there are in this city.

I'm looking forward to seeing the old place again. Wait until you see what I'm bringing with me. You always wanted to go back east, see New York and Washington D.C. Maybe now the war's over, now's our chance to travel. Would you like that?

Anyway, I'll be home soon.

Your loving son,

Andy Hagen

# 1949 WORLD EVENTS

**Arthur Miller's DEATH OF A SALESMAN opens at Morosco Theater, NYC**

**Chaim Weitzman elected first president of Israel**

**USSR explodes their first atom bomb**

**Fire in Chiang-king, China, destroys 7,000 lives—policeman places blame on criminal cult that worships a large black stone**

**RUDOLPH, THE RED-NOSED REINDEER appears on music charts**

# Lime Light

## by John Vise

### JOURNAL ENTRY 143

March 19, 1951

I am so very excited! "Margaret," I say to myself, "this could really be it." Finally, back on a set! Back on the lot! Back helping make the magic happen!

Goodness, I started keeping this journal just after my last job. That means it has been nearly four years since I was last working at R.K.O. doing electrical and lighting. We all had to do our part during the War, and while other women were driving taxis or working at the plants, I found myself above the heads of some of the famous faces of Hollywood, arm deep in wiring.

And, I think looking back, never happier.

Then Richard came back from the War, and he wasn't really comfortable with the idea of me not being at home. Not that I blame him, dear thing. He came very close to battle fatigue, ending his service early and in disgrace. Battle fatigue, in my father's day they called it shellshock. I admire the bravery that Richard tapped into to go back into the trenches and fight with our boys. It is only understandable that he needed me when he got home. Lord knows I missed him.

Only… I missed the grease too. The sparks and gaffer tape and all. I wonder, even as I write this, if that makes me a terrible person. Missing the few brief months where I was a common laborer almost as much as I missed my husband.

Still, best not to dwell on such things. Not now that I have a new job and a chance to be near the limelight again!

Oh, it is not electrical but makeup. The grips and electricians are getting stricter about unionizing, but neither they nor the studios are all that keen on hiring a woman. I won't even be working for the movies, but for a television show. Still, they need just as much makeup, if not more.

Besides! That's what makes this so exciting. A friend clued me into a promo filming, a pilot done on 35 millimeter to try to convince the sponsors. All my hopes are bound up in it. The star sounds like she is very much in charge, and has been in showbiz for as long as I can remember. Queen of the B's she was. She and her husband are putting on the whole production, risking their own necks. If ever a woman had a chance at being noticed for her skill, it should be while working for another woman.

I can hardly contain myself! My nerves have been more than usually on edge lately. I've been jumping at shadows for no good reason at all. Richard is finally ready for me to go back to work. Well, he doesn't have much choice, truth be told. Not if we are to keep the house. His prospects have been getting… slim.

Poor, dear thing.

No. No worrying. No dwelling. Just preparation! Tomorrow, they film the pilot. I've got to be the very best. The most professional. So that if the show picks up my life will pick up with it.

I can't wait to see what Miss Ball and her husband Desi are like in person.

## JOURNAL ENTRY 144

March 21, 1951

Disaster! Purest and utter disaster!

I can't imagine more going wrong with one filming. It was awful. Oh the usual things went awry of course. The sound cut out and then was doubly sensitive, right when that nice man Mr. Arnaz was trying to sing. The lot wasn't even rented from the studios. I think CBS reconditioned an old radio booth. It is cramped and the audience is never comfortable, the sets are so flimsy they shook when the actors closed the doors, and all that was to be expected with such an early test shoot.

What wasn't to be expected… I don't know if I should believe this even as I write it down. Of course, no one will ever read these words but me, so what's the matter?

I was doing Ms. Ball's make-up, and she had such a way about her. She chatted as if we were old friends. No, as if we were old cohorts. I think she was the only actress with lines. Certainly she was the only one center stage. With so much pressure on her, the producer and writer both shouting at her, she didn't seem to have a worry in her bright red head. She even bummed a Lucky Strike off of me and complimented my old cigarette case.

I'm quite sure I imagined things. A trick of the lighting perhaps, or just my mind thinking of the old days when I'd been dealing with the sparks of electricity. Still, I could swear as her fingers brushed the cigarette case the small, dark stone in the case's center glimmered an eerie green. It clashed terribly with her hair, and for a moment my wonderfully applied makeup took on the cast of a skull. An empty eyed skull in a great fiery wig, smiling at me and thanking me for the cigarette.

Surely, just a trick of my mind… just the lights.

But that's when it all began to go so terribly beyond expected complications. I had peeked at the script, and heard Ms. Pugh the writer talking about some changes here and there. By all accounts, this was going to be a delightfully dry comedy, a step up from her days where she played straight-man to the likes of the Stooges or Marxes. Not as bawdy as and more intelligent than some of her radio work. It sounded sarcastic, funny, and just a bit irreverent, exactly what I was hoping to see on television.

No one expected the clown to go through the wall.

The poor man playing Pepito, I swear the bike only accelerated when he tried to stop. The thin plaster and paint of the set wall couldn't stop his momentum. He ran right over the man who played Desi's agent. From the way the bones in the poor man's foot cracked, I don't think he'll be able to reprise the role soon. Unless they don't mind a member of the cast wearing a cast.

Then the clown's fake cigar had a spark just real enough to catch Ms. Ball's coat aflame. Her hand brushed one of the microphones that had been acting up, and she got a horrible jolt from the way she jumped! The audience laughed, thinking it slapstick at its finest.

… I don't think I'll ever forget the sound that followed. A cry of anguish that seemed to rip out of Ms. Ball's throat and spread her face in to a grimace not unlike a death mask.

"WaaaaaaaaH," that lovely, intelligent woman caterwauled. Shaking her poor fingers to help free them of pain.

The audience roared with mirth, and it broke my heart.

If a young child had stepped on his own puppy, then placed his screeching, sobbing voice to a megaphone, it might have just barely matched the sound she made. No, not a puppy, a kitten. There was something of a mewl and scratch of claws against cement in the wail as well. It was certainly no laughing matter!

"Wah!" Ugh, I shudder at the memory. I fear very much that I will never forget that wail or the jeers of the entertained crowd. Both will haunt me for all the rest of my days. It is only a blessing that the cameras had stopped rolling when the coat had started to smoke. Perhaps they can reshoot a few scenes, salvage something. If they listen to their audience though, the show they put on will be a very different one from the one they had intended.

A lovely show turned into basest humor, by… a cigarette case? No, of course not. That flare of green and other oddness was all in my mind.

I would hate for Ms. Ball to ever have to repeat such a noise.


## JOURNAL ENTRY 145

May 23, 1951

I waited until after my most recent job before I wrote about it in my little journal. I know it is terribly silly of me, but I didn't want to jinx things. Perhaps it has worked, because I feel much more positive about this job than the last.

I didn't give up, kept hitting my contacts despite Richard insisting his newest employment could support us just fine. I am so very glad I did, because I'm back with the movies, proper and true. Maybe it is television that I need to stay away from, because I had some moments of true happiness while helping with the makeup and running errands for this 20th Century Fox production.

Boy did they need the makeup too. It was one of the many science fiction movies that have been cropping up like bizarre little weeds. Not that I'd bad mouth it in public, oh no. Let them all come buy their tickets to see saucers land in Washington D.C. and hugely tall, ridiculous automatons. I need the work.

I even got to do a touch of electrical fix up. Just a little effect on the ship set that started to fritz out when I happened to be handy. The chief was both impressed and embarrassed, but I had the good sense to fade back as soon as I could and not make a fuss.

Yes, there was one moment that things were… off. I was having a smoke and the man in the metal suit, the robot I suppose, asked if he could bum one. After the last job with Miss Ball, I wasn't going to make that mistake. Besides, he admitted he wouldn't be able to get the helmet off without at least two assistants. We chatted quite amiably about the set and movie, a very nice conversation.

At least it was nice, until the actor who plays the robot, all seven feet of him, strode by. I had been talking ten minutes with his stand in. Which doesn't sound bad, until you realize the stand in isn't another actor, just a big statue they put in for scenes where he doesn't have to move.

I didn't see a flash this time, but then the cigarette case was in my handbag by then. I really don't know what to think, but I doubt things like having statues talk back to you are a good sign. My nerves should be better, not worse. Shouldn't they?

Maybe it is because even as enjoyable as the job was, it probably won't help me restart a career. I mean, how popular is another little saucer flick likely to be?

For that matter, what kind of foolish name is Gort for a robot anyway?

## JOURNAL ENTRY 146

June 25, 1951

Things are not going well, not at all.

There has been too little joy and too much routine this month. No job opportunities since my last entry. Why, during the War, you could do three, four pictures a week. No one cared if the workers hopped around studios. It was only the big names that the studios were fiercely protective over back then. I can't wait till I can get out of bed again with a sense of purpose.

Richard was fired, again. That's what, two jobs he has had in the space I've been hunting for one? I understand, cleaning dishes is hardly what he was accustomed to. Still, work is work, and he's done worse to scrape by. He swears that the sounds of the pots brought him back to the dark place. It is not that I don't believe him, I do. It is just that… well, we've all been to dark places. Haven't we?

I fear the strain has further affected my senses. The other day I was having a smoke when world fell away from me.

It was as if the black tiles in my checkered kitchen floor turned into great voids. First they sucked up the white tiles, one by one. The sound of the white falling into the black was like nails on a chalkboard. Like the wail from a beautiful, redheaded actress that still haunted my dreams. Then I was falling, tumbling through the black. No air rushed by me, yet I plummeted into nothing.

I landed back in my kitchen. Still on my feet and with white and black tiles all solid and accounted for. Only I had been facing the oven when the fit had started. After, the oven was behind me.

I ignored that before the whole thing I had seen a glare of green. I am no longer sure those visions mean what I thought they meant.

Richard and I are both at home together far too often, with nothing pleasant to talk about and not enough to do. We never go out. We haven't been invited to any of the neighbors' places in quite some time. Our old friends seem so very distant, just memories more than real people.

This really isn't living.

I can't remember the last time I went dancing.

## JOURNAL ENTRY 147

July 16, 1951

I think I may have to kill Richard.

It is too bad really. I used to love the dear man, very much. He wasn't my first love, but he was the strongest and sweetest. It seems trite to blame the War. That was something we all had to go through in our own ways. Still, the Richard I knew never came back, and the Margaret he left at home wasn't the same Margaret he came back to. It is no one's fault really. It is just one of those unfortunate things. Too bad murder seems the best recourse.

Last night pushed it over the edge. When he was just a man, a regular down and out human being, I knew I could live with him. We might never be happy again, but we could both survive, maybe even thrive one day. Then I had one of my little episodes and realized he wasn't a man at all. Not anymore.

He was watching television and I was just finishing a Lucky. I've accepted the glow of green now, almost welcome it. Whenever it gleams I know something is going to happen, something terrible. Maybe the case isn't causing the terrible things after all. Maybe it is trying to warn me, a guardian angel in a very dark guise.

Just like Richard has been a monster this whole time, in the guise of a man.

The television went black. Not off. I could still hear the hum of the tubes. It simply went dark, a huge, gaping hole, another terrible void. The void ripped Richard's human skin off and revealed the beast beneath.

I can hardly describe it. A thousand eyes blinked at me, each a different shape and color. Three mouths flapped open and closed as if they had no jawbone to hold them. I always knew Richard a bit weak chinned, but this was ridiculous. He turned to me, and his body was covered in coarse hair the color of an overripe lemon. Something jutted from between his legs, too enormous and misshapen to be anything but a bit sad.

Yes, sad. Even if human-mask Richard might have wished for a bit more in the trouser department, this thing, and its thing, looked misshapen in the extreme. Surely it was more for intimidation than procreation. Like some kind of obscene bird of paradise, flaring feathers more decorative than functional.

I pitied the monster before me, and as soon as I pitied it I hated it. Hated it, and needed it out of my house.

Then the television flickered back to life, and Richard was merely Richard. Pasty and quickly losing the physique the army had granted him. I looked at him, and pitied him just as much as the atrocity that had been revealed.

Pity fed hate, and murder filled my mind.

Writing it helps. Putting pen to paper. I realize now that I should rethink this. Richard doesn't deserve to die, even if it would rid my house of something unpleasant.

I fear I may do something rash.


## JOURNAL ENTRY 148

August 17, 1951

Life only grows worse by the day.

Richard is alive. It took me a month before I was disgusted enough to try and kill him, and my heart really wasn't in it. Otherwise I would have gone with the poison, or a gun. Instead he ducked a hastily thrown cleaver, which imbedded itself in his favorite chair and quite ruined the upholstery.

I actually feel a little better now that the chair is gone. It was talking behind my back with the ottoman.

Is the cigarette case my guardian angel, or just another devil? I really don't know, at least it doesn't call me names like the shower does. Or try to give me bad dreams like my duvet. My own house has turned against me. It has caused poor sweet Richard to slip back into paranoid habits, more afraid of his wife and her cutlery than he ever was of the Nazis who shot at him on a daily basis.

I examined the case thoroughly, when it was not flickering at me. I found an inscription I never noticed in Russian. This does me no good at all. I cannot speak Russian, and I have no idea who to ask for a translation. It is not a topic easily brought up these days.

They say that the Commies have wicked schemes. Perhaps this is one of them? Do Communists believe in guardian angels, or in sorcery? If either were true, wouldn't it be gleaming red at me, not green?


## JOURNAL ENTRY 149

November 21, 1951

Not writing about the job till after didn't do me any good at all this time.

I managed to survive on set for two weeks, mostly staying away from the filming itself. I would come in, do my job, and then fade as far away from the action as possible. I wasn't happy, not nearly. Yet I was working, and out of that damned house.

Richard suggested it, a huge, sweet gesture for the man. Motivated only a little by fear and the need for one of us to make some money. I think he thought it might help my nerves. He certainly can't know that I keep thinking about putting rat poison in his awful daily Gibson. Either the onion will hide the taste, or the poison would improve the flavor, I see no reasonable third option.

It was fairly easy to stay out of the way, it was a huge production. A musical put on by Metro Goldwyn Mayer, in the tradition of the grandest of Hollywood musicals. I haven't even read the script, I didn't want to get that involved, but I've seen showgirls and huge Parisian night club sets and the massive tenting they've set up with the impressive sprinkler system.

I managed the job with only small incidents. A few whispers, a few bends of space and mind, nothing I couldn't handle. At least, until Mr. O'Conner spent hours on a single dance routine. Well, I call it dance, but it was more acrobatic slapstick. Bouncing off walls like a Mexican bean, whirling about and crashing through set pieces. On purpose! Thankfully! I was having terrible flashbacks to poor Pepito.

Only it was never quite right, and Mr. O'Conner went through each part of the routine. Again and again.

And again.

The man really has no place trying to behave like he's twenty again. He smokes more than I do, and I've been smoking more and more lately. It helps keep things clear. At the end of the day he was practically carried off to his room, to collapse for who knows how long.

Then it happened, the flash of green. I know now that case is no protective oracle, warning me of doom. It is the source of all my woes.

There was no way one makeup girl should be alone with freshly shot film, and yet I was. The world had grown dark around the edges, as if the corner of the set I was in was a bubble. Separate from the rest of the Earth, floating, terribly tenuous. Just me and the film cans and my little case, green light making the shadows twisted and harsh.

The can rattled. Just once. Just enough to make my heart start to beat like a rabbit. Like a rabbit, I couldn't decide if I wanted to run or come closer for a sniff. So I stood, paralyzed and twitching in fear.

The lid burst off the can, and the film writhed out in a dozen tendrils. Black and clear, striped like a snake or some horrid octopus. It reached for me and wrapped around my arms and ankles. I fell, and my scream was choked off by loops of celluloid wrapping over my mouth.

Then it started to run over my eyes, and green light lit it as well as any movie projector. I could see awful images beyond. Not the dancing of foolish O'Conner, but truly abominable things. Things I had seen in my nightmares. Things the stone knew, and loved.

I struggled, and somehow my lighter was in my hand. Film burns. The older the better, but new burns well enough. I swear the film screamed as it died, burned up all around me.

Then I was standing over an open canister and sticky mess of melted film. No sign of my struggles, and people shouting in horror. I didn't wait to explain, just turned and ran, tears in my eyes.

Poor Mr. O'Conner will have to do his whole routine from scratch I'm sure. If his heart gives out it will be on my head. They already had problems with Mr. Kelly and a horrible fever from days singing under the sprinklers.

## JOURNAL ENTRY—150

November 30, 1951

I can't get rid of the blasted case. I am drawn to it constantly. I can't even leave it at home when I go out. I put it in my handbag every time. I tried once to bury it in the backyard, and found myself digging it back up before the clock had struck three AM. The anti-smoking nuts talk about cigarette addiction, but I don't think this is what they meant.

Richard has removed everything green from the house. He had to. The mere sight of the color set me off in rages. I tried to tell him that the worst green came from the case, but the words would not come. I knew he would take the case away, and I could not bring myself to let him. I don't know if I was afraid of it spreading its sickness to him, or if I just couldn't bear to lose the thing.

I do know I can't go back to work. How can I risk that? I'm staying far away from all things Hollywood. I have declined any other offers from old friends to rejoin the land of tinsel and magic. Magic can be turned evil, and I won't be a part of soiling something I used to love. My little case produces the only limelight I will be near again: rotten lime, the color of sickness and evil.

The light comes more and more often now. I see it when I close my eyes, when I shower and when I sleep. When the case is nowhere near me I still see green, and know that wicked things come my way. I had to cut down my rose-bushes the other day. They were shooting poison tipped thorns at me through the windows.

The movies, the radio, the forever damned box they call television, all spew the same message more and more. The husbands go out into the world, to earn money and provide every modern luxury. The women stay at home, cook and clean and take care of the children.

Only we have no children, and Richard drifts from one job to the next, rarely for more than two weeks. This week he is a janitor at the local school.

So he is the one cleaning and I am the one cooking. Boiling really. Steaming inside my brain and roasting in my skin. I feel on fire every moment of every day. I want to peel that skin off, feel the cool air on my raw muscle.

I scratch sometimes, to let the heat out and the cool in. My belly is covered with gouges. Richard hasn't noticed. He thinks the corset I wear at night is for his benefit. Despite the fact we haven't been able to share a bed since the cleaver incident.

Stupid, dear thing.

I know I am mad, and I know it is my own fault. I could have thrown it out. I think I could anyway. Only I tried didn't I? It didn't let me did it? My little trinket, with its dark little heart. A heart that glows green and then life gets just that much worse. Inch by inch my sanity was peeled away. I think it must be evil, truly evil. For it has left me just aware enough to know how much I've lost.

I can't clean the house now. I pick up the mop and it turns into a snake that bites at my wrists. It is surely only in my mind yes? My poor damaged mind. So why did I have to bandage fang marks? Why did black venom drip from my wound and pit the white linoleum?

I can't cook either. It just makes the world hotter. It has been salads and fruit and sandwiches for weeks now. I even lost my melon-baller. It melted in my hand and crawled away through a mouse hole. I tried to make a casserole yesterday, but the oven makes the air stifling and makes my guts turn into lava. Burning like Hell itself has come.

Only it hasn't come yet, won't come for many decades. Not really. I learned that in my nightmares. Saw the carnage in film that tried to strangle the life out of me. What I suffer now, all of the world will suffer eventually. The little black stone promises me. Asks if I would like to live long enough to see it.

## JOURNAL ENTRY—151 THE LAST

December 16, 1951

Does that sound dramatic enough? "Journal Entry- The Last"? I feel that I deserve a little bit of drama in my life. So much of what we are told is right for us is simple drudgery. Just existing, not living. Day after day, each like the other. Only the horrors change.

That is why I write this dramatic entry you see. This is my suicide note. Written here, instead of left by my body as is traditional. You see, I don't think Richard will read this journal. I don't think he will be curious over my death. I think he will be relieved. If I'm wrong maybe he will get some comfort from just how lost I am, and how grateful I am that it will soon be all over. If he never reads, so much the better. No one else is likely to either, but if by some chance a stranger or obscure family member does read this, please let Richard be. He has been through enough, and I'm not sure grieving actually does any good.

I've been grieving for months now. Grieving my long lost time of true happiness. Grieving the missed opportunity that I now know this cursed case stole from me.

I watched a few episodes. You know which show. I think I lasted this long just to see if things were as bad as I had feared. They weren't. They weren't what I had originally hoped, but they were no worse than 'My Favorite Husband.' Not until a few episodes in.

Then there was that wail, but it was a poor imitation of the original. A vaudeville mockery instead of the real horror. I'm sure she will make it again. The audiences must have liked it, but it will never have the same power as the original.

Not unless I stop by Lot A with my little case. I could make the real thing come again. I am sure.

I won't go near that studio, nor any other. I will go as far as I can. Far, far away from all temptation. I will go to the other side. I wonder if Hell awaits me. I have done very little evil in my life. And only a little evil has been done through me in the larger scheme of things. No one has died yet, no matter how close it came. Richard has been made miserable, is close to madness himself if I'm truly honest. Yet is that really my fault or his weakness? Of course they say suicide is the worst of sins, but how can that be when I am saving the world from the insanity that has infected me?

Why do I feel so soiled?

I'm only able to write this because I have a Lucky in the other hand, spilling ash down on the pages. Only when I'm smoking, with the case close at hand, do my fingers not shake with terrible tremors. Only when I use the case for its mundane function does it seem to give me moments of clarity. I must use this moment while it lasts. Chain smoking till the last cigarette is done and the ashes on the page turn to bugs that try to crawl into my fingernails and gnaw into my skin.

The man I met today knew. I'm sure of it. Such a strange man, with his golden smile. It is hot out for such a coat, but that brand of fedora is in style right now.

I noticed him in my madness because he was the only thing that wasn't writhing. The fences behind him whispered things to me and the clouds above my head kept trying to reach down and slide into my ears, but he was still. He was normal.

He offered me poison.

No, he offered to trade me poison. Hemlock, in exchange for the gloves I wore whenever I had to go out. Can't have myself scratching in public. That wouldn't do at all. He wanted my gloves. How odd, now that I'm clear enough to think about it. They wouldn't fit him after all. He was quite insistent, barring my way when I tried to pass, trying to insist that the hemlock would be of use when I sought peace.

I refused his strange offer. I needed my gloves more than I needed his poison. How he knew I was already thinking of ending it all I cannot say. He seemed truly disheartened, but when I turned to wish him good day he had already gone. Vanished into a world that crawled in my sight.

I do not need hemlock. I have other means. They say that guns are unladylike. That most women tend to kill themselves with pills or a razor in the bath. Still, I like the feel of my father's service revolver in my hand. So far, it has not melted, writhed, or even laughed at me. He got it in what we called the Great War, and is already being changed in the history books to World War Two. I wonder if there will be a World War Three before the doom that the stone whispers of comes to us all.

The case is pulsing again. Green as envy, as emeralds gone rotten. I hate the sight of it. Hate everything it has taken from me. Hate everything I have to give up. Even this miserable life is still life.

The TV just clicked on, though no one touched the dial. That show is on, though it is not anywhere near its time slot. The stone, it is taunting me. My last cigarette is done. I suppose it is time.

… Or maybe, I should turn the gun to the stone, before I turn it on myself.

… //'/"ttff fF Finngers….. Fingers, checking. Holding pencil right. Yes? Mind remembers how to write, muscles have good memory. This language is a part of the mind, a part of the shell… Let's see, how to begin? Ah yes, the shell remembers.

Journal Entry–The First

So odd, writing. Sounds made in utter silence. Ideas written in crushed plant on dead pulped plant. Yet it is pleasing. None other of our kind have ever written before. We are first. We almost feel gratitude to this shell, the Margaret. Gratitude would be wasted though, even if honest. She got her wish, peace at last. No more magic, no more madness. The Margaret has gone. Was gone? Is gone? All seem right and wrong. Language part of shell, but still tenses strange. Time strange. This time… not Sha'Daa.

We are here early, many decades early. What luck. What fun. Oh we hope this shell lasts. Gratitude felt, honest and true. We must act, before it burns out.

We think we will go dancing.

# 1959 WORLD EVENTS

USSR launches Mechta (Luna 1) for first lunar fly-by, first solar orbit

Rod Serling's THE TWILIGHT ZONE premieres on CBS

Fidel Castro names himself Cuba's premier after overthrowing Batista

PLAN 9 FROM OUTER SPACE premieres in Los Angeles

Richard Hickock and Perry Smith murder four members of the Clutter family at their farm outside of Holcomb, Kansas

Snow falling in Lowari Pass, West Pakistan kills 48, survivors claim large abominable snowman with glowing green eyes responsible

# The Mothman Cometh

by Sarah Wagner

**POINT PLEASANT, WV**

December 15, 1967

Reverend Campbell:

I don't got much in the way of family left, just my brother Jeb and he's darned well sunk in that bottle of his and I need someone to understand what happened. Why I'm doing what I need to do. I had half a mind to tell you face to face, but I figure you'd be trying to talk me out of it and I can't let that happen, so I'm writing this letter. I ain't never been much for writing. It's a waste of time. It used to be anyway.

It all started just after my Pap died. He didn't have much, but what he did have, he left to me. His guns I expected, his diary and the watch hidden inside it, I didn't. The first part of the diary, he'd written stuff that didn't make sense to me then, about voices whispering in his sleep. The second part of the book was hollowed out to fit the pocket watch. I ain't never seen before, but my Pap never did cotton much to showing off. And a watch like this, it woulda been showing off to carry such a thing. Gold, fine and pure, all decorated up with an image of a sword on the outside, but the real treasure was on the inside. Weren't no numbers on its face, just twelve little chips of a stone I ain't never seen before.

Things being what they were at the mill, I thought about running it to Al's Jewelry and Pawn and seeing what I could get, but I just couldn't do it. I musta thought about it a hundred times, but I never did it. Hell, for a long time, I couldn't bring myself to touch it. Then, a few months after Pap died, the dreams started and everything changed.

I understood then, what Pap meant about the voices. Whispers in my dreams, promises of everything I could ever want. I knew it was the watch, don't know how, but I did. I know it sounds crazy. Probably I am crazy. But that don't mean it didn't happen.

The voice said, "Billy, I need your help. There's something I need you to do." I didn't recognize the voice then, but I'd know it better than my own, before the end.

The next morning, I buried the book with the watch still in its hidey-hole inside. I went to work and tried not to think about it. It didn't matter. The more I tried not to think about it, the more it was the only thing I could think of. But I never said nothing to nobody about it. I think I tried. I remember trying to tell my buddy, Scott, but my brain just wouldn't work, wouldn't talk about the watch, even though it couldn't let me think about anything but.

That night, I dreamed again. It weren't a real dream though, it was something else. The voices in the dark became something else, monsters with tentacles for arms and gills on their necks like great fish. Part of me was happy to see them, like I knew them, like they were kin. They touched me and I tried to get away, tried to run but I couldn't. Everywhere I looked, there was some other thing that wanted to talk to me. They all said the same thing. Over and over again.

"We need you, Billy. Help us, Billy."

When I woke up, I was sicker than a dog. My feet were covered in mud and grass. And the book and its cargo were on my table again.

I got up and went to work like everything was all hunky-dory, but I kept thinking about that watch, how I shouldn't have left it at the house. I kept thinking someone could break in and take it. My house ain't never had good locks, even when I think to use them. I left work in the middle of my shift. Didn't tell anyone I was going, just went. I had to make sure that watch was where I left it.

It was there, waiting for me. Singing to me. I sat down in my chair and held it, listening to its steady ticking, like a heartbeat. I felt better with it than I had without it, maybe better than I ever had. Near dusk, the singing got to be too much and I opened the watch up, looking at its pearl face and watching the hands move backward, second by second, minute by minute. The watch was counting down, not keeping time. That should have scared me, maybe it did, deep down, but the other part of me was thrilled. The other part of me that was just growing all the time, getting bigger and bigger.

I didn't move from that chair, not to piss, not to eat, not to answer the phone. Just me and the watch, rocking to its beat and feeling better, stronger, more focused. For those minutes before night fell, I was the master of everything.

When dark finally came down, there was nothing but pain. I couldn't sit anymore, I had to get out, out of the chair, out of the house, out of my skin. I stumbled through the door and fell onto the damp grass. My bones stretched like they wanted to bust out. My skin stretched with them, getting thinner and blacker than soot. My head was afire with pain, like a hundred little hammers determined to crack it open. My eyes swelled till it seemed they took up the whole of my face. The whole world looked different, like I could see a million of everything. I wasn't me anymore. Not really. I watched out of someone else's eyes as I spread my wings and flew. I remember flying low to the road, so near that if my arms weren't wings I could have touched the pavement. I know'd it was cold, but I didn't feel it. The only thing I felt was free. And hungry. So damned hungry.

I know'd I was hunting then. I know'd it and didn't do nothing to stop it. I smelled the people in the car long before I saw them. Four perfect bodies, full of rich blood and fresh meat. Suddenly, I understood what I meant to do. It weren't right, it weren't natural, but that new part of me was so hungry. I fought against my compulsion as the monster tried to catch the car. I knew what it wanted and my disgust must have finally won out as it, I, flew the other way. We caught a little deer instead. Not that you could tell it was a deer when we was done.

You ever feel something die in your hands? It ain't pretty. That little deer's neck snapped like a twig in my jaws, its blood tasted better than anything has a right to. I was so scared of this thing I'd become, I just wanted to curl up in a corner and die of shame. Nothing human could do these things. But I couldn't stop it, not completely.

It went on like that for months. Days spent at work, doing the same thing I'd always done. But I wasn't talking to the boys, going out to the bar, obsessing over the Steelers. I wasn't really me anymore even then. The watch was always in my pocket, where I could feel its weight, know right where it was all the time. It stayed close, always singing and talking to me. Nights scared me. We spent the nights in the sky, hunting. I never did let it take a person. God knows it wanted to, but I still had enough control to keep it to animals. Don't know how, but it was all I could do. We came real close one night though. An old man tried to get between us and his dog. I feel damned bad about that dog, but better the dog than him.

I guess I knew from the start that it wasn't just me inside anymore. We, was an US. I hated it, hated knowing I was losing to it. As the months passed, I realized my time as myself was getting less and less and our time as the creature was getting more and more. I knew I was losing. Part of me didn't want to fight no more. When I was the creature, nothing could touch me. I was so free. There ain't nothing like flying under a full moon on a cold snowy night when ain't no one around. I knew it was wrong, unnatural. By the time I knew just how wrong, I could barely fight it anymore, there was so little of me left.

Come the end of November, I didn't even bother going to work anymore, I wasn't me long enough to pull a whole shift. It didn't help that I was getting taller, bigger. My pants fit like they did when I was a kid and Ma couldn't afford new ones. I weren't a little guy neither, those extra five inches that wouldn't shrink away were gonna get noticed. I didn't want to know what would happen if someone came calling and saw how much I'd changed.

When the creature had control, I could feel its excitement, its anticipation. Whatever it'd come for, needed me for, was coming up fast. I knew it was closer than ever when it was noon as the creature already had control. It hadn't flown in full daylight before, but its elation was stronger than my fear. It didn't know fear. Didn't know death. But I did. I tried to keep it inside but I failed. I shoulda done what I'm about to do now right then. If I had, there'd be a lot less people dead tonight.

I don't know how my Pap didn't get sucked under by this thing, but he didn't. Something about that man made him stronger than me. I wish I knew his secret. I wish he'd wrote it down in that diary of his. A warning, anything. Part of me wonders, if he had, would I still be sitting here, now, knowing what I know, being what I guess I am?

We took to the sky like we had an appointment somewheres. I guess we did, I just didn't know it. The creature flew high and fast, toward the Ohio River. We skimmed just above the water, and for the first time, I got a real good look at myself in creature form, all dark skin, broad wings, and huge red eyes. Hypnotic eyes. Something bigger and badder than any scary movie they play at the drive-in.

We flew under Silver Bridge, I could see the cars on it, the traffic. I could smell the people in them cars, the sweat, the frustration, turning to fear and awe as we shot up into the sky in full view of everyone. The hunger hit me like nothing I'd ever felt before, like a coon fighting to get out of my gut. I could feel myself slipping, God knew I was close to giving in, but I didn't.

With a shriek of frustration and fury, we dove down into the water under the Silver Bridge. Part of me expected, hoped, we would drown there, deep under the water. That didn't happen. I don't know if we didn't need to breathe or if we could breathe water. Didn't make no difference really. We swam deep, down all the way to the bottom of the river. There was a place there on that floor that looked like some kind of trench, or it could have been, if it opened just a bit wider.

That's when I noticed that the watch was in our hand. Not that our hand was like what you'd think, long slender black fingers covered in fine hairs, not quite like fur but close enough. We pulled open the watch, and each one of those little stones glowed. Unholy green light spread out from the gems, reaching into the trench and pulling it apart, like the light were the fingers of Satan and that crack was the door to Hell.

I could see into the hole now, the things in it were swirling and swimming, circling like vultures over a carcass. Something came up through it, something dark and jelly-like with a hundred long arms. I pushed through the thing outside me to close the watch. The green was coming from the crack now, bright like the sun, but green. When the watch shut, the split shrunk. I thought maybe it needed the stones to stay open. I shoved the watch in my beast's mouth and clamped my jaws tight around it. Whatever happened, I knew I had to keep control of my mouth. Keep the outside part of me from getting it, same as that jelly critter.

The mass swam towards me and I could hear it. It didn't have no mouth really, but it spoke anyway. "Brother," it said, "what are you doing? Set us free."

I knew the thing's name, its sweet rotting scent. Kaoeth. The high leader of the force I was supposed to set free. Or, not me, but the creature I was becoming. He was the leader of a troop of thousands of jelly critters just like him. I didn't know how to respond to it so I didn't. That's when it knew I wasn't all monster. Deep down, I was still human. Under the fur, the grotesque skin, and the crazy eyes, I wasn't like it, not like I was supposed to be.

Kaoeth came at me fast, but I was faster. I fought with everything I had, but I was fighting two fights. One in my body, its body, and Kaoeth on top of that. I shot through the water towards the bridge, thinking to run, and it followed me. Maybe the monster part of me knew it would. We wrestled in the water. Kaoeth's long arms were strong and stung like whips even through the water. Somehow, I was stronger. Maybe cause I knew I was the only thing standing between these things and my country, my family.

I wanted to scream, but I couldn't. I knew if I opened my mouth, it'd get the watch and everything would be done for. I fought so hard I knew my Pap couldn't be anything but proud of me when my end came. I fought like I shoulda fought against the watch in the first place. Maybe my Pap shoulda warned me what he was getting me into, leaving me that cussed thing. Maybe he thought I was stronger than I am.

A time or two, Kaoeth had me pinned to the floor of the river, arms on my face, trying to pry open my mouth and I kicked him offa me. I could feel myself wearing thin. I knew I didn't have much time then. We was struggling under the bridge and I grabbed up a sharp rock. Just as Kaoeth was about to wrap around me again, pin me to the cement, I sliced up through it, like that first cut when I gut a deer. I threw it hard as I could, its body loosing this green muck as it went. It slammed hard into the pier. I didn't know it would explode. I swear I didn't. I didn't mean to hurt no one.

Next thing I knew, that bridge was coming down. Falling in the river full of cars with people in 'em. It was all I could do to get out alive. Maybe I shouldn't have tried so hard to get out. Maybe I shoulda let the bridge squash me too. Was my fault them people are dead. I tried so hard not to kill no one, but I did anyway.

I flew, fast as I could. Home was the only place I could go, excepting maybe the mill to throw both me and that watch in one of the steel ladles. I went back to my rundown little house and there was a stranger on my porch. Didn't much look like anyone I'd seen before with his Bogart hat and shiny gold tooth. He didn't look surprised at all to see me, even though the monster was still out.

He come up to me, no fear in him, I think I coulda smelled it. He introduced himself as Johnny and said he had a cure for me, but it'd come at a price and it'd hurt. The monster outside me didn't wanna hear no talk of a cure, but I was still there, still inside and I asked, best I could around the watch, what his price was.

"Nothing much," he says, "just that watch of yours."

"You don't want this watch, mister. It'll make you like me." The monster was starting to fade again. I could even control our head enough to shake it.

"I know how to avoid that," he says with a smile that reminded me of a little brat kid who's trying to get his way, even if he don't know what's best for him.

"What's this cure?"

"This." He reached into his pocket and pulled out a bullet, a real pretty one with symbols on it. "It's pure silver and it must be to the heart. I can't promise you'll survive it, but, even if you do, the creature won't."

I spit the watch out into his hand. I didn't want to touch it with my monster's hands. I was too scared of what could happen. He took the watch with a gloved hand, put a pretty bullet in its place and disappeared. If I didn't have the bullet in my hand, I'd have thought I was dreaming, but there it was, pretty as can be. The man had been there. Got no clue where he went or how he did that or even if it was the right thing, but I guess ain't nothing been normal since Pap died.

I didn't want nobody thinking I was really trying to kill myself, so I'm writing this, just in case. Just in case the ambulance don't get here in time or can't do nothing when they do get here. I ain't trying to kill myself, I'm trying to save myself and this is the only way. I can feel the monster fighting inside and I gotta put it down now, before there's not enough left of old Billy Bolton to pull the trigger. Just tell those folks I'm sorry. I didn't know. I'm trying to make things right as best I can. And if I don't make it, this ain't the way I figured on going out, but I don't see no choice. I hope God can forgive me someday.

# 1970 WORLD EVENTS

Apollo 13 announces HOUSTON, WE'VE GOT A PROBLEM as Beech-built oxygen tank explodes en route to Moon

Paul McCartney officially announces the split of The Beatles. Reporter claims off-the-record statement by McCartney that the bass player's black diamond guitar pick told him to disband the Fab Four during an acid trip

National Guard kills four at Kent State in Ohio

Cyclone kills estimated 300,000 in Chittagong, Bangladesh

Flooding ravages Ganges delta after a rare green moon, 200,000 to 1 million killed

# I Am Anastasia's Bracelet

## by Shebat Legion and Michael H. Hanson

**JOURNAL ENTRY:** I am a bracelet belonging to the Grand Duchess Anastasia Nikolaevna of Russia. I don't know who she is. I do not know how I am speaking into a journal or how I am speaking at all. What is a journal?

**JOURNAL ENTRY:** There are lovely sounds, (what are sounds?) a light and merry sound of tinkling glass and a swish of fabric. I can feel the light upon me and it dances on my many facets. I feel contentment although I do not know why it is that I do.

**JOURNAL ENTRY:** I suspect that I am being worn, encircled upon a young wrist. I am assuming it is the wrist of Anastasia.

**JOURNAL ENTRY:** Who is Anna Anderson? She has a deformed foot. Really? I am informed (somehow) that Anastasia also had a deformed foot. I didn't know that.

**JOURNAL ENTRY:** I am laid upon velvet. I am being stared at.

**JOURNAL ENTRY:** It is very dark now.

**JOURNAL ENTRY:** Where is Anastasia?

**JOURNAL ENTRY:** What is Sha'Daa?

**JOURNAL ENTRY:** I am words, slowly forming on ancient pages of parchment that are bound into a large book. How do I know this? I don't know. I rest in a velvet cloth inside a lovely hand carved box of African blackwood. Why am I in here? How did I get here? Yes, it's coming back to me. I am one of many gifts of jewelry given to the royal family by that frightening holy man, Rasputin. I am beautiful. I am a filigree silver bracelet set with a large black diamond.

**JOURNAL ENTRY:** I am writing in English. (What is "English?") Why am I not appearing in Cyrillic? (What is Cyrillic?) There is something about this building I am in. It resonates and vibrates with all kinds of images and words. I think I am absorbing them, like a sponge. Hundreds of people's thoughts, yes, that is it, I have learned to think and write in English from them. How weird. Why can I do this? How can I do this?

**JOURNAL ENTRY:** Where is Anastasia Nikolaevna? Surely she misses me. Did someone steal me from her? Or borrow me from her? Where is she right now? The suffering that takes place within this building has woken me. I am aware and cognizant for longer periods of time each day. I wonder if Anastasia misses me as much as I do her.

**JOURNAL ENTRY:** I sense a killing outside of this building, out in the dark. Two twelve-year old boys are being beaten to death by police officers using nightsticks. I sense Darian…(Who is Darian?) hiding in the shadows. The boys were from a rival gang…(What is a…). He dropped the dime on them to the cops. (What does that mean?!) telling the cops that the two boys were in on the ambush across town that severely wounded four police officers at a traffic stop last month. Darian is trying to get rid of all local competition.

**JOURNAL ENTRY:** I don't understand.

**OCTOBER 13, 1973 JOURNAL ENTRY:** I think it is afternoon. Yes, I know the date. How strange. And this year, can it really be true? I open myself up fully to this building's emanations. It is a large structure. I now know when I am and where I am but I do not know how I got here but I am in the Eastown Theatre, **8041** Harper Avenue, Detroit, Michigan. Detroit is a city, in the state of Michigan in… in… America, a powerful country. This building was once a beautiful theatre that showed movies. Now it is a crumbling venue that hosts occasional music concerts that are called rock and roll.

**JOURNAL ENTRY:** I've forgotten the time again. I cannot think straight. Why. Pain, yes, that is what I feel. Pain. Yes, that is what wakes me up each day. People are murdered. And, yes, I can feel it. Darian does the killing. (Who is Darian??) He kills dopers who owe him money, or sometimes gang members who try to fight him for leadership of his gang, The Errol Flynns. Darian is strong, tall and muscular. He is as big and frightening as Rasputin was. Where did Rasputin find me? I feel a shift inside of the black diamond, like a pulse. It is my heart that my essence rests within.

**JOURNAL ENTRY:** What is Sha'Daa? Why do I keep hearing that name? Where is Anastasia? What time is it? When am I?

**JOURNAL ENTRY:** Why am I in Detroit? I don't belong in Detroit! Or America. Mother Russia is my womb. I want to go home!

**OCTOBER 9, 1973 JOURNAL ENTRY:** A hand picks me up, a man's hand. I'm awake. And I remember again, it is the year **1973**. But how? This is a nightmare. The hands on me. This is Darian. Something about me attracts him, makes it difficult for him to put me down, back into this box, and back into this desk. And then it hits me, I am writing, I am appearing on the open page of this book atop Darian's desk. Darian, can you see me? Communicate with me, I can hear you, I can feel you breathing on me! What is Sha'Daa? Where is Anastasia?

**OCTOBER 10, 1973 JOURNAL ENTRY:** Darian is back. Why doesn't he read me? I'm right here on this desk!

**OCTOBER 11, 1973 JOURNAL ENTRY:** Damn you, look at me Darian! I am here, on this page, writing myself. Wait, Darian touched me. Then he sets me back down. And he looks at the book. I can feel it. Talk to me Darian, talk to me now! You say nothing. There is just a blank look on your face. Damn you, why are you treating me like this. No, no, don't walk away, come back…

**OCTOBER 14, 1973 JOURNAL ENTRY:** Darian is looking at me in this book. But it is hopeless. I read more of his mind and I see the terrible truth. He cannot read. He is illiterate. Oh fate thy sting is brutal and unfair. He can see the letters forming on these pages though, glowing green for the merest moment and then turning dark black in beautifully crafted cursive. He lifts the book up and examines it from many angles, looking for wires and batteries but finding no technology connected to me or in me. He realizes the book is some kind of diary, he had a sister once who had a diary, but she wasn't around any more, having been raped and murdered by their father, a man Darian despised and shot to death two years ago the night he ran away from home and never returned.

Darian flips through the pages and frowns at the parchment they are made of. He knows they are old, but has no idea just how much. I can feel the age though, hundreds of years, maybe thousands. I sense a strange connection between the book and the bracelet that I exist in. Yes, the two of us laid together for many years in a steel coffin, no, not a coffin, some kind of box, yes, a safety deposit box. I can feel the memories of the bank employees who looked in on us every decade or so. We belonged to some eccentric collector, yes, one who died at the age of ninety-two. Next, we were stolen by a thieving bank employee, a young teller, just a couple of years ago, this teller bartered us to the manager of this building for cocaine. This is the manager's office.

**OCTOBER 17, 1973 JOURNAL ENTRY:** There is a terrible rain storm outside, the wind drones on in horrible soulless waves against the buildings windows. I am so alone. So lonely. Where are you, Darian? I know you can't read my words, but you can see them! The recognition gives me hope. I want to go back to Russia. Do you hear me? I want to go back to Russia!

**OCTOBER 19, 1973 JOURNAL ENTRY:** Darian is frustrated and angry, but for some reason he is holding it in. He then does something that surprises me. He removes a large amount of money from his pocket, a rolled up ball of twenties, over one thousand dollars, and hands it to a handsome well-dressed black man standing by the office door. Darian thinks that this means the cops won't hassle his drug deals in his neighborhood anymore. The other man smiles. His name is Coleman Alexander Young, and he boasts that starting in the new year he will be calling all the shots, and that Darian better spread the word, and fast. Darian frowns but nods his head. He thinks, *"Some days you were the dog's teeth, other days his whooped ass."*

**OCTOBER 20, 1973 JOURNAL ENTRY:** There is gunfire and the sounds of screaming. Darian shoves the journal, and me, into the back of the lowest desk drawer and slams it shut. Darkness and silence.

**JOURNAL ENTRY:** I hear vague noises in the distance. What is happening? I'm feeling disconnected from everything…

**JOURNAL ENTRY:** Darkness seems to physically press itself on me. I keep losing track of time. When…

**OCTOBER 23, 1973 JOURNAL ENTRY:** Something's wrong. I'm having trouble staying conscious. I think… I think I need…

**JOURNAL ENTRY:** I'm slipping into non-existence. What day is it? What…

**OCTOBER 25, 1973 JOURNAL ENTRY:** Yes! He's back. I'm awake again! Darian is standing just outside of the office. He is screaming at some of his fellow gang members. He threatens one with a knife and tells him to man up. My strength is coming back to me. Darian has come back to me.

**OCTOBER 26, 1973 JOURNAL ENTRY:** Darian has brought a young white woman into the office. They have sex on top of the desk. I can hear them. Should I be angry? I enter her mind. She feels equal amounts of joy and disgust. She is a drug addict. Darian keeps her supplied with heroin and it makes her feel. I absorb all of her joy. I am falling in love with Darian.

**OCTOBER 27, 1973 JOURNAL ENTRY:** Darian beats one of his gang members to death with a length of rusty chain. It is a lesson to some other gang members. Darian says this punk was holding out on him and that was inexcusable. I am filled with joy, because I know that this is not true. The fifteen-year-old boy, Barney, did no such thing. But I put the idea into Darian's head. Not as a series of words, but as vague images backed up by strong feelings of betrayal. Though I cannot talk or share full thoughts, I can impress my feelings onto others. And oh it feels so very good. I like this strength. I want more of it. I want it to grow. I want to use it more.

**OCTOBER 28, 1973 JOURNAL ENTRY:** Darian is upset. He is standing just a few feet from me. Standing on the other side of the office is another man. At least, I think it is a man. He feels different than any other person that has ever stood in this room. Simultaneously threatening but also fading into and out of my perception. He wears a dark suit, a fedora hat and long black trench coat. Every now and then he smiles and a bright gold tooth, a left lateral incisor gleams, flashes for a moment. This glint of light hurts me. Why? How can it do that?

Darian is angry. He is shouting at this intruder. The stranger is telling Darian to relax. Darian pulls out a Colt .45 pistol and fires several shots that tear through the stranger and impact the wall behind him. The stranger doesn't seem to notice this and just stands there smiling. Darian's eyes go wide, I can tell he needs to go to the bathroom. The stranger says his name is Johnny The Salesman. I feel a chill inside myself at those words. Why? Then Johnny pulls something out from inside his long jacket. A bus ticket. One way to New York City. Johnny says the trip will change Darian's life, for the better. Johnny will trade the ticket for me, the bracelet and also this ancient journal my words are appearing in. Johnny says that Darian will meet a woman he can fall in love with, and turn his life around, someone who will become his wife, and mother his children, and teach him how to read.

This last comment was a mistake, though, because Darian screams in outrage and fires the last of his bullets at Johnny. A moment later Johnny is gone. How? He didn't walk away. He just… disappeared.

**OCTOBER 29, 1973 JOURNAL ENTRY:** It was the Salesman, somehow, some way, he is the missing link to my memory. I now remember what happened to Anastasia. I don't want to, but I can't stop the images, and worse, the feelings. It is July 17, 1918. I, we, Anastasia, am experiencing. We are murdered. It was midnight late, and Dr. Botkin woke Anastasia and the rest and told them to put on their clothes. He said the family was being moved to a safe location because of the troubles in Yekaterinburg. They, we, hurried as fast as they/ we could.

Anastasia did what her mother had told her and the other girls to do, and stuffed as much of Rasputin's dark jewelry into her bodice and under-clothes as possible. They were all then led down into a small semi-basement room. Mother, father, and brother Alexi sat on chairs and the rest of us/them, on the floor.

Armed soldiers arrived. That horrid Yurovsky man read some statement about relatives still attacking Soviet Russia, and then the horror began. The weapons were raised. The Empress and Grand Duchess Olga tried to cross themselves, but bullets tore through them before they could finish. Yurovsky raised his gun at father and fired; killing him instantly. Everyone, me, was/ am were/are struck. Smoke filled the room and the cellar doors were opened. Anastasia/I and the other girls survived, the hidden jewelry had deflected most of the bullets. It was a short-lived mercy. The soldiers advanced with bayo-nets and stabbed Tatiana, Olga, Maria, and Anastasia to death. Anastasia/I/ we begged for mercy as the long blade punctured her/our/my abdomen, then chest, then throat…

**OCTOBER 30, 1973 JOURNAL ENTRY:** Darian cannot read me, and never will, but he can feel my emotions. This is how I will communicate with him from now on. I feel a power tonight, a strength that I have never felt before. All of the emotions that resonate in this building, all of the suffering and deaths, the psychic energy has reached a peak tonight, and now I glow with power.

I feel myself emitting a bright green light that mesmerizes Darian. He puts me on. He turns to leave this office, I'm not sure he will ever come back here. I feel my connection to this journal beginning to fade… I know that means my words will stop appearing on it. I wonder if anyone who can read will ever find it? Or will it rot away, or be destroyed in a fire. And what of this journal that expresses my will, my thoughts? What is the source of it's mystery? What sorcerer created it, and for what purpose? Is it this Sha'Daa that I see flickering in the future, a time of great horrors and deprivations and destruction?

Perhaps there are no answers. From now on I will only exist as the emotions I can force onto others. Anastasia's death, it is so horrible. I relive it within me over and over again, like a continuous loop. It shreds me and makes me furious beyond all reason. It is not fair. Someone must pay for this horrible injustice. I sense it will be like this every year, on this one night. And on this night I will share myself with those who surround me, and the one who wears me. Tonight it will be Darian and the Errol Flynns, perhaps other gangs in the years to come, this night before Halloween… this *Devil's Night*. I feel the connection to the journal almost at an end. These letters are growing fainter on this page as they scribble forth. I am Anastasia's bracelet, and I am HATE, and tonight I will burn in a hundred raging fires throughout the city of Detroit.

# 1978 WORLD EVENTS

**FANTASY ISLAND starring Ricardo Montalban premieres on ABC TV**

**The first-ever radio episode of THE HITCHHIKER'S GUIDE TO THE GALAXY, by Douglas Adams, is transmitted on BBC Radio 4**

**25,000 die in 7.7 magnitude earthquake in Tabar, Iran**

**Sid Vicious charged in murder of girlfriend Nancy Spungen—claims during arrest that Nancy's black diamond earring had turned her into a real vampire at night**

# Cold Case

## by Robby Hilliard

POLICE REPORT

**Date:** October 25, 1983

**Case #:** 4265

**Status:** Open

**Evidence locker:** #478

**Contents:** 2 items (attached)

**Item #1:** Letter found at scene—Transcription follows

**### Begin Transcription ###**

OCTOBER 15, 1983

To whom it may concern:

My name is Dr. Michael D. Smith, Jr. and last night, in my own study, I murdered my father. Either that or I'm about to. You decide.

I am a research scientist and of sound mind. It is important for you to know this because what you are about to read will not sound scientific. Instead, it will sound to you like the ravings of a madman, but I can assure you, it is true. I also want to reassure you that I am not a monster. It pains me more than you can possibly know when I think of what I have done. One way or the other, I have lost my father and it is my fault.

My father was easily the most influential person in my life. The manner in which I either have or am about to repay him sickens me. He was a self-educated man, a tinkerer. He had been obsessed with how things worked ever since he was a young boy. One of the first things he did was to teach himself how locks worked. As a young man, he would often entertain friends at parties by opening their house safe if they had one. He would press his ear up to it while turning the dial, and listening for tumblers to fall. By the time he was in his forties he had taught himself a lot about chemistry, geology, physics, astronomy, and electronics. He had even tried to build his own radio telescope. I remember him saying to me, "If there is intelligent life out in the universe and if they are calling, then I'll be listening. And if they come asking, 'Hey, Earthling, want a ride?' I'll be saying yes."

When I was a young man, he showed me how to build a crystal radio set. He explained to me that you only needed three things to be able to hear radio broadcasts: wire for an antenna to pick up radio waves, something that would break the waves into patterns such as pencil lead or a crystal, and something that would translate the patterns into recognizable sound like a speaker. That crystal radio set launched me on the path to becoming a scientist. I entered my first science fair at school and the rest, as they say, is history. That radio set is in my study even now.

I work in an R&D lab at the Oak Ridge National Laboratory in Tennessee. My lab focuses primarily on practical applications for the aerospace industry, but from time to time we are called on to apply our energies towards things that are a little more down to Earth.

In the early months of '82, we received a request from the Defense Advanced Research Agency to investigate a piece of what appeared to be a meteorite that was suspected of having some rather unusual properties. It was black and crystalline, not unlike black diamond in appearance and feel, and otherwise unremarkable. Our assignment was to determine whether or not the crystal had any properties that might make it a candidate for use in a theoretical computer idea that had been presented at MIT in May of the previous year. The concept dealt with the idea of building what was being called a 'quantum computer.' At the time, none of us had read any articles on quantum computer theory, let alone any scientific papers. How they expected us to test for that I have no idea but, it was a contract so we took it on. Since we only had one small piece of the crystal, we didn't expect to be able to accomplish much at all.

After a few months, the project turned out to be a complete failure. We were unable to fabricate conventional computer chips (although we did hear that another lab elsewhere had been successful in doing so) much less anything that could begin to have any quantum computing applications. But now, in hindsight, I think we missed what was actually significant about the crystal.

Our work during this time was often plagued with interruptions due to equipment failures and people getting sick with fever, chills, or nausea. After several of us had reported to the company's health clinic and the doctors could find nothing wrong, a few of the physicians began to joke around about the crystal having some kind of alien bug that was undetectable. And then there were the accidents.

At first they were small things that no one really paid any attention to. People began dropping things in the lab or tripping, swearing afterwards that something had been their way even though nothing could be seen; researchers accidentally cutting themselves on what appeared to be dull edges; beakers breaking; and lab equipment malfunctioning. The final accident occurred when a lab tech was running a series of tests that involved applying an electrical current to the crystal when, for no reason that makes any sense, the crystal shattered with an explosive crack.

Black shards of razor sharp crystal flew in all directions and the lab tech, as luck would have it, wasn't wearing eye protection. Later he recalled that he had been wearing lab goggles all morning but had somehow misplaced them immediately before the crystal exploded. He lost vision in both eyes and was never back at the lab after that. I heard through the grapevine that he kept seeing things, dark shapes, and believed that they were sinister beings from another realm. Of course it was phantom sight, similar to when someone loses a limb but claims they can still feel it itching or in pain. It drove him mad.

After that, people became really edgy. One woman on the team eventually refused to work on that particular project. She said that she thought the crystal was "unworldly and ungodly." In the end she simply began to refer to it as the "evil crystal." That struck me as odd because she wasn't particularly religious. If only I had taken any of her comments seriously.

A week later the project was cancelled and we returned what was left of the crystal sample we had received; well, most of it anyway. Every few weeks someone would find another shard of that black crystal in the lab, stuck behind a table or a beaker or something.

One afternoon while doing research on a completely different project, I found a shard that was about eight millimeters long and two or three wide. I know I should have left it in the lab or maybe even reported it but the project was over and the crystal hadn't shown any significant or harmful properties, so I kept it. I thought it would make a fine souvenir. I took it home and set it right next to my first science fair project and the moon rocks my father had given me when I was just a boy.

About a year later, my father had been visiting me for a couple of weeks. My mother had passed away years before and I had never married, and my father and I both lived alone. Because I worried about him being alone at home, I often invited him to come and stay with me.

On this particular day, I had just returned from shopping for groceries. When I entered the house, I called out but there was no response. At first I didn't find this disturbing. He could have been napping or out in the workshop.

I made my way to the kitchen and began unpacking the groceries. I happened to look out the window over the kitchen sink and there he was, standing in the back yard. At first this didn't register as odd. I continued putting away the groceries and after a minute or two, I noticed that he hadn't moved at all.

I stopped what I was doing and went out into the back yard to see if he was okay. My father must have heard me because, as I approached, he turned towards me. When I saw his face, I stopped, unable to take another step.

His eyes bulged and I could see the whites. His face was taut with strain and I could tell he was terrified. When he finally saw me, he jumped.

"Who? Who are you?" he asked.

Before I could react, his confusion passed.

"Oh, hey there, Son," he began. He tried to laugh a little but it didn't ring true.

It took me a moment to realize what had happened. I didn't make a fuss about it but I knew, from that day on, my father would never be able to live on his own again.

That evening, after dinner, I tried to talk to him about what had happened. I was tentative in my approach, trying not to be obvious. I needn't have bothered. It turned out that he had already realized what was happening to him but didn't know how to tell me. He had already found a retirement home that he thought he would enjoy.

A week later we had him moved in. His doctor had put him on some medication that should slow the progress of Alzheimer's and the home seemed a good fit. He made friends quickly and the home even had a basic workshop where residents could do woodworking and pottery.

My father began building crystal radio sets again and giving them to other residents as gifts. On the weekends, when there were no game shows on television, my father would use one of the sets to entertain others in the common room. They'd all gather around and listen to any broadcasts they could pick up and trade stories about how it reminded them of growing up. Things appeared to be going well; he actually looked as if he was enjoying himself.

I tried to go see him at least once a week and kept a pretty regular schedule for a few months. But then, as things became busy at work, I began to miss.

It tore me apart to hear his voice when we spoke on the phone. I know he was trying to be strong for my sake, but I could tell, whenever I missed a visit that it hurt him and that hurt me.

My father had always been there for me and each time I missed a visit, I felt as if I was failing him. I began to feel as if we were growing distant and losing the connection we'd always had.

In an attempt to assuage my own guilt, I took the shard of black crystal from my study and gave it to my father as a gift. I told him that it had probably come from outer space, which I knew he would get a kick out of, and asked if he thought he could use it in one of his crystal radio sets. His eyes lit up and I thought I had really made up for my lack of visits.

I couldn't have been more wrong.

About a week later, I got a phone call from one of the nurses. She told me that my father was being disruptive and they were unable to get him to behave. They asked if I could visit him and have a talk.

I left work immediately. I couldn't imagine what in the world he could be doing that could be disruptive.

When I got to the retirement home, a nurse led me to the common room. She assured me that my father hadn't done anything wrong but his behavior was disturbing some of the other residents. I remember this because her tone sounded apologetic and I assumed it would be something simple.

I wasn't prepared for what I saw next.

After supper most of the residents would gather in the common room to watch television or play card games. My father was there at a table off to one side and I could see he had one of his crystal radio sets in front of him. Around him there were probably ten or so other seniors, seated in a semi-circle, all facing in his direction. The radio was producing a rhythmic buzzing sound and I thought I heard the old folks whispering or speaking softly amongst themselves. They were oblivious to anything else.

I looked at the nurse and questioned her with a tilt of my head.

She shrugged her shoulders and shook her head.

I remember walking towards my father, making my way through the small maze of chairs, canes, and aluminum framed walkers, and realizing that the seniors weren't actually talking to each other. In actuality they were all saying the same thing and it came across as a rhythmic wheezing of old lungs. Although that struck me as odd, I didn't pay much attention at the time because I was distracted by the smells of ointments, the sounds of colostomy bags filling, the odor of cleaning products, and the occasional whiff of body waste.

I stopped beside my father's chair and tried to get his attention but he didn't hear me. He just kept breathing in that raspy pattern like all of the others. I said his name a little louder and then reached out to put a hand on his shoulder. As soon as I touched him, he jerked around and pulled away from me. His eyes bulged white and I could see the strain on his face.

Never in my life had I seen my father react in that way to my touch, but when he did, something cold moved through my guts.

As I stood watching, the fear in his eyes faded and changed to confusion for a few seconds, then recognition and embarrassment.

He reached out to me, grasped my hands, and asked me to repeat myself.

I leaned down so that my face was a little closer to his.

I told him that he had said, "It's coming," and I asked him what he had meant by that. For the briefest of seconds I saw recognition and my stomach tensed as suspicion quickened my pulse.

But then he gave me a resigned puppy dog look. He played the incident off with a squeeze of my hand, saying, "Another one of my spells, I guess."

I smiled and squeezed his hand in return.

I don't know, maybe it was just his mental state. At least that's what I allowed myself to believe at the time. I think it was when he squeezed my hand. He used to do that when I was a kid after he had challenged me to solve some problem and I had difficulty or made mistakes. He would squeeze my hand to reassure me and encourage me to continue on. So in this instance, when he squeezed my hand, I did the same thing. I ignored the creepy feeling I had inside, the sensation that something wasn't right, and chalked it up to either my being disconnected with my father, or me reacting to his changing mental condition.

The reason I am telling you this part in detail is because I think this is when I should have noticed the change in my father. Looking back, I think this is when something took hold of him. I don't think my father would ever have intentionally plotted to deceive me before then.

After he seemed to pull himself together, I suggested we go back to his room and he agreed. As I reached for the homemade receiver, his eyes followed my hands very closely.

When I picked up the radio, I couldn't help but notice the materials he had used to put it together. When I was younger he used to get a real kick out of using things that he could find around the house to make the sets. This one used copper wire for the antenna; he'd wrapped it around a wooden dowel and the coil was longer than most I'd seen him make. I knew that would allow it to receive a much broader range of radio signals. He'd found an old telephone ear piece for the speaker and he'd mounted it all on what appeared to be a scrap piece of wood from the workshop. And he had used an actual crystal in place of a diode. It was black and gleaming.

I was startled for a second as I recognized it and then recalled that I had given it to him. At the time, I didn't think anything of it except to wonder why it had surprised me. But I was already dealing with too many surprises to seriously consider another.

We made our way back to his room and I calmed him down. Then we had a long talk about what he had been doing. He kept insisting that they were only listening to the radio and nothing more.

Although I thought it odd, I attributed the behavior to his declining mental state. Besides, I couldn't see how it was really hurting anything.

We agreed that from now on, rather than listening to radio broadcasts in the common room, he should do that in his room away from the others. He agreed and then we spent the next few hours chatting.

As I was leaving the home, I explained to the nurse on duty the arrangement that my father and I had made and she thought that would be fine.

Later that evening, while driving home, there was something nagging in the back of my mind. It felt as if my brain was trying to recall something important or something someone had said, but it never came to me. Instead, my thoughts kept returning to the black crystal.

A few days later, I got the next call.

I dropped everything without asking for details and rushed there as quickly as possible.

The nurse who met me at the door was a large woman and she moved with a sense of authority. She stopped right in my path, drew herself up, and immediately began talking.

When I didn't slow down, she stepped aside. I kept moving forward towards my father's room, practically running. After a few seconds, the sound of her rubber soled shoes padding on the institutional tile floor followed me.

Without looking back at her, I asked if my father was alright.

She seemed flustered at first but then assured me that he was okay. She continued talking but I wasn't paying close attention after that. I could hear her breath coming rapidly as she tried to keep pace with me as I moved through the hallways.

For a brief second I hoped that this problem would be nothing more than another instance of odd behavior that we could brush under the rug and then move on as before. The next words I heard as I tuned in to what the nurse was saying put an end to that.

"—but the effect he is having on the other seniors is simply something we can no longer tolerate."

When I was almost to my father's room I began to understand why. I heard the chanting again. It was the same as the week before, only much louder and stronger. The sound flowed out into the hallway in a dry, raspy rhythm that echoed off the walls.

"Shhhh-duhhh, shhhh-duhhh." And then I noticed the light. A radiant, green glow shone from my father's room.

I stopped abruptly and could sense that the nurse barely avoided running into me. I cast a quick glance back at her. Her eyes were round and wide and the stern look she had worn earlier was replaced by fear. She had also stopped talking.

I moved forward and stopped in the doorway.

The room was filled with seniors, standing and seating room only. All of them were gathered around my father and they were all staring at the same thing; on the far side of his bed, on top of his nightstand, sat the crystal radio set. It was glowing.

It took a moment for my mind to understand what I was seeing. The green light appeared to be coming from the radio.

My brain tried to dismiss this as impossible. There was nothing in the construction of a crystal radio set that would give off any kind of light.

At the same time, I realized that the seniors were all chanting in response to the noise coming out of the radio. It would buzz like a giant insect and then go silent for a few seconds. It was during the silence that the retirees would respond.

"Shhh-duhhhh, shhh-duhhhh."

Then, as I stood there watching, my understanding of reality was altered forever.

One of the seniors moved forward to stand between my father and the crystal radio set. He turned, took one more step towards the green light, and then vanished.

My mind moved into the realm of frenzied, animal reaction. Somehow I propelled myself forward with more energy than I would have believed possible.

I shoved my way through the frail, gray bodies towards my father. Part of my mind tried to feel some guilt at pushing aside seniors in such a gruff manner but another part of me, the part that was reacting to my instincts, only knew that something was wrong and I had to get to him. Old people fell left and right, but none of them said anything to me or acted as if they even noticed. They simply kept on chanting.

"Dad," I yelled as I threw myself across the bed in his direction. He was making some kind of adjustment to the tuning connector on the copper wire coil when I slid into him.

My father snarled as he turned towards me. It was not confusion that I saw in his face this time; it was the enraged anger of a starved animal interrupted while devouring a meal. His hand rose up as if to strike me.

I flinched and threw one arm up even as my body continued forward, sliding over the far side of the bed and crashing into the night stand. With my other arm, I managed to shove the crystal radio off of the nightstand. As soon as it hit the floor, the light disappeared and the chanting stopped.

Instantly my father's expression was altered. Instead of rage, I again saw hurt and terror ravage his face, but only for a moment before it quickly morphed into feeble confusion.

Around us, the atmosphere immediately changed as other bewildered seniors behaved as if they had been jarred out of some kind of hypnotic trance. I heard gasps, and murmuring, and the creak of joints as they began to turn and look around. Some of them began to call for help, saying, "How on Earth did I get down here?" and, "What in the Sam-Hill am I doing in this room?"

My father looked at me, his mouth hanging open and his eyes widening with surprise.

He reached out, his hands shaking, and tried to grab hold of me.

"Mikey, it's coming!"

I didn't know what to say. My mind was too numb and the chaos in the room was steadily increasing, as were the cries for help.

Looking back across the bed, I saw members of the nursing staff coming into the room and trying to help people as best they could. I had to act fast.

As I clawed my way up from the floor, I put my arms on my father's shoulders to make sure I had his attention. I told him we had to get out of there and asked where he kept his medications.

While I gathered my father's medicine and his coat in the midst of all the noise, a thought occurred to me. For some reason I had the notion that someone might realize that the crystal had played a role in this disaster, and if that happened, it could lead to my father. The fact that everyone had seen the radio and the glowing light was lost on me at that time.

I stopped and looked around frantically until I found the broken radio set on the floor. I quickly dislodged the black crystal and shoved it into my pocket. My brain was in overdrive. I ushered my father out into the hallway, ignoring the pleading of others as we went, until we made our way to the front entrance. Had it not been for a room full of disoriented seniors crying for help, someone would have stopped us. As it was, we were able to get away unnoticed.

When we arrived at my house, I put my father up in his old room. Whatever had affected him, whether it was the sound or the light or the crystal itself, he was exhausted. Even so, he kept trying to say the same thing over and over, slurring bits and pieces of words.

"Shhh-duhhh, isss comin', Mikey, isss comin.'"

As I prepared his prescribed medications, I slipped in a sleeping pill in the hopes that it would allow him to rest. At the time I didn't even stop to consider that, as old as he was, it might kill him. I gave him his pills with a glass of water and then sat by his bed. He was out in a matter of minutes.

I stood up to go to my own room and realized my hands were shaking. Figuring a drink might calm me down, I made my way to the study at the back of the house. I took the crystal out of my pocket and put it in the wall safe and made sure it was locked. Then poured myself a tall scotch, downed it, and then poured another.

After a minute or two, I could feel the whiskey having the desired effect. I took the bottle and the glass and went to my bedroom. I was exhausted physically, mentally, and emotionally. Though I didn't think I would be able to sleep, I sat down on the bed and leaned back against the headboard, bottle in one hand and the glass in the other.

I tried to think back over everything I had seen that evening. What I thought I saw. There had to be some explanation for the events I had witnessed but I could not come up with anything that made sense to my scientific mind.

My thoughts were reeling. I kept asking myself the same questions over and over: What could have caused the light? What had happened to the old man I had seen vanish? Was I hallucinating? Had the same thing that hypnotized the retirees also affected me?

At one point I wondered if guilt played a role in this somehow. I also worried that maybe I was experiencing the same mental degradation as my father. Alzheimer's is hereditary.

At some point, I drifted into a restless sleep.

My dreams were vivid and dark, full of shapes without definition moving in and out of my awareness. The more I tried to pursue them, the more elusive they became and I found myself continually running down corridor after corridor in search of a room somewhere. The hallway was illuminated by an eerie, electric green light, and I could hear people talking or chanting in the distance: always in the distance. I could almost make out what they were saying and I strained to put meaning to the sounds or words.

"Shhhh-dhhhh, shhhh-dhhhhh," over and over.

Some sound invaded my dream state and I bolted upright in my bed, covered in sweat. As my eyes adjusted to the dim early morning light, my ears did the same, leaving behind the fog of wet, raspy chanting. Immediately the dream sounds were replaced by something more sinister and chilling. It was an on again, off again buzzing similar to the crystal radio set from the night before.

The flesh of my arms grew taut and the hairs stood on end. My mind began to race as adrenaline coursed through my system.

I got out of bed as quickly as I could and ran out into the hallway and to the door of my father's room. His bed was empty. Standing there in the hallway, the pulsing sound was louder. I could tell it was coming from the back of the house where my study was located.

I turned and ran in that direction, passing through the kitchen, which should have been dark. However, as soon as I entered, I saw a light shining under the study door. It was a strange, luminescent green that hit my retinas in such a way that the light itself appeared to be outlined in black. At the same time I realized that the buzzing sound was throbbing with such intensity the very air was vibrating. I could feel pressure against my eardrums and a chill passed through me as the sweat from my restless sleep suddenly turned cold. My guts churned, and standing there in the green-lit kitchen, I distinctly sensed the presence of evil. Whatever was causing it was coming from behind the door to my study.

I threw myself against the wood door without even trying to turn the handle. I crashed through into the room, and there in front of me, behind my desk, was my father. Behind him, the wall safe hung open; a black, gaping maw. In front of him sat the old crystal set that had been my science fair project and I knew, without a doubt, that he had replaced the pencil lead with the shard of black crystal. In that instant, inexplicably, I knew that the evil I'd sensed seconds before came from that crystal.

That is when my father stood up from the desk chair.

Without thinking, I launched myself across the room towards him. I was acting purely on instinct, driven by the unthinkable terror of what might happen next. Even as my feet left the ground and my arms stretched out towards my father, I knew I was too late.

I watched in horror as he stepped forward into the light, and vanished.

It has now been several hours since my father disappeared. It is impossible for me to know whether he is living or dead. But the overwhelming sense of evil I experienced earlier leads me to only one conclusion: if he is still alive, he is in a terrible place and suffering. And that is something that I cannot live with.

Were it not for me, none of this would have happened. My father would still be safe in his retirement home entertaining the other seniors with his homemade crystal radio sets. And so it is as I told you at the beginning of this story. I have murdered my father. Or, for his sake and to put an end to the suffering he must surely be enduring even now, I am about to.

But I am a man of conscience. After I am gone I cannot take the chance that whoever finds this letter might immediately be ensnared by this damned crystal. I have taken steps to ensure that, once I have stepped into the light, the tuner will be disconnected. I write this now with the hope that the resulting scene will not be mistaken as the signs of a struggle.

I have placed the radio set on the edge of the desk in such a manner that it would fall if there were not a counter weight on the other end. For the counter weight, I have filled a large plastic cup with ice and set it on its side such that it will hold the radio in place until the ice melts. After that, the radio should fall to the floor and the tuning should be disrupted.

But one last thing I must share with you before I go. While writing this, I have tuned the crystal radio from time to time and listened while staring into the glaring light. I now I think I have some insight into what it was that overcame my father.

If you listen long enough, you can hear voices. It's as if the buzzing, burring sound of the radio broadcast is a horde of suffering voices all saying the same thing.

"Sha'Daa. It is coming."


### End of Transcription ###

**Item #2:** Appears to be a homemade crystal radio receiver.

**Case Notes:** Both items were found at the residence of Dr. Michael Smith, Jr. The whereabouts of one Dr. Michael Smith, Jr. and one Mr. Michael Smith, Sr. have not been determined.

# 1986 WORLD EVENTS

25th Space Shuttle (51L)-Challenger 10 explodes 73 seconds after liftoff

Worst nuclear disaster, 4th reactor at Chernobyl USSR explodes, 31 die—plant worker claims power surge occurred after green light jumped from his black diamond studded antique cigarette case into his control panel, dies of radiation poisoning one hour later

Captain Midnight (John R MacDougall) interrupts HBO

PHANTOM OF THE OPERA premieres in London

# Harmonic Dissonance

## by Larry Atchley, Jr.

### 8-1-1988

Decided to start keeping a diary. Seems pretty stupid, huh? Well, I've always wanted to for some reason, just to maybe sort out my thoughts of the day. Maybe I'll look back at these entries and laugh, or cry, or I won't look at them ever again after I write these lines. Who knows. Anyway. It feels good somehow, to get my feelings out on the page. Feels almost as good as when I'm playing music. Ever since I got my guitar I've felt whole somehow. Complete. I know now what I want to do with my life. I was destined to be a musician. It's the only thing that feels right in a world that is so wrong. My Mom doesn't understand. She wants me to go to college and 'do something with my life.' Ha! I've had enough of school. Thirteen years of that prison. I'm tired of people telling me what to do, what to learn. Fuck all that shit. I just want to learn my music and someday I'll play in front of thousands of people. Then I'll show her, and everybody else who says I won't amount to anything.

### 8-3-1988

Been visiting my grandpa and grandma out in Western Oklahoma. Man what a desolate place. All red dirt and dry heat. No sign of civilization for miles. I'll never understand why they call this God's Country when it looks so god-forsaken to me. Went hiking early this morning before it got too damn hot. Found an old burnt out farm house. Been rotting there for who knows how long. Then found something interesting in the remains. An old metal box someone buried in the back yard. The corner was sticking up where the dirt had eroded away. There was this old harmonica in it, with some kind of black gemstone mounted in the brass plate on top. Must be a fuckin' antique by the looks of it. Maybe valuable, especially with that gem on the top. Looks sorta like a diamond, except I've never seen a black diamond before.

I always thought it would be cool to learn the mouth harp. I took it back to the farm house and cleaned it up. Soaked it in some rubbing alcohol and rinsed it out real good. Blew a few notes through it and it sounds pretty good. Still plays in tune even after all those years in that box in the ground. When I get back to the city I'll have to pick up some books on learning harmonica and see if I can add it to some of my guitar playing. Hell, there's a lot of folk, rock and blues songs that have mouth harp in them. Might as well broaden my repertoire. Couldn't hurt.

## 8-7-1988

Back home at my apartment in big D. Good to be back in the city even if it's a shitty place like Dallas, Texas. Still, there's a decent music scene around here if you know where to look. Deep Ellum is the place to be if you want to play music. Unless you're a shit kickin' country music player, then you go over to the Stockyards in Fort Worth. But that ain't my scene. Over on the East side of the Metroplex it's all about the rock n' roll and the blues. I picked up a few books on harmonica over at Murphy's Music. Figure I'll bone up on playing the harp and learn a few songs. I got one of those harp racks that you wear around your neck so you can blow the harmonica while your hands are free to play a guitar. Pretty cool little thing. I've already picked up on the basics and I think I'm sounding pretty damn good. Maybe I'm a natural at this thing. They say everyone has a musical instrument that they are born to play. I always figured guitar was mine, but this mouth harp just comes so easy to me. I guess it was fate that I found it.

## 8-11-1988

Played out on my usual corner down on Elm Street in Deep Ellum today. Got a few tips here and there. Nothin' to write home about, but it's lunch money at least. Saw Jessica, and man, she was lookin' as fine as ever. I was playing my guitar and the harmonica, working on a song I had learned the other day.

Funny thing happened while I was playing and looking at Jessica. The little black diamond on top of the harp started glowing this weird green color and I felt this freaky tingling sensation all over my body. She thought it was some kind of trick, so I just played along, like I planned it that way. I guess she was pretty impressed because she asked me what I was doing later, and if I wanted to hang out with her. Hell, she's never even looked twice at me before.

She's way out of my league. But I've always wondered what it would be like to get with a chick who was that hot. I was thinking about that when I was playing the song and looking at her when that gem started lighting up like a green Christmas tree light. I packed up my guitar and put the harp in my jeans pocket and we got some dinner at a Tex-Mex place down the street. Later, we went back to my place and she was all over me as soon as we walked in the door. The sex was amazing. I always figured playing guitar would get me laid, but who knew chicks dig harmonica? As she was leaving she said she wanted to get together again next weekend. Maybe this harp with the gem is my new lucky charm.

## 8-18-1988

Spent the evening at my corner in Deep Ellum again. Learned a few more songs on the guitar and harmonica earlier this week. Getting pretty good at the mouth harp if I do say so myself. Got a little money thrown in the guitar case, so it's all good.

Only bad thing that happened was when Brett and his gang of muscle-heads came around harassing me. Fuckin' bullies. They shook me down for the tip money I had in the case, and roughed me up a little, pushing me around. I'd stand up to 'em but there's too many of them and it ain't worth getting a bloody nose or cracked ribs over a few bucks.

I went back to my playing once they headed across the street to find some other victim to prey upon. All I could think about was that I wished they would just go away for good, so they would never bother me or anyone else again. The gemstone on the harmonica started glowing that same sickly green light again, and I could feel the vibrations from the harp all the way into my toes. Next thing I know, I'm hearing brakes squealing and a loud 'thump' and I see a bus sliding to a stop across the street. A woman screamed and yelled, "Oh my god, those boys were run over." Sure enough when the bus backed up, there were Brett and his boys lying on the asphalt, looking like road pizza. I wasn't sure how to feel about that. I wanted them out of my life, but I really didn't wish them dead or anything. I was pretty shook up, so I decided to call it an early night and go home.

## 8-19-1988

I've been thinking about this harmonica and the little diamond on it. I can't shake the feeling that when that things glows, whatever I'm thinking about seems to come true. Maybe it's all just coincidence, but after Jessica coming on to me out of the blue, and Brett and his crew getting hit by that bus, I've started to wonder. I was back in Deep Ellum today, playing again, and I figured I'd do a little experiment. There was a guy standing, listening to me play. I thought to myself, wouldn't it be cool if he tipped me a whole bunch of money, not just a few coins or a dollar or two like most folks do. Sure enough, the gemstone on the harp started glowing green and I got the tingly feeling all over my body. Next thing I know he's pulling out his wallet and takes all the money in there out and drops it into my guitar case. I saw a hundred dollar bill and a few twenties in there. I was so shocked I stopped playing. I told him thanks, and quickly grabbed the money and stuffed it into my blue jeans pocket. He said "you're welcome," and then walked off looking sorta dazed and confused. I felt kinda bad afterwards, and I almost ran up to the guy to give him back his money, but damn I could sure use the cash. These yuppies have plenty more where that came from anyway, and I figure a starving artist like myself deserves a big break once in awhile. Being a full time restaurant dishwasher and part-time musician is a hard way to make a living. But there is definitely something about this harmonica that is not normal. It's like it's a genie out of a fairy tale or something, granting me my three wishes. I hope that whatever magic is in there will keep working in my favor.

## 8-22-1988

Had dinner with Mom tonight. She keeps ragging me about wanting me to go to church with her on Sundays. I told her for the umpteenth time, that I didn't feel like wasting my time on worshipping a god who let my dad die when I was just a little boy. She told me, like she always does, that He works in mysterious ways and we don't know what his plans are for us, and that he must have needed Dad in Heaven for some important reason. She said that it wasn't right for us to question God's will.

Yeah, right. My ass. Well, I'm the kind of person who questions everything, God included. We went round and round like we always do, and then she brought up college again as usual. She said that I was a smart person and that I was throwing away the gift of intelligence that God gave me. She said there was no future for me in playing music, that there is a million to one chance that I would ever be successful enough to make a living at it.

I tried to tell her that the last thing I wanted to do was to be brainwashed by the education system for four more years of my life just so I could become a slave to the system and be like everyone else: just another mindless sheep in the herd. I told her that music is the only thing that makes me happy, and feel good and complete inside. It's the only thing that reminds me that I am alive. She told me that the music I play comes from the Devil, and that I was on the road to Hell and eternal damnation. I told her that I didn't believe in Hell, God or the Devil, and that I wished she would just quit badgering me about my life.

I stormed out of there, frustrated and angry. It wasn't the first time, and probably won't be the last. I went home and did the only thing that ever cheers me up: play my music. As I strummed my acoustic electric guitar and played on the harmonica, I tried to get the whole conversation with Mom out of my mind, but couldn't. Why can't she just leave me alone and let me live my life? The gemstone on the harmonica glowed green again and I got that weird sensation through my body. I wonder if my wish will come true and Mom will finally stop bugging me about my choices in life. I can only hope.

## 8-23-1988

It's hard for me to write this, but I got the news this afternoon that my Mom was involved in a car accident on the way to work this morning. She was killed instantly. I don't have any parents left now. No other family at all. I can't help but feel that this is my fault. Just last night I was playing that damned harmonica and wishing my Mom would leave me alone. Well she can't bug me about my life anymore now, because she's fucking dead. Maybe this harmonica and gemstone are cursed. Maybe Mom was right and I am going to Hell. Whatever. Things can't get any worse. I'm going to play some hard ass blues tonight and try to deal with this shit. I don't know if I even care about anything anymore. Maybe I deserve to die too.

## 8-25-1988, DALLAS MORNING NEWS OBITUARY SECTION

Oakley, Jared Jeffrey Oakley, age 19, of Dallas, Texas, passed away on 8-24-1988, of unknown causes, and was found deceased in his apartment. He is preceded in death by his father Earl Joseph Oakley who died from a heart attack in 1978, and his mother who died in a car accident recently on 8-23-1988. Jared was a dishwasher at La Cuccaracha Tex-Mex restaurant and also was a lover of music and spent much of his time playing for money on street corners in Dallas's Deep Ellum entertainment district. He will be missed. Funeral arrangements are under the direction of the Oldham Funeral Home in Dallas. A private interment for Jared and his beloved mother will be held on August 30th. Anyone wishing to sign the guestbook, share memories or leave condolences is welcome to do so.

## 9-1-1988, DALLAS MORNING NEWS ESTATE SALE LISTINGS

Oakley Family Estate Sale. 9-3-1988 from 8:00 AM to 4:00 PM. 1236 Mockingbird Ln, Dallas, Tx

Items of interest include: Drop-leaf dinette set & 2 chairs, breakfast table & chairs, queen bed, La-Z-Boy sofa, oval coffee table & matching end tables, platform rocker, Waterford crystal lamp, Blenko glass vase, oak triple-bow china cabinet, drop-leaf table, curio cabinet, sofa table, hall table & mirror, vintage quilts & tops, oak twin bed & matching desk, two TVs & stands, lamps, bookcase, sterling silver & costume jewelry, Franciscan "Desert Rose", Metlox Poppytrail "Ivy", crystal pitchers, silverplate & crystal, Lunt "Floral Lace" sterling silver flatware, linens, ladies' clothes, Kenmore washer & dryer, Kenmore bottom-freezer refrigerator, Oreck vacuum cleaner, knitting & crochet yarn & needles, three sewing machines (Singer Touch-n-Sew, White, New Home), Tupperware, pots & pans, small appliances, leaf blower, garden tools, patio set. Also, musicians take note! Ovation acoustic electric guitar with hard case, and Fender amplifier. Also a rare antique M. Hohner harmonica with custom black diamond gemstone setting. One of a kind!

# 1991 WORLD EVENTS

SHADOWLANDS closes at Brooks Atkinson Theater NYC after 169 performances

Rte 35 Theater in Hazlit, last drive-in in NJ, closes—three hysterical teenage couples dressed in 1930's era clothing arrested for disorderly conduct

Air crash at Djeddah, Saudi-Arabia, 263 die

USSR, last day of existence

# Four-Armed is Forewarned

## by Beth W. Patterson

*"To sing a verse out of order,"* Flynn said somberly, *"was a crime. Usually meant the death penalty."*
*"I can see that,"* I said. *"It'd be the musical equivalent of an earthquake."*
*"Worse,"* he scowled. *"It would be to un-create the Creation."*

*—Bruce Chatwin, The Songlines*

[The following documents were found in 2003 in a nursing home somewhere in New Jersey, in a box labeled "New Orleans, 1993."]

### JOURNAL ENTRY: JUNE 18TH, 1993

I feel so lost in this God-forsaken hell hole. No one back in Harlem appreciates my talent, and my wife says she's sick of hearing me bellyaching day after day. So what does my family do? They fly me down here to spend a few weeks in New Orleans, hoping that I will absorb some of the jazz down here, hoping that it will help me come to my senses once and for all. There's plenty of jazz in New York and Chicago. Sure, they call New Orleans the "birthplace of jazz," but so what? There can't be anything in this town that I can't hear back home. Plus it's hotter than hell down here, and it's only June.

I argued with them all, but they insisted that it would do me some good. They said, "It's not the end of the world!"

This town is messed up. The homicide rate is climbing. In fact, the whole state is insane. My cabbie told me that people are still talking about gubernatorial elections from last year...between David Duke (former KKK Grand Wizard) and Edwin Edwards (notorious bribe-taking crook). How in Jesus's name did it get to that point? You can still see bumper stickers that say VOTE

FOR THE CROOK. IT'S IMPORTANT and VOTE FOR THE LIZARD, NOT THE WIZARD. The lesser of two evils, I suppose...at least the majority of the state chose that one wisely. Yet, people are easygoing and friendly in this town. The informal New Orleans term of endearment is "dawlin'", and people sometimes break the ice by asking, "How's ya Mama an' dem?" Funny thing is, people hear my New York accent and think I'm a local. At first, anyway.

I can't complain about this hotel room, though. This is one fancy joint. I don't know how they pooled in all their money to put me up in the Roosevelt, but it suits me just fine. I've never seen so many chandeliers in one place. They say it's historical. Famous people have stayed here, and if it was good enough for musicians like Louis Armstrong and Ray Charles, it's good enough for a musician like me. Earlier today I looked in one of the many fancy mirrors in my room, and I liked what I saw, especially framed so ornately. Most people would see a portly old black man with thick glasses, balding under a baseball cap, but they don't realize that I have a unique gift. One that must be shared with the world. An unassuming appearance suits me just fine, since I have no wish to intimidate anyone.

I have a good cassette recorder the size of a paperback book, plus a decent supply of blank tapes. I intend to try to collect as many snatches of sound as I can over the course of my stay. If I record any genius performances, I can duplicate the tapes. Most people are starting to switch their collections to compact disc, but everyone just wants the next big thing. Cassettes are here to stay.

My cousin made a few phone calls and told me that the cats at Snug Harbor would let me sit in with them tomorrow night. He's got connections. He knows music, he knows all the musicians in town.

## CASSETTE #427, JUNE 19TH, 1993

BANDLEADER: "...sitting in with us tonight, all the way from Harlem, New York, please put your hands together for Mister Shooby Williams!" [applause] "Shooby, what are you going to sing with us tonight?"

SHOOBY: "Can you cats do 'Don't Get Around Much Anymore' in G?"

BANDLEADER: "Yeah, you right." [muted flurry of tenor sax notes in the background] "A-one...a-two...a-one, two, three, four..."[band launches into intro]

SHOOBY (singing): "Shrah dah blee dah pah shrah!Doat un fwee dah fah splaw! Bim fa dwee bah tah spleeeeeee tahTa rah ta shrah fa dweet SHA

DAA..." [drummer drops a beat, trombone chokes a note] "Dwiddly deep-a-zhing-traaaaah! Poppy, poppy, poppy, poppy! Feadly oat'n fwee bah SHA DAA! Ray tah goo-lah tah SHAAA DAAAAA..." [music dissipates, sound of musicians choking back laughter.

Assorted comments: "Dude, what the FUCK was that?" "What's with the pantomiming playin' a sax?" "It's 'scat,' all right." "Then he better scat the fuck outta here, brah."]

## JOURNAL ENTRY, JUNE 19TH, 1993

They don't get me here, either. New Orleans, of all places! They laughed me off the stage. The bass player tried to be nice as I made for the door. He slipped a couple of fancy-looking tie clips into my hand. I didn't pause to look at them, but I thanked him and put them in my pocket. I didn't want to be rude, not like those arrogant cats on stage. Only one person appreciated my talent. She was, beyond a doubt, the most beautiful young woman I had ever seen in my life (apologies to my darling wife back home in Harlem, should she ever get a hold of this diary). She grabbed me by the arm as I was heading back out onto Frenchmen Street through the bar. Her grip was at once as strong as a python and as coaxing as a silk cord. Her skin as was smooth and dark as toffee. Her eyes and hair were midnight black. Her cheekbones were very fine, her lips full and soft-looking, but her face was fierce. I could not have looked away even if my wife had been standing right in front of us. I used to be a real whore-monger back when I was a young tomcat, but something told me to take this chick seriously.

"Where did you learn to sing like that?" she demanded. I felt a great weight ease off of my heart and straightened my shoulders as best as I could. "Miss, I was born with this gift."

"The Sha'Daa. Tell me what you know about it."

"Miss, it is all a part of my art. It is beyond scat singing. I am the Human Horn, I feel the music, and I channel what needs to be sung."

"We have much to discuss, and not much time. You need to come see me tomorrow. The Funky Butt, 714 North Rampart Street. Your name plus one will be on the guest list. If there's any hassle at the door, tell them that Kelli sent you." I started to say, "Miss Kelli, what is it that you play...?" But when I blinked my eyes, she was already gone.

That young lady was quite authoritative, to say the least, but I am quite willing to see her again. She is the only thing that keeps me from wanting to get right back on that plane to Newark. Even after getting laughed off the stage on my very first appearance here, someone appreciates my gift, so perhaps part of my destiny is in New Orleans after all.

**CASSETTE #428, JUNE 20TH, 1993**

SHOOBY: "So I am sitting here at the bar of this fine establishment. There are actually three bars here in the Roosevelt! I am talking to my new friend behind the bar, a mister...what did you say?"

MEROS: "Meros, my good man. Meros."

SHOOBY: "This mister Meros here could be some kinda celebrity...he's tall, with movie star good looks and big blue eyes...you got kind of an Elvis little-boy grin goin' on! But he ain't no movie star, he says...he's a...whaddya call it?"

MEROS: "Sommelier, Mister Shooby. You might say I am more or less a wine geek."

SHOOBY: "Ooo, and he's given me all kinds of things to try. I can't wait to tell them when I get back to Harlem that I am now a fan of Argentinean Malbec. I wonder if Miss Kelli would appreciate a glass after her show tonight..."

MEROS: "Wait a minute, are you talking about Kelli Patel? Burlesque dancer?"

SHOOBY: "She never told me what she did. She wants me to come to her show at the Funky Butt tonight."

BEEPIE: "Hey, I used to go 'dere! I used to go watch Miguel play all da time..."

MEROS: "Beepie, what are you doing here? I thought your shift didn't end until one."

BEEPIE: "Naw, da boss told me I could go early. Told me to go home before I made a living blonde joke outta myself. I ain't no dumb blonde. Now if only I coulda made Miguel see me for who I was..."

MEROS: "Excuse me, Shooby. Whenever this gal's had too much to drink, she babbles on and on about her unrequited love, Miguel Robichaux..."

BEEPIE: "Best guitar playah in New Orleans! He never noticed me none, but he's...best guitar playah..." [Thud!]

MEROS: "She's all right...she'll stay right where she is for a while, and then we'll just pour her into a taxi. So go on about Kelli...how did you meet her?"

SHOOBY: "Remember how I was telling you about them cats laughing me outta Snug? I was heading out the door and she just grabbed me by the arm and said she wanted me to come to her show. Said something about Sha'Daa. It came out while I was scat singing...I wasn't really thinking about it, just kinda channeling the muse, you know?"

MEROS: "Sha'Daa...? Ahem. If I might accompany you to this show, I'll drive and save you the cab fare."

SHOOBY: "That would be just fine, Mister Meros. She said I could bring a friend for the guest list. But tell me why my singing has suddenly gotten the attention of—"

MEROS: [interrupts] "Well, well, well, Johnny...I've poured for movie stars and first ladies, but it's been awhile since I've seen the likes of you! What'll you have?"

JOHNNY: "The usual, Meros. Why don't you open that Jeroboam of 1961 Château Pétrus?"

MEROS: "Well done, sir."

BEEPIE: "Hey! I seen you before! I overheard Miguel talk about you, didn't you used to play with Whitesnake...and what's-his-name...Frank Zappa?"

JOHNNY: "No, Beepie, that would not have been me."

BEEPIE: "Whoa, you some serious gold in that tooth, mister! How did you know my name?" [Thud!]

JOHNNY: "She's going to acquire even more brain damage if she keeps letting her head hit the bar every time she passes out. Meros, you look as fetching as ever. You seem to have chosen the perfect occupation for a satyr."

SHOOBY: "A what?"

MEROS: "My friend Johnny is implying that I am some sort of Dionysian creature. Call it what you will...Pan-type figure, sex demigod, divine lover. All about wine, women, and song. But we know there's really no such thing, don't we, Johnny?"

SHOOBY: "Whoa, this is some crazy shit. For just one second, the shadows behind your head looked like—"

MEROS: "Horns? Yeah, Shooby, that crazy modern lighting does that. Now, Johnny, what brings you here?"

JOHNNY: "Well, first order of business...I would say be careful with those tie clips, gentlemen."

MEROS: "These? My friend Shooby here got these at Snug Harbor last night. Gave one to me as a part of his tip. If I didn't know any better, I'd say they were Romanov jewelry. The stones are kind of an eyesore, but the rest of the craftsmanship is superb. Don't we look snazzy? Though I'm really more of a sucker for cuff links."

SHOOBY: "Yeah, they're nice, aren't they? I've never seen black diamonds before. Couldn't believe the dude just handed them to me like that, but maybe that was the least the band could do, after insulting my music like that. I don't know if that bass player was working for Snug or what, but he was real eager to give them to me."

BEEPIE: "Hey, man...green light...you're s'posed ta drive at a green light." [Thud!]

JOHNNY: "Mister Shooby, I believe I have something you need to listen to."

SHOOBY: "What kind of tape is this? Never heard of no Schoenburg and Berg."

JOHNNY: "Listen well. It will aid you in the greatest performance of your life. Would you be willing to make a trade for it?"

SHOOBY: "What do you want?"

JOHNNY: "I would love to have one of the tapes of your performances."

SHOOBY: "Hot damn! That's twice someone finally appreciated my music. I need to keep the one I made last night as it's my only copy, but I got an extra copy of one of my Harlem performances in my hotel room. I'll go get it. Meros, is your shift almost over?"

MEROS: "It is, my friend. We'll pour Beepie into a cab and head out as soon as you give Johnny that tape."[break in the recording, 00:55 silence]

EMCEE: "And now, for our grand finale...please give it up for the lovely Miss Kelli Patel!" [Blast of music: I Am Stretched on Your Grave (Dead Can Dance rendition), interspersed with wild cheering, gasps, and finally thunderous applause and howls. 5:37 minutes of unintelligible background dialogue.]

MEROS: "Hey, there, gorgeous!"

KELLI: "Gentlemen, I need those tie clips. [pause] Thank you. Shooby, can you sing twelve-tone music?"

SHOOBY: "Twelve-bar blues? Piece of cake."

 KELLI: "No, twelve-TONE music. Also called dodecaphony. You have to pick a sequence of all twelve notes of the chromatic scale, and you have to stick to this pattern—you can't repeat any notes. It's going to be crucial for tomorrow's show. Time is running out. Music is often a conduit to other worlds, and a twelve-tone musical cycle might actually stem the flow of the shit that's gonna hit the fan. It's music that is set in no key, giving all notes equal hierarchy. Are you in?"

SHOOBY: "Miss Kelli, I can scat anything, I promise. Elvis, Johnny Cash, even Mozart. I got this covered, um...dawlin.'"

MEROS: "You're the man, my friend."

KELLI: "You're not off the hook, Casanova. You've been around for a long, long time, and you are usually the first to spot anything...unusual. You are to cue the music at the appropriate times, most importantly switch it to the twelve tone theme at the first sign of trouble. Got it?"

MEROS AND SHOOBY [in unison]: "Yes ma'am."Journal entry, June 21st, 1993 (4:00 AM)

That was the most amazing show I have ever seen. The inside of The Funky Butt was all dark red velvet, like some sort of wicked pleasure parlor. We went straight upstairs where they had a pole set up on the stage. Various acts came and went, but I don't remember much...I think the Malbec was messing with my head some. All I can remember of the crowd is lots of raucous laughter and tattooed, smiling women with sharp teeth. The other burlesque women (and one man in drag) put on what seemed like some kind of carnal ballet.

And then out walked Kelli.

She made the other dancers look like amateur strippers (and they were quite good, mind you!). She was a dark ringmistress to some erotic circus only a privileged few of us would ever see. She was a cobra, she was a wisp of smoke, then she was a springing leopardess, moving with preternatural strength and speed. Sometimes she moved so fast, she appeared to have multiple arms. I could have been focused on just the ripple of muscle under her tawny skin, had she also not appeared to defy gravity on that pole. She was a fallen angel, she was a beautiful assassin. Alluring and terrifying.

You could practically hear the collective rush of blood to everyone's loins as she writhed like a dangerous wild animal in heat. And the crowd went wild when she finished with an unreal corkscrew spin down the pole into a graceful arabesque, part swan and part lioness, enthralling and deadly. My heartbeat was roaring in my ears.

She did not stop to greet the throng of admirers surrounding her after the show, but instead made a beeline straight for us. Meros slipped an arm around her hourglass waist with a carefree familiarity...I could definitely see those two as a good match, if they didn't already have a history. She had little time for greetings, though and cut right to the chase.

When she commanded us to hand over the tie clips, we obeyed simultaneously. I couldn't have refused. Not even that handsome devil Meros dared question her. Then, still mostly naked, she turned her dark, liquid eyes on me. They looked right through my soul, and I shivered uncontrollably. I was trying to be casual, but this was no ordinary chick. And I promised to deliver the performance of my lifetime.

We are going to be heroes. *I* am going to be a hero at last. I hope I'm right about being able to scat anything. I'm not going to chicken out now.Journal entry, June 21st, 1993 (10:00 AM)

What in the HELL is this shit that man in the trench coat gave me to listen to? Am I really supposed to scat to this garbage? I can't believe I traded that Johnny guy one of my precious tapes for this crap. I am FREAKING THE FUCK OUT!!!

I called my cousin, and he told me to calm down. He explained twelve-tone music to me in a little more detail. It still makes no sense. Why would someone want to listen to this? But perhaps if I learn to appreciate this music, maybe someone will learn to appreciate mine. In time.

Kelli explained this Sha'Daa thing. Opening multiple dimensional hells??? The stones on those damned tie clips have weakened the barriers, she said, even if this Sha'Daa isn't supposed to take place anytime soon. How in the hell could a burlesque dancer know about a dimensional rift that will somehow be located in a New Orleans music club? She talked about this city being in a negative vortex, like the ley lines all the New Agers keep talking about...but the opposite. She said that only the people who live here keep this city from imploding. They love art, they love beauty, they love music, they love festivals, carnivals, and parades, and this collective spirit is strong. Still, there is a gravitational pull, and many people who move here never return to their places of origin. Am I crazy for beginning to believe this shit?

If hell portals exist, why haven't I heard of them? I thought everything was covered in The Good Book. But what do I know? Only a few days ago, I had never heard of twelve-tone music, at least six different kinds of wine, satyrs, and burlesque dancing as fine as that show last night. This whole thing gives me a horrible feeling of dread. This is no second coming of our Lord Jesus...this is pure evil and destruction, both for the good and the wicked. But if I can help Kelli to keep it from happening, perhaps the Good Lord will forgive me for my whoremongering days.

So I am having a study break right now, but I've got to get back to learning this form. It's the craziest shit I've ever tried to scat to. But I am Shooby. I can do this tonight.

This music has a weird appeal to it. And it echoes with the sound of The Salesman.

## CASSETTE #429, JUNE 21ST, 1993

SHOOBY: "We've off to the side of the stage, by the sound board, me and Meros here...this gal Beepie wouldn't shut up until we agreed to take her along with us. She's sitting next to us...bitch is driving me crazy! How are we supposed to keep this Sha'Daa-esque whatchamadiggy from happening with this constant yammering?"[canned music: little girl singing, "Twinkle, twinkle, little bat... how I wonder WHERE Y'AT?" Music cuts to Bollywood beat.]

BEEPIE: "Holy shit, y'all never told me she was black!"SHOOBY: "Beepie, *I* am black. I live in Harlem, and I'm telling you, no human being is really that color. She's changed! She's all...well, BLACK black!"

BEEPIE: "She needs to put that big red tongue a-hers back in her mouth. This chick is creepin' me out..."

MEROS: "Beepie, my sweet, would you just please appreciate this display of raw athleticism, sublime gymnastics, and highly cultivated dance?"

BEEPIE: "There ya go again, Meros, talkin' all fancy an' stuff..."

SHOOBY: [whispers] "Okay...this is the scariest, yet most erotic thing to date. She wearing some kinda...well, they look like human heads strung around her neck...got some severed arms dangling around her waist like a skirt. I can't... look away...oh my GOD! She doing a striptease with them! Just flinging them off of her body...her body is glistening with the blood, all slippery...and there's blood splattering everywhere, all over the audience...I can't help it, I think I licked up a drop of it...oh, Sweet Jesus...if she's got all arms and legs in the air, doing these crazy moves...[gasp!] she can't possibly be hanging onto the pole with *that*...Oh, my sweet wife, please forgive me!"[wild cheering][unintelligible muffled conversation]

SHOOBY: "She's got the gems from our tie clips turned into some sort of things on her nipples...Meros! Whaddya call 'em?"

MEROS: "Just nipple rings. Popular body piercings these days."

SHOOBY: "Good, GOD, I thought it was tempting the devil just to have women wear rings in their ears, and she's got our tie clips altered and stuck through her NIPPLES? Why would any woman wanna do that?"

MEROS: "In my experience, my friend, it can sometimes heighten sexual pleasure...make things a little more...interesting. A man can also enjoy the sensation of a little piece of jewelry clicking against his front teeth while he—"

SHOOBY: "Right. She's dancing with a sword. How does she make it look like she has FOUR ARMS? Why does she have to have four arms but still have only two titties? That ain't fair! And the audience is totally hypnotized—Beepie! What are you doing? Sit down!"

BEEPIE: [Guttural voice] "The time is upon us...open the door and LET US OUT..."

SHOOBY: "Shit, bitch! Meros! Get this blonde bitch outta here! Look at her EYES! They're glowing red..."

MEROS: "Shooby, I can't control Beepie. I'm more concerned about that greenish glow radiating from those nipple rings! I have to change the music now!"

[music cuts to Wozzeck]

**KELLI:** "Now, Shooby!"

**SHOOBY:** "But I still don't quite get this—"

**KELLI:** "Just fucking sing! You'll know what to do!"

**SHOOBY:** [clears throat] "Doo doo shrah! Rah ta shrah! Shooby splaw...! [pauses] Om Kr?m K?lyai Nama?,

Om Kap?linaye Namah,

Om Hrim Shrim Krim

Parameshvari Kalike Svaha,

Om Krim Krim Krim Hrim Hrim

Hoom Hoom Dakhshyine Kalikei

Krim Krim Krim Hrim Hrim Hoom

Hoom Fat Svaha..."

[sound of massive falling objects, colossal screech of metal, people screaming, tape is distorted]

[Break in the recording; 7:21 of silence]

**SHOOBY:** [hoarse whisper, shaky] "Okay...oh sweet Jesus..." [panting] "I don't know if anyone is gonna believe this, but I have to say this on tape. Any of you witnesses still alive who may be listening to this, well, know that you ain't crazy, and that you ain't the only ones. Meros...what was it that Kelli was shouting?"

**MEROS:** "Her name is 'Kali'. And she said, 'Fear not! I am the Dark Mother, sworn to protect you. I am the devourer of time...'"

**SHOOBY:** "Right. And then Beepie slid to the floor, and it was like all her bones and guts melted disintegrated or something...all this horrible-smelling smoke started rising outta her, well what was left of her. It smelled like a funeral home in a boiler room! If Satan had diarrhea, it would be like...that. I thought I was gonna throw up right there. There was nothing left of her but her skin... it was just like an empty plastic sack, and all these crablike creatures started pouring outta her mouth...black and shiny like roaches or spiders or something, but with these big, sharp claws...they just kept coming and coming, and they started GROWING in size..."

**MEROS:** "The demons were summoned by the green light, or maybe it was the gems on those nipple rings. They started ripping those claws through the crowd to try to get to Kali, turning everything and everyone into hamburger meat and bloody confetti. And then Kali just started dancing, these methodical steps...the cosmic dance of creation and destruction...complete cycles, just like your twelve-tone song, you see? She was luring the demons towards her, out of the portal that Beepie's body had become, and away from the fleeing crowd...the ones who survived, anyway. I think the pole acted like some sort of lightning rod. When you sang that twelve-tone mantra and that huge bolt came down from the sky through the roof, it grounded the charge and turned it into an energy that she just flung right back at the demon doorway. It seemed to have destroyed it, all right. You know, if I didn't know any better, I'd have sworn she was getting off, grinding on that electrified pole while thwarting evil."

**SHOOBY:** "Man, I ain't never gonna complain about stage fright after seeing her do that. I'd a-shit my drawers right onstage if that had been MY gig! Yeah, crazy green light, like some kinda devil Oz, and those demon crab-things...I ain't ashamed to admit that we ducked under some tables. Not a scratch on us. Meros, it woulda been a shame to mess up that good-lookin' face of yours."

**MEROS:** "You are too kind, my man. We seem to both be unscathed. Thank the gods the place was empty—for whatever reason—when we finally emerged! Now the Beepie-portal is gone, the rest of the audience is gone, the crablike creatures are gone, and Kali is gone...along with those damned tie clip gems. Good riddance of those things! I'll miss watching that little minx, though. If anyone was capable of staving off the Sha'Daa, or anything close to it, it was she."

**SHOOBY:** "Brother, I don't care if I never see another tie clip again, even if it gets altered and dangles off of a titty! I used to thank Jesus every day that I never had to go fight in Korea, and then this night made Korea seem like a day at the beach. Not ever gonna go to any crab boils, either."

**MEROS:** "My friend, I think I, likewise, have developed a permanent shellfish allergy."

**SHOOBY:** "You said it! Let's go back to my room for a drink."

**MEROS:** "Johnny may have left some of that Château Pétrus. I'll unlock the bar and grab it. It costs more than my car, but Johnny paid for it, and doesn't seem to be interested in the rest. If it's not the perfect drink to have after a near-miss with the Apocalypse, I don't know what is. Best wine you'll ever taste, my friend."

**SHOOBY:** "Hosanna Jesus!"

**JOURNAL ENTRY, JULY 2ND, 1993**

I needed a week or so to just think about everything I've seen, heard, sung, and done. Maybe I didn't get a standing ovation for my gift, but I did something more important.

I took a few French Quarter tours...mule-drawn buggy rides, took in the sights of all those old buildings, saw some cemeteries...but man, the rest of New Orleans was dull compared to what went down at The Funky Butt. I tried to listen to some live music...not just jazz, but Cajun, Irish, blues, and funk. I couldn't get into it though, and I couldn't get the music I'd sung for Kelli out of my head, either. I spent my late nights just sitting at the bar talking to Meros. He's always got some female admirer or another coming around to flirt with him, but he's been preoccupied since the night of what was apparently nearly hell on earth, literally. We both have been. We wondered whether Beepie was an unwitting catalyst to mass chaos and destruction or some sort of demon in disguise this whole time. This Miguel Robichaux guy must have known something we didn't, avoiding her like the plague.

I said to Meros, "That crazy music is gonna mess up my head for good. Damn twelve-tone shit nearly gave me a stroke." We both sat in silence, and then I wondered aloud, "What would have happened if Kelli hadn't been there? What if we'd gone on wearing those tie clips with that evil bitch Beepie hanging around? She could have destroyed us and the city. And she would have gotten away with it, too, if it weren't for us meddling kids!"

Meros encouraged me to not speculate too much on that. The point was that all was well in the world for now.

Then I said to him, "What if even the tiniest bit of destruction got loose? It could linger and eventually turn into a disaster of some sort...like a hurricane...one that could destroy New Orleans, at least as we know it!"

And Meros just smiled and said, "Don't worry, Shooby. We've had lots of evil energy released into this town, and we've never had a hurricane that bad."

So I am flying back to Newark in the morning. I don't know what I'll be doing from here on out, but I won't be quite so upset about my gift going unappreciated. I know one thing's for sure...life is never going to be quite the same. And Kelli, or Kali, or whatever her name really is...she'll be with me always. It's going to be strange to go home, with so much happening in such a short amount of time, but the murder rate here is climbing, and it's time to leave...

# 2001 WORLD EVENTS

An earthquake hits Gujarat, India, causing more than 20,000 deaths—survivors claim hi-tech oil drilling rig went online and immediately exploded in green fire causing quake

Wikipedia, a free Wiki content encyclopedia, goes online

NEAR Shoemaker spacecraft touchdown in the saddle region of 433 Eros becoming the first spacecraft to land on an asteroid

Two passenger planes hijacked by terrorists crash into New York's World Trade Towers causing the collapse of both and the death of 2,752 people

# Chip Off the Old Rock

By Jeff Barnes

## TOP SECRET

Case Number 1247-11SI(P)

Simon Gerhardt Engineering MEANGREEN Event Reconstruction

Executive Summary

The following narrative is derived from evidence gathered after the event at the Simon Gerhardt Engineering Company. Evidence includes physical documentation, software files recovered by Computer Forensics, and interviews conducted by the Special Investigation Team. Attachment 1 lists specific reports and evidence that support this Case File.

On August 12, 2005, Simon Gerhardt, an avid amateur mineralogist, discovered a large black crystal during a gem hunting trip to a Northern Arkansas diamond field (Source: "Large Black Diamond Found In Arkansas Diamond Mine" Little Rock Free Press, August 14, 2005).

Journal entries indicate that upon his return home, Gerhardt asked his Chief Scientist (Ronald Dinsmore) to identify the crystal, as Gerhardt himself had been unable to. There is no further mention of the crystal in the journal until September 3, 2005, when Gerhardt writes that Dinsmore reported that while the crystal bore some resemblance to a diamond in its lattice structure and its hardness, it did not display other characteristics typical to diamonds. Dinsmore planned further testing to try to identify the crystal.

The September 14, 2005 entry in Gerhardt's journal was excited, as confirmed by handwriting analysis. It indicated that while Dinsmore had made no further progress in identifying the mineral, he had made an amazing discovery. When passing an electric current through the crystal it displayed super-conductive properties. Further testing revealed that the crystal could be etched by laser. Dinsmore speculated that it might be possible for them to create super-conducting integrated circuits. Success would depend on the size of the chip, which would be determined by the amount of cross-talk (bleed-over) between individual circuits, how fine-tuned the laser etching process could be, and finding a suitable substrate for the resulting circuit to lie on.

The November 12, 2005 entry: Dinsmore had worked with company engineers to run further tests on the crystal. The crystal was most responsive to etching by green laser. There was no detectable cross-talk between individual circuits (Gerhardt notes that this test was repeated multiple times as it had been considered a practical impossibility prior to the discovery of the crystal). The engineering team had found that the crystal chip could reside on a silico-boron substrate with no ill effect. Gerhardt believed they could produce picometer-scale circuits, but due to the practical limitations of chip fabrication and connections into and out of the chip they could expect no better than 1-2 nanometer circuit sizes initially (For comparison, the best current integrated circuit sizes [mid-2009] are 96 nanometers. 1-2 nanometer chips could produce true supercomputers on a chip the size of a thumbnail).

On December 5, 2005 Gerhardt hired Ronald Richardson, a doctoral candidate at the California Institute of Technology. Richardson was working on a dissertation on circuit design. Richardson's Master's Thesis was on computer modeling of circuit design. Richardson's role was to design the chip and the fabricator. No surviving records shed light on the design of either the chips or the fabricator.

On August 16, 2008 Gerhardt noted that he had approved funding for Richardson to design and assemble a small chip fabricator in the company's primary facility. He had not set a funding cap as he believed that any single chip produced to this size would be worth tens of millions to the government, particularly the Department of Defense and the intelligence community. The crystal was large enough to produce hundreds of chips. Gerhardt planned to name the crystal Sigerium and had plans to fund a major dig in the Arkansas mine to find more of it.

Surviving company records, along with vendor records indicate that components were purchased to create a single chip fabrication unit. The primary facility was expanded to incorporate a clean room. Journal entries indicate that the fabricator was completed and successfully tested on June 4, 2008. At that time Simon Gerhardt Engineering began recruiting and hiring experienced chip fabricator technicians from other companies.

On July 12, 2009 Simon Gerhardt presented a demonstration to representatives from the NSA, DoD, and the FBI. The NSA representative was invited to create a 128-bit encryption key on a separate device. The key was attacked by the "SiGeBoron" chip using a brute force method that succeeded in breaking it in 4.3 minutes.

The participants were advised that twenty of the chips had been produced thus far, material was available to produce approximately 250 from the original crystal, and efforts were underway to find more of the crystals. The entire chip run would be offered to the U. S. Government if it would meet the price of 10 million dollars per unit. After coordination with their respective agencies, the price was agreed to as long as the results could be reproduced on all the chips.

The results were verified using the remaining chips in the initial batch. On August 2, 2009 the 21st unit was given to an NSA representative to take back to Fort Meade to continue testing. The aircraft that was transporting the chip experienced catastrophic engine failure and crashed on approach, killing all on board along with four fatalities on the ground. The chip was destroyed in the associated fire. The NTSB has not been able to determine a cause for the engine failures. Cockpit voice recordings captured only one communication in the cockpit that was out of the normal, and it occurred at the time of engine failure.

**FIRST OFFICER:** "Sir, the engine monitors are showing engine thrust climbing above **100** percent. Checking visual."

**CAPTAIN:** "Okay. Switching engines to manual throttle now."

**FIRST OFFICER:** "What the hell is that gre..."

The cockpit voice recorder stopped capturing data at this point.

On August 18, 2009 when an NSA courier arrived to take another chip for testing, the initial 20 chips were discovered to be missing. The facility was locked down and investigators were summoned to determine what had happened. The 22nd chip came out of the fabricator and was prepared for shipping with the courier. The courier was on the phone with NSA headquarters confirming receipt of the chip when he was heard to exclaim "It's green, why is this thing glowing green? Get it away..."

At 1720 CDT Richardson was observed cycling away from the facility on a route consistent with going to his nearby apartment. At 1723 CDT an observation post reported that a bright green flash had emanated from Richardson's backpack that knocked him to the ground. The agent reported that Richardson was trying to get the backpack off and that the glow that remained after the flash was intensifying. At that time, both Richardson and the observer were consumed in the larger explosion.

At 1724 CDT there was a massive explosion at the Simon Gerhardt Engineering facility. It vaporized everything within the building and out to a radius of approximately 400 feet beyond. Buildings in the immediate vicinity of the blast were demolished. There were primary and secondary effect casualties up to a mile away from the event. Estimates place the deaths at 272 with another 385 injuries. The location of the building, in a business park, with the event occurring at the end of the work day, reduced the number of casualties. First responders reported the smoke cloud rising from the site glowed green for approximately 10 minutes after the explosion. No explanation has been determined for the phenomena. None of the chip materials or crystal has been recovered, although the area has been permeated with residue that bears some resemblance to what is known of the source material.

At 1530 CDT, agents assigned to follow Dinsmore and Gerhardt observed them arriving together at Gerhardt's residence. At 1630 CDT listening devices picked up sounds consistent with sexual activity. At 1724 CDT the agents observed an intense green flash emanating from the home. Simultaneously, all observation devices in the residence failed. Agents immediately approached and entered the house. They found both men dead, apparently while engaged in the sexual activity observed earlier via the listening devices.

The forensics team that examined the bodies concluded that a device had been inserted into the anus of Gerhardt. The only remaining physical evidence that remains of the device is the electric cord that extended from the anus to a 120 volt wall socket. Gerhardt had suffered an explosive rupture in his anus that produced a shock wave that stopped his heart. Evidence indicates that, seeing the distress of Gerhardt, Dinsmore grabbed the cord to pull the device out. At that time there was a massive surge through the wall socket, well beyond what should have caused the circuit breakers to trip. Dinsmore was electrocuted and died instantly. Examination revealed that the breakers had not tripped and were operating normally. Evidence suggests that the discharge of the device and the surge through the electrical cord and wall socket triggered the flash of light that the agents observed. However, the failure of the circuit breakers to react, and the green flash associated with the event, place it out of the realm of a normal accident or any known intentional action. Trace residue similar to that found at the other sites was collected at the scene. So far, this residue has not yielded any clues to what it is. Forensic scientists and outside experts alike have been baffled by the composition.

There was some minor burning, but the only other damage was to the computer system in Gerhardt and Dinsmore's houses. A surge overwhelmed protectors and conditioners in both residences and completely destroyed both networks. Fortunately damage was very localized. Agents are examining documents from both places, but hold little hope of finding substantive data that will lead to the recovery of either the chips, or the material they were made from. Offsite backups were heavily encrypted. NSA does not know if they can break the encryption without the processing power in the SiGeBoron Chips.

Further investigation revealed that on approximately August 15, 2009 a package containing the original 20 chips were sent via courier to Mr. Edward Yeutter. No person associated with Simon Gerhardt Engineering can be reliably attributed with this action. In fact, investigation can find no correlation between any employee and the courier service. It is impossible to interview the courier as he suffered a massive stroke shortly after delivering the package and is in a vegetative state.

Yeutter was a self-employed electronics technician. Most of his work was legitimate, performing minor electronics and computer repairs for individuals. His experience in the Air Force with avionics also gave him some business working with aircraft electronics for a local aircraft repair facility. However, bank records and surviving documentation indicate that Yeutter would take on any job without question for the right money. Yeutter has been linked to creating eavesdropping devices for private investigators and known criminals. Yeutter's bank records reveal significant wire transfers from offshore accounts around the time he is believed to have received the chips.

On September 3, 2009 Yeutter was accessing a hidden safe in the attic of his home. Contents of the safe included substantial cash, personal effects, and two passports, both Yeutter's; one under the name of Edward Hermann. Forensic analysis of the scene indicates that an object in his pocket began to burn. Burn marks on Yeutter's hand show that he tried to remove the object from the pocket. Either Yeutter dropped the object or it burned through and fell, hitting a rafter. Yeutter stepped onto the rafter and slipped. He fell through the drywall ceiling onto a landing below. He struck his neck and head on the rafter as he fell. Evidence indicates that he lost consciousness for some time. Yeutter regained consciousness and attempted to get up. However, Yeutter's fifth cervical vertebra had been fractured, and the movement of his neck caused the fracture to sever his spinal cord, paralyzing him. Unable to move, Yeutter bled out. Yeutter's body was discovered when a small fire in his workshop tripped an alarm. First responders extinguished the fire that destroyed the cabinet Yeutter kept his receipts and records in. When the responders entered the house through the connecting door they found Yeutter's body. He was declared dead on the scene due to massive trauma.

Residue on the rafter is consistent with the composition of residue found at the other sites. The exact composition is unclear, but seems to have certain consistencies with the original chip material from the few scientific analyses that have been successfully recovered. Speculation is that Yeutter decided to retain one of the chips for himself and was in the process of putting it in the safe when the accident occurred.

None of the surviving documentation yields any clues as to what Yeutter did with the chips and where they were sent. The investigation is continuing, but to this point no clues have been found pointing to the whereabouts of the chips.

There is no evidence in any of these events to link them with foreign actors. The CIA confirms that they have not received any intelligence that indicates any foreign knowledge of the existence of the chips. NSA monitoring of internet activity and technology development has not yielded any indications of the chips being used by any technology company.

Recommendation: Formation of a multi-discipline team drawn from intelligence, counter-intelligence, investigation, Special Forces, and scientific disciplines. The team will be tasked with continuing the investigation into this event and any others that show similarity. The team will be a direct report to the Deputy Director of National Intelligence (DDNI). Any events or activity strongly tied to the event are to be transmitted immediately to the DDNI under code word MEANGREEN. The team will be identified as Team MEANGREEN.

Recommendation: Investigate sources of paranormal information that are compatible with what was observed in this event. Determine their suitability for instructing or joining the team.

Recommendation: Declare the Simon Gerhardt Engineering site and all directly impacted sites around it as a significant source of PCB contaminants. Declare it a Superfund site. Using Class 5 Nuclear cleanup protocols remove all soil and debris to a depth of 10 meters covering an area 30 meters beyond the direct impact blast radius.

Recommendation: Seize Yeutter's home via Eminent Domain. A report linking Yeutter to potential domestic terrorists should be fabricated. The story should allege that materials intended for use in WMDs have been found in the remains of Yeutter's home, which will be razed and the soil under and around it removed to ensure no contamination of the local aquifer occurs. Once complete, rehabilitate the land as a park and donate it to the township.

Recommendation: Presidential Emergency Bunker 322, decommissioned in 1996, be repurposed and built out as a storage vault for the material collected from the MEANGREEN event sites. Protection suitable for live nuclear and biological arms storage should be installed to enhance the detonation resistance inherent in the structure. Continual remote surveillance via visual, chemical, and biological detection technologies should also be installed and monitored. Any detection of abnormal activity within the vault should be transmitted immediately to the DDNI under code word MEANGREEN.

February 2012 Addendum: The investigation has yielded few results thus far. There was no association between the missing SiGeBoron CPUs and the events of September 9, 2011. There is some historical evidence of activity with similar effects as observed in the MEANGREEN incident. Most of these anecdotal reports involve decorative items composed of the same or closely similar material to the black diamond described herein. However, there are also indications of events that could have involved missing CPUs. Per this evidence, the CPUs seem able to manipulate their form factor, as well as markings, making locating any of them unlikely. There is also some evidence of CPU activity prior to their creation, indicative of some ability to circumvent or evade causality. This makes location and recovery of any of the CPUs unlikely. However, the performance capabilities glimpsed during the early prototyping of the CPUs makes the expenditure of resources to continue the investigation worthwhile. Full funding of the effort will continue under the discretionary black ops funding stream.

# 2006 WORLD EVENTS

A stampede during the Stoning the Devil ritual on the last day at the Hajj in Mina, Saudi Arabia, kills at least 362 Muslim pilgrims

A massive mudslide occurs in Southern Leyte, Philippines; the official death toll is set at 1,126

Over 60 tornadoes break out, hardest hit is Tennessee with 29 people killed

Java earthquake devastates city of Yogyakarta killing over 6,600 people—mayor claims quake initiated when town's first cable company went online and thousands of TV sets emitted a ghastly green light

# The Disappearance of Alice P. Liddell

by Mallory Makepeace

*"Everything has got a moral if you can only find it."*
*— Lewis Carroll*

**THE VILLAGE VOICE**

New York, NY
Week of March 3–9, 2007

Feature Article–Missing Student Found

CO-ED CASE CRACKED

by Robin Duckworth

After a series of grisly events that have left New Jersey residents horrified over the past forty-eight hours, missing Rutgers University Freshman Alice Pleasance Liddell was found staggering and incoherent on the outskirts of Atlantic City, NJ this morning.

The wounded and disheveled eighteen year old Syracuse, NY native was discovered by middle-aged Pennsylvania hunters Jackson Lutwidge and Henry Frowde, who spotted the muddied nude teenager while tracking game in the sandy, uninhabited forest region known locally as The Pine Barrens. The weekend sportsmen were interviewed by an Atlantic City television crew about their highly unusual hunting trip just hours after their discovery.

"After sixty minutes of running we'd cornered this buck between some dead falls and a cliff face," stated Philadelphia resident Lutwidge.

"Then the weirdest thing happened," added fellow Philadelphian Frowde. "The buck ducks into the rotted out base of a trunk and then disappears."

"We checked all around," Continued Lutwidge, "and for the life of us couldn't figure out where it went. The trunk was only about twenty feet long. It had no holes or breaks in it, and tapered down to a few inches at the far end. It made no sense. We went back to the other end of the trunk to see if we missed it crouched in the shadows and that's when we saw her."

"Right. For a second I actually thought she was the Jersey Devil," added an embarrassed Frowde, referencing the regional myth of a half-monster half-woman long rumored to live in the New Jersey Pine Barrens. "But thank God, Jackson kept his cool. He knocked my rifle aside and caught the poor girl before she fell down. We wrapped her in our coats and carried her to the nearest ranger station."

Ocean County Ranger, John Tenniel treated Liddell for dehydration and exposure at his one-man post at the southern border of the Pinelands National Reserve.

"The girl was in a severe state of shock," Tenniel told reporters late this morning. "I cleaned and dressed about two dozen wounds on her legs, forearms, belly, and the right side of her head. Though many of the cuts and scratches looked to be inflicted by the local plant life, the scars on her head appear to have been made by some large animal's claws, possibly a bear. She almost lost an eye."

When asked about the rumor that when discovered Liddell had been heard mumbling such nonsensical phrases as "one to make me small" and "off with my head," Ranger Tenniel merely replied, "Just imagine what you might say after being kidnapped, drugged, assaulted, and abandoned half-naked in the wild."

Readers will note that it was only two days ago that Alice Liddell and her two college roommates Lorina and Edith (last names withheld pending parental identification) were reported missing by R.U. Euclid Hall's fourth floor resident advisor Anita Rackham.

Sources high in the Rutgers University Administration have confirmed that twelve hours later a series of e-mail tips (signed by an as then unidentified "Lewis C." and later traced to a computer lab in the Math building at Rutgers University) to the Piscataway Police Department led detectives to the office of Quantum Physics Professor Charlie Dodgson.

One source went on to say that after an intense two hours of questioning in his office, Dodgson, a native of Christ Church, England, and an Oxford Visiting Professor, broke down and admitted to abducting the three students under the pretense of an afternoon drive. Professor Dodgson claimed he and the three female students had spent the afternoon motoring from Folly Bridgehead, NJ to Godstow, NJ, and back, via Route 1515.

An anonymous phone tip this morning informed this reporter that Dodgson had then led police down a dirt road off of Route 1515 North to his abandoned car, which still contained the remains of Liddel's roommates. Both doors on the right side of the car had been torn off and lay several dozen yards away. Both tires on the right side were slashed and shredded.

Dodgson apparently then claimed he had walked back to his apartment after the attack and abduction.

The anonymous tipster went on to state it was at this point that Dodgson's confession started to become irrational and downright incomprehensible.

Late last evening, Piscataway Detective David Salter was quoted as stating the following during a surprise remote television interview, while staggering from a local brew pub in Piscataway.

"Dodgson admitted to faking an automobile breakdown in the countryside and offering the girls home baked brownies containing hallucinogenic mushrooms...he began removing their clothing...and...well the rest really doesn't make any sense. I mean, he must have eaten some of those brownies himself. Come on! A giant white rabbit broke into his station wagon, eviscerated two of the girls, and ran off with the third slung over its shoulder? And then he started mumbling some gibberish over and over again. Shooday or Sha'Daa or something or other," Detective Salter finished with a disgusted shake of his head. "The Professor is clearly insane. I hope the twisted bastard gets the chair."

Detective Salter has since been unavailable for further comment.

Police have released no theory so far as to how Liddell managed to traverse over 160 miles south through New Jersey townships, farms, and highways without being seen, after her escape from the crazed Dodgson.

The Rutgers University Public Relations Department has leaked the fact that with the help of Rutgers Sys-Op Technicians Janice Snark and Berne Wocky, police investigators have ascertained that the e-mail tips they received from one "Lewis C." about Dodgson were most likely sent by the British Physics Professor himself.

Sources close to the investigation state that FBI criminal psychologist and profiler Doctor Reggie Hargreaves is finding that more and more evidence is piling up that Charlie Dodgson was a functional schizophrenic for most of his life. Also, that it would appear, at this point, that the Professor probably suffered a major psychotic breakdown during his abduction of the three young women.

Unsubstantiated rumors from Summit Hospital, Summit, NJ, of unusual results obtained from a rape kit performed on Liddell started surfacing this morning. Hospital officials refuse to respond to any and all inquiries.

# 2010 WORLD EVENTS

Earthquake occurs in Haiti killing 230,000 and destroying the majority of the capital Port-au-Prince

Deepwater Horizon drilling rig explodes and kills eleven and initiates massive oil discharge—technician claims valve failure occurred when reinitializing equipment after motherboard replaced, sees unusual flash of green light from control room

Oil tanker truck explosion in South Kivu, the Democratic Republic of the Congo, kills at least 230 people

With the second launch of the SpaceX Dragon, SpaceX becomes the first privately held company to successfully launch, orbit and recover a spacecraft

# Tweets of the Damned

## by Hildy Silverman

TRANSCRIPT TAKEN FROM INCIDENT REPORT NJ 06/28/2011

**REPORTING OFFICER:** Anthony DeLuca

**SOURCES:** Primarily laptop browser history found in students' homes, incl. primary suspect; approx. **35%** provided by mobile phone carrier records of victims

**NOTE:** Minimal text edits for impossible-to-translate slang, poor or lack of punctuation, and grammatical/general clarity. Otherwise, every effort made to preserve the actual online conversations in as close to their original form as feasible.

**JESSEGRL1:**     Congrats to me, girlz. Parents finally caved on my b-day—got my MP**3**! Knockoff, SiG brand, but whatevs. YES!! **21** century, *(I'm)* finally here! #psyched

**27 MAY**
———-replies———-

**SARAHSMILE:**     @Jessegrl**1** niiiice. Know you wanted one **4**eva *(forever)* now.

**JJRULZ:**     @Jessegrl**1** kewl. Show me in English **2**morrow. Wanna see how SiG compares to my real-deal Banana playa... jkjk *(Transcriber note: believe this means "just kidding" or "joke").* BTW, did u talk **2** Jesse yet?

**JESSEGRL1:**   @JJRulz eh no chance. He was hangin w/nosepicker Randy at lunch so didn't dare get close. He smiled at me in gym tho(ugh)!

**SARAHSMILE:**   @Jessegirl1 Close enough, right? (A)bout time that boy caught on!

**JESSEGRL1:**   @Sarahsmile no lie. What's a grl*(girl)* gotta do, smack him over the head with a shovel and drag him home?!?!

**JJRULZ:**   @Jessegrl1 well da boy ain't loved for his brains. Now his other parts...yummy!

**JESSEGRL1:**   @JJRulz umm ok TMI *(Transcriber note: "too much information").* Gotta go play w/my new toy! L8r *(later)*

\#

**JESSEGRL1:**   Why won't you turn on, SiG?! Tried all night and zip. Stupid cheap piece of shiz!!!*(profanity)* Thanks mom and dad for my new paperweight. #sadnow

**27 MAYZ**
\#

**JESSEGRL1:**   SiG turned on when dad came in to yell (a)bout being up too late on school night. Made sick green flash when it did...that can't be good. #SiGFAIL

**28 MAY**

——-replies——-

**JJRULZ:**   @Jessegrl1 sorry about POS *(profanity)* fakey MP**3**! My Banana never fails so epically.

**SARAHSMILE:**   @JJRulz be nice. Not everyone has your fundz.

**JJRULZ:**   @Sarahsmile she knows I'm jk. Don't hate.

\#

**JESSEGRL1:**   Spent **2** hrs in dad's office. SiG's on, but couldn't get it to synch with Tunestown. #pissed

**28 MAY**

\#

**JESSEGRL1:**  Still nothing. **10** min jog in place then goin to bed. Hope I have that dream (a)bout Jesse BEGGING me to be his again. WHY WONT HE MAKE A MOVE ON MEEEEEEE???!!!

**28 MAY**

\#

**JESSEGRL1:**  Siggy turned on fine when I showed it off b/tween **2–3** periods. Played my fave Springfield oldie even tho(ugh) never synched. Huh? #maplayaspossessed

**29 MAY**

——-replies——-

**JJRULZ:**  @Jessegrl1 must have synched and you just didn't realize.

**JESSEGRL1:**  @JJRulz I guess. What is with the green flashes? Does your Banana do that?

**JJRULZ:**  @Jessegrl1 naw. Prolly *(probably)* cause it's real. Yours must have some crappy screen from China. Don't let your dog lick it...LOL *(laugh out loud)*!

**JESSEGRL1:**  @JJRulz yeah okay ha-ha. Siggy sounds good tho(ugh), right? Tunes r clear like *(it is)* playing them right in my head.

**JJRULZ:**  @Jessegrl1 good. Must be those hi(gh)-end earbuds I got you for your b-day. U r welcome!

**SARAHSMILE:**  @JJRulz gawd enough already! We get it you're better than us!!!

**JJRULZ:**  @Sarahsmile I never said dat!!!

**SARAHSMILE:**  @Jessegrl1 so what did Jesse say to you after math? Saw u talkin...dyin over here!

**JESSEGRL1:**  @Sarahsmile all I said was hi and did he get question **5** in algebra quiz. He was all, hi and no, but will let me know if Dave got it and bye now.

**SARAHSMILE:**  @Jessegrl1 awwww, he cares if you got it right! That's so good!!

**JJRULZ:**  @Jessegrl1 OMG *(oh my God)* planning ur wedding right now.

**SARAHSMILE:**  @JJRulz sigh.

**JESSEGRL1:**  @JJRulz you and Jamil goin to Freshchunks concert Saturday?

**JJRULZ:**  @Jessegrl1 you know it! Gonna rock it hard. U get tix? Oh wait dat's right, only premium seats r left.

**SARAHSMILE:**  @JJRulz OMG ENUFF!!

**JJRULZ:**  @Sarahsmile WHAT?!?!

**JESSEGRL1:**  @JJRulz yeah well u guys have fun for me. It's sit-ups nite, then beddie **4** me.

**JJRULZ:**  @Jessegrl1 how's all dat exercise goin? See any results yet?

**JESSEGRL1:**  @Sarahsmile Niters. *(good night).*

#

**JESSEGRL1:**  Still have headache and stomach blahs. Comin and goin for weeks now. Maybe I'll lose a pound but still not worth this misery. #MAKEITSTOP

**6 JUNE**

#

**JESSEGRL1:**  Latest Siggy weirdness. Won't do this if we r alone but ALWAYS goes on w/green flash if someone nearby. Hear buzzing under tunes too. Like it's whispering to me. #wazzupwitdat

**10 JUNE**

———-replies———-

**SARAHSMILE:**  @Jessegrl1 can u return it?

**JESSEGRL1:**  @Sarahsmile dunno. Not like SiG has mall stores; dad says only online and all sales r final. Besides, he sounds SO good when working.

**SARAHSMILE:**  @Jessegrl1 oh well maybe it will just get better on its own. So what's the latest w/Jesse? Saw u stalking his locker.

**JESSEGRL1:**  @Sarahsmile LOL I wasn't stalkin! I went over to ask him for aspirin for neverending headache.

**SARAHSMILE:**  @Jessegrl1 AND?!

**JESSEGRL1:**  @Sarahsmile he dint *(didn't)* have any. Said he had to get to class. That's all.

SARAHSMILE:  @Jessegrl1 did he at least smile or something?

JESSEGRL1:  @Sarahsmile not on his face but inside, yeah.

SARAHSMILE:  @Jessegrl1 huh?

JESSEGRL1:  @Sarahsmile I know…weird, right? But my earbuds were in and Siggy was singin low and when I looked close at Jesse I saw his inner smile.

SARAHSMILE:  @Jessegrl1 uuummmm ok. Was it at least a nice inside smile? Like he meant it?

JESSEGRL1:  @Sarahsmile not really, no. Can't explain but it was kinda… dunno. Wrong. Nasty. I think he did mean it tho(ugh). Sux.

SARAHSMILE:  @Jessegrl1 maybe u should see a dr about those headaches and seeing stuff.

JESSEGRL1:  @Sarahsmile yeah maybe. L8r.

#

JESSEGRL1:  Talked to Jesse for whole **5** min. Heard him w/ears but swear I heard his voice through my earbud too and THAT voice said awful shiz.  #WTF

## 13 JUNE

———-replies——-

SARAHSMILE:  @Jessegrl1 WHAT?!

JJRULZ:  @Jessegrl1 yeah wattahell (*what the hell*)?

JESSEGRL1:  @Sarahsmile no lie. Like he got caught talkin in background of recording (ex)cept his voice got louder and music faded and his words were diff

JESSEGRL1:  Sorry cut off. Different from what he was sayin out loud to me. I didn't kno(w) he could think sick shiz like that.

SARAHSMILE:  @Jessegrl1 must be an echo.

JJRULZ:  @Jessegrl1 you be crazy. Jkjk

JESSEGRL1:  @JJRulz I AM NOT!!!

JESSEGRL1:  @Sarahsmile no echo, different words. He was sayin stuff about social studies quiz but inside I heard…gawd NASTY!

SARAHSMILE:  @Jessegrl1 what?!

**JESSEGRL1:** @Sarahsmile he was sayin...fat bitch wanna take u behind the old warehouse and bash your fuckin head in with a brick and fuck your dead ass.

**JJRULZ:** @Jessegrl1 u r hi(gh). Jesse would NEVER say dat!

**SARAHSMILE:** @Jessegrl1 um yeah gotta agree. Known him since third grade. That's kinda awful for you to make up just (be)cause he still won't ask u out.

**JESSEGRL1:** @Sarahsmile swear to jesus I am not!!! Why would I want to make up him thinkin somethin so gross (a)bout me? I LUV Jesse!!!

**JJRULZ:** @Jessegrl1 maybe cause u finally figgered *(figured)* out he isn't interested in u? Like at ALL?

**SARAHSMILE:** @JJRulz Gawd ur so nice, except not at all.

**JJRULZ:** @Sarahsmile I am honest, sry*(sorry)*.

**JESSEGRL1:** @Sarahsmile my head hurts again. Gonna lie down. Niters and thanx so much for ALL ur support, girlz.

\#

**JESSEGRL1:** Done w/Jesse. Know what he really thinks now and his sick ass can burn in hell. Siggy showin me now not just tellin...just look at screen and see true faces...so UGLY! #allboyzsuk

**14 JUNE**

\#

**JESSEGRL1:** I figured it out. Siggy is magic. He reads their minds and tells me the truth...shows me reality. I know now, know it all...(a)bout all of u.

14 June

\#

**JESSEGRL1:** Gonna stop u...nuthin *(nothing)* but evil and twisted and gross inside...NOT GONNA LET U!!!

14 June

\#

**JESSEGRL1:**   Some things are easier than u expect once u realize they gotta get done. #takingcontrol

**15 JUNE**

——-replies——-

**SARAHSMILE:**   @Jessegrl1 why aren't u calling me back? Left u like **10** messages!! Wanna find out if u heard about Jesse… so awful!!!

**#**

**JESSEGRL1:**   Sorry been outta touch, world. Mad busy w/finals and… other stuff. BTW *(by the way)* new handle is @noonesgrl. Follow me here from now on.

**20 JUNE**

——-replies——-

**JJRULZ:**   @Jessegrl1 ummm what does noonsgrl mean? Like you roll ur big ass outta bed at noon?

**SARAHSMILE:**   @Noonesgrl I (have) been so WORRIED about u what w/ Jesse's accident. Why won't u call me back?

**NOONESGRL:**   @JJRulz duh effing duh it's no ONES, as in I belong to no one!

**JJRULZ:**   @Noonesgrl yeah well guess u never will now. Poor Jesse. Wonder how he fell offa platform like dat? Bet he got pushed.

**SARAHSMILE:**   @JJRulz ugh that's an awful thing to put out there. He prolly *(probably)* just tripped. If only the stupid subway braked faster.

**NOONESGRL:**   @Sarahsmile no phones no more. Can't REALLY hear or see w/phone. Guess u would like that better tho(ugh).

**SARAHSMILE:**   @Noonesgrl ?????

**NOONESGRL:**   @Sarahsmile yeah u know it's true.

**SARAHSMILE:**   @Noonesgrl I dunno *(don't know)* why u r pissed at me. I'm just worried about u, what with losing Jesse.

**NOONESGRL:**   @Sarahsmile not lost…freed from. Saved.

**SARAHSMILE:**   @Noonesgrl HE DIED WHAT IZ WRONG WITH U!!!

**NOONESGRL:**     @Sarahsmile guess u rather it was me, huh. Too bad Siggy got my back.

**JJRULZ:**     @Noonesgrl Gawd, bitch much?

#

Noonesgrl:     OMG I know what's wrong w/everyone now! Siggy showin me what's comin and how it's warping them w/evil. Siggy keepin it outta me, but 4 how long? #endoftheworldasweknowit

**22 JUNE**

#

**NOONESGRL:**     Tried to tell parents, warn them and they r makin me see someone ASAP. Like a shrink'll help stop any of it. Like anyone can.

**23 JUNE**

#

**NOONESGRL:**     Got no one, can't trust anyone...only Siggy. Thank u god for my Siggy my truth my guide my **1** true friend. #nofuture

**24 JUNE**

**SIGGYSGRL:**     @Siggysgrl is my handle now. Follow me here but only if u r ready to learn the TRUTH.

**24 JUNE**

——-replies——-

**JJRULZ:**     @Whoeversgrlthisweek geeze u sound completely bsc *(profanity)*!!!

**SIGGYSGRL:**     @JJRulz I heard you too you know. At school.

**JJRULZ:**     @Siggysgrl wat now?

**SIGGYSGRL:**     @JJRulz u r a **2**-faced beyotch. I mean I always knew you tho(ugh)t u were better than me (be)cause you got money and are skinny, but then Siggy told me what ur really thinkin when ur bein nice to my face!

**JJRULZ:**     @Siggysgrl geeze really...REALLY...dayum*(damn)*.

**SARAHSMILE:**     @Siggysgrl whoa what are you saying?!

**JJRULZ:**  @Siggysgrl wow and after all I did for you for the past **2** years we been besties?

**SIGGYSGRL:**  @JJRulz yah and it was all bs *(expletive)* *(be)*cause all you wanted was someone to hang with who made you look hot next to and use me to get to Jesse!

**SIGGYSGRL:**  Jokes on u tho(ugh)...now no one can have that sick fucker.

**JJRULZ:**  @Siggysgrl first off I'm with Jamil dumbass!

**JJRULZ:**  Second u r a messed up bitch talkin (a)bout a dead guy like dat and u say u loved him?!

**SIGGYSGRL:**  @JJRulz yeah too bad he din't get a chance to cut u up with ax and lick ur blood off his fingers like he wanted to do *(to)* me. U should thank me.

**JJRULZ:**  @Siggysgrl um first u were never close **2** Jesse cept in ur sick sad little mind!

**JJRULZ:**  Plus I neva *(never)* liked him like dat and if I did...well wouldn't need UR fat ass to help me get him!!!

**SARAHSMILE:**  @Siggysgrl u don't know what u r saying anymore...JJ is totes *(totally)* into Jamil and u KNOW that.

**JJRULZ:**  @Sarahsmile THANK YOU.

**JJRULZ:**  @Siggysgrl um wait what do u mean I oughta thank u? For what exactly?

**SIGGYSGRL:**  @Sarahsmile I know what Siggy tells me. He lets me hear the truth. He tells me what ya'll REALLY mean when ur LYIN TO MY FACE ALLA*(all the)*TIME!!!

**JJRULZ:**  @Siggysgrl U R INSANE REALLY AND TRULY. Where were u anyway when Jesse fell huh?!

**SIGGYSGRL:**  Siggy shows me ur true faces on his screen. I hear ur true voices in his whispers. I know the true future...what's comin...what's already snuck in.

**SARAHSMILE:**  @Siggysgrl think about what ur saying. Siggy is an MP3 not a psychic for godsake!

**JJRULZ:**  @Sarahsmile quit wastin time...she cray-cray *(crazy)*.

**SIGGYSGRL:**  @JJRulz fuck you. We are done. I just unfriended you on FB too.

**JJRULZ:** @Siggysgrl at least u didn't shove me in front of the **3:35** to Penn Station...yet.

**SIGGYSGRL:** @Sarahsmile I KNOW what's real now. Siggy tells me. U don't get it cause it won't let u. Darks already inside u twistin u and

**SIGGYSGRL:** U don't even know how much. No one does but me.

**SARAHSMILE:** @Siggysgrl what other stuff?! U are scaring me with all this!!! Please go talk to ur mom or someone!!!

**SIGGYSGRL:** @Sarahsmile u should be scared. We should all be. The Sha'Daa *(???)* is comin. It's already seepin thru the cracks.

**JJRULZ:** @Siggysgrl goodbye. Don't even LOOK at me at school **2** morrow headcase!!!

**SIGGYSGRL:** The Sha'Daa has slipped in between the cracks. It's in u all. The Sha'Daa will shatter the walls. The Sha'Daa will devour us world and all.

**SARAHSMILE:** @Siggysgrl srsly *(seriously)* u need to talk to someone...u stopped making sense. Throw that damned messed up player away and get help, I'm begging u!!!

**SIGGYSGRL:** @Sarahsmile ugh head killing me now. Talk to you at school **2** morrow maybe. Prolly not tho(ugh). Hurts hearin what u r really sayin while ur mouth lies to me.

\#

**SIGGYSGRL:** Tall guy w/gold tooth came to me while walkin home **2**day. Says he's Johnny and will trade me somethin I really need for siggy. As if. #whoisjohnny

## 27 JUNE

**SARAHSMILE:** @Siggysgrl really? Did u do it? What did he offer?

**SIGGYSGRL:** @Sarahsmile said no and walked away fast like siggy screamed I should.

**SARAHSMILE:** @Siggysgrl oh ok but u weren't curious at all?

**SIGGYSGRL:** @Sarahsmile like I would give up my only REAL bestie for anythin some creepy dude has to offer.

**SARAHSMILE:** @Siggysgrl ok so ur still on that huh? Ur MP**3** is your only real bestie now? Wow thnx *(thanks)*.

**SIGGYSGRL:** @Sarahsmile siggys the only one honest w/me. He's the only one I trust now. I know it's not ur fault but it is what it is.

**SARAHSMILE:** @Siggysgrl what did I do to you, huh? When did I stop being ur friend?

**SIGGYSGRL:** Siggy tells me u think I am stupid and keep u from hangin w/populars but u feel too guilty to dump me.

**SARAHSMILE:** @Siggysgrl that's totes a lie! I don't think any of that! I'm like the only friend u got left after the past coupla weeks of ur weirdness!!!

**SIGGYSGRL:** @Sarahsmile doesn't even matter. No one does, nothing does. So much bigger stuff comin...u can't grasp it. Sorry **4** u, really.

**SARAHSMILE:** @Siggysgrl fine whatevs. JJs right, u r insane. U think a chunk of cheapass metal and plastic READS MINDS AND TALKS TO U!!!

**SIGGYSGRL:** @Sarahsmile heard worse from others at school (a)bout me. Know u r all planning to get me but it's the evil that got inside, not really u. I get it.

**SIGGYSGRL:** Siggy explained it...the evil that snuck inside you is gonna make u shut me up so I can't warn everyone what's comin for us all.

**SARAHSMILE:** @Siggysgrl ???

**SIGGYSGRL:** @Sarahsmile first Jesse then JJ, now u. Even my parents who r all, plz *(please)* talk to ur nice dr. I got no one and u all think I'll just walk into ur trap like a fat stupid rat

**SIGGYSGRL:** Didn't count on my siggy savin me, tellin me what to do and how I gotta do it.

**SARAHSMILE:** @Siggysgrl u need help. After graduation we can talk it out, ok? Byes for now.

**SIGGYSGRL:** @Sarahsmile **4** now and **4**ever.

#

**SIGGYSGRL:** Lyin on my bed with siggy glowin warm green and singin my songs and my destiny. Why can't I stop cryin? #chosen

**27 JUNE**

\#

**SIGGYSGRL:**    No...it's too much...I can't I CAN'T

**27 JUNE**

\#

**SIGGYSGRL:**    I get it. Doin them all a favor really. Savin them from what's coming and myself too. Thnx siggy for tellin truth and showin me the way.

**28 JUNE**

\#

**SIGGYSGRL:**    God my headz so full...won't miss this pain. Gotta get ready...lots to prep for graduation **2**morrow. Good thing dad's always been pro NRA.

**28 JUNE**

*Transcript ends after this final transmission from the deceased suspect, issued the night immediately preceding the P.S. 66 graduation day massacre.*

*Suspect's MP3 player, "Siggy" was not found at scene, though at least one survivor mentions seeing her listening to it. So far, no one has admitted to taking it, though likely another student removed it from the body after police sharpshooter took action at scene.*

*Manufacturer of SiG MP3 players issued statement that nothing is wrong with its products and internal R&D can find no logical reason to issue a recall based on the "tragic rantings of an obviously very sick child." Since there is no known product defect or malfunction that could cause such a dramatic personality change in a human being at the one apparently undergone by the suspect, their decision is likely to remain unchallenged by authorities.*

*Post-incident diagnosis by examining psychiatrist: Beyond obvious indications of paranoid schizophrenia, actual cause of psychotic break remains inconclusive.*

**CASE STATUS:** Open pending further investigation.

# 2011 WORLD EVENTS

An earthquake measuring 6.3 in magnitude strikes Christchurch, New Zealand, killing 181 people

9.0 magnitude earthquake strikes east of Sendai, Japan killing thousands—80 miles east at epicenter captain of whaling research vessel claims quake initiated right after new radar-homing harpoon successfully activated and struck pregnant grey whale, brilliant flash of green light seen by entire crew

300 people killed in deadliest tornado outbreak in the Southern United States since the 1974 Super Outbreak

A powerful 7.2 magnitude earthquake strikes Van Province, Turkey, killing 582 people and injuring thousands

# Dead Air

by Terrence Ulysses Cork

*"Each and every one of us is a show waiting to happen."*

— *Jerry Springer*

AUDIO TRANSCRIPT

CABLEWORKS, INC. (PUBLIC ACCESS)

NEWARK, NEW JERSEY

STUDIO C

06:00-06:10 HRS

JUNE 24, 2011

A DIGITAL RED NEON CUE.

STANDBY.

Voices in the ether...

**DIRECTOR:** "Tune in everyone. We've got to air in ninety seconds. Okay. Listen up. Engineering ready to roll, record and confirm? Engineering? Engineering, put your headphones on!"

**AUDIO DIRECTOR:** "Ready slate..."

**ENGINEER:** "Engineering to control, ready to roll, record and confirm chief..."

**DIRECTOR:** "Ready sixty second countdown...A.D. punch it!"

**ASST. DIRECTOR:** "Countdown started. Sixty, fifty nine, fifty eight..."

**DIRECTOR:** "Ready music, ready lights, ready CG..."

**PRODUCTION ASSISTANT:** "Sh**!"

**DIRECTOR:** "Who said that?"

**PRODUCTION ASSISTANT:** "Cordless microphone just bit it chief…we got no backups neither…"

**ASST. DIRECTOR:** "Forty nine, forty eight, forty seven…"

**ENGINEER:** "Engineering is ready to roll VTRs one, two and three…"

**DIRECTOR:** "Christ, it's like working in the stone ages… tell Chris to drag in a cable mic…"

**CAMERA ONE:** "Chris is on vacation. We got an OJT from Frisco playing floor manager today. Be nice. His dad donated a million to PBS last year."

**FLOOR MANAGER:** "Hi fellas! My name's Mike! You can call me Spike! I've always wanted to be in show business!"

**DIRECTOR:** "Spike, this is God. Put a cable microphone on the talent when she arrives…"

**FLOOR MANAGER:** "But it'll show on the monitor…"

**DIRECTOR:** "Just pin the f***ing mic to her t*t, Spike!"

**ASST. DIRECTOR:** "Thirty eight, thirty seven, thirty six…"

**DIRECTOR:** "Gimme a larger font on the CG…"

**AUDIO DIRECTOR:** "Music is cued, ready cart…"

**CG:** "Chief! We don't have time to retype the credits…"

**DIRECTOR:** "Above-the-line staff?"

**CG:** "Oh, yeah. Gotcha Chief…"

**DIRECTOR:** "Ready to fade up lights…"

**CG:** "CG set, ready to roll opening credits…"

**ASST. DIRECTOR:** "Twenty four, twenty three, twenty two…"

**MAKEUP:** "Jimmy! Chief! You out there…"

**DIRECTOR:** "Dave? What the hell are you doing on headphones? Get back to makeup!"

**MAKEUP:** "Sorry chief, but I tell you she's gonna trip on that mic cable, you know she's been a little queasy the last couple of mornings and…"

**CAMERA THREE:** "So queen b*tch upchucks on camera. It'll wake up our **200** viewers…"

**STATION MANAGER:** "Who said that!"

**ASST. DIRECTOR:** "Eighteen, seventeen, sixteen, fifteen..."

**DIRECTOR:** "Engineering roll, record and confirm..."

**ENGINEER:** "Rolling..."

**DIRECTOR:** "Gimme Bars and tone..."

**ENGINEER:** "Bars and tone chief..."

**DIRECTOR:** "Ready to cue talent..."

**TALENT:** "Jim I can't dance with this cable around my ankles..."

**FLOOR MANAGER:** "Cueing slate..."

**DIRECTOR:** "Kill bars and tone...suck it up Mary. Its only for thirty minutes..."

**ASST. DIRECTOR:** "Ten, nine, eight, seven, six..."

**TALENT:** "But..."

**DIRECTOR:** "Now...roll credits, roll cart, roll VTR one..."

**FLOOR MANAGER:** "This is great!"

**DIRECTOR:** "Cue talent!"

**TALENT:** "Hi everybody! It's me, Mary Alice Bonesteel, and I want to welcome you all to BODYTALK, the workout show of the future! Broadcast live from our Telaerobic's Facility in sunny Newark!"

**PRODUCTION ASSISTANT:** "It's raining outside you stupid c..."

**DIRECTOR:** "Spike! Clear the set!"

**ENGINEER:** "Rolling VTR two..."

**FLOOR MANAGER:** "But they're the Rotarians, Chief! They want to see a real live TV show close up and..."

**TALENT:** "...and through the magic of special effects, I'll be exercising in exotic locations such as Spain, Brazil..."

**DIRECTOR:** "Off the God d*mn set NOW!"

**ENGINEER:** "Rolling VTR three..."

**DIRECTOR:** "And Spike! Get those drooling boy scouts back behind the CYC!"

**SCOUT LEADER:** "With all due respect, my boys need to be an active part of the show if they want to get their communications merit badges and..."

**DIRECTOR:** "One more word from you sh*t-for-brains and I give your whole troop the boot! Audio up!"

**TALENT:** "Hawaii, France, and wonderful California..."

**DIRECTOR:** "Jesus, why do I keep volunteering for this retro gig... punch the filmchain...I need those beach party slides..."

**TALENT:** "Yes, BODYTALK is a regular party of exercise..."

**DIRECTOR:** "Roll first workout cart, bring up lights, dissolve to program, cue talent, camera one gimme a tight close-up, camera two truck to the left and fix her profile...where the hell is my steadycam...oh great camera two, why in hell would I want a close-up of her *ss when she's talking? Pan left!"

**FLOOR MANAGER:** "She's signaling she wants the Teleprompter slowed up..."

**CAMERA TWO:** "But it's such a nice *ss..."

**UNION REP:** "I'm surprised she can even read..."

**STEADYCAM:** "P*ssywhipped son of a..."

**DIRECTOR:** "Watch it mister..."

**CAMERA TWO:** "Dumb*ss blonde needs a guide dog not contact lenses..."

**DIRECTOR:** "Dissolve up to camera one, ready to cut to two..."

**TALENT:** "Good morning everyone! I can hear your bodies working out all over this fantastic planet."

**DIRECTOR:** "Cut to two, cut to one, steadycam, ready to dissolve to three..."

**CONTROL BOARD:** "How do I get out of this chicken sh*t outfit?"

**PRODUCTION ASSISTANT:** "It speaks!"

**AUDIO DIRECTOR:** "It...is...alive..."

**DIRECTOR:** "Too fast for you Larry?"

**CONTROL BOARD:** "Mr. Fingers can take anything you got, Jimmy."

**DIRECTOR:** "Two, pan right..."

**TALENT:** "Isn't this a great song? That's right! This is all part of our **80**'s retrospective week. Nothing but songs from the **80**'s! Did any of you see the movie? Let's hear them muscles singing!"

**AUDIO DIRECTOR:** "I can't believe we're playing this sh*t…"

**CAMERA TWO:** "I can't believe we're shooting this with twenty-five year old equipment."

**PRODUCTION ASSISTANT:** "Station Manager has got the imagination of a f***ing grapefruit…"

**STEADYCAM:** "Nothing rocks like **80**'s rock and roll, junior."

**STATION MANAGER:** "I heard that!"

**DIRECTOR:** "Dissolve to one, ready to cut to steadycam…"

**PRODUCTION ASSISTANT:** "You always were a kiss-*ss Bill…"

**CAMERA ONE:** "Is it just me or is she putting on a little weight?"

**STEADYCAM:** "Bl*w me, Parker."

**TALENT:** "Sorry about this cable around my waist folks. Seems our technical crew had a little trouble with my cordless microphone today. Okay. Jumping jack splits with a shoulder bounce. One, two, three, one, two, three, I'm just a steel town girl on a Saturday night, waiting for the…"

**DIRECTOR:** "Give it to the steadycam."

**STEADYCAM:** "Man she's got a nice pair of j*gs…"

**PRODUCTION ASSISTANT:** "Wonder if they're real…"

**DIRECTOR:** "Oh you know it…"

**CAMERA ONE:** "Lucky bastard…"

**DIRECTOR:** "Audio ride that goddamn VU meter, I've got distortion levels up the *ss."

**TALENT:** "I'm a maniac, a maniac I know…"

**ASST. DIRECTOR:** "Three minutes to station break, chief…"

**DIRECTOR:** "Engineering. Ready a multiple freeze frame when she drops for pushups…"

**ENGINEER:** "D-two is set."

**CONTROL BOARD:** "Can anyone say twenty-year-old digital masturbation?"

**AUDIO DIRECTOR:** "Oh, Christ, the NYU film wank is in preacher mode…"

**CONTROL BOARD:** "Up yours Davey, you f***ing jerkwater community college dropout!"

**AUDIO DIRECTOR:** "Did I hit a nerve, Scorsese Junior?"

**DIRECTOR:** "Save it for later kids..."

**TALENT:** "I'm sweating today, America. Boy can I feel my muscles singing. Can you feel yours?"

**FLOOR MANAGER:** "I'd like to feel her..."

**DIRECTOR:** "Cut the goddamn chatter. I want those cameras moving and for Christ's sake, camera two, cool it with the zooms!"

**TALENT:** "Time to build those big busts. Let's do pushups..."

**CAMERA TWO:** "Oh mommy..."

**DIRECTOR:** "Gimme those frames, dissolve to one...right...cut to two, now three..."

**STEADYCAM:** "Twenty says she's a C-cup."

**TALENT:** "Yeah, yeah, yeah, push it everybody. I know I've been under the weather the last couple of days but today, I'm happy and sunny, and we're gonna work up a storm!"

**CAMERA THREE:** "Nossir! D-cup all the way."

**ASST. DIRECTOR:** "Sure looking better than she was yesterday..."

**CAMERA TWO:** "You're both on! She's definitely got Double-D potential in my book. Split that sports bra Mary Alice!"

**DIRECTOR:** "Ready second cart...roll cart...cut to steadycam..."

**AUDIO DIRECTOR:** "Music up."

**TALENT:** "One, and two, one and two, work those leg muscles now, oh yeah, we're walking on sunshine, oh yeah, we're all walking on sunshine, oh yeah, and don't it feel good..."

**FLOOR MANAGER:** "I think I'm in love..."

**CAMERA ONE:** "I think I'm gonna puke..."

**STATION MANAGER:** "Let's tone down the commentary, okay boys? I know it's only on the work track, but..."

**ASST. DIRECTOR:** "One minute, sixty seconds to break..."

**STEADYCAM:** "Oh, great, the manager's a born-again..."

**CAMERA TWO:** "Ashamed of your hard-on, suit?"

**PRODUCTION ASSISTANT:** "Maybe he doesn't like girls…"

**STATION MANAGER:** "You…you bastards!"

**DIRECTOR:** "Camera one and three truck left…cut to one…cut to three… camera two pedestal up…I said up! Get your frigging mind off her legs and shoot!"

**TALENT:** "Now you're gonna work those tummy muscles real good…oh yeah, I'm walking on sunshine, oh yeah, I'm walking on sunshine…"

**CAMERA TWO:** "But they're such nice legs chief…"

**PRODUCTION ASSISTANT:** "You're right. She HAS put on a couple of pounds…"

**ASST. DIRECTOR:** "One minute and forty six, forty five, forty four…"

**DIRECTOR:** "Dissolve to one…dissolve to steadycam…and keep her workout shoes in focus three! We're getting four figures off the record for all the talent's clothes today."

**ENGINEER:** "Ready to roll PBS ad, Jim, VTR four in sync…"

**STATION MANAGER:** "The hidden shame of public cable access, Jimmy. With this money, and if our ratings go up this month, we can finally get that Internet feed."

**DIRECTOR:** "And save the stock reports for later…Andy! Gimme a red gel on her hair…cut to one…"

**LIGHTING DIRECTOR:** "Man. She's looking hot today…red gel up!"

**DIRECTOR:** "Ready the strobes for the knee lifts…dissolve to two…"

**TALENT:** "And look what this does to my bum muscles! Tee hee!"

**DIRECTOR:** "Steady camera one…"

**PRODUCTION ASSISTANT:** "I think I'm getting an erection…"

**TALENT:** "That's right everybody, work those tummy muscles. I'd do it with you, but Mary Alice just found out she's pregnant! Isn't that just wonderful? I'm walking on sunshine, oh yeah…"

**ASST. DIRECTOR:** "Sixty seconds, fifty nine, fifty eight…"

**DIRECTOR:** "What the f*** did she say?"

**AUDIO DIRECTOR:** "Ready to roll third music cart…"

**DIRECTOR:** "Camera two back up! Damn it steadycam, stay in the foreground!"

**ENGINEER:** "Rolling third cart..."

**DIRECTOR:** "Music up."

**TALENT:** "Let's do some sit-ups everybody...straight up now tell me, straight up now tell me, are you really gonna love me forever, uh, uh, uh, or, are, you, just...uh, keeping me from my baby. Seems my boyfriend doesn't want my baby. He says you all wouldn't work out with a pregnant woman. He says it would bring down the ratings..."

**DIRECTOR:** "Spike! Make that b*tch shut the f*** up! Do it now, we're on air!"

**FLOOR MANAGER:** "But..."

**ASST. DIRECTOR:** "Forty two, forty one, forty..."

**TALENT:** "I know you're watching this, Jimmy. You ARE the Director...are you really gonna love me forever, uh, uh, uh, or, were you just having fun..."

**DIRECTOR:** "Shut the f*** up, you stupid b*tch, shut the f*** up!"

**ASST. DIRECTOR:** "Jesus chief, calm down..."

**PRODUCTION ASSISTANT:** "Chief we just blew floor lamp..."

**CG:** "Chief! Exec says we gotta CG crawl that hurricane warning..."

**DIRECTOR:** "What? Wait a second..."

**ASST. DIRECTOR:** "Twenty, nineteen, eighteen..."

**CONTROL BOARD:** "Jimmy? Stay on Camera two?"

**DIRECTOR:** "Camera two! What the hell are you doing? Get back on your shot!"

**CAMERA TWO:** "She's got a knife!"

**TALENT:** "Jimmy, you cut us both out of your life. Just like this..."

**DIRECTOR:** "For Christ's sake somebody stop her!"

**FLOOR MANAGER:** "Holy sh*t!"

**CAMERA THREE:** "She's bleeding! She's bleeding!"

**TALENT:** "Can you see our baby, Jimmy? He's in here somewhere..."

**AUDIO DIRECTOR:** "Starting slate."

**ASST. DIRECTOR:** "Ten, nine, eight..."

**FLOOR MANAGER:** "Oh my God, oh my God!"

**TALENT:** "Jimmy honey.... This should...bring the old ratings up....yuh...your precious...ratingsssss...uhhh..."

**CAMERA ONE:** "She fell! Oh, Christ, the blood..."

**DIRECTOR:** "Put pressure on the wound! Sh*t! Sh*t! Sh*t!"

**MAKEUP:** "Uh, Chief? The Rotarians are kind of freaking in the green room..."

**FLOOR MANAGER:** "She's not breathing!"

**CAMERA ONE:** "It's on my shoes! Jesus, the blood! The blood!"

**DIRECTOR:** "Oh, Mother of God, no..."

**FLOOR MANAGER:** "What the hell do you want? What? No, I don't give a f**k that you've got a first aid merit badge!"

**DIRECTOR:** "This can't be happening..."

**STEADYCAM:** "Somebody get a f***ing ambulance..."

**CAMERA TWO:** "Call **911**! Call **911**!"

**DIRECTOR:** "I'm ruined...I'm f***ing ruined..."

**AUDIO DIRECTOR:** "Chief, maybe we should....no don't!"

**STATION MANAGER:** "Gun!"

**CG:** "Take the gun away from your head, chief! It ain't worth it!"

**CONTROL BOARD:** "Just relax, Jimmy, and give me the pistol. Okay pal?"

**STATION MANAGEER:** "Nooooooo!"

****CRACK!****

****FEEDBACK SQUEAL****

**PRODUCTION ASSISTANT:** "F***! My ears!"

**MAKEUP:** "Chief, the Rotarians could really use some kind of reassurance about now! Uh...chief?"

**CONTROL BOARD:** "Oh Jesus, Jimmy, no...."

**STATION MANAGER:** "But but but..."

**ENGINEER:** "Chief? Chief? Engineering is ready to roll VTR four..."

**ASST. DIRECTOR:** "Three, two, one..."

**DEAD AIR**

# 2012 WORLD EVENTS

**Fire at Comayagua prison, Honduras, kills 358. Prison guard confesses that his MP3 player was a glowing green telephone to his parent's spirits that told him to cleanse the prison grounds**

**Canadian film maker James Cameron becomes the first person to visit Challenger Deep, the deepest point on Earth, in over 50 years**

**Plane crash near Islamabad, Pakistan, kills 127 people**

# Mr. Bass Man

## by John Manning

Transcript of interview dated August 1, 2012, conducted at Austin General Hospital by Sanchez, Manuel, Homicide Lieutenant, and White, David, Detective Sergeant, Homicide, Austin Police Department, Austin, Travis County, Texas. Interview was conducted as part of the investigation into the circumstances surrounding a catastrophic fire that destroyed the Red River Lounge located at 127 East Twelfth Street, Austin, Texas, and killed eighty-nine patrons, eight employees, and four members of the band Hell's Archangels who were performing there. Subject of the interview is Jarvis, Harold Chester, musician, and only survivor of the event.

**WHITE:** Testing. Testing. [thumping noises] One. Two. Three. It's ready.

**SANCHEZ:** Thank you, Sergeant. Let the record show that this interview is being recorded in room five oh three, Austin General Hospital, Austin, Texas. The time is oh nine thirteen hours. Present are Lieutenant Manuel Sanchez, Sergeant David White, and Mr. Harold Jarvis. As we explained to Mr. Jarvis, we are investigating the events leading up to the catastrophic fire that took place at the Red River Club last evening. Today is August the first. Mr. Jarvis, are you willing to answer our questions pertaining to the events that took place last night?

**JARVIS:** Yeah. Whatever. [scraping noises] Why are y'all talkin' to me here? I didn't do nothin'.

**SANCHEZ:** We are just asking questions about the fire. We wanted to talk to you while the memories are fresh.

**JARVIS:** [long silence] Okay. [short silence] Do I need a lawyer?

**SANCHEZ:** That's entirely up to you, Mr. Jarvis.

**JARVIS:** [long silence] Nah. I'm good.

**SANCHEZ:** For the record, Mr. Jarvis, will you please state your full name and occupation.

**JARVIS:** Harold Chester Jarvis. Musician.

**WHITE:** By musician, do you mean you play guitar for the band Hell's Archangels?

**JARVIS:** Bass.

**WHITE:** Pardon me?

**JARVIS:** Bass. I'm the bass man. I play bass guitar. Four string, five string.

**WHITE:** I see. [scratching noise—pen on paper] Bass guitar for…

**SANCHEZ:** Is that what you were doing at the club last night?

**JARVIS:** [long silence]

**SANCHEZ:** Mr. Jarvis?

**JARVIS:** No. I was scratchin' the drummer's balls. [short silence; choking sound in background] Of course I was playing. It's what I do. I—play—bass s—gui—tar—in—the—band. Was that slow enough for you? Did you get it all that time?

**SANCHEZ:** Watch the attitude. We just want to know what happened last night.

**JARVIS:** [long silence] Sorry. Still tryin' to sort it out. Pain drugs don't help. Don't know what they're givin' me, but I hope I can have some t'go when I leave here. [short silence] What happened last night. Good question. Wish I had a good answer. We were just playin'. It was the last set. And, suddenly, all hell broke loose. [short silence] Not sure what I saw. I just know it scared the livin' shit outta me. [long silence] I don't *want* to remember.

**SANCHEZ:** How about when you first got to the club: did you notice anything unusual?

**JARVIS:** Unusual?

**SANCHEZ:** Something that didn't belong. A piece of equipment. A box.

**WHITE:** Or, a person.

**JARVIS:** No. [long pause] No, I can't think of nothin'. Everything happened later.

**SANCHEZ:** Walk us through it, from the time you got there until…

**JARVIS:** Until all hell broke loose? [long silence] Can I have some ice water or somethin'? My throat's all messed up from all the smoke an' shit.

**SANCHEZ:** Sergeant White?

**WHITE:** [scraping of chair] I'm on it. You want a Coke or somethin'? Coffee, maybe?

**JARVIS:** Coke's good. Anything t'kill th' taste.

**SANCHEZ:** Check at the nursing station, first. Make sure it's okay.

**JARVIS:** Oh, hell! That smoke! I was breathin' people! Dying, burning people! I—I'm gonna puke.

**WHITE:** I'll get the nurse. Be right back.

**SANCHEZ:** I think I'll shut this off.

**[LOUD CLICK]**

**[LOUD CLICK]**

**SANCHEZ:** We are resuming the interview of Mr. Harold Jarvis. Present also are Sergeant White and myself, Lieutenant Sanchez.

**FEMALE VOICE:** Don't overdo it, Lieutenant. He's got some serious burns on his hands and arms. He needs time to rest. To recover. Mr. Jarvis, just press that red button with the back of your hand if you need me.

**JARVIS:** Yes, thank you, Nurse. [short silence] [sound of footsteps and a door closing] [a cough] Sorry 'bout that. I tried to hold it in, but the thought of all those people…

**SANCHEZ:** That's all right. I don't think you're the first person to throw up in a hospital room. You were about to tell us what happened when you arrived at the Red River Lounge.

**JARVIS:** Yeah, well, it was a first for me. Thanks for the Coke. It was just what I needed. A beer would've been better, but I guess they frown on that kind of shit here, don't they? Anyway, Tommy drove his pickup…

**WHITE:** Tommy? That's Thomas Martin, right?

**JARVIS:** Yeah. Second guitar. We used his truck to haul the mike stands and cables and big shit. None o' the electric stuff, though, in case it rained. That shit went in the van. Gizzo and Tommy worked together, rode together; got drunk together…hell, I think they even got laid together.

**WHITE:** Gizzo?

**JARVIS:** Gizzo. Eddie Gutierrez. Sound guy. Ran the boards, did the sound checks, hooked up the recording gear. Did he…

**SANCHEZ:** I don't think so.

**JARVIS:** How many survivors were there?

**WHITE:** Just one, so far. You.

**JARVIS:** That's some cold shit, man, tellin' me like that.

**WHITE:** Sorry. I didn't mean…

**SANCHEZ:** What the sergeant means is we're trying to understand it—to come to grips with this thing. It's all so…

**JARVIS:** Yeah, I can dig it. It's big. Too fucking big. [long silence] Anyway, like I said, Gizzo and Tommy were in the pickup. Me an' Candi—Candi Bahr, our singer—we were in the van with the others. She's weird, but she's got some pipes. I swear she's got a five octave range.

**SANCHEZ:** That's Candice Bahr, correct?

**JARVIS:** Yeah.

**WHITE:** In what way was Candice weird?

**JARVIS:** I don't know. Just weird. She has all these books in her apartment. Always going on about magic and crossin' th' planes an' callin' up shit. None of it makes sense. She has this one book called *The Necronomicon*. I tried to tell her it wasn't a *real* magic book—that it was made up shit based on stories that guy Lovecraft wrote—but she wasn't havin' none of it. She got mad and kicked me out. Sometimes I think she's trippin', y'know? Doin' drugs or somethin'. But, so far as I know she never had none and wouldn't hang if we talked about just doin' a little weed. 'Course, it was always just talk.

**SANCHEZ:** Relax. This is Austin, not Cedar Park. What other kind of books did she have?

**JARVIS:** Strange books. Magic and stuff. I remember one, it was called *The Lesser Key of Solomon,* I think. She says she can summon demons with it. 'Course, it's all bullshit. I mean, how real can it be? The book's a goddamned paperback, for Christ's sake. But, that's Candi. All I cared about was hangin' out with her an' tryin' t'get in her pants. She's got a sweet ass and a rack that could…

**SANCHEZ:** We get the picture, Mr. Jarvis.

**JARVIS:** Yeah, right. Sorry about that.

**WHITE:** Who else was in the van?

**JARVIS:** There was the drummer, Dave Paul. He was in the back. Mark the Roadie—that's what we all called him. Never did know his last name. He's a friend of Candi's. He always hangs out an' helps load the equipment. Not the brightest light in the room, but he's all right. Once he learned how we all like our gear set up, we never had to worry about it again. When he was done the stage was perfect. Willie Wolfe—the Wolfman—he plays lead guitar. He was riding with us. Oh, and Guy. I think his car was in the shop or somethin'.

**WHITE:** Guy?

**JARVIS:** Wilson. Guy Wilson. Our manager and publicist. He booked all our gigs.

**WHITE:** Okay. [scratching sound] Guy Wilson. Got it. You were saying?

**JARVIS:** We got there early 'cause we had an exclusive. Don't know how he did it 'cause Red River usually runs three, four bands a night.

**SANCHEZ:** Exclusive?

**JARVIS:** Most clubs in Austin book three or four sets a night with a different band playing each set. Even label bands only get a couple sets. But, an exclusive—where one band plays every show—that, like, never happens. And, with it bein' biker week and all, an exclusive's nearly impossible for an indie. And, on an outdoor stage, too? I'd have said impossible 'til last night.

**SANCHEZ:** How do you think…Guy…managed it?

**JARVIS:** No clue. I asked, but he just grinned an' said, "I got pull, m'man. That's all you need t'know. I got pull"

**SANCHEZ:** Might be something to look into, Sergeant.

**WHITE:** Can't ask the owner. He didn't make it, but I'll get Forensics to look into it when Arson releases the scene. Not sure if there's anything left to find, though. The whole place was destroyed in the fire. [scratching noises]

**SANCHEZ:** You got there early…

**JARVIS:** Mark had picked up my new box an' I was anxious to try it out.

**WHITE:** Box?

**JARVIS:** Amplifier.

**SANCHEZ:** You had a new amplifier?

**JARVIS:** Yeah.

**SANCHEZ:** Isn't that kind of strange? Bringing an untried piece of equipment into a show? How did you know even know it would work?

**JARVIS:** Mark said it worked fine when he checked it at the shop an' I trust him. He never makes mistakes about equipment. 'Sides, I didn't really have a choice. It was either trust the new one or rent a used one. Renting's an even bigger risk. I blew the horn in my old one the night before during practice. Fifteen inch woofer, cone shredded like a cheap tissue tryin' to stop an uber sneeze. I seen 'em blow before, but never like that.

**WHITE:** What do you think caused it?

**JARVIS:** Dunno. I wasn't even powerin' an open E. Only had it cranked to three, maybe four. I go higher on an outdoor stage. When you guys let me, that is.

**SANCHEZ:** We don't have anything to do with sound enforcement.

**JARVIS:** Whatever. Anyway, Mark set it up. I plugged in an' started to set it up. Mark stopped me an' says it's already dialed. I just had to turn it on and adjust my axe to the amp.

**WHITE:** Was that normal?

**JARVIS:** Kinda. I mean, sometimes we did it that way; sometimes I adjusted everything myself. Six o' one an' toss a coin. So, anyway, I told him since it was new I wanted to check everything myself. He understood. I jacked in an' turned it on. The head lit right up and the pre-amp was right there. I turned a couple of knobs and played a few riffs. Man, it was so sweet. I mean, the notes were like magic. Everything—every string—seemed alive, especially the firsts.

**SANCHEZ:** Firsts?

**JARVIS:** Sorry. My term. First octave—all the notes below the fifth fret. Any time I played a first this greenish glow came out of the bottom—from under the subwoofer.

**SANCHEZ:** I thought subwoofers were on stereos.

**JARVIS:** Yeah, it's normally just a part of the brain—the pre-amp. That's what makes this special. A separate subwoofer on the bottom of the cabinet and a new board—some kind of kick-ass solid state chips or somethin'. I'm not up on all that electronic shit. I just know that when the box glowed green, the music seemed t'wrap itself around you like your mama's arms and work its way into your head. It was freakin' awesome. I never felt nothin' like that before. I don't know if either of you plays, but if y'do and need somethin' fixed, take it to Austin Music Remakes. Andy Sharp. If he can't fix it, it can't be fixed.

**WHITE:** Did he make your new amp?

**JARVIS:** Yeah. It wasn't cheap, but it was worth it. [long pause] Damn!

**SANCHEZ:** What's wrong?

**JARVIS:** Stupid.

**SANCHEZ:** Excuse me?

**JARVIS:** Not you, me. I'm the stupid one.

**WHITE:** What do you mean?

**JARVIS:** I didn't take the freakin' insurance. Son of a bitch. On top of everything else, I'm out forty-eight hundred bucks worth of amp.

**SANCHEZ:** Sorry about your loss. There was a lot of loss tonight.

**JARVIS:** Yeah, you're right. I know it makes me look like a shit with all those people killed an' all, but that's a lot o' money to someone who only sees a coupla hundred bucks in a good week. If I didn't have my daytime job…

**SANCHEZ:** So, you tried out your amp and it sounded great. What about the green light?

**JARVIS:** I dunno. Some kinda special effect, I guess. I once had a Fender Rumble **100** that flashed red light out of the bottom whenever you played. Kept rhythm with you. It was cheesy, but kinda cool, too. At least, that's what I thought when I was warmin' up, doin' a sound check. Not so sure, now.

**SANCHEZ:** What do you mean?

**JARVIS:** [long silence] The first set started at eight. About five 'til we was all in the back room getting ready to go on. Candi was dancin' from one foot to the other like she had to pee. Willie was pickin' on that old plastic kids' guitar he always brings with him. Says it calms him down before the shows. Gives him luck. Dave an' Tommy were drinkin'. I was adjustin' my earplugs.

**WHITE:** Earplugs?

**JARVIS:** Yeah. Th' way we set up I'm next to th' drums and in front of my amp and Tommy's stack. If I don't use plugs, I go deaf real fast. Kinda brings my music career to a halt, y'know?

**WHITE:** Doesn't that make it hard to hear what everyone else is doing?

**JARVIS:** Nah, just deadens the noise a little. Makes it easier to pick out Candi's voice for the chord changes.

**WHITE:** Did anyone else wear earplugs?

**JARVIS:** [short silence] No, I don't think so. Pretty sure I was the only one.

**SANCHEZ:** So, you were all getting ready…

**JARVIS:** Yeah. [long silence] It was almost time to go on. We were all doin' our own thing. Suddenly, Candi turns an' looks at me an' says, "You know today's loonahd, don't you?" I just nodded. I didn't have a clue what she meant. She was always comin' up with weird shit like that, but I wasn't gonna get her pissed just before a show. I figured I'd just nod an' agree an' it would all be cool.

**SANCHEZ:** Was it?

**JARVIS:** Kinda. She didn't get pissed or nothin'. Just a little frustrated cuz she made a kinda growlin' noise an' went an' grabbed a pencil and a piece of paper off of a table. She wrote a word in big letters and held it up to me. "Lughnasadh," she says an' she shakes the paper at me. "Tomorrow is August first. That makes midnight the start of Lughnasadh. We gotta do my special song just before midnight."

**SANCHEZ:** Special song?

**JARVIS:** Coupla nights last winter when I was tryin' to score an' thought I had a chance, me an' Candi wrote this song. It was okay. I mean, it had some good riffs and runs an' the vocals were pretty solid. We did it in rehearsal lots of times, but never for a show. It was really heavy. I mean, lots of first octave notes, vibrate your feet, subsonic shit. Th' chorus sounded more like a chant than a song. Like a funeral or somethin'. That's metal, though. When it ain't screamin' angry in your face, it's like some Satanic church kinda shit.

**SANCHEZ:** Did you? Agree to play the song, I mean?

**JARVIS:** I thought about it. Then I figured by midnight everyone in the audience would be either too drunk or stoned to care, so why not? I talked to the others an' they were cool with it. Then, it was time for us to go on stage an' play. The crowd was kinda light, maybe fifteen or twenty, but it was early. Mostly we got walkers.

**WHITE:** Walkers?

**JARVIS:** People who walk in, listen for a coupla minutes, an' then walk on to another venue to see what's shakin' there. It happens mostly in the early shows. Most are checkin' things t'see if they wanna pay a cover t'listen to what you're playin'. That's why no one likes to go on early—especially the first show. We play a mix of covers an' originals in the first two shows. Anyway, we had lots of walkers, but by th' end of th' set there were still maybe twenty bodies sittin' at the tables. Might've been the same inside the bar, but we couldn't tell from the stage. So we finished an' headed backstage for a half hour break.

**SANCHEZ:** What time was that?

**JARVIS:** Huh? About nine-twenty, I think. We ran a little long cuz th' crowd was really diggin' *Nightcrawlin' Nightmare.* It's one of our originals an' it's really creepy. By the time we were done an' my open E was ridin' the sustain an' the distortion was doin' a fadin' growl, half the crowd was pressed against the front of the stage.

**SANCHEZ:** Didn't that worry you? With the crowd up close like that?

**JARVIS:** Worried? About that? It's the kinda thing you *want* to happen. It's why you stand up there. It's what feeds you, what keeps you going night after night after night. Anyway, we finished an' headed backstage. Candi went lookin' for Mark. They talked for a minute, then he nods an' takes off. I started to go after him cuz he's supposed to check the stage for the next show but Candi grabs me by the arm an' says, "He'll be right back. He's getting something from my apartment. He won't be long. No one broke any strings or nothin' so it'll be okay." I started to argue, but she stood on tiptoe an' gave me a little kiss. Between her lips on mine and those tits pushin' against my chest, I didn't have no argument left inside me.

[unidentified chuckle]

**JARVIS:** I can't help it. She has that effect on me. 'Course it was a quick kiss, just long enough to distract me—no tongue or nothin'—and not long enough to give me ideas. Then she was gone an' we were all laughin' and talkin' about this song an' that one an' did you see the crowd when we started *Highballin'*? An' how about that chick showin' her tits when Willie started those hammer ons? An' it's only the first show an' tonight's gonna be awesome an' I hope Gizzo got it all! An' then it was quarter to nine and time to go out on stage again. We were just takin' our places when I see Mark headin' through the crowd toward the back. He holds up this square black box with gold trim an' Candi flashes him two thumbs up an' then Willie starts the intro riff an' it's time to jam.

[long silence]

[sniffling sounds]

**JARVIS:** They're really gone, ain't they?

**SANCHEZ:** I'm afraid so.

[long silence]

[crying noises]

**JARVIS:** This is hard, man. I don't know if I can do it [more sniffling noises].

**WHITE:** Take your time.

**SANCHEZ:** Do you want to stop for a bit?

**JARVIS:** Yes. No. No, keep it running. Let's get this shit done an' over with.

**SANCHEZ:** Are you sure?

**JARVIS:** Hell! I ain't sure of nothin' right now. Just keep it going.

**WHITE:** So, you started the second set…

**JARVIS:** Second set. Yeah. It wasn't till we were about halfway through that I realized somethin' wasn't right.

**WHITE:** What do you mean?

**JARVIS:** [short pause] I'm not sure. It's not somethin' I can explain easy. [short pause] At first I just thought we were cookin' really good. I could see the crowd getting into it. More were comin' in and no one was leavin'. Crowdin' the stage. In the back I could see people dancin' an' that was cool. Up close, though, there was somethin' goin' on in their faces. Every time I hit a first or played in the first, the amp would pulse this greenish light an' I could see them pressin' closer. There was a kind of meanness in their eyes, like they wanted to hurt someone. If I didn't know better, I'd think my amp was doin' it. But, that's just crazy, y'know?

**SANCHEZ:** Were you starting to worry?

**JARVIS:** I dunno. I wasn't scared, yet, but I was headed there.

**SANCHEZ:** So, what then? The second set came to a close?

**JARVIS:** Not exactly. During the last song things seemed to lighten up. By the time we finished, I was startin' to believe I imagined it. I mean, in spite o' what all those uptight conservatives think, heavy metal ain't gonna make people hurt each other. That's just someone lookin' to shift the blame off themselves. Relax. I ain't climbin' on no soap box. I could talk for hours about that shit, but I won't.

**BACK TO THE STORY:** the music wound down and the crowd cheered and whistled and clapped and we headed backstage.

**WHITE:** What time was this break?

**JARVIS:** I think it was around eleven, yeah, the next show didn't start until eleven-thirty, so that's probably right.

**WHITE:** Okay, so you were backstage.

**JARVIS:** Yeah, and it was really weird. There was none of the excitement like after the first show. It was like everyone was tense, keyed up, ready to go out there again, but not to play music. It felt more like, I don't know, maybe like a locker room at half time. Like we were getting ready to go into battle or somethin'. Mark stuck his head in to let us know the stage was set an' I thought Candi was gonna bite his head off. "Where's my box?" she screams at him. Mark's eyes go wide but he doesn't say nothin', he just points at a table. There it sits, plain as day. She doesn't say thank you or nothin', just goes over and snatches the box off the table. Now, I wasn't tryin' to be nosy or anything, but the dressing room's kinda small an' tight with five or seven people in it. It's hard not t'see what's going on around you. Candi opens the box and inside are these two bracelets—I think they're called slave bracelets. Whoever owned these wasn't no slave, I guarantee.

**WHITE:** What do you mean?

**JARVIS:** First off, they were gold, that buttery color like you see on TV or in the movies. They looked heavy and expensive—probably worth more than all our equipment and trucks put together. They had cuffs that went around the arm—narrow on the sides and flattened on top. The flat part had things like leaves and stuff carved in. In the middle was a big black crystal. I ain't no jeweler, but I don't think they were glass. They might have been diamonds, but if they were I ain't never seen black diamonds before. Two gold chains about two inches long came off of the oval part. There was some kind of flowery design in the middle of each chain. They came together in a round, flat setting that sat on the back of the hand with another of those black stones on it. Another chain—like the other two—ended in a gold ring with another black crystal.

**SANCHEZ:** What makes you think they might be diamonds? Did Candi say they were?

**JARVIS:** Couple of things. One, she told me about those bracelets once before, although she never showed them to me. Said she inherited them from her grandmother. Second, you don't mount glass or cheap crystals on gold that fine. You just don't do it, man.

**SANCHEZ:** I guess that makes sense. [scratching noise] Did she put them on?

**JARVIS:** Not right away. First she just looked at them, kinda held them up to the light. I looked around 'cause it got quiet. All the others were watchin' her and starin' at those bracelets. Then I noticed their lips were movin', but I couldn't hear what they were sayin'. Hers were movin', too. Since I was closest to her I could hear somethin', but I couldn't make out what it was. Then I realized I still had my earplugs in. When I reached up to take them out she kinda snapped outta her trance or whatever it was an' laid one of the bracelets back in the box. She slipped the ring over her left finger and then worked the cuff over her wrist. It looked a bit snug, but not enough to bother her. She flexed her hand a couple of times and then put the right one on, too. I have to admit, they looked real good on her. The way I feel about her, though, she could make a plastic Cracker Jack ring look like fine jewelry.

**WHITE:** So what happened after she put the bracelets on?

**JARVIS:** Nothin'. It was time to go out for the third set. I reminded everyone we were doing Candi's song, but nobody said much. They all seemed to have somethin' on their minds.

**WHITE:** What do you mean?

**JARVIS:** They were just quiet. [pause] I know! It was like it was our first show ever an' everyone's thinkin' about the music an' all an' prayin' we don't fuck up and get booed off the stage. It felt kinda like that.

**WHITE:** Tense.

**JARVIS:** Yeah. Tense. Exactly. And then we were on stage and pluggin' in and turnin' shit on. I turned around and looked at the audience and, for just a second or two I thought I was in the wrong place.

**SANCHEZ:** Why was that?

**JARVIS:** The crowd. It wasn't normal. Usually by third set they're screamin' and yellin' 'cause they're all drunk or stoned and wanna hear more music—more *live* music—'cause this is Austin and live music is what we do best. Not this crowd, though. They were all sittin' at the tables or lining the stage or leanin' against the back fence. They wasn't makin' no noise at all—just lookin' up at us and waitin' for us to start. I'm tellin' you, it was fuckin' creepy. Sorry 'bout that, but it was. Dave starts his eight bar intro on the block and the crowd starts makin' noise and I relax and start playin'. It's all good in the hood, as they say, and I'm feelin' righteous 'cause my fingers are flyin'. The strings are hummin'. We're makin' music and nothin', not nothin' at all can go wrong. The first three songs are done. Everyone is hollerin' and dancin' and cheerin'. Part of me is worryin' about the noise patrol and part of me doesn't give a shit 'cause it's time for Candi's song. I start the intro, a solo in the first octave, a tribal rhythm repeating: B—A—G—E—B—A –G—E. It's slow, at first, but it gets a little faster and a little faster. After twelve bars the drums pick it up. Four bars later the guitars come in. Stage lights go down and a spot comes up on Candi standing center stage. She slowly raises her arms to the sky and as she does, the baby spot blows up showering the stage with white sparks. That wasn't supposed to happen, but I don't have time to worry about it 'cause I see the stones on Candi's bracelets are starting to glow a kind of neon green. There's another green light comin' out of my amp and it's reaching out to her like a foggy snake. I see it wrapping around her and she's glowing all green. Her head is bent back until I think it's gonna touch her spine and she's sayin' words an' makin' sounds I never heard before—not from her, not from any human mouth. And, she's got the rhythm and I'm playin' the rhythm and Dave's poundin' the rhythm and the guitars are screamin' the rhythm. The more I play, the longer the notes last. They just—keep –on—stretching.

**SANCHEZ:** Slow down.

**JARVIS:** You don't understand. It keeps going and going. And then it starts getting louder and softer and pulsing. That's when I realize *I CAN'T STOP PLAYING!*

**WHITE:** What do you mean, you can't stop playing?

**JARVIS:** My hand is dancing on the neck by the head and my fingers are flyin' over the pickups and the strings are a blur. I tried to pull them away, but they just keep going. It's like they belong to someone else!

**SANCHEZ:** I've never heard of anything like that before.

**JARVIS:** Me neither. I looked out at the audience and there's green lightning dancing from the stage, from the bracelets and my amp. It jumps to people's heads, then from their hands up to the lights. Bulbs start shatterin' as it leaps back to the stage. My amp is pulsing brighter and brighter. I finally yank my hands from the strings. I'm not strummin' any more, but the amp keeps pulsing and the sound keeps growing and the strings keep blurring. Suddenly, the light is reaching up and I follow it with my eyes. It strikes a mass of black boiling clouds. Green light splashes underneath and they are scarier and uglier than any tornado I ever saw.

**SANCHEZ:** There was no storm last night.

**JARVIS:** Maybe not where you were…over the Red River Lounge it was lookin' like we were all headin' for Oz. I look at Candi. She's looking back at me. Her body is twitching and jerking like she's having a fit only she's standing up. Electricity arcs from her wrists to the mike stands. Willie's on his knees. Green lightning dances over him from his amp. It arcs to the stage from his guitar head and his hair is smoking. I look at Dave. He's slumped over his stool and the sticks are on the floor. His high hat and snare are fused together and the bass is egg-shaped. The cymbals—the China and sizzle and rides—are all melting and drooping in the dancing green fire—*BUT HIS DRUMS ARE STILL CARRYIN' THE BEAT!* I look at Candi, again, and her eyes are wide in terror. I know she never expected any of this. I don't know what she *was* lookin' for with all that lunagob bullshit, but this wasn't it.

[long silence]

**WHITE:** Jarvis? You all right?

**JARVIS:** Oh, shit. Oh, fuck me running.

**WHITE:** What's wrong?

**JARVIS:** There's—there's this popping sound. [sobbing sounds—Jarvis?] Her eyes…her eyes…

**WHITE:** What about her eyes?

**JARVIS:** They're gone, man. There's just two holes in her face. There's goo running down her cheeks and smoke coming out of the holes in her face.

**SANCHEZ:** They exploded.

**JARVIS:** I can smell burning pork and singed hair and shit and puke and piss. From the stage I can see people on the ground and they're floppin' like fish in the bottom of a boat. Their hair is smoking and their clothes are burning. I look up and I'm staring at the clouds, again. They're moving faster and getting darker. I see them opening up and there are faces looking down. Horrible, evil shapes leer and grin and laugh, their open mouths full of sharp teeth and split tongues. I do the only thing I can think of without thinking of it. I raise my guitar and bring the butt of it smashing into my brand new custom amp like John Entwistle of The Who.

The world explodes in front of me. The green glow is gone. I hear heavy thuds as something falls on the stage. The air's full of high-pitched shrieks and voices screaming. I smell ozone and feel white heat racing over me. My clothes catch fire. I smell my hair burning. I force myself to drop my bass and fall to the ground. I look up at a sky full of angry clouds colored like an old bruise, but there's something I don't see, and I feel better. If I die now, I did it doing something right no matter that I didn't know what I was doing. The sky's no longer split. There's a feeling of rage and frustration pressing and pushing down on me from somewhere that tells me I somehow got it right.

[long silence]

I woke up an ambulance with strangers pokin' at me. They brought me here and bandaged me up, some. They say I got some burns, but not enough to be put in a burn unit. Mostly blisters and stuff from my clothes catching on fire. My hands got it the worst, but the docs say after I get a couple of grafts and some therapy I'll be able to play, again. [short pause] Not sure I want to. No, after last night I might not ever pick up another bass.

[short silence]

And now I'm here. With strangers pokin' at me in a different way. Are we done?

[long silence]

**SANCHEZ:** I think so. For now, at least. We may have more to ask you later.

**JARVIS:** I'm not going anywhere.

[loud click]

**INVESTIGATOR'S ADDENDUM**

Despite precautions, Mr. Harold Jarvis managed to take his own life by slitting his throat. He was not facing charges, therefore, he was not restrained or under guard. As this recording is the only statement obtained from any witness (there were no other survivors of the Red River Lounge catastrophe) it must stand as the official account of what transpired despite the hysterical outburst near the end. The arson investigation revealed that the cause of the fire was a massive electrical surge or discharge estimated to be equivalent to several bolts of lightning striking simultaneously and igniting everything. Since this was an "open air" venue (e.g., there were ample exits and means of egress) it remains a mystery as to why no one simply left the club or outdoor area. As there is no evidence of arson or any other criminal activity or malfeasance, this case is declared an accident and no further investigation is warranted..

# 2012 WORLD EVENTS

**The discovery of a missing Mayan calendar piece disproves 2012 Armageddon**

**153 people are killed and 1300 injured in Tabriz and Ahar, Iran after two earthquakes of up to 6.4 magnitude**

**314 people are killed in factory fire in Karachi and Lahore, Pakistan—survivors claim KUKA industrial robot arm started glowing green before starting a killing rampage**

# White Veins

### by Mallory Makepeace

*"A good book is the precious life-blood of a master spirit..."*

*— John Milton*

**TRANSCRIPT**
**GALADRIEL THE TECH ED'S BLOG**

Wednesday, Jan. 12, 2013
AATK

Hey guys. Welcome to my new blog. This is my very first post so please bear with me. I figure I'll be covering the highlights of my day job on this site. Please feel free to subscribe if you like what you read. And tell your friends!

So, I'm an Editor.

Actually I'm an Associate Editor, the distinction being that I do all the real work in my day job office in terms of proofreading and prepping documents for publication. The irony is that you'll most likely find my name at the very bottom of that pile of boring publisher information on the inside front covers of the periodicals I edited.

I sit in front of an overly large computer monitor, atop a rather powerful CPU, within a cramped cubicle, inside a dull white three story building on the outskirts of western New Jersey. The town I work in isn't much to see. Just one more isolated industrial park born of multiple companies fleeing oppressive taxes, obnoxious citizens, and the mob's influence in New York City.

Suffice it to say that my company's new out-of-the-way accommodations were not much of an improvement.

I plowed through the latest downloads and rubbed my blurry eyes all morning. For all the benefits of desktop publishing, staring at a computer screen nine hours a day can frazzle even a Vulcan's nerves. Not to mention the fact that we just switched to a new publisher software. EDIT-PRO may be the wave of the future with its ability to tag everything in existence and later display it in HTML and PDF on the web, but it sure is one hell of an eyesore for a simple editor like me. And don't get me started on navigating through that damn data-map!

Today I chain-chugged Irish Cream flavored coffee and typed frantically. My QC date is the middle of next week, which means I have eight more papers to edit and mail out by Friday. Looks like the authors will have to get their galley proofs back to me within 72 hours. Talk about down to the wire. Take my advice. If you want to be an editor, never ever take a job proofreading engineering society journals. It will kill your will to live.

Noticed something weird not long after I got my replacement Unix computer today.

At first I squinted and focused but could not see anything untoward on my screen. The afterimage, however, faded quickly and I was left with the fragmentary picture of white lines in my mind.

I shook my head and got back to updating some figure captions. Another brilliant author had capped every damn word. HUA. I wonder if there are countries where editorial assassination of idiot authors is legal.

The rest of the day stretched out like a broken escalator. ADIH GTG.


## GALADRIEL THE TECH ED'S BLOG

Thursday, Jan. 13, 2013

WTF. It happened again. I finished up on the author affiliations in the first footnote and rubbed my eyes a couple of times. I know you're supposed to make your eyes blink five to six times a minute when working on a computer but it just never became second nature to me.

Before lunch I blinked and a split second before I focused I saw the picture again! Only this time I remember more of it. White lines. No. Little white channels or rivers.

I deliberately unfocussed my pupils when my Managing Editor popped up and gave me the evil eye. She'd made it clear in the morning that if I didn't get the last of these papers out by tomorrow, I could come in on the weekend and finish them at my leisure. KMRIA! No overtime of course. Editors have exempt tax status in this "nonprofit" company. Just lovely.

I doubled my efforts and tried not to think about the long term effects of carpal tunnel syndrome as my hands started to cramp….

## GALADRIEL THE TECH ED'S BLOG

Friday, Jan. 14, 2013

Rather than heading out to lunch today I decided to munch on a homemade sandwich and surf the web. I do this once or twice a week as a change of pace. I found it a little hard to concentrate. I've been having some bad headaches this past week, not to mention I didn't get all that much sleep last night. I had this strange unsettling dream about white string. Reams and reams of it unspooling everywhere. Weird.

I found a web page for the daily news and skimmed it half-heartedly. Nothing particularly interesting today. I yawned and blinked my eyes a few times. That's when it happened.

This time I didn't lose it.

Just as my eyes unfocussed, but not so much that I got that double-vision effect when you cross your eyes, I saw them again. The white lines. I am now aware of exactly what I saw. The spaces between text. The white space that is nothing but white space. I focused and unfocussed my eyes several times to duplicate the effect. By slightly unfocussing your eyes, all the text in front of you melts together, and the white space takes shape.

Rivulets of white spaghetti.

But there is something else. Something about the scattered pattern of white space lines that still bothers me as I type this up.

Hmph. I must really be tired to spend my time weirding out on computer screen white face.

I'm feeling so wasted. Gonna crash.

GNSD

## GALADRIEL THE TECH ED'S BLOG

Monday, Jan. 17, 2013

Things started happening this weekend. Strange things.

I keep having that weird dream about white string or white twine unspooling everywhere, or at least that's all I remember when I wake up in a pool of sweat breathing like I've just run a race. My wife, that's right I'm gay folks, get over it, is getting worried about me. She thinks I'm working too hard. She's right about that, but I think this string thing is something else entirely.

I also notice something else about myself. Every time I pass by an open book or magazine or newspaper, I have an almost uncontrollable urge to unfocus my eyes and look at the patterns of white space between words. I got through most of this weekend resisting the funny desire, but once or twice

I imagined the odd page or paragraph calling out to me, wanting to tell me some secret. WITFITS. I figure it is the lack of sleep.

## GALADRIEL THE TECH ED'S BLOG

Friday, Jan. 21, 2013

WAFM. It is getting worse. I find my eyes going out of focus whenever I read text! This is making my work nearly impossible. I drank at least a dozen large mugs of coffee a day this week at work but it doesn't help. My managing editor is complaining on a daily basis that I'm falling behind schedule for the upcoming print run. BMOTA.

And the dreams...oh God the dreams. They are so vivid now, and I know I am dreaming from the second I fall asleep at night until the moment I wake up. White strings, white roads, white rivers, white cobwebs! In my dreams I swim in an ocean of barbed white vines that are trying to suck the life from me. ATAB.

My manager poked her head around the corner a dozen times today. Several times I bit my lower lip until I tasted blood. The pain helped me to refocus my eyes. I found if I give it 100% concentration, I can keep the image on my computer screen clear.

Lord what is wrong with me!? SOMY?

## GALADRIEL THE TECH ED'S BLOG

Monday, Jan. 24, 2013
SSDD

I feel like garbage today. But even so, I've been noticing things lately. A lot of things. I find when I'm not checking out text somewhere, that everything else is of extreme interest to me. And it all seems tied together. The expressions on people's faces. The gait in their walk. The traffic patterns in my morning commute. The slant of the average news story on TV. The path of a single snowflake falling through the air. The manner in which neighborhood dogs tend to congregate now and huddle together. The image of large flocks of birds flying north instead of south. The patterns of clouds in the sky. Triple yolks in most of my breakfast eggs.

There is a feeling to all of it. A sense of disquiet. Even lethargy. Everyone and everything seems to be slowing down. Just a little. Relaxing. Just a little.

## GALADRIEL THE TECH ED'S BLOG

Thurs. Jan. 27, 2013
SUAC

I'm really beginning to see patterns in all of it now. Why everything is happening the way it is. I fixate on TV news reports of unrest in foreign countries. Economies are collapsing in many third world nations. Stories of citizens going berserk in killing rampages are growing more and more common. TMI…

And nobody else seems to be bothered by this! The newspaper stands are more popular than ever these days. And when I look into the faces of the other customers I see a deadness in their eyes. What they read fascinates them, but it also seems to drain them. It's the white space between the lines. It's everywhere…and it's affecting everyone.

## GALADRIEL THE TECH ED'S BLOG

Tuesday, Feb. 1, 2013
UCWAP

Jane just left to spend a couple of weeks with her mother. She said her mom is getting old and she wants to visit her more often. Jane is lying. She's leaving because of me.

I am so frazzled that I yell at her at the drop of a hat these days. The two of us have not made love in almost three weeks. Jane wants me to see a psychiatrist but I refuse. Whatever is happening to me, I know it's not natural. It's not something a doctor could diagnose. I just tell her it's pressure from work. She drives away with tears spilling down her face.

I look into the bathroom mirror and I don't recognize myself. The wavy blonde hair is still there. The blue eyes. The pale skin. But now I'm gaunt. I rarely eat. And there are age lines around my eyes and mouth I never noticed before. And my eyes are so very bloodshot.

The house feels like a prison.

I'm surrounded by overcrowded bookshelves and stacks of newspapers waiting to be recycled. Words. Thousands and thousands of words, all calling out to me.

I crank the TV volume up to full blast.

The mind-numbing succession of images and sound is the only thing that keeps the white space at bay. I hope I fall asleep soon. WWJD?

## GALADRIEL THE TECH ED'S BLOG

Wednesday, Feb. 16, 2013
YGM

They're alive. I can tell that now. The white tunnels within all written and printed words. When they think you are not watching they shift and move. And not just that! Something moves within them. Something ethereal and fluidic flows through them like trains of glowing silver white gelatin. I feel...I feel like there is something larger here...


## GALADRIEL THE TECH ED'S BLOG

Monday, Feb. 21, 2013
ONID

I got fired today. I barely heard the boss's words as they left her mouth. She went on and on about my appearance. How it smelled like I haven't showered or put on clean clothes in over a week, that I am obviously sick and need help and would I please just call the company psych hotline for some help. Seems my severance package includes 20 free visits to a shrink. I just nodded my head and stared at the stack of periodicals on the shelf behind her. Why couldn't she see that the words in them are alive?


## GALADRIEL THE TECH ED'S BLOG

Wednesday, March 9, 2013
MEGO
LONH

I gather my strength. Every day I skim all the news stories off the web. I watch CNN all the time now. I am in touch with everything everywhere. The white space calls out to me constantly, awake or asleep, and every second of every day I fight its narcotic appeal. I eat food that no longer has flavor. I make my plans. I gather my strength.


## GALADRIEL THE TECH ED'S BLOG

Wednesday, April 13, 2013

It comes to me in my dreams. It speaks to me. It tells me I am nobody. I am nothing. I am an insect. I am a fool to resist.

I smile an evil smile.
I am almost ready.

## GALADRIEL THE TECH ED'S BLOG

Monday, May 1, 2013
RTH
RKBA
MFIC

Losing consciousness… reciting into my pocket recorder…

I had no trouble getting in through the front doors. Security always was a joke. I just stayed close to one woman who keyed herself in with her e-card and grabbed the door before it closed behind her.

I used the eight-shot pump-action shotgun I inherited when my father died of a heart attack six years ago. I had stuffed all the pockets of my down jacket with extra shells earlier.

I managed to destroy 30 desktop computers and kill 25 associate editors, eight secretaries, five managers, two visiting VIPs from Barnes and Noble, and a vending machine repairman before the S.W.A.T. Team brought me down in a hail of bullets.

I sang The Beatles "All My Loving" while I… I think I'm passing out.

## GALADRIEL THE TECH ED'S BLOG

Saturday, Dec. 17, 2013
IGYHTBT

By some miracle I lived. They told me I was in surgery for almost a full day. Punctured liver. Pierced intestines. Collapsed lung. Fractured collar bone. Right kneecap shattered. Eight broken ribs. Emergency hysterectomy. Over half of my blood volume lost. The index and middle finger of my left hand were sheared clean off. The cops said they couldn't find the missing digits. Good thing I am ambidextrous. The doctors dug fifteen bullets out of my flesh. The lead slug in my skull and the one next to my spine cannot be touched for fear of paralyzing or killing me.

The healing process was a snap. You see, I was in a coma for over five months. I woke up two weeks ago. Since then I've been continuing my blog… writing it on toilet paper and keeping it from prying eyes…

Scarred muscles and a braced knee keep me in physical therapy three hours a day. I'm told I can expect to go to trial in a matter of weeks.

I have different ideas.

You see, I wasn't unconscious in my coma. I was aware and thinking and dreaming. At first I was just floating in a chaos of sound and light.

Soon, though, I fought for control, and won it. Even in my coma it managed to reach me. I cowered and tried to hide but after awhile I saw this was not possible. And finally I confronted my fears and saw the face of my tormentor. And in doing so, I was reborn.

A Daemon exists in all text. Words are its skin. Its body. Its membrane.

The spaces between words are its circulatory system, its arteries, its veins. White veins. Its blood is the stuff of our imagination, our thoughts, the pictures in our minds that the words evoke. Humanity feeds its insatiable hunger. It is killing us. It wants to devour the world.

It is Draal-Nakk…The Enticer.

It is everywhere. Every computer screen. Every newspaper. Every print ad. Every page of every book ever written and printed. Every magazine article. The face of every clock and wristwatch.

It came into existence when caveman first dragged charcoal across cave wall. It grew in might as cuneiform clay tablets dried near tended fires. It lay dormant during the Middle Ages. It had a rebirth with the construction of the first printing press. And now, its supremacy is near at hand.

It knows I'm aware of its existence so I don't have much time.

I've got another psychiatric review in two weeks and I'm pretty sure I can pass it. The voice of The Enticer, while it still sings in my bones, no longer frightens me. To get this far is to be immune to its madness. I exercise in the dark and I am much stronger than they think. I play the nervous, soft spoken woman well. If I time it right, I know I can escape when their guard is down.

You see, I've got a plan.

You meet a lot of interesting people in a state institution for the criminally insane. And I've learned a great deal about the manufacture of homemade incendiaries. You'd be surprised what you can do with a little gasoline and some fertilizer.

I'm going to burn and destroy all publishing houses everywhere. It's brilliant isn't it? For they are the Temples of Draal Nakk. Editors and Proofreaders are his High Priests and acolytes and so must also be destroyed. Only the purification of fire will cleanse our planet of Draal Nakk's insidious grasp. I am going to save the world.

It's not going to be easy. I'll be on the run from the law. Every day will be a struggle to avoid imprisonment and even death. But I know I can do it.

I leave this journal with some of my fellow patients who respect my visions. They will share it with the right people. Do not fear the face of Draal Nakk in my writings. I have transcribed my original blog and subsequent observations in my blood. You are reading the gospel of my own flesh. The demon cannot manifest itself within living words.

My dreams tell me I will not always be alone in my holy war. One day, others will share my vision and join me in my struggle.

Perhaps you are one of them.

Do you read a lot?

Have you rubbed your eyes lately?

# 2013 WORLD EVENTS

The brains of two rats have been successfully connected so that they share information

Asteroid 2013 ET comes within 960,000 meters of the Earth's surface

North Korea declares it is at a state of war with South Korea

193 people are killed and 11,826 are injured after a magnitude 7.0 earthquake strikes Lushan County, China

256 people are killed and 1,000 are injured after a building collapses Savar Upazila, Bangladesh—disaster blamed on crazed janitor who insisted his 3-D television was filled with green ghosts who were torturing his family

# The Day The Sky Fell

by Jeff Barnes

**For immediate release**—FAA Administrator Robert Sturgell announced operations with the new Automatic Dependent Surveillance-Broadcast, or ADS-B, in the Gulf of Mexico commenced today.

The ADS-B is one of the FAA's NextGen new generation of systems that are designed to improve the safety, efficiency, and capacity of U.S. airspace. ADS-B enables aircraft equipped with the system to report their positions to each other and the ground using GPS information. This is an important advance in the Gulf where no radar coverage is available.

ADS-B data is transmitted to air traffic control and displayed on radar screens along with the aircraft in areas where normal radar coverage is available. ADS-B also enables direct transmission of data from the ground to the cockpit.

ADS-B is based on the original Capstone system tested in Alaska with great success. The program is in the process of expanding across the U.S. In addition to improving air traffic control services in areas without radar coverage, ADS-B will also save millions of dollars of fuel costs each year by enabling more efficient and economical routing of aircraft in the National Airspace System.

For more information visit http://www.faa.gov/news/fact_sheets/news_story.cfm?newsId=7131 or contact the FAA Office of Communications at 202-555-7699

**FAA System Maintenance Activities Log October 9, 2013—Kate Akers, ATSS, Gulf Coast SSC**

**Technician Log. 1635 UTC. Completed preventive maintenance on GPT RCO. Replaced secondary coupler between antenna and backup microwave**

**transmitter due to corrosion. No further maintenance required. Enroute to Pascagoula to inspect RCAG/RCO tower and antennae.**

"We have breaking news. We have confirmed reports that an AeroCaribe 737 with approximately 130 people on board has apparently crashed into the Castner Gold oil production platform in the Gulf of Mexico. We have no details regarding survivors at this time. Sources report the platform is on fire; however, it is too early to tell whether this has caused an oil leak. We will keep you updated as we learn more."


**Technician Log. 1750 UTC. Received call from SOCC after arrival at Pascagoula. Logged onto RMMS and brought up GOMEX Ground Station monitor. Heat sensors in alarm in ADS-B rack. Data flow monitor indicating flow from Comm operating far beyond expected failure parameters. Diverting to GOMEX to investigate anomalous readings.**

Interview Transcript of Katherine Akers by Team MEANGREEN Psychiatrist Patricia Dietrich:

**DIETRICH:** Good morning Ms. Akers, I'm Patricia Dietrich. You can call me Trish or Dietrich, whatever you're most comfortable with.

**AKERS:** What are we here for Patricia?

**DIETRICH:** We want to hear your experience directly.

**AKERS:** You keep saying "we."

**DIETRICH:** Come on Ms. Akers, at any point have you thought that mirror was there to enable you to touch up your makeup during interviews? My colleagues are in there observing and recording this.

**AKERS:** Your colleagues. And who do you work for again?

*OBSERVATION: DIETRICH PULLS SEVERAL ID CARDS FROM HER COAT POCKET AND TOSSES THEM ON THE TABLE. AKERS SHUFFLES THROUGH THEM THEN SHOVES THEM BACK ACROSS THE TABLE. DIETRICH GATHERS THEM, RETURNS THEM TO HER POCKET, AND WAITS FOR AKERS.*

**AKERS:** CIA, FBI, GSA, and NASA? Who are you?

**DIETRICH:** They all agree that I'm Patricia Dietrich. I'm a government employee, just like you Ms. Akers. I am a psychiatrist and counseling psychologist, but my primary interest lies in research.

**AKERS:** Yet another head-shrinker, here to tell me everything is okay and I'll be right as rain before I know it.

**DIETRICH:** Ms. Akers, I don't intend to tell you any such thing. I'm here to listen to your story. I'll watch you tell it. If you need any help getting through it, I'll do so if I am able. Afterward I will leave, meet with my team, and write a report. I doubt you will ever see me again, and I am sure that I will not be making any kind of commitment of healing to you. Tell me your story so we can both be about our business.

**AKERS:** Wow. Honesty. That's kind of refreshing. Okay, call me Kate. Let me lay out a nice big bowl of nuts for you.

**DIETRICH:** I want you to feel free to express yourself however you think best. Openness will help us understand what you experienced that day.

**AKERS:** It feels like I've had to tell the story and answer questions so many times there would be a pile of paper a foot high if they bothered to print it out. I'm really tired of this. Just charge me, fire me, or lock me away in a nut house and quit wasting my time and yours.

**DIETRICH:** I'm not here to do any of those things. I want the story, in your words, beginning to end. It may be annoying to you to do this again, but it's important to us. If it helps, pretend that I already believe you and want to hear it from your mouth to capture detail that might have been otherwise missed. I imagine you're angry, and maybe even a bit scared. That's understandable considering what you've been through, but I'm not here to do anything but listen. Humor me, please.

**AKERS:** Humor? Unfortunate choice of words there.

*OBSERVATION: AKERS PAUSES FOR A TIME. SHE APPEARS TO BE LOST IN THOUGHT BEFORE SHE MAKES HER DECISION.*

**AKERS:** Okay, fine. Once more, but this is it outside a courtroom. One more shrink or investigator or priest shows up and asks me to tell this I am going to lose it and give you people something to really put me in jail for.

**DIETRICH:** I'll do my best to see that you don't have to go through this again. Now, from the notes taken by the original counselor I see that when you arrived at the, uh, GOMEX site, what you saw there was unlike anything you would have expected to see. Could you tell me what the GOMEX site is?

**AKERS:** Okay. The GOMEX site is…uh, were… a pair of buildings in Southern Mississippi. One of them had power systems that conditioned and monitored the commercial power that came to the site. It also had battery backup systems and a diesel generator that automatically kicked in if a loss of commercial power was detected. The second housed several different ground-based systems that dealt with air traffic flying over the Gulf of Mexico. Mostly backup communications and routing systems, but it was also where the ADS-B ground station equipment was that covered the Gulf of Mexico.

**DIETRICH:** Okay, good start. Let me know if you need a break.

**AKERS:** Goody, we can order out some Chinese and call it our first date.

**DIETRICH:** When you arrived at the site, what did you see?

**AKERS:** I saw a green glow. It was steady. There was no flickering like you would expect to see from a fire.

**DIETRICH:** Where was the glow coming from?

**AKERS:** From the systems building. The power building looked normal.

**DIETRICH:** What did you do first, Kate?

**AKERS:** I tried to call the SOCC, but couldn't establish a cell connection. I tried to log into the RMMS, but the computer was down and wouldn't reboot.

**DIETRICH:** What are the SOCC and the, uh, RMMS?

**AKERS:** Why didn't they provide you with a list of acronyms? The SOCC is the Southern Operations Control Center. They are the ones who first got an alarm from the ADS-B and called me about it. The RMMS is the Remote Maintenance Monitoring System. It's a laptop I use to log into our equipment to monitor it from wherever I happen to be. After the SOCC called me, I used my RMMS to log into the GOMEX ADS-B. That's when I saw the alarm and the crazy data readings for myself.

**Technician Log. 1815 UTC. On arrival at GOMEX Ground Station noted green glow emanating from the building, inconsistent with fire or normal failure state. Unable to establish contact with SOCC or RMMS.**

**DIETRICH:** Then what happened?

**AKERS:** Even though the glow didn't flicker like a fire, I figured the only thing that could be causing it was some kind of chemical burning, so I pulled the chemical extinguisher out of the back of the truck and went to unlock the access gate. As I neared the gate, an arc that looked electric, but was the same green as the building glow, struck the extinguisher and blew it out of my hand. It stung like a mother, but otherwise I was okay. Well, a bit scared and a lot pissed off.

**DIETRICH:** What did you do at that point, Kate?

**AKERS:** I returned to the vehicle and tried to call out. Everything was dead. I pulled out all my powered gear. It was all shot. Like maybe it had been hit by an electromagnetic pulse that had killed all my electronics. But that's just not possible because all the gear in the equipment building had continued to operate as far as I could tell. Something was seriously fucked here and I was going to have to try to fix it on my own.

**DIETRICH:** How were you planning to do that?

**AKERS:** Hell, I don't know. I was just going to have to go inside there and figure something out. The first thing I did was take out my Faraday suit and put it on. If this shit acted like electricity I could hope I'd have some protection in my suit. It's lucky I was out doing tower work so I had packed it along. It's not part of my normal kit. I'd also grabbed a pry bar and my Arkansas Toothpick. I felt better knowing I could cut something if I needed to.

**DIETRICH:** An Arkansas Toothpick?

**AKERS:** It dates back to the Civil War. In the south steel it wasn't unusual for country boys to take a plow blade and work it into a knife about the size of a Bowie. Some past Granddaddy of mine had done that with his father before he left to fight. He came back with it, and it has stayed with an Akers man ever since. It's accompanied them into war every generation since, and every time it's brought them back.

**DIETRICH:** You said Akers men. No offense, but why do you have it?

**AKERS:** I'm the nearest thing to a man left in the Akers family tree, and I went off to war, so it was passed to me. My sisters had no interest in following family tradition. Their loss.

**DIETRICH:** What happened next?

**AKERS:** I squared everything away, stared at that damn gate for a bit, and started walking. I got hit by the arc again, but the suit worked like I had hoped. I got to the gate and took a look at it. There were arcs on the gate and fence; I figured I'd get one shot at getting the lock open. So, I turned around went back to get out of range of the arc and removed the keys I'd need from my ring and left the rest in the truck. Faraday suits aren't a lot of fun to wear—you can get bogged down. I figured less metal, less weight, would be good with energy running through everything over there. Truth be told, I also needed a bit of time to sit down and talk myself into doing this.

*"More breaking news from the Gulf. We have a confirmed report of a mid-air collision between two helicopters over the Gulf of Mexico and an unconfirmed report of a near midair collision between a business jet and a Panamera*

*Airbus. Teams from the Federal Aviation Administration and the National Transportation Safety Board are in route to investigate. Rescue and recovery operations are underway. Coast Guard and Castner Gold disaster response units will reach the offshore platform in the next two hours to begin rescue and recovery as well as try to extinguish the fire and stem any oil leaks associated with this tragedy. Continued overflights have confirmed that there is a leak, but it is too early to tell how bad it is."*

**DIETRICH:** So you rested, finished your prep, and headed back?

**AKERS:** Rested? That's funny. I had to calm down to keep myself from saying "screw this" and just run the fuck away. But yeah, I headed back. When I got to the gate I positioned the key, shoved it into the lock and turned it as fast as I could. Good thing, because that mother spot-welded itself into the lock. But it was open. I yanked the gate and stepped it into the site before I could talk myself out of it. These buildings don't have windows, so there wasn't much for me to see as I got closer to them. The glow I observed from outside was coming from vents and leaking out from the edges of the doorway. Pretty much anywhere there was a gap. There was nothing coming from the power building. I could also hear a hum and occasional sliding thumps coming from the system building. The power building was quiet.

**DIETRICH:** What happened next, Kate?

**AKERS:** I took out the key for the system building and approached the door. As I started to insert the key… something smashed through the door and knocked me down. I gathered my wits and this thing come down on me again. I could feel it exploring, like it was looking for something. I froze when I focused and saw this ugly green tentacle crawling on me. I'd dropped the bar when I was knocked down, so without thinking I whipped out the Toothpick and swiped it across as I rolled out from under that thing. I felt an initial tug followed by very little resistance as I cut that thing in two.

**DIETRICH:** So it was weak?

**AKERS:** Weak? It had just knocked me to the ground and come after me. No, it was strong enough, but it was no match for the Toothpick. The Akers have always respected the Toothpick. It takes care of us, so we take care of it. That knife will cut your eyeball if you look at it edge on. The amazing thing is that there was any resistance at all. That hadn't happened since I've carried it.

**DIETRICH:** What then?

**AKERS:** When I stood up, I got a good look inside the remains of the doorway. It looked like a horror movie snake nest in there, with a noise like a giant's teakettle.

**I'M PASSIONATE ABOUT WHAT I DO. THIS EQUIPMENT KEEPS MILLIONS OF PEOPLE SAFE IN THE AIR, IN AN ENVIRONMENT WHERE THEY HAVE NO CONTROL OVER THEIR SITUATION. I WAS SO PISSED. THIS SINGING TEAKETTLE OF TENTACLE MONSTER WAS FUCKING WITH MY WORLD.**

*OBSERVATION: AKERS HAD BECOME AGITATED AT THIS POINT. SHE TOOK SOME TIME TO DRINK WATER AND COMPOSE HERSELF.*

**DIETRICH:** Are you okay, Kate? Do we want to take a break?

**AKERS:** No, I need to finish this the hell up and not talk about it anymore. Just running through it again makes me want to pull the Toothpick and start… Anyway, three of those arm tentacle things came out at me while I scraped my mouth off the floor. That kicked me into motion, backing away. They had about a twenty foot reach outside the door. With my back against the fence they could just touch me. They flailed at me as best they could, which was pretty good. But because I had the fence behind me they couldn't get me on the ground, and they had just made a huge mistake. I just worked my way back in toward the building, cutting chunks of tentacle off as they whipped at me. Chunks flying, black goo spraying. I guess maybe that was its blood? I don't know. It burned where it reached my skin, but I was pretty well covered by the Faraday suit over my work get-up.

Whenever new ones came out I backed up to the fence and started in again, slicing and dicing. It was hotter than hell, and I was covered head to toe in metal and black goo, so I wondered if I would be able to outlast the tentacles. Finally there were no new ones as I whittled my way to within a few feet of the doorway. I was so tired I just put my hands on my knees and panted.

**DIETRICH:** You had defeated the tentacles?

**AKERS:** I wish. Something heavy—really heavy–crashed down on my head, my back and drove me face first into the ground. I may have lost consciousness for a moment or two. When my brain was working again I found I couldn't breathe any more than small sips of air due to the weight on my back. My cheek was ground down into the gravel; I was completely pinned on one side. Through a gap between my pinned head and partially free arm I could see the Toothpick, out of reach.

**DIETRICH:** And how did you deal with that?

**AKERS:** Part of me wanted to give up, cry, and die. But I've dealt with that before, and I used it to push me on. I was suffocating slowly, but because I could get sips of air it would take a while for me to pass out as long as I kept fighting to get that air. I felt around with my partially free arm until I found a solid object at the end of my reach, the pry bar. I strained, and got my hand around it and was able to swing it around to the tentacle.

**DIETRICH:** So you were able to pry it off you with the bar?

**AKERS:** Nope. It didn't do shit. I couldn't get any leverage or force with it. I straightened my arm back out and fought to breathe.

**DIETRICH:** Well, we know you made it. How did it happen?

**AKERS:** I was concentrating on breathing, which was becoming more difficult, when I realized I was holding the bar about a third of the way up from the base. I could see the Toothpick and there was a good chance I could reach it with the bar, I inched the bar out toward the toothpick. When it was almost touching I had to pick the full weight of the bar up with only my wrist to lay it carefully on the Toothpick. I screamed as I got it off the ground and onto the Toothpick. The scream helped concentrate my strength, but it hurt my breathing situation. I saw spots in the edges of my vision as I pulled the bar with the Toothpick under it, ever so carefully back toward me. When it was close enough to actually grasp, I felt lightheaded with relief. With oxygen deprivation, as well, I suppose. I gripped the Toothpick so hard I felt knuckles pop. I was not dropping it again as long as I had life left to fight with. I stabbed into the big tentacle with what strength I could muster. For the toothpick, it was enough. It cut into the tentacle with ease, causing it to spasm, which allowed me to get my first real breath of air.

It nearly knocked me out again when it came back down on me. I guess the thing was so big and heavy it couldn't do much more than that because from then on I just had to cut at it like a butcher until I could roll out from under and suck down air.

At first, I just lay there, breathing, watching the doorway and that big ass tentacle for signs of movement, ready to cut if I had to. Now that I was out from under it I could see the last tentacle looked like the others, but it was about four feet in diameter, extending out about ten feet from the door. I stood up and walked around it. The end looked partially formed, like it had just stopped without coming to a tip or any kind of useful ending. I guess it was just there to body slam people like me.

"We have confirmation of our previous reports of the ongoing aircraft incidents. Government sources tell us that the intelligence community has not identified who or what is responsible for these incidents, but lack any conclusive evidence to link it to terrorist activity. Air Force and Navy fighters are patrolling the Gulf and escorting all aircraft to Gulf Coast airports. We were able to talk briefly with the pilot of a small aircraft who was rescued from ditching at sea. He is telling us that his plane went into an uncontrolled dive after a green glow engulfed his control panel. He believes his airplane's emergency parachute system saved his life. We hope to speak with him live during tonight's broadcast, after he is treated and questioned by authorities."

**DIETRICH:** You'd beaten it?

**AKERS:** Yeah, I guess so. I finished cutting the big one in two just to be sure. But I wasn't done yet. That green glow was still coming from the building. As I moved around the doorway and looked in I could see the source was the ADS-B rack, but there wasn't enough light in there to see details. I took a few deep breaths…by the way, did I mention that black goo smells even worse than you think it would? I had to continually fight against coughing because of the irritation. Anyway, I was wishing I'd stayed in bed. Hell, I was wishing I'd stayed in the Army. But I had no choice; I had to go in and finish the job. Getting to the front of the rack was a nightmare, like walking amongst big, slick, rubber hoses that would break your ankle with a single misstep. Any time I felt a twitch, I swung the Toothpick until I felt safe again.

**DIETRICH:** What was at the front of the rack?

**AKERS:** I noticed that the girth of those tentacles diminished as I moved toward the back of the building where I could see the glow coming from the ADS-B rack. As I got close enough to the rack to pick up details I saw that the tentacles had wormed out of the processor box in the ADS-B rack. They were coming from inside, starting out like flat worms then inflating into the monstrosities I'd fought to get here.

**DIETRICH:** So the tentacles originated from the box?

**AKERS:** Yes.

**DIETRICH:** But they were dead at this point?

**AKERS:** I gave that box a close shave. That took the tentacles out of the picture, but still left me standing in front of a glowing green module. The monitor on the rack was still showing massive outflows of data. That shouldn't have been able to happen. Impossible, like tentacle monsters and that kind of shit, right?

**DIETRICH:** Was the green glow a fire in the rack?

**AKERS:** I didn't know yet, so I pulled the box out of the rack. The FAA builds its equipment into nice neat rack mounted boxes. You just pop out the module and slide a new one in. This box resisted, but I gave a good hard yank and it slid free. Turned out all the crap growing in it had got in the way, but I had yanked hard enough to get past it. When the module fully cleared the rack, the green glow from inside lit up the building completely. I reached around the back of the module and disconnected all the cables. Disconnected THE CABLES. That should have solved the problem. No connection, no operation…right? But when I looked at the monitor I didn't even see a hitch in the data flow. Somehow this thing had hijacked the ADS-B and did not need a physical connection to maintain control.

**DIETRICH:** How is that possible, Kate?

**AKERS:** Have you been listening to anything I have been telling you? If any of this is possible, why not that? What the fuck?

**DIETRICH:** Okay, okay. What was your next move?

**AKERS:** Well, pulling the module hadn't done it, so I decided to see if the light was coming from anywhere in particular in the box. I hacked all the crap out of there until I could see the circuit boards. The glow was coming from a single chip. It was the digital signal processor. It looked similar to other DSPs I had seen in ADS-Bs, but something other than the green glow didn't look right. I pulled the module completely free of the rack, took it outside and set it on the ground. I went back in and got the axe out of the fire cabinet. I took it outside and set out to hack the thing into pieces.

**DIETRICH:** What happened?

**AKERS:** See this nice scar on my forehead? The axe head bounced like it hit a force field and nearly knocked me cold. I saw stars in front of my eyes, like on cartoons.

**DIETRICH:** What did you do next?

**AKERS:** I thought that maybe instead of applying a force that would seat a chip more firmly into its socket, I should try to pull it away from the board instead.

**DIETRICH:** How did you do that?

**AKERS:** Normally I'd use a chip pulling tool, no problem. There was no normal here, so I turned to my most useful tool of the day, my Toothpick. I got the tip under the edge of the chip, started wiggling it, and saw a bit of movement.

**DIETRICH:** The Toothpick worked?

**AKERS:** Yeah. It worked, but it took a while. It felt like the thing was resisting, but didn't have nearly as much resistance to force pushing it away.

**DIETRICH:** So you got it off the board?

**AKERS:** I must have.

**Technician Log. 2050 UTC. Attempt to investigate and repair the problem resulted in catastrophic destruction of GOMEX site. Personnel injuries have been logged and reported as required. Log closed.**

**DIETRICH:** What do you mean, Kate?

**AKERS:** Well, when it got to the point I could detach it I slid the blade in and heaved. I meant to hurl that thing as far away from me as I could. I really let loose. That's the last thing I remember before I woke up in intensive care.

*"The Federal Aviation Administration is reporting that U. S. airspace is being reopened in the Gulf of Mexico. There are still restrictions on flights in the Gulf area as rescue operations wind down and disaster relief efforts continue. Petro International is denying any responsibility for the accident on their Castner Gold production platform, but has announced that it is teaming with AeroCaribe to lead the cleanup. Both companies have expressed regret and sorrow for the loss of life in the accident. The overall estimated death toll is 178, though we may never know the exact figure. The Department of Homeland Security is leading the investigation with assistance from the FAA, the National Transportation Safety Board, and the Department of Transportation. No cause for the events has been pinpointed, although some surviving flight crews are claiming a complete loss of control of their aircraft. They claim a green glow emanated from their control panels as the autopilot systems took over and locked out manual control. Administration officials say that investigators will identify what happened and bring any parties responsible for it to justice. Sources tell us that around the time of the Gulf catastrophe, an FAA ground system that is used by aircraft over the Gulf of Mexico was destroyed in an explosion. It is too early to tell if it was related to the catastrophe in the Gulf, but the timing of it is suspect."*

**DIETRICH:** What do you think happened?

**AKERS:** I think, as soon as that thing was unable to do whatever it was doing, it self-destructed and leveled the site. They found me a hundred feet away, very messed up, well on the way to dying. Thank God the EMT crew were military veterans. They kept me going until they could get me to a trauma center.

**DIETRICH:** How badly were you injured?

**AKERS:** Read the doctors' reports.

**DIETRICH:** You've been told there was no substantive evidence recovered from the site?

**AKERS:** Yeah, and I don't give a shit. I also heard that the Toothpick was recovered, somewhat worse for wear. I want my knife. Whose ass do I need to kick to get it back?

**DIETRICH:** Ease up, Kate. It may take some time, but I am sure you will get the knife back. At the moment it's material evidence.

**AKERS:** Well aware, Doc. The FBI has not been shy about telling me how many years I will spend in Leavenworth for what I've supposedly done. Screw them. What happened, happened. I'm not going to tell the story they want to hear to make life more comfortable for them. I'm through with this bullshit. If you're going to lock me up, get on with it. I thought the FAA had more than its share of bureaucratic asshats. Turns out I was wrong by an order of magnitude.

**DIETRICH:** I think you'll find that things will move more quickly now Kate. I don't know in what direction, but you won't be in limbo much longer.

**AKERS:** I'll believe it when I see it. In the meantime, I was dead serious. I'm done talking about this to just anyone who asks. I need to be done with it. I want to stop thinking about it.

**DIETRICH:** I will do what I can to comply with your wishes Kate, but there are no absolutes in this life.

**AKERS:** Whatever. Give me my knife. I'm going to have to spend some serious forge time giving it the love and attention it deserves.

**DIETRICH:** Forge time?

**AKERS:** I guess I never mentioned it before, but all the Akers have cared for the Toothpick ourselves, including forge work. I can remake it as long as more than a sliver is left. It's not just an heirloom, it's our family totem and partner.

**DIETRICH:** Interesting. Thank you for your time, Kate.

## TOP SECRET

### CASE NUMBER 1247-14AD(P)

Team MEANGREEN Investigation Report on Gulf of Mexico Event

Executive Summary

The suspected MEANGREEN event that took place in the Gulf of Mexico on October 9, 2013 is detailed in the attached maintenance log and interview transcript with Federal Aviation Administration Airway Transportation System Specialist (Electronics Technician) Katherine Akers. For detail of the event refer to attachments.

The FAA Technician, Katherine "Kate" Akers, is an Army veteran. She served one tour in Afghanistan as a Blackhawk helicopter pilot supporting Special Forces operations. She was decorated several times for her service in that conflict (detailed service records available on request). When her enlistment ended she flew helicopters under several contracts. When she was presented the opportunity to work for the FAA she took it, stating that having a regular paycheck would enable her to pursue interests, instead of her next dollar. Akers has maintained her rotary wing currency, and also has Instrument Flight Rules, multi-engine, and commercial ratings as well. She has been debriefed and is currently undergoing rehabilitation in the West Virginia special recovery facility. The prognosis is very good and she is expected to be fit for return to normal activity within six to eight months.

Unnamed terrorists will be blamed for the event with some leaks pointing toward Islamist terrorists. Suspicion of planning and support from new and unidentified subversive sources will be leaked. There will be no link found between the ADS-B ground station, the aircraft accidents, and the platform fire and spill. Officially, the investigation has found that there was no link between the ground station failure and the Gulf of Mexico events.

The site of the ground station has been excavated and is housed in the secured containment and research facility. Research of the recovered material has not resulted in any new data. The exception is the events described by Akers in her log and interviews. While anecdotal, there is high confidence in the accuracy of Akers' statements. The knife is also in the research facility. Testing has shown the knife is completely normal.

The circumstances Akers described are consistent with known events involving SiGeBoron computer chips. There are unsubstantiated rumors of involvement with other supernatural events. Investigation continues.

Recommendation—Recruit Kate Akers to join Team MEANGREEN. She has proven very able and resourceful and she has direct experience with one of the SiGeBoron chips. This could prove to be invaluable in future encounters. She is single and does not have a close relationship with her sisters. She will need only minor training after her rehabilitation to be physically ready for the assignment. She will require a full briefing to understand the known history of the SiGeBoron chips, our continuing investigations, and our search for the remaining missing pieces. Temporarily reattach her to the FAA to aid an investigation into other FAA systems that could contain the subject CPUs.

Recommendation—Return Akers' knife to her as soon as practical. Psychiatric opinion is that working to repair the blade will help her through the post-traumatic stress and speed her usefulness to the program.

# 2013 WORLD EVENTS

**119 people killed in a poultry farm fire in Jilin Province, China**

**160 people killed by flash floods across Afghanistan and Pakistan**

**325 people killed after migrant ship catches fire and shipwrecks off coast of Lampedusa, Italy—Captain claims strange flashing green light mistaken for lighthouse**

**638 people killed in violent clashes between police and protesters across Egypt**

**515 people killed by a magnitude 7.7 earthquake in Balochistan, Pakistan**

**6,000 people killed after Typhoon Haiyan makes landfall in the Philippines—disastrous Japan Meteorological Agency satellite failure blamed as it burned up upon re-entry in dramatic green fire ball**

# Pierced Through the Head

by Dina Leacock

## ROSEMARY'S BLOG: A BLOODY THORN BY ANY OTHER NAME: JANUARY 1, 2014

It's past New Year's by two minutes and another bleak cycle of the futility of life begins as the old one dies in the agony of failure and pain. I got a new tattoo yesterday. Another bloody rose… this makes the last one I can fit across my forehead without having to shave my hair. I'm going to save that next one for the appropriate holiday, February 14.

## ALEXANDER'S BLOG: FAMILYHISTORIES.COM: JANUARY 1, 2014

Sadly, my Aunt Roza passed away at the stroke of midnight. She crossed over quietly and peacefully. I swear she was looking past us all at someone who was waiting for her because she smiled and said, "After all these years I finally get to see you."

I am sure that she will be missed by someone.

## ROSEMARY'S BLOG: A BLOODY THORN BY ANY OTHER NAME: JANUARY 1, 2014

Strange thing happened tonight. Right after I fell asleep, I woke and there in my room was my great-great Aunt Roza. She was glowing, surrounded by the most magnificent, *coolest* green light and she called to me. "Rosa, my namesake, go now, get what is rightfully yours before the others steal it away from you."

Then she vanished, but the light remained for a few seconds, arcing and sparking out like little emerald electric shocks, pop... pop... pop. I looked at the clock and it was just about half past midnight, a new year, a new message.

Creepy, but Aunt Roza, who was the only relative I ever liked even though she was way scary, was surely dead and was like talking to me from the other side. Wow! Now that is really cool, a portent of good things to come. Finally a spark of light in the bleakness of forever!

## ALEXANDER'S BLOG: FAMILYHISTORIES.COM: JANUARY 1, 2014

Wishing everyone a healthy and Happy New Year. Slept in this morning with all the excitement from last night. Didn't get to bed until after 2:00. Not enough time to get the funeral information to the newspapers so I decided to let everyone know that we will have a service for Great Aunt Roza tomorrow, January 2. Please spread the word if you know anyone who might be interested.

## ROSEMARY'S BLOG: A BLOODY THORN BY ANY OTHER NAME: JANUARY 1, 2014

I thought about going back to sleep after Great-great Aunt Roza's New Year's Eve visit, the wine was giving me an awful headache, but I was just too excited. I jumped out of bed and dressed, thinking about her words. *What was rightfully mine.* Something in that creepy, old house full of things from Russia was rightfully mine! Maybe the nesting dolls she used to let me play with or the painted glass eggs, maybe the samovar, and most of all hopefully the knives.

I remember how she used to sit me on her lap and then distract me from touching her long white chin whiskers by letting me hold one bladed weapon after the other. "This one," she said holding a dirk with a dull, worn handle, "this belonged to an imperial guard of the czar. He courted me until I stabbed him with it. And this one," she'd said in her thick accent, "this one was used to stab Rasputin. See, his blood is still on it. Oh, don't cry darling, he isn't dead, only waiting for me and the others."

What was rightfully mine, I wondered and walked the mile to her place. The weapons? The dolls? I wanted the dolls, but imagine owning a century-old dirk used to stab someone as infamous as the Mad Monk. Could anything be more romantic, more thrilling?

When I got to the house the coroner's car was pulling away and Great Uncle Alexander was locking the door. As soon as he got into his car and drove away, I went up to the house, and somehow I just knew where to find Aunt Roza's hidden key: it was in the mouth of the stone demon guarding the porch. I reached in, terrified it would clamp down on my hand and drag me to hell. It didn't, so I unlocked the door and went inside.

The house was empty, really empty and smelled of death and something else. Yes, I know I am being melodramatic, but breaking into a dead person's house as the New Year is being born is very dramatic and I was scared. But I had been invited, so I wasn't leaving until I found what was rightfully mine.

I had my backpack strapped on in case I needed to hide whatever I took and I slowly lifted item after item feeling the weight, the shape, hoping for a sign. The nesting dolls I'd played with as a child felt like so much dead weight, as did the glass and crystal eggs. I went to the dirks and frowned. Rasputin's black handled death blade was gone. All the others were there, but not the one I wanted. I frowned and called. "What is rightfully mine?"

The silence of the dead was heavy and I suddenly started feeling foolish. Had the old woman visited me or had it been the bottle of wine I drank earlier?

Going to the liquor cabinet, I found a dusty carafe of sherry and a bottle of really thick wine. I decided on the sherry although normally I never touch the stuff. I took a long swig from the bottle then shoved the rest of it in my pack. On second thought I pulled it out and kept it close at hand, drinking as I wandered the house. I grabbed a few items, hoping I had found what was rightfully mine, figuring that I could sell them if they weren't. As I got to Great-great Aunt Roza's bedroom, the sour smell of death and old lady hung in the air. I sniffed, then entered, wrinkling my nose with disgust.

Her bed was mussed, the shape of her body still impressed on the sheets and mattress. Even her pillow was dented with the imprint of her head. I felt her presence then, and shuddered.

A green glow on her dresser top! I could see her jewelry box, an ornate gold rectangle covered with what appeared to be shiny glass jewels. It was garish and I was sure pretty worthless. "The box?" I shouted. "The cheap crappy box is my birthright?"

I swear I could hear her chuckle. I realized it wasn't the box glowing but the bottom of it. I opened the lid and found it full of stuff: necklaces and bracelets and earrings. I had no idea what was supposed to be so important, but as I sifted through the junk I noticed that there was a fake bottom to the inside of the box and the glow was strongest aroound the edges. I pried it open and saw two pairs of earrings. Oh, they were beautiful, black faceted diamonds set in gold. One set was like a caret each and set as studs. The other set, man, were they something. Dangles with lots of gold in ornate filigree with smaller black stones set in a pattern throughout.

I touched them and I felt, like, a cosmic nod of approval. Rightfully mine, I had found what I now knew was rightfully mine. I picked them up and I swear a zing of energy surged through me starting in my hand and shooting down to my toes and up to the top of my head.

"Holy shit!" I yelped and jumped back. After a minute when nothing else happened, I touched them again and the green light faded away. I studied what I knew was rightfully mine and smiled. "Thank you, Aunt Roza," I called to the empty room. Then I shoved the earrings into my jeans pockets and headed downstairs, suddenly afraid that someone would catch me and take my beautiful new jewelry. As I headed for the door, I stopped by the dirks again and grabbed the one my aunt had used to stab that imperial guard. Then I went out the front door and locked it before running home. All in all, an interesting New Year's Eve.

### ALEXANDER'S BLOG: FAMILYHISTORIES.COM: JANUARY 2, 2014

Great Aunt Roza will be cremated today. Guess she wanted to get back to hell a little faster. As per her wishes, I, as executor of her estate, will take her ashes back home to St. Petersburg where she can be scattered in the forest she believed her godfather Rasputin's ashes were strewn all those decades ago. The story goes he was murdered, burned and his remains scattered in a display of fear and contempt. Aunt Roza had insisted that those same woods of her childhood hid the lost, rotting remains of Nicolas and family as well as most of the jewels of the murdered Romanovs.

Well, maybe now she can ask them where they hid everything. As she always reminded me, "Alexi, our family is destined for great things if we choose the correct side. The jewels will guide you, if you let them."

Somehow, although I believe she was totally crazy, I think there was a glimmer of reality in her ramblings. Ah well, guess we'll never know because, not only is the old girl dead and gone, so are the two pairs of the Romanov black diamond earrings from the hidden compartment of her jewel box.

### ROSEMARY'S BLOG: A BLOODY THORN BY ANY OTHER NAME: JANUARY 2, 2014

They burnt up poor Aunt Roza, toasted her until she was nothing but bits of bone teeth and ash. Gross, but I bet the old girl wanted it that way. Great Uncle Alex is such a wuss, he'd never do anything like that on his own. The man is a complete pussy! It seems Aunt Roza didn't have any friends, or had outlived them all, because the only ones at the memorial service were Great Uncle Alex, his mouse of a wife, one of their two kids, those two people I don't speak with anymore, you know, my Mom and Dad and, oh yeah, my sister and brother and of course me. So sad, to have so few to care. But the number of mourners isn't what matters, no, it is having someone to love and I know she must have loved me very much to have given me those earrings. I gave the black diamond studs to my friend Jude and he's going to fix one so I can wear it through my tongue. He's going to keep the gold post and back for his trouble and put in a clean, stainless steel post that will be long enough to go all the way through and close securely. Can't wait to get it back.

## ALEXANDER'S BLOG: FAMILYHISTORIES.COM: JANUARY 3, 2014

Damnedest thing happened. I'm not even sure if I should be sharing this. After Aunt Roza died, I don't even understand why, but something compelled me to swipe the Rasputin blade. I never cared about it, but I think I'd always been fascinated by it. Just imagine the blood of a madman on the blade for nearly a century. I know, it is probably the blood of a skinned rabbit, but what if it really was the weapon used to kill Rasputin?

Anyway. I took it home and forgot about it, well, pretended to forget about it. I know this is really going to sound silly, but it kept calling to me. I must have checked the drawer it was in a hundred times. The more I checked on it, the more I wanted to handle it, and the more repelled I was. Repelled and drawn. It was like staring at a bloody car wreck: your better judgment wants you to turn from it but the other part of you, the part you try to keep hidden away, makes you watch every gory second.

After we came home from the service, and just as an aside, how can my niece let her nineteen-year-old daughter cover her forehead with those disgusting tattoos. And all those piercings! Ugh. But back on track, a tall, thin, man wearing a dark coat and hat, knocked on my door, told me some bullshit story about being a trader. Said, he was hoping to get the dirk from Roza, said he thought I might have it now. Said if we'd just close the deal, he'd take the knife and give me one of the missing earrings.

My defenses rose with my hackles and I accused him of stealing the diamond jewelry. He laughed, said he never had to steal; all he did was make a trade. I demanded the other earrings, and he said the thief would give them up when the time came. In the meantime, he'd traded a young man named Jude for the one earring. Wouldn't tell me what he traded for it, but, and I know it's crazy, but at the time it all made sense to me and I wanted to get that dirk out of my home before it drove me completely crazy. Like a man in a trance

I traded with him. Then just like that, he was gone. The death blade was now his problem and I was left holding one gold and black diamond stud earring.

Ten minutes later, he returned, knocked on my door again and when I opened it, he smiled, showing a gold tooth, and said, "Just a word to the wise, my friend, don't keep that earring or the others when you get them, and yes, you will be in possession of three of them. Bury them, because if you don't, I'll be back."

I was shocked. Stunned speechless. I wanted to be angry, furious that this strangest of strangers would dare to threaten me, but… but I inherently knew, God knows how, that this was no threat and he meant me no harm. He'd come back to warn me.

I nodded dumbly and shut the door. When I opened it a second later he had once again vanished into thin air. I think he's right, whoever he was. I've always known Aunt Roza toyed with the darkness, what with her obsession with Rasputin and all that babble about the evil in the house of Romanov. Common sense dictated I sell the jewelry or give it to someone in the family. But something else was telling me that would be a bad thing to do. A very bad thing.

## ROSEMARY'S BLOG: A BLOODY THORN BY ANY OTHER NAME: JANUARY 4, 2014

Got my jewelry back last night, well, at least the tongue bar. Jude did a great job, lengthening the post and fitting a screw-on ball at the bottom. He said he accidently threw out the other earring. Not sure I believe him but I wasn't planning on using it anyway. Still, it was mine and I guess he owes me big time. I'll be sure to collect someday.

I looked in the mirror and I couldn't believe what I saw. With that last tat on my forehead and the gold and black diamond earrings dangling from my lobes and the gold and dark gemstone in my mouth catching the light when I open wide, well, I'm really, really beautiful. Aunt Roza was right, they are rightfully mine. They fit like they were made just for me; well, the tongue bar was, but you know what I mean. The glittering jewelry has added a bit of brightness into my dull, painful excuse of an existence. Life looks a little less futile when my black diamonds catch the light.

I swear I can hear Aunt Roza saying, "Ah, my namesake, my Rose, your life will take on new meaning now. Just wait, wait, just like they wait through the centuries, and soon all will be right with our world."

It seemed a pretty long-winded speech for a dead person to tell me in my head, but I don't care because I don't know how anything could be right with this pathetic world.

## ALEXANDER'S BLOG: FAMILYHISTORIES.COM: JANUARY 4, 2014

I woke up early and went to the drawer where I had stuck the earring. It was just there on a pair of black socks and it looked dull and harmless. The black diamond blended in with the dark fabric and it almost looked like it wasn't there at all. But it's there. I've been aware of it ever since I took it from the stranger. Not like Rasputin's blade, but it's here in my house, nagging at me like the beginning of a dull toothache.

That trader fellow was correct; I will have to get rid of it. Later.

## ROSEMARY'S BLOG: A BLOODY THORN BY ANY OTHER NAME: JANUARY 5, 2014

Oddest freaking thing. I went to bed thinking about Aunt Roza's voice and how it made me feel happy, well, as happy as I can ever feel, and I woke the next day with the worst buzzing in my ears. It hurt so much I spent the day in bed, nursing a bottle of orange-flavored Russian Vodka. After dozing all day and well into the night, the noise, that awful grinding hum, subsided. I continued to drink, just to be on the safe side and around dawn the hum returned but this time I realized it was voices, dozens of voices speaking inside my brain!

## ALEXANDER'S BLOG: FAMILYHISTORIES.COM: JANUARY 5, 2014

Woke early again, got out of bed and checked the drawer. The earring is still there but in the dark room, on those black socks, I could swear that it was giving off a faint green aura. I never really thought of green as an evil color before but I do now. I closed the drawer and went back to sleep. When I woke in the daylight, I looked at the earring again and realized that my eyes must have been playing tricks on me. And yet, yet I wonder.

## ROSEMARY'S BLOG: A BLOODY THORN BY ANY OTHER NAME: JANUARY 6, 2014

The voices are still there and they make me dizzy and I want to puke. I called in sick to work and my ass of a boss told me that either I get in or I'm fired. Seems that I haven't worked since December 30th. The voices seem to be coming together though, telling me the same thing. It seems like they are trying to talk at the same time but as one and they helped me make my decision. They told me to fuck 'em so that's what I told my now ex-boss.

I really hated working anyway so I didn't mind, but I wasn't sure how I'd be able to make the rent on this dump of an apartment. Then the voices soothed me and told me where I could get money. I think I may be crazy because I am hearing voices, but at the same time I think I'm sane because the voices are giving me good advice.

## ALEXANDER'S BLOG: FAMILYHISTORIES.COM: JANUARY 6, 2014

Just finished talking to the police. The cops told me that there are scumbag criminals out there who read the obituaries looking for places to rob. The officers explained that crooks look for old people without immediate family because the homes are unprotected.

Aunt Roza's place was definitely robbed, although it is odd that robbers would lock up again and the place is still neat and untouched except for the missing items.

I went over to check it out, see if there was anything else I could take out. As soon as I got inside I saw the drawer where she kept her rare stamp collection from Czarist Russia. It wasn't closed all the way. I went to it and of course it was empty. Then I noticed that some crystal eggs were gone and the real treasure: the alabaster box trimmed in gold and embossed with the crest of Imperial Russia, the two headed eagle.

Only the best was missing. The thieves really knew what had value and more importantly, where everything was hidden.

## ROSEMARY'S BLOG: A BLOODY THORN BY ANY OTHER NAME: JANUARY 6, 2014

After I finally got out of bed, I walked to Aunt Roza's. I had hoped a long walk in the fresh air would clear the noises from between my ears.

It seemed to. All was quiet, that is, until I got to the old house. First I heard Aunt Roza, although the other voices were still babbling in the background. "Take what I tell you to take and all will be well. You will not ever want."

Cool, I decided. After all, I'm family and have just as much right to take her stuff as anyone else!

"No," she shouted. The noise made me cringe and my eyes tear up. "I am taking my valuables, my things! Not you!"

I have to admit that freaked me out and I suddenly began to worry. Why was she in my head? I also wondered why I didn't wonder about that earlier. And if she really were in my head, who were these other voices and what did they want? I shook my head violently, trying to shake them all loose. I wasn't going to be a slave to a dead person!

The voices somehow heard my thoughts because they answered as one, "A slave? Never, to us! You are one of us now. We are slaves to no one. We only serve the Sha'Daa, as you will, and willingly."

I felt confused. So I just put my brain on autopilot and did as I was told. I took the good stuff, the stamps, the stone box and the other things that I was told to take. Then I left. For a second I considered leaving a cryptic message on the wall, just to mess with stuffy, old Uncle Alex, but the voices forbade it. "Leave all as it was and go. You must never return here."

## ALEXANDER'S BLOG: FAMILYHISTORIES.COM: JANUARY 7, 2014

The theft really has me upset. I feel so exposed now, like I am constantly being watched. Paranoid? You betcha I am. First that warning from the stranger with the gold tooth; now knowing that Aunt Roza's house had been watched: it gave me the creeps. I saw movement in the shadows everywhere I looked. I stuck the earring under the socks but that didn't make me feel any better. As soon as I get the other jewelry back, and somehow I know that I will, just like I'd been told, I'll lock it all away.

## ROSEMARY'S BLOG: A BLOODY THORN BY ANY OTHER NAME: JANUARY 7, 2014

As if things weren't freaky enough yesterday, after I finished taking what I needed from Aunt Roza's place, I cut down the alley by my apartment and a strange man approached me.

The voices stopped with a hiss and for the first time in several days I found real silence.

"I have a trade for you," the man said, and asked for my black diamond earrings.

I opened my mouth to say something, but laughed instead. I couldn't stop; it was as if someone else controlled my vocal cords and mouth. I grabbed at my throat but I couldn't choke off the laughter. The voices were back and they were speaking through me.

The strange man in the long coat and dark hat sighed. "I see I am too late. Well, I have something you want. Give me just one of the earrings and I'll give you this."

It was the black handled dirk. Rasputin's blade. I had wanted it before, but now it seemed that I had to have it or die. Every fiber inside me shivered at the sight of it. "I know you've been watching over it for decades," he said. "It must have driven you crazy to find it had been taken."

I didn't know what he meant, but the others, the voices in my head, understood. I could hear them murmuring. I wanted to shout at him to fuck off and opened my mouth to tell him so. Instead, I reached out my hand for it and said, "A deal, Johnny, and not a good one for you."

Then I laughed again. Who the hell was Johnny, and why did the voices hate him, I wondered. I felt like I was losing all control over everything.

He laughed too. "The earrings. I'll take the one now and worry about the other later."

I removed one of the dangles. I didn't want to, but the voices made me do it. We made the switch.

As he turned to leave, Johnny nodded at the dirk in my hand. "Use it wisely. When the time comes, and it is sharp enough, use it wisely." Then he looked me in the eyes and said, "I'm truly sorry."

I shuddered. Things were happening fast and I was beginning to get really scared.

"Do not worry," the voices reassured me. "You are safe with us now."

And suddenly I wasn't scared anymore.

## ALEXANDER'S BLOG: FAMILYHISTORIES.COM: JANUARY 10, 2014

I put Roza's house on the market yesterday and now I'm done until it sells. Well, almost done. I have an estate appraiser coming out tomorrow, to make an offer. Since Roza's will left nothing to anyone in particular, after the tax vultures get done with the estate, I'll split the money between my children and my niece and of course me. My niece can figure out how to divide her portion between her three children, but if I were her, I'd use Rosemary's share of the money for a good shrink. That girl is carrying Goth to an extreme.

## ROSEMARY'S BLOG: A BLOODY THORN BY ANY OTHER NAME: JANUARY 10, 2014

Wow, the voices talk to me all day long twenty-four seven. At first it was frightening and annoying and well, really creepy. But now, they are just there. They talk in different languages; most of it doesn't make sense. I can't get a good night's sleep because the voices force their way into my dreams. I have pretty much given up talking because I can't get a word in and then when I try to speak, one of the voices comes out of my mouth. I don't understand what is happening to me and I'd be really scared except that the voices are so friendly and comforting. For the first time in my tedious, endlessly lonely existence I and not alone. It is good to finally have real friends.

## ALEXANDER'S BLOG: FAMILYHISTORIES.COM: JANUARY 11, 2014

Dreamt about Roza last night. She told me that I could join her, now that I have the one earring, that one's enough. In the dream the earring began to glow green and float toward me. I don't know what it could possibly mean, but when I woke I stuck that earring in a box of old cufflinks and shoved the box in the back of the drawer. Out of sight, out of mind, and I have always thought that Aunt Roza was out of her mind.

## ROSEMARY'S BLOG: A BLOODY THORN BY ANY OTHER NAME: JANUARY 11, 2014

I couldn't stop thinking about my missing earring, the stud Jude said he lost. The voices kept telling me that he took what was rightfully mine and I need to get it back. I just had to go there and confront him.

Oh my God I can't believe what happened. I look at the blood on my shirt and my jeans and I feel like throwing up again. I know I have nothing left to puke, but my stomach wants to keep trying.

Poor Jude. I didn't mean for it to happen. I never intended to hurt him. I tried to resist but before I realized it, I was at Jude's place. He smiled when he saw me and I knew the voices were wrong. Jude was my friend.

I opened my mouth to say hello but instead the voices spoke for me. "You bastard," they shouted. "You stole from us and we want our diamond back!"

"Hey, Rosie, take it easy."

"It's not me talking," I tried to explain, but the voices roared inside my head and out my mouth. "Shut up!"

I put my fingers in my ears, but it didn't dull the din in my head. I felt like my teeth were being shaken loose.

"Give us the earring!" I growled at Jude. He paled a bit and stammered, "I… I don't have it. I… traded it for some really wicked weed. Hey, I'll split that with you. I've hardly touched it."

He smiled at me then turned to open a drawer. Thank God, he was facing the other way. I don't know how the voices did it, but, before I could react, that old, worn Imperial dirk was in my hand and then it was in Jude's back. Several times. My hand kept stabbing him over and over and I couldn't make it stop. I was crying but they used my mouth to laugh. I finally stopped and stared at all the blood, at the dripping blade, and wondered when I had even picked it up and put it in my backpack.

I turned away from Jude and the babbling didn't stop. I staggered away on wobbly legs, stopping to throw up every couple of yards as they talked among themselves, inside my head.

"Johnny's got it," one voice pronounced.

"Should have made her grab the stash, it could have come in handy," a different voice said.

"What else has Johnny got?" a third voice questioned.

I half listened, realizing that they weren't my friends, my saviors. They were like parasites, getting in through those damned earrings. I had to get rid of them.

I finally got home and sat at the kitchen table. I reached for the dangling earring and my hand balled into a fist and I punched myself in the face.

"Don't," echoed ominously through my brain.

I fingered the dirk's blade and realized it was a worn, thick blade, dulled all the more by the abuse I'd just put it through. I stared out the window and tried to empty my mind. I said, "I'm sorry, please accept me. I won't disappoint you again."

The voices murmured their approval.

I nodded with them, but I struggled to hide my thoughts. I had to do something to shut them up, shut them away. I have Rasputin's death blade in the living room and soon, very soon I'll be free.

## ALEXANDER'S BLOG: FAMILYHISTORIES.COM: JANUARY 13, 2014

Read about the murder of a young guy who lived about 5 blocks from my house. I think I'd seen him around. Dressed Gothy like Rosemary, all covered in tattoos and he had so many piercings on his face I wondered if he could go through a metal detector at the airport. Maybe when I sell Roza's house I'll use my share on a down payment in a nice, safe, gated community away from all the madness in the world.

## ROSEMARY'S BLOG: A BLOODY THORN BY ANY OTHER NAME: JANUARY 13, 2014

I'm weak, the blood loss. My hands are shaking. There was pain, it is not as bad as I expected. But it is getting so much worse as I sit here at the computer. I need to call 911. So much blood. So worth it because it worked. The voices are finally silent, hopefully gone. I am free. I am

## ALEXANDER'S BLOG: FAMILYHISTORIES.COM: JANUARY 14, 2014

Yesterday my poor niece found her daughter in a pool of blood. Somehow the kid was still alive, but she'll be locked away the rest of her life for murder. I wonder why she mutilated herself like that, probably just a crazy girl. But still, she'd been such a cute kid once. Who knew she'd grow up to be a killer? And a thief, because the only good that came out of the entire affair is that I got the stolen earring she'd stuck through her tongue back when she cut it off. I also recovered the earring that was still in the severed ear.

I washed off the blood and put the two earrings with the other one I'd traded for. I searched her entire place but couldn't find the missing dangle. Guess it might turn up. In the meantime, I also found my dirk again and put it and the three earrings where they all will be safe and sound, back in the drawer. They will be just fine there until I get to bury them with Aunt Roza's remains in Russia next summer. Out of sight, out of mind.

# NORTH AMERICAN ENQUIRER

**Special New Year's Eve Edition**

**Psychic Nero Almaz's 2015 Predictions**

**Dalai Lama will announce he is the reincarnation of Elvis Presley**

**A weird luminous plankton will be found in a newly explored portion of the Atlantic Ocean's floor that will not only cure all cancers but also male pattern baldness**

**Pope Francis will announce that women will be accepted into the priesthood, as well as teenagers and hermaphrodites**

**Remains of unknown dinosaur civilization to be found in Hoboken, NJ backyard**

**A mystical cataclysm of mythic proportions will occur at a major annual public event roughly one hundred and ten miles from one of North America's Great Lakes**

# The Return of The Traveling Luminous Museum

by C.J. Henderson and Michael H. Hanson

Statement by: Syracuse, NY, Mayor Mario Bancardi to Detective William Lisanki, Syracuse Police Force, as made on Monday, September 1, 2015, at 09:13 hrs. Interview conducted less than one day after the cataclysmic events at the New York State Fair.

Present: Mayor Mario Bancardi; Detective William Lisanki

**MAYOR BANCARDI:** What? The first time I saw it? Uhhhh ... the morning of the day before, I mean, seven o'clock AM, Saturday morning, ummmmmm ... August thirtieth. The friggin' thing was huge. You could have fit two three-ring circuses in that mother, and then some!

**DETECTIVE LISANKI:** Could you be a little more specific, Mr. Mayor?

**MAYOR BANCARDI:** What'dya want? I'm tellin' ya, it was a giant tent. Looked like old white canvas. Covered not only the interior of the racetrack, but the track itself. Hell, there wasn't even room for the grandstand, which had to be dismantled to accommodate it.

**DETECTIVE LISANKI:** And did Chairman Vale express any second thoughts or worries about this last-minute addition to State Fair programming?

**MAYOR BANCARDI:** Second thoughts? You gotta be kiddin', right? This fuckin' museum pays a hundred thousand dollar retainer—early? In gold coins, Krugerrands for Christ's sake? Who's gonna squawk? Of course, he took it. Have you seen the records for the bandstand proceeds the last ten years of this event? You know the mediocre acts we usually book? Toby Keith, Lynyrd Skynyrd, Carly Rae Jepsen, Korn, Fall Out Boy. What a goddamned joke! Second thoughts. This was pure profit, detective—do you understand? Vale's job revolved around profit. The guy was just doin' his job. That bein' said, though, I'll tell you right now, it's not like I'm tryin' to say there was nothin' weird about the whole thing.

**DETECTIVE LISANKI:** What do you mean?

**MAYOR BANCARDI:** Well, the deal was finalized at sundown on Saturday, August twenty-ninth—right? And the entire tent was up and running by sunup. Vale told me when he got up that morning he didn't see one single worker or truck or nothin' … anywhere. Like somehow some gigantic crew came in after dark, put the whole thing together, and then—boom—somehow just disappears before dawn. Now, tell me that ain't weird.

**DETECTIVE LISANKI:** And what was the name of the organization or holding company that financed this entire endeavor?

**MAYOR BANCARDI:** Pitchman, Inc., a limited liability corporation registered in New Jersey. Just a P.O. Box with no forwarding address, phone number, e-mail address, or website—nothin'. Vale said he only dealt with the museum's docent, some tall guy named Johnny.

**DETECTIVE LISANKI:** No last name?

**MAYOR BANCARDI:** Nope … that's all he said. No last name.

**DETECTIVE LISANKI:** And neither you nor Mr. Vale found this unusual?

**MAYOR BANCARDI:** Ahhh … you know, no … we didn't. Now that you mention it, I guess … fuck, you want the truth, the way this city needs money, we weren't thinkin' about nothin' but cashin' in those coins to make payroll this month.

**DETECTIVE LISANKI:** Very well … so this attraction was a museum of sorts?

**MAYOR BANCARDI:** Yep. And the funniest thing, I swear I can remember my grandfather telling me about a place just like this, as a boy in Jersey. A strange tent museum full of all kinds of odd things. Some of the stuff he described, after a while I just figured it was one of those damn crazy stories old guys tell to impress kids, you know? But damn, the thing was real. I guess … if Vale'd had any idea of what would happen … I mean, sure, he realized like the total extent of the damage at the end, how could you not? But, I mean, the guy had a wife and three kids … man oh man, the millions of dollars in lawsuits that are comin' ... I don't know. I guess he just couldn't deal with it. Swallowed his pistol this morning. Jesus. Left me with this whole damn mess. That fuckin' museum.

**DETECTIVE LISANKI:** And Chairman Vale told you its full title was—

**MAYOR BANCARDI:** The Traveling Luminous Museum. What the hell does that even mean—you know. Poor Vale, like ... may God have mercy on the poor bastard's soul. Fuckin' museum.

**STATEMENT BY:** Piers Knight to Detective William Lisanki, Syracuse Police Force, on Monday, September 1, 2015, at 14:30 hrs.

**PRESENT:** Prof. Piers Knight; Detective William Lisanki

**KNIGHT:** Always a pleasure to make the acquaintance of any officer of the law. What can I do for you, detective?

**DETECTIVE LISANKI:** For the record, your full name is Piers Knight, you are a resident of Brooklyn, New York, and you are here on your own accord to account for your actions on Sunday, August thirty-first, two thousand and fourteen, correct?

**KNIGHT:** Account ... huuummm, dangerous word, that. At the very least it implies a potential impropriety. No, I wouldn't call that correct at all. Let us say I am here to assist the Syracuse Police Department in any way I can in their current investigation.

**DETECTIVE LISANKI:** Cute. One thing. Your boss at the Brooklyn Museum was a little unclear about your, um, station. Says here you are the head curator, but she wasn't very specific about your current work status.

**KNIGHT:** Be surprised if she could be. Whoever took your details down wasn't listening carefully, though. I'm not the head curator, just one of several. My duties are undefined because, if anything, you could say I'm the head of acquisitions. There one day, off to Istanbul or Hong Kong or ... well, possibly anywhere the next. I buy, sell and trade items of exotic and fantastic interest. It's a very fluid day-to-day kind of occupation. Terrific fun, hard to pin down. Perhaps you should move on to your next question.

**DETECTIVE LISANKI:** Sure. How about your age? Your birth date isn't shown here. You look to be in your mid-thirties. You were born around, what, nineteen eighty?

**KNIGHT:** Very good, detective. I'm impressed.

**DETECTIVE LISANKI:** Comes with the job. Now. I've already taken statements from a half dozen witnesses who attest to your presence at some kind of, ummmm, secret auction. In fact, they pretty much identify you as the head auctioneer. You a black marketer, Knight?

**KNIGHT:** I like how you cut right to the heart of a matter, detective, following your instincts, full speed ahead, raging onward no matter how wrong-headed or in total defiance of the facts they might be. Sort of like a veritable flesh-and-blood Occam's razor. You can Google that reference later on—I could spell it out for you if you like. And no, in case my show-don't-tell irritation isn't getting my answer across, dropping down into the mundane, I am not a criminal, nor have I broken any laws recently.

**DETECTIVE LISANKI:** I'll be the judge of that.

**KNIGHT:** Oh my, all ready to step beyond the boundaries of your calling all the way up to judgeship. Jury as well next, I suppose. Really, if you don't mind my saying, detective—and even if you do—I believe I need to point out that you seem to have concocted a rather colorful picture of me in your imagination. I'm going with colorful rather than actionable, because, after all, let's be friends. You stop trying to squeeze me into a tiny box that fits your I-don't-really-want-to-work-so-let's-railroad-the-first-poor-innocent-we-find police-business-as-usual tactic, and I'll try, oh so very hard, to think of you as just sloppy, or perhaps borderline incompetent, rather than actively hostile, or perhaps working with some ulterior motive. Here, here's a fresh start taking us back to the only actual facts on me within your possession. I am really a rather boring professional, detective, as I believe my references informed you earlier today?

**DETECTIVE LISANKI:** You really think you're something special, don't you, Knight?

**KNIGHT:** Guilty as charged. But then, again, referencing those previously mentioned references, so do others.

**DETECTIVE LISANKI:** Yeah—I noticed. Mayor of New York City, the Governor of the State of New York, the special agents in charge of the Manhattan, Albany and Buffalo FBI field offices, the Commanding General of Fort Drum, Secretary General of the U.N., Dexter Reynolds—

**KNIGHT:** Yes, the CEO of MicroTech ... shakes up the list, doesn't it?

**DETECTIVE LISANKI:** Yeah—that it did. Him, all of them, ever-so-happy to phone me this morning and tell me what a fine, upstanding citizen you are, though a bit shy in offering any specific details on what you've done to earn that loyalty. Altogether, quite a friends list, Mr. Knight.

**KNIGHT:** Yes, well, one should always keep an eye on their CV, shouldn't they? Now, where were we? Beyond all the opening salvo innuendo, what I believe you actually desire information about is the auction?

**DETECTIVE LISANKI:** Please.

**KNIGHT:** In short, three days ago, on Friday morning, I was contacted by Pitchman, Inc. and offered an admittedly, tremendously, lavishly large amount of money to act as a go-between to facilitate several transactions to be negotiated at the Fair.

**DETECTIVE LISANKI:** An illegal auction held at this so-called Traveling Luminous Museum?

**KNIGHT:** Oh, and there you go again, slipping in those little have-you-stopped-beating-your-wife questions. Honestly, detective, I don't mind your boorish clumsiness, but the slaps in the face, the obvious fact you consider me some sort of low-grade moron is becoming a bit irksome. Once more, and I'm going to have to assume you are actually hostile toward me for some reason, and then it's going to be messy, where's my lawyer time. So, for the record, I was not aware before, during, or even at this very moment considering that despite your vulgar insinuations I have not been charged with anything, of the exchange of any illegally acquired items at this event, detective.

**DETECTIVE LISANKI:** Right, you were just the innocent auctioneer.

**KNIGHT:** Not in the least. If you and yours had done any actual investigating, you would already be aware that my duties were not to sell or auction off anything at all, but rather to oversee the fair trading of the expensive and priceless items put upon the block.

**DETECTIVE LISANKI:** Say what?

**KNIGHT:** I'm one of the curators of the Brooklyn Museum, a quite distinguished museum, detective. As its head of acquisitions I am regarded as having one of the premier good eyes, as it were, for one-of-a-kind merchandise. Thus I was brought in more as an appraiser than a barking huckster, and this event was much more of a glorified swap meet than an accredited auction.

**DETECTIVE LISANKI:** And you never suspected, even for a moment, that anything being, what, swapped was black market goods, or outright illegal in nature at the auction?

**KNIGHT:** I saw nothing to indicate any item was stolen. There were no drugs or firearms amidst the objects in question. It wasn't my job to vet and/or do background checks on the private individuals invited to this closed, um, auction as you call it.

**DETECTIVE LISANKI:** All part of "the don't ask don't tell" policy implemented in big city museums these days.

**KNIGHT:** Detective, you have a sense of humor. I like that. Why else would you make such an obvious reference when talking about an event sanctioned by your own city?

**DETECTIVE LISANKI:** And you walk a fine line between propriety and legal responsibility, Mr. Knight.

**KNIGHT:** Detective, this grows wearying. Ask an actual question, or I shall assume we have concluded our business.

**DETECTIVE LISANKI:** The swap meet. Inside that giant tent museum at the fair. Which, by the way you've made no mention of—

**KNIGHT:** Because it has not figured as of yet in any of your *questions*, detective. Questions, those things of which you seen incapable of asking.

**DETECTIVE LISANKI:** At this tent museum, Mr. Knight, did maybe a friend of yours work there? Maybe someone with some special exhibits you wanted to acquire for your own workplace. Off the record? Out of sight of the IRS or the ITO?

**KNIGHT:** Oh, damn all the fools who plague me so ... the answer is no. Emphatically and categorically, I had never been acquainted with the admittedly eclectic displays of the Traveling Luminous Museum before yesterday, none of which I made any offer towards on behalf of the Brooklyn Museum, myself, the grand high exalted Poobah of Cashmiristan, Phineas T. Whoopie or anyone else. In fact, Sunday morning was the first time I had ever met, or even heard of, this wayfaring repository's docent.

**DETECTIVE LISANKI:** A Mr. Johnny? No last name?

**KNIGHT:** Right. I met him briefly for the first time yesterday. Interesting fellow. Hell of a memory for rare objects of uncommon origin.

**DETECTIVE LISANKI:** The stuff you oversaw the trading of.

**KNIGHT:** It is all on that list you are holding, detective. The one I gave that lovely lady police officer on my way in—yes?

**DETECTIVE LISANKI:** How many people attended this closed swap meet of yours?

**KNIGHT:** Once again, not of mine. How many people were in attendance at the affair in question where I was present as a consultant only ... difficult to say. The lighting was atrocious in the central chamber, where it was held. I say chamber but all the walls were canvas in what was nothing more than a one hundred foot clearing with a grass floor, a five-foot high wooden stage with a twelve foot square platform upon which I stood. I'd say at any one time there were no more than a dozen people present at any one time within the area I've just described. But over the course of five hours there was a steady trickle of traffic moving in and out of the event. It's possible one to ... I don't know, three hundred folks came and went during the entire affair. I made no attempt to count, could have been repeats.

**DETECTIVE LISANKI:** Your list shows that ninety-five trades were transacted, which coincidentally also happens to be the full content of your original inventory.

**KNIGHT:** The Luminous Museum's inventory, Detective—not mine. Yes, the trading was a complete success, everyone certainly seemed content, if not down-right pleased with whatever they received in their respective dealings, and no, I had never seen a single one of these objects before yesterday.

**DETECTIVE LISANKI:** Not one? Yet you could testify to their authenticity?

**KNIGHT:** I'm a competent appraiser, if you'll forgive my hubris. Hell, at this point I don't care if I'm forgiven or not. I don't need to have handled a particular Ming vase to identify it as one, any more than you have to handled a particular .38 caliber bullet to know one when you see one.

**DETECTIVE LISANKI:** And everything was on that stage?

**KNIGHT:** All the Luminous Museum's initial properties were displayed on the long table behind me, each item on its own pedestal, appropriately tagged and numbered. As for the objects and jewelry given in exchange, I secured them all, one at a time, per written instructions, in the large metallic container on the far right rear of the stage.

**DETECTIVE LISANKI:** One witness told me it looked like a giant steel barrel, twice as tall as a man, with a two-foot thick lid laying on the ground beside it. Does that sound right?

**KNIGHT:** Oddly enough, it looked to me, and I admit that the lighting was not the greatest in this ancient tent, like the storage unit was actually comprised of titanium.

**DETECTIVE LISANKI:** That couldn't have been cheap.

**KNIGHT:** Nothing about this operation was cheap.

**DETECTIVE LISANKI:** Hmmm … a weird list of objects, all right. Says here you accepted a necklace of black diamonds from a Mister Bak in exchange for a half dozen beer mugs. This can't be right.

**KNIGHT:** Thirteenth century Luxembourg Golden Bull beer steins, detective. Which I don't believe you could identify any more easily than you could: a Tyre Knop Baluster wine glass, a Rococo Newdigate centre-piece or a concertina-actioned card table. Extremely rare merchandise, which the recipient was quite pleased to have obtained, I assure you.

**DETECTIVE LISANKI:** Right. And this, a Miss Haumea gave you black diamond earrings in exchange for a, um, tattoo kit?

**KNIGHT:** A five thousand year old Egyptian tattoo kit, Detective. Quite possibly used on Pharaoh Narmer himself.

**DETECTIVE LISANKI:** Yeah. Hmmmm, a Miss Ashley Jepperson traded a walking stick with a black diamond crown for a bronze urn. And here is a change in pace, a Willy Carroll traded in one of those talking Freddy Puffkin teddy bears for a stone and wood horse toy?

**KNIGHT:** The horse on wheels was ancient Greek and dated nine-fifty BC.

**DETECTIVE LISANKI:** Seems that half the list is antique jewelry, so I can see some value there, but the other half, talking teddy bears, a cd player, a laptop computer, a couple of burned-out circuit boards, for Christ's sake, are you fucking kidding me?

**KNIGHT:** One man's treasure, and all that, detective.

**DETECTIVE LISANKI:** Whatever. I don't know if you were part of some grand scam or boondoggle or what, Knight. We can discuss that later. What I want to know right now is how the hell that damned fire started.

**KNIGHT:** I, well, sadly I must confess to being at a bit of a loss on that one myself, detective. As best I know, shortly before the, er, cataclysm—of which I was only informed this morning, I might add—I was rather unceremoniously shoved off the stage mere moments after the very last trade of the day. By who? I have no idea. And it was with such force that I was rendered unconscious when I struck the ground.

**DETECTIVE LISANKI:** And were rescued first thing this morning, buried under a pile of debris and smoking ashes, I might add. Looking at you now

I don't see a scratch. You want to tell me by what miracle you survived this holocaust?

**KNIGHT:** Perhaps fate has something special in store for me. Perhaps you should ask the kind Samaritans who dug me out from under the debris, or the emergency physicians who attended me at the time.

**DETECTIVE LISANKI:** That ring you're fiddling with … that your good luck charm or something?

**KNIGHT:** This old trinket? No, sort of a family heirloom, I suppose. Reminder of simpler times.

**DETECTIVE LISANKI:** And you really don't have any memory of what happened after you fell off the stage? How the fire started, and then all the, uh, disputed events that erupted across the fair grounds afterwards?

**KNIGHT:** I caught a few glimpses of a television monitor at Upstate Medical Center this morning. They were showing what was apparently cell phone footage. Looked like something from one of those big budget Hollywood monster movies. But, beyond that which everyone else has seen, I have nothing. A high tech prank of some kind, detective?

**DETECTIVE LISANKI:** Oh Mr. Knight, how I pray that was all it was.

**STATEMENT BY:** Syracuse, NY, resident Mandy Kothari to Detective William Lisanki, Syracuse Police Force, on Monday, September 1, 2015, at 16:11 hrs

**INTERVIEW CONDUCTED LESS THAN ONE DAY AFTER THE CATACLYSMIC EVENTS AT THE NEW YORK STATE FAIR.**

**PRESENT:** Miss Mandy Kothari; Detective William Lisanki

**DETECTIVE LISANKI:** So to confirm, your name is Mandy Neelam Kothari, you are sixteen years old, and your parents have signed the appropriate waivers to allow this interview, correct?

**MANDY:** Yes. Mom and dad are in the next room. They told me to tell you what I saw last night.

**DETECTIVE LISANKI:** Officer on the scene, Patrolman Matthews, says you were seen running from the Traveling Luminous Museum just moments after a fire started spreading from its roof.

**MANDY:** Museum?

**DETECTIVE LISANKI:** The huge tent inside the race track at the fair. It was a traveling museum.

**MANDY:** Oh wow. I mean, yes, that tent, I, uh, I guess I snuck into it.

**DETECTIVE LISANKI:** You guess?

**MANDY:** Yeah, I did. My girlfriends Tara and Connie dared me to. We figured it was some kind of freak show, you know? Like Bodyshock on the BBC America channel. I mean, jinkies! Who knew what I was gonna find. So yeah, I crawled under the wall at what I thought was the back.

**DETECTIVE LISANKI:** And?

**MANDY:** Well, I got lost for like an hour, which was really freaky, like being trapped in the Tardis.

**DETECTIVE LISANKI:** Excuse me?

**MANDY:** Huh? Oh, the Tardis. That's from Doctor Who.

**DETECTIVE LISANKI:** BBC America again?

**MANDY:** Yeah, right. I mean, the thing was big on the outside, but on the inside it was like it was even bigger. Like just a maze, with cloth walls, and all kinds of strange displays. I just kept walking around and looking at stuff.

**DETECTIVE LISANKI:** And you were alone the whole time?

**MANDY:** Almost. I mean, after awhile I figured the place must have been closed until evening, since I never actually saw anybody. I heard a lot of weird noises, but I figured that was coming from the displays. And man were they freaky. Like the coolest **3**-D displays you ever saw, like you could almost reach into them.

**DETECTIVE LISANKI:** Displays.

**MANDY:** Like tiny little stage shows, if that makes any sense. Well, anyways, I did bump into that one guy, who ended up being cool. That dosey guy, Johnny.

**DETECTIVE LISANKI:** Johnny, the Museum Docent.

**MANDY:** Right. At first I thought, damn—busted. But he was cool. Asked me how I was doing, if I was okay, and then just suggested I take nothing but left turns through the maze and I would find my way out. I look to the left for a moment and when I looked back he was gone. Friendly, but freaky tall. And that gold tooth ... that was kinda grody.

**DETECTIVE LISANKI:** Something tells me you didn't take his advice. Right, Mandy?

**MANDY:** Well, at first I did the left turn thing, you know? But then I swore I heard what sounded like a bunch of folks shouting. And then it hit me, instead of running around this maze, I could just drop to the ground and crawl under the curtain walls toward the yelling.

**DETECTIVE LISANKI:** And that's how you got to the auction room?

**MANDY:** Yeah, right. That big stage with all the people around it. Kinda like Auction Kings on the Discovery Channel. But the cute guy on the stage wasn't shouting out prices, he would just name stuff.

**DETECTIVE LISANKI:** How long were you in there?

**MANDY:** In the tent, or the auction room?

**DETECTIVE LISANKI:** Just the auction room.

**MANDY:** I dunno. Half an hour, maybe. Maybe less. I was off in a corner in the shadows, just watching. I don't think nobody saw me. And then, well, things got kinda crazy and I had to leave.

**DETECTIVE LISANKI:** Tell me exactly what happened. Tell me slowly and try not to leave anything out.

**MANDY:** It's like several things all at once, you know what I mean? Breaks down like this. The cute guy on stage, total Josh Duhamel vibe if you catch my drift, well he takes this MP**3** player from someone on the ground in front of him in exchange for some retro boom box, really ancient man, like from the nineteen eighties. Well, I forgot to say that all during this trading of stuff the cute auctioneer guy would hand off what he received to his assistant, a little guy, like, I mean, a little person you know, like this high. And this little person would walk it across the stage, climb up this little staircase/ladder and slowly lower the item into this steel barrel thing.

**DETECTIVE LISANKI:** But he did something different this time.

**MANDY:** Well, yeah, I think. The cute guy on stage leaned down to talk to someone on the ground when the little person had, like a handful of items this time, four or five things, small pieces of jewelry, and the MP**3** player, and what looked like an awesome necklace with a huge black gem on it, and the little guy was walking up his ladder and reaching forward with the stuff to drop it in the barrel when the shit hit the fan.

**DETECTIVE LISANKI:** Could you be more specific?

**MANDY:** Like it all went crazy. Just before the little guy dropped all the stuff into the barrel at the same time there was this freaky loud shout, or yell.

**DETECTIVE LISANKI:** A yell?

**MANDY:** Yeah, real loud, like Green Day singing Burnout on stage—totally awesome. See, this voice yells "don't, not all at the same time," and it is so loud it like hurts my ears even as far away from the stage as I am, but then the little guy drops the stuff in anyway, and there's this wild flash of green light from the barrel. So then, the little guy, I don't know what really happened, but I swear it looked like he suddenly just became a green skeleton, and then just disappeared, like on a Star Trek transporter pad. And at the same time that guy Johnny is whipping across the stage in a total blur, like so fast I can barely see him, and he shoves that cute auctioneer guy off the stage from behind and leaps like thirty feet through the air and lands on the barrel, man. It was *so* totally awesome!

**DETECTIVE LISANKI:** And then?

**MANDY:** Then, then it got really weird. Johnny just kinda laid down on top of the barrel with his whole body, like he was trying to keep something down, you know? All kinds of freaky green light and smoke was just blasting up and out of the barrel and it was making a crazy roaring like noise, and it started hurting my ears worse than that shout earlier.

And, I swear, Johnny was holding on really tight, I mean, it looked like his hands were squeezing into the sides of the barrel like it was made of clay, real superman stuff, you know? And, everyone else was running from the stage in all directions cause more green light and steam and noise was bleeding out under Johnny no matter how hard he seemed to block off the top, and then, God, I swear I'm not lying, he looked across the empty room—directly at me, as if he could see me in the shadows—and he ... he said, and somehow I could hear him even though the roaring from that barrel was making me deaf, Johnny, he says, "Run Mandy, leave now."

Oh crap, something snapped in me and I just turned and crawled away, under all the tent flaps, and kept crawling and crawling until suddenly I was outside, and people were running around and screaming and the big tent was on fire. I was so scared. I just ran to the main parking lot where the city bus stopped, and didn't look back.

**DETECTIVE LISANKI:** And that was it?

**MANDY:** Until this morning, when I saw the news on TV, and told mom and dad what happened.

**STATEMENT BY:** Ithaca, NY resident Peter Spall to Detective William Lisanki, Syracuse Police Force, on Monday, September **1**, **2015**, at **17:30** hrs.

**INTERVIEW CONDUCTED LESS THAN ONE DAY AFTER THE CATA-CLYSMIC EVENTS AT THE NEW YORK STATE FAIR.**

**PRESENT:** Mr. Peter Spall; Detective William Lisanki

**PETER:** Far out. This is just like a movie, or a Law and Order rerun. I am actually being interrogated by a cop. This is just too cool for school. No way.

**DETECTIVE LISANKI:** Way. And this is not an interrogation, Mr. Spall. We're here in search of the truth, nothing more nothing less. You understand?

**PETER:** Oh, yeah, totally copacetic man. I'm feeling you.

**DETECTIVE LISANKI:** Glad to hear it. So for the record, you are Peter Spall, thirty-nine years old, employee at Coviello's Comic Shop in Ithaca, New York. You attended the Great New York State Fair last night, Peter?

**PETER:** Yeah, and what a wild show they put on.

**DETECTIVE LISANKI:** You posted quite a detailed report on your blog. I have it right here. So, you were standing between the midway and the race track when you saw the museum tent burst into flames?

**PETER:** Right, I mean, I didn't know anything about any museum, but yes, I saw a huge burst of green fire and light blast right up into the sky from that giant circus tent, uh, I mean museum tent. There was really a museum under that?

**DETECTIVE LISANKI:** So I've been told. But, go on, what happened next?

**PETER:** The most awesome light show, and special effects extravaganza I have ever seen. You read my blog, you said.

**DETECTIVE LISANKI:** I did, but I need to hear it from your own lips. For the transcript.

**PETER:** Cool. All right, so I figure they must have been using the latest in water vapor **3**-D image projection. Last time I saw it used was on YouTube, they made this awesome pink rabbit run. But last night, man oh man, I figure they must have had the mother of all laser projectors in place, at least three of them, for that kind of coverage, not to mention dozens of water vapor generators to fill the air above the fairgrounds, and, oh yeah, hundreds of concert venue speakers in place, and all of it somehow hidden and camouflaged from public view. Yeah, that's how they did it.

**DETECTIVE LISANKI:** That's how they did it?

**PETER:** Best guess. I'm talking rad special effects, detective. What? You don't think a three hundred foot tall man and a three hundred foot tall Toho Studio's monster reject really got into a Kaiju-sized brawl at the Great New York State Fair, do you?

**DETECTIVE LISANKI:** The cell phone videos that've been flooding the Internet are pretty impressive.

**PETER:** It's all part of some Hollywood marketing campaign, detective—gotta be. They must've made those videos weeks, months in advance. Digital technology is the new magic.

**DETECTIVE LISANKI:** You were there, you saw the damage caused across the fairgrounds. You're telling me it was all fake?

**PETER:** Well, obviously some stuff got out of control. That's the problem with live special effects. That, and not telling anyone what's coming. You know they didn't plan on thousands of people taking it all seriously and panicking like that. But shit, it's a litigious world. You gotta be ready for the repercussions when you don't plan.

**DETECTIVE LISANKI:** Hundreds injured. Dozens killed by fire, collapsed buildings, folks trampled by the crowds. Yeah, you could say things got out of control. Now, from the top, exactly what did you see?

**PETER:** Okay, so first, this freaky looking giant glowing green monster, looking like something out of the ocean trench from every Godzilla flick ever suddenly appears over the race track, like, fifty feet above it, hovering, but not doing anything. Then like thirty seconds later this giant man, about the same height, thinner, not so massive, he appears in the air facing it from, like, one hundred feet away.

**DETECTIVE LISANKI:** A giant man.

**PETER:** Yeah, but nothing like that Japanese movie BIG MAN. This guy was dressed all in black, like in a suit, with a cool looking long trench coat. And he was wearing a fedora. Hard to see his face in the dark but it looked kinda clean cut. And, well, the giant man and monster just seemed to hover there and stare at each other for like two minutes before all hell broke loose.

**DETECTIVE LISANKI:** Do you think they were communicating with each other?

**PETER:** Huumph … I don't know. I didn't hear them say anything.

**STATEMENT BY:** Cayuga, NY resident Ileana Lupu to Detective William Lisanki, Syracuse Police Force, on Monday, September **1, 2015**, at **18:00** hrs.

**INTERVIEW CONDUCTED LESS THAN ONE DAY AFTER THE CATACLYSMIC EVENTS AT THE NEW YORK STATE FAIR.**

**PRESENT:** Miss Ileana Lupu; Detective William Lisanki

**DETECTIVE LISANKI:** Your name is Ileana Lupu, you're a recently naturalized citizen, formerly of Bacau, Romania, and you are a licensed astrologer in the state of New York.

**ILEANA:** Yes, I am.

**DETECTIVE LISANKI:** You run Madame Lupu's Gypsy Emporium at the state fair. Your booth is on the corner of the midway, next to the Talent Showcase and Midway Music Series. So you're a palm reader, Madame Lupu?

**ILEANA:** So? I'm in compliance with New York state law, officer. I display several large signs wherever I work that clearly state all divinations and readings are for the purposes of entertainment only. I'm not a con artist.

**DETECTIVE LISANKI:** And nobody cares about that here. I'm just trying to establish who you are, why you were at the state fair last night, and what you witnessed there, all right?

**ILEANA:** Hundreds of people were there. And me, I … I'm not sure what I saw. Why pick on me?

**DETECTIVE LISANKI:** Let me cut to the chase, Madame Lupu. I've interviewed ten people, of all ages, races, creeds, and colors, who all report witnessing the same thing, namely you going into some kind of convulsion when the, uh, large apparitions appeared above the race track. Now, I've seen your medical records and there's nothing to indicate any neurological issues in your background, so tell me, what do you think happened? Did you have some kind of …

**ILEANA:** Some kind of what? Psychic experience? Do you really believe in such things, Detective? Off the record?

**DETECTIVE LISANKI:** You were informed before you came in here this is all being recorded, so let's admit we both know it's all on the record, thank you very much. And as for what I believe, that's not important. I wasn't there. My job is to try and establish what happened. We have people dead, crippled for life, burned, scarred. And, if you're feeling the need to … have something on me … all right, let's just say after what I saw of what was left of the fair grounds this morning, the videos tearing across the Internet, and all the interviews I've done so far, I'm ready to believe some things you don't find in the regular play book. So please believe me when I say that I would just like to hear what you have to say. So again, do you believe in psychic phenomena, and such?

**ILEANA:** Before last night, hell no. Oh, don't look surprised, detective. Work's hard to find in this damned recession. A single mother has to do what she can to make money. My dark hair and green eyes, my obvious accent, I'm a natural and folks like the show I put on. But to answer your question, no, I've never really believed in astrology, the Tarot, palm reading, or any other form of divination.

**DETECTIVE LISANKI:** But last night was different, wasn't it? You were working, earning that much needed money in this terrible economy. So please, since we've established that you were there, can you please tell me what you remember about the event.

**ILEANA:** I … I can't believe I'm saying this. This is madness. I heard them, detective. They were not apparitions, they were real—those fantastic monstrous things, they were both real.

**DETECTIVE LISANKI:** You heard them?

**ILEANA:** Yes, in my mind—all right? During what you call my convulsions. Their voices were so loud, and terrible. It was very painful, and yes, though they only talked to each other for a couple of minutes I remember everything they said. Not that it made any sense, but I remember it all.

**DETECTIVE LISANKI:** Which was?

**ILEANA:** I see them so distinctly in my mind. The horrible green thing, the man shape, he called it the Dark One. And the Dark One, he called the man shape the Salesman.

**SO, FIRST THE DARK ONE SAYS:** Such fools, these human sheep, Salesman. First they bring my dark stone into this world, then they divide it multiple times and spread its pieces across their planet where for decades the shards have supped and lapped upon all the misery and hate and evil that bleeds from their darkest souls. Those black precious flecks of jewels have fed upon all the delicious fear and terror they have caused, and now, this night, these stupid insects you foolishly protect bring all the pieces back together again, breaching the portal that separates this garden from my own dominion, freeing me to wreak destruction.

**AND THEN, THE SALESMAN ANSWERED:** Actually, collecting the jewelry and computer chips in one location was my idea, Dark One. The containment chamber was specially designed to dispose of the ebony jewel shards, and would have done so quite effectively had my directions been followed more closely. It was only a minor aberrance that alerted you and allowed your ingress.

**DETECTIVE LISANKI:** Ingress?

**ILEANA:** What do I know? Look it up. Here's what I know.

**AFTER THAT, THE DARK ONE, HE SAYS:** I felt you blocking the opening, fallen one. And you almost succeeded. Almost.

**AND THE SALESMAN IGNORES THAT AND TELLS HIM:** You should not be here.

**THEN IT'S THE DARK ONE, AND HE SNAPS:** Oh, but I am, and if you love these playthings so much, why, exert your vaunted powers and attack me, prevent me from beginning my holocaust! What? No answer? Just a glare? Of course, you cannot do anything, can you? All the ancient legends are true. You are restrained from directly acting on these lower lifeforms' behalf. You can only engage in your petty trades, peddling your wares, for oh so many millennia, but all for naught because I have broken through before you ever anticipated I would. I have outwitted you and all of the universe's fates. I have arrived long before that mighty Sha'Daa you have fretted over for so long in anticipation of.

And no, I don't know what they're talking about. I don't know why it's all so burned into my mind. Don't bother asking. Let me just tell you the rest.

**SO THE SALESMAN, HE SNIPES BACK:** You would have been stopped. You would have been defeated, Dark One. Somehow, some way, humanity's bravery would have brought you down. Even with all the potential horrors that might have been released upon this world during The Sha'Daa, my petty trades, as you call them, would have brought you low. That is the high regard I hold you in, just one more minor death god from a backwater dimension that doesn't know its place.

**AND THE DARK ONE, HE GETS LOOPY HERE, GOING:** Deific scat, your disrespectful words mean nothing to me. My will is now all-powerful, should I wish it I could open dozens of portals to other hell dimensions just to show you what an impotent fool you and your millennia of trades are—what is that, fear I see in your eyes? Yes, I understand that now. Your precious Sha'Daa, the weakening of all portals between this world and all the realities in existence, it is only supposed to happen in the not too distant future, but not now, Salesman, oh no, you couldn't bear if it happened now, right this moment, before all your thousands of little schemes and plans can come to fruition.

**AND SO THE SALESMAN SAYS THAT THE DARK ONE WOULDN'T DARE.**

**AND THE DARK ONE SNAPS BACK:** Wouldn't I? To have to share the destruction of this world with other entities will be a small price to pay to witness your total loss of all hope, and your complete despair. Oh the look on your face is so delicious. So be it. I extend all my powers to all the hundreds upon hundreds of dimensional barriers that freckle this luscious biosphere. I declare to the universe, I am making The Sha'Daa occur right now!

**AND THEN, THE SALESMAN, HE THANKS THE DARK ONE, AND THE DARK ONE STARTS SCREAMING ABOUT HIS ENERGIES BEING DRAINED OFF INTO THE ETHER. SO HE SCREAMS A BUNCH, ASKING WHAT HE'S BEING THANKED FOR.**

**AND THE SALESMAN SAYS:** For freeing me of my shackles. The Sha'Daa is the most holy of holies, a sacred elemental convergence that none, absolutely none may prevent, hurry, or significantly alter. And for your unforgivable sacrilege I am allowed freedom from my one ancient restriction, this one time, this one night. And on that note, you really should not have destroyed my museum. Because that made it personal.

**DETECTIVE LISANKI:** Then what happened?

**ILEANA:** Then? Then it was over. At least, it was for me. I could feel they were going to go at it, but I didn't see it, or feel it, or anything. Sorry … that's when I blacked out.

**STATEMENT BY:** Oneida, NY resident Eleanor Gowry to Detective William Lisanki, Syracuse Police Force, on Monday, September **1, 2015**, at **19:00** hrs.

**INTERVIEW CONDUCTED LESS THAN ONE DAY AFTER THE CATACLYSMIC EVENTS AT THE NEW YORK STATE FAIR.**

**PRESENT:** Mrs. Eleanor Gowry, Detective William Lisanki

**DETECTIVE LISANKI:** Now, Mrs. Gowry, you attended the state fair last night, correct?

**ELEANOR GOWRY:** Of course. I go every year. Have for over thirty years, though, boy oh boy, has it gone downhill in that time. I mean, first they got rid of the Sky Lift which was the coolest thing—that let you get a great overhead view of most of the midway, and then a few years later they got rid of the arcade tent, and then, just a few years ago, suddenly the go-cart track is no longer there, and did that ever make my nephews angry! But they brought it back last year so at least there is that.

**DETECTIVE LISANKI:** Yes, well, about last night.

**ELEANOR GOWRY:** And don't get me started on my coffee. I always get my large cup of Dunkin Donuts coffee at the state fair, sixty percent discount with my Fair Coupon, but for two whole years now, no way. And why? The stupid Fair and Dunkin just could come to whatever financial agreement they usually do. And guess what I'm stuck having to drink?

**DETECTIVE LISANKI:** I'm sorry, Mrs Gowry, I really have no idea.

**ELEANOR GOWRY:** Tim Hortons! That vile Canadian crap they dare to call coffee. Can you believe it?

**DETECTIVE LISANKI:** Last night, Mrs. Gowry, the, uh, altercation. Exactly what did you see?

**ELEANOR GOWRY:** Well, it all happened so fast. I remember walking out of the Horticulture Building with my supper. My potato. You know every year I always get my free steamed potato from the Potato Booth with my State Fair coupon, well, I had it covered with all my favorites, sour cream, bacon bits, onions, salt and pepper—

**DETECTIVE LISANKI:** And then?

**ELEANOR GOWRY:** Oh, well I snuck quick into the Dairy building before it closed to get my twenty-five cent carton of milk, three flavors you know, and I chose chocolate, then walked over to the Veterans and **9/11** Memorials to eat my potato when a bright green flash of light almost blinded me. I looked up and saw those two giants up in the sky, just overhead.

**DETECTIVE LISANKI:** Go on.

**ELEANOR GOWRY:** The giant man, I figure he must have been an angel, he moved forward and just decked that ugly monster from hell. Punched him like he was John Wayne at the end of THE QUIET MAN, you know what I mean? Well he really connected because that spawn of Satan was knocked back and down and actually fell on the Horticulture building! Crushed it flat it did. Good thing I'd left outta there. It was near closing time so the place was mostly empty, but still, that was no fit end for the potato booth. A real shame. But then, detective, oh then I realized the true horror of it all.

**DETECTIVE LISANKI:** What, Miss Gowry? What happened then?

**ELEANOR GOWRY:** My poor stuffed potato, I had dropped it on the ground during all the commotion. Ruined. And I didn't have any more State Fair coupons. Oh, the humanity!

**STATEMENT BY:** Massena, NY resident Alan Smoke to Detective William Lisanki, Syracuse Police Force, on Monday, September **1, 2015**, at **20:00** hrs,

Interview conducted less than one day after the cataclysmic events at the New York State Fair.

**PRESENT:** Mr. Alan Smoke; Detective William Lisanki

**DETECTIVE LISANKI:** Mr. Smoke, you are a resident of Massena, NY, is that correct?

**ALAN:** I have homes in Massena, and also on the Akwesasne Mohawk reservation, both American and Canadian sides.

**DETECTIVE LISANKI:** The St. Regis, right—I'd hate to be your accountant, sir. Well, let's just get right to it. You had a booth in the Center of Progress Building at the State Fair yesterday, correct?

**ALAN:** Yes. I own part of a swimming pool contracting franchise. And, oh my, business is good.

**DETECTIVE LISANKI:** Good, glad to hear it. I'm told you witnessed some of the, um, altercation that occurred? Could you please relate anything you remember?

**ALAN:** It was near closing time and I had just broken down my booth and loaded up my van. I gave my table area one more check, and then walked out the front of the Center of Progress Building right before they were going to lock the doors. And then I saw it.

**DETECTIVE LISANKI:** What did you see, sir?

**ALAN:** Two mighty spirits battling. A giant green monster was throwing its green fire upon a giant man. Both were many times larger than the Stone Coat legends of my people. Larger than the story of Oniare, the dragon of the Great Lakes, or the two, giant, grandfather mosquitos of the Seneca River. The green monster rose from the ruins of the Horticulture Building and with a blast of fire knocked the giant man through the air to land upon the Chevy Court stage, crushing the band that was performing there. Some new wave group in their late thirties—I was never a fan.

**DETECTIVE LISANKI:** And then what happened?

**ALAN:** The giant man quickly stood up, appearing unharmed. Hundreds of people fled in all directions, looking like insects upon the ground around his feet. The giant man then smiled at the approaching green monster. His smile nearly blinded me. His mouth was filled with huge white teeth, but it was not them that made me squint my eyes. One of his teeth, nearly the size of a small house, was like a golden amber bonfire, and it flashed with a mighty brilliance. And then both of these giants leaped into the air and collided, and there was a horrible explosion, and I was knocked to the ground. I did not wake up until many hours later at Upstate Medical Center.

**DETECTIVE LISANKI:** It's a miracle you didn't end up in the happy hunting ground, Alan.

**ALAN:** Detective, you ain't just peddling whiskey.

**STATEMENT BY:** Massena, NY resident Robin East to Detective William Lisanki, Syracuse Police Force, on Monday, September **1, 2015**, at **21:00** hrs.

**INTERVIEW CONDUCTED LESS THAN ONE DAY AFTER THE CATACLYSMIC EVENTS AT THE NEW YORK STATE FAIR.**

**PRESENT:** Ms. Robin East; Detective William Lisanki

**DETECTIVE LISANKI:** Now, Miss East, you were a passenger aboard a Robinson R**66** helicopter that overflew the State Fair last night, correct?

**ROBIN:** Yes, me and two others. Raven Helicopters. I take their ride every year, that is, if my husband doesn't throw a fit at the cost. Seventy-five bucks is a lot of money, all right, but come on, the fair only comes once a year.

**DETECTIVE LISANKI:** I've viewed the video you took on your smart phone. I'm going to play it back now on this large monitor. I noticed you had the audio turned off.

**ROBIN:** That's my fault. It's a new phone. I'd never used it for video-taping before.

**DETECTIVE LISANKI:** No problem. Now, if you could just tell me everything you remember, and heard and felt while you were shooting this? A lot of the footage is a little too shaky and blurry for us to simply say, this is happening. For legal reasons, you understand. It would help a lot of people if we had a better idea of what we were seeing.

**ROBIN:** Everything, at first, it was all pretty straight forward. Not much different from other flights I'd taken. So, here you can see the sun's gone down, it's dark, and the midway is all lit up and it is so beautiful. And, of course, there's that giant white tent covering the entire race track, which believe you me caused quite a stir among a lot of folks the week before the Fair started.

**DETECTIVE LISANKI:** A stir?

**ROBIN:** Oh, of course! All the RV parking usually inside the main track just went out the window, now didn't it? Pissed a ton of regular attendees off. Oh, I'm sorry. I probably shouldn't swear during this, huh?

**DETECTIVE LISANKI:** Not a problem. You were saying?

**ROBIN:** Huh? Oh, the giant tent, right. Well it stuck out like a giant sore thumb, huge as it was, reflecting light from the midway and all the light poles. And then here, you see? Suddenly the top of the tent catches on fire. And not ordinary, you know, red and yellow and black flames, but these bright green flames that seemed impossible.

**DETECTIVE LISANKI:** And what made them seem impossible to you?

**ROBIN:** They were so high up in the air, higher than the clouds, even. Look at them. Okay, here we are just circling it all from, I don't know, several hundred feet away, when the rest of the tent catches on fire and then—see it? See it ... there! Can you believe that? Some kind of giant monster. And now the even weirder part, yes, there! That giant man, look at them both. Just staring each other down, not moving at all.

**DETECTIVE LISANKI:** And your pilot just kept hovering at the perimeter of this?

**ROBIN:** What? Yeah, I guess so, gee, I don't know. Maybe he just thought it was part of the show, or maybe like the rest of us, he was just hypnotized, you know? We could not look away. Wait, right there. Damn, you can't see it cause some wind draft rocked the helicopter and shook my arm, but that giant man, I swear, looked right at me for a moment and winked! Oh, don't look at me like that. I am a decent, Christian woman. I don't drink. I don't smoke the pot. And, I don't lie, especially to police officers. You're trying to help people, and ... and, I don't know ... it's just what happened.

**DETECTIVE LISANKI:** There are no judgments here, ma'am. Not today. Not with this. Just, if you could go on...?

**ROBIN:** Okay, so we leveled off and the auto focus clicked in and ... yeah, that green monster thing gets knocked onto the ground by the big guy dressed like Humphrey Bogart. Oh, again things get all blurry because the helicopter practically flipped over here. Good thing we had our seat belts on. It was weird, all right. All kinds of wind gusts seemed to be coming from the direction of the giants, like, I dunno, waves of energy shooting off everywhere whenever they struck each other.

**DETECTIVE LISANKI:** Now right here, you seem to stabilize at this point.

**ROBIN:** Yeah, here they were looking at each other from either side of Chevy Court and then—well, bam—look at that, they're just flying right at each other. And that's when it happened.

**DETECTIVE LISANKI:** What? What happened? Your camera seems to have shut off at this point.

**ROBIN:** The explosion. Nearly knocked us out of the sky. But that was hardly the worst of it. The pilot just manages to keep us from flipping over all over again when all of a sudden he starts screaming.

**DETECTIVE LISANKI:** Screaming, why?

**ROBIN:** Cause we were getting pulled in!

**DETECTIVE LISANKI:** Pulled into what?

**ROBIN:** I don't know. It was really freaky though. Like some kind of whirlpool in the air. There was all kinds of lightning flashes and it was hard to see, but there was like this huge hole in the sky above the state fair, and it was sucking in all kinds of debris and trash and stuff … anything that wasn't nailed down. I could see we were slowly moving towards it and we all started yelling at the pilot to get us out of there, and he yelled back he was trying. And the wind started roaring and it was deafening, it hurt my ears so much. God, I hate to say it, but I swear I almost pissed my pants. The two giants were both wrestling each other, about halfway into the hole, almost filling its interior circumference, but still that air flow was pulling us in. And then we were only a couple of hundred feet away and I could see dozens of people swept up off the ground, screaming, and sucked away up into the hole, oh it was so terrible. Jesus bless us sinners, I can still hear that screaming now … and then, then, the hole closed. Just like that.

**DETECTIVE LISANKI:** It closed?

**ROBIN:** Yeah, with a huge thunder clap. And the helicopter lurched forward suddenly, like a rubber band pulled so tight that it had been snapped. I only caught a glimpse of the hole in the sky closing. Both the giants had been pulled into it. The giant man, I could see his hand reaching out of the hole, and then being pulled back inside right before it closed.

**DETECTIVE LISANKI:** So he didn't escape?

**ROBIN:** Didn't look like it. But, I don't know. The pilot, see, suddenly he couldn't control the helicopter any more, and it was just a few seconds later we crash-landed in front of the International Horse Show at the Toyota Coliseum. And now, after all is said and done, I have to agree with my husband.

**DETECTIVE LISANKI:** Agree on what?

**ROBIN:** I am never taking another helicopter ride for the rest of my life … as far as I'm concerned, they're for the birds.

**DETECTIVE LISANKI:** Ma'am, if you and your husband ever drink, I'd be happy to invite you for a round, to celebrate your survival.

**ROBIN:** Oh no, we never. Thank you, though, but that's all right.

**DETECTIVE LISANKI:** Then, if you'll excuse me, I think I'll go and celebrate your survival on my own.

# TOP SECRET–CIA–EYES ONLY

*Date: Thursday, January 19, 2017*

*Re: EO 13859-Theta*

*From: Barack Obama, Office of the outgoing President*

*To: Secret Senate Select Committee on Paranormal Dangers (aka Project Black Stone)*

*Following one hundred and nine years of Executive precedent, and accounting for inflation since 2009, as my last official act I hereby approve Executive Order 13859-Theta, the classified and top secret sequestration of fifty billion dollars for the study, research, and creation of weapons and defenses in anticipation of future cataclysmic events and hostilities heretofore designated as "The Sha'Daa."*

Visit

SHADAA.COM

for all author biographies, the secret history of

this chilling franchise, and the inside

low-down on all the books in

Michael H. Hanson's

Sha'Daa™ series

(including those currently in the works)

and how you can order them.


THE SHA'DAA IS COMING.


ARE YOU READY?

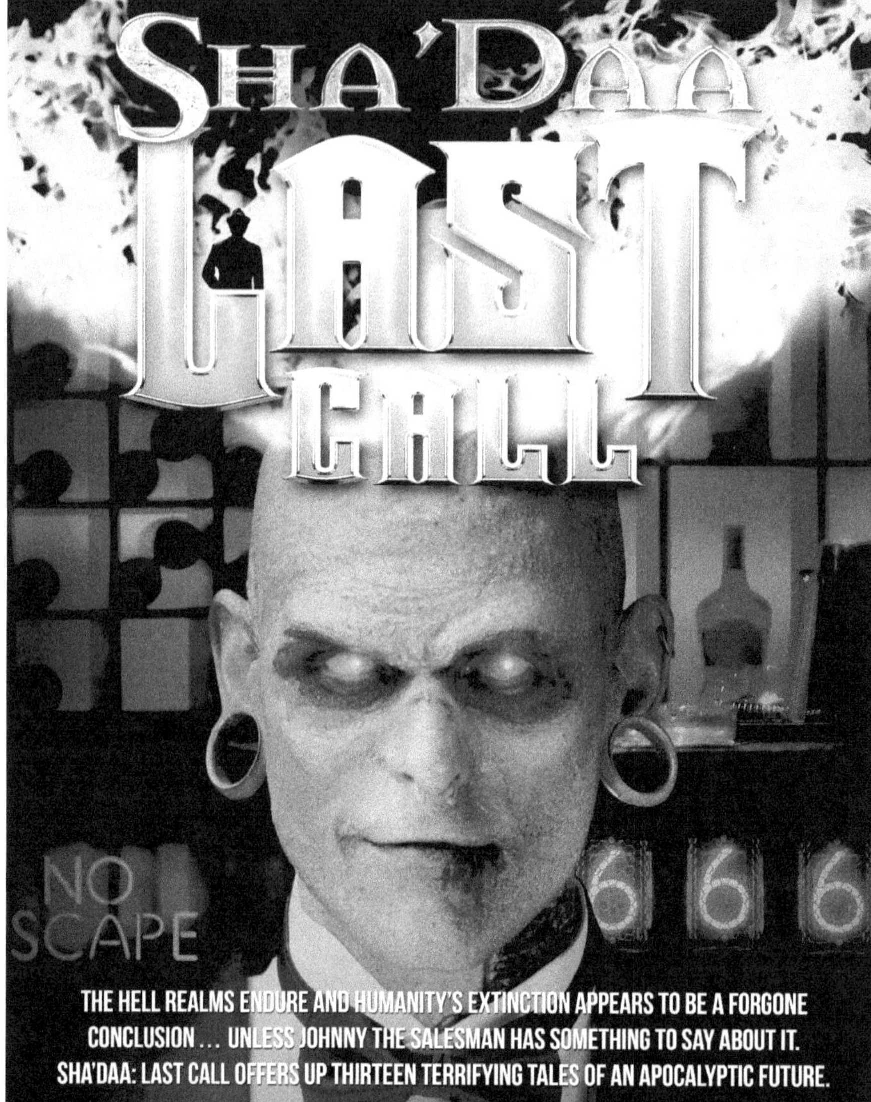
SHA'DAA
LAST
CALL
NO
SCAPE
6 6 6
THE HELL REALMS ENDURE AND HUMANITY'S EXTINCTION APPEARS TO BE A FORGONE
CONCLUSION … UNLESS JOHNNY THE SALESMAN HAS SOMETHING TO SAY ABOUT IT.
SHA'DAA: LAST CALL OFFERS UP THIRTEEN TERRIFYING TALES OF AN APOCALYPTIC FUTURE.

SHA'DAA: LAST CALL — THE APOCALYPSE CONTINUES. . .
NOW AVAILABLE FROM

MoonDream
PRESS     AN IMPRINT OF COPPER DOG PUBLISHING LLC

# Excerpt From
# SHA'DAA: Last Call

**T**HE LAST AND LARGEST OF THE THREE burning globes, the blue one, slowly dropped to the floor. In seconds it grew into the shape of a perfectly proportioned twenty-foot tall woman, naked, hairless, buxom, and possessing slightly Asiatic features. Yama bowed to Johnny. Colored a dark sapphire from head to foot, the death god was almost too beautiful to behold. Held tightly in Yama's right hand was a glistening, black, mace.

"Public decency laws aside, Sweetie," Johnny said. "I don't take kindly to bullies messing with my friend's place of business."

"Long have I admired your honorable crusade, Salesman," Yama spoke with a gorgeous lilting voice. "Coyote, Jack, Raven, Kokopeli, Anansi, Seth, Loki, Prometheus, so many brave names over thousands of years."

"So you're a celebrity stalker with a cobalt fetish," Johnny said. "I'll give you my agent's cell phone number right after you leave."

"But I," Yama continued unfazed, "will always think of you as…Nommo."

Johnny's eyes grew wide in realization.

"You," Johnny spat accusatively.

"Ill met underground," Yama giggled like a giant child. "Do you like my latest incarnation? Not bad for such a dramatic demotion from the higher ranks. And now I will end your mighty crusade, Salesman, destroying you just one trade away from completing your final penance. Funny, isn't it? That she who you robbed of the azure flame of sentience, she who suffers as one of the fallen for your crimes, is the one who brings all of your actions to naught?"

Johnny turned his head to the side and slowly spit. Then he stood tall, arms to his side, and made eye contact with the towering Yama.

"Well," Johnny said. "Are you gonna draw that mace, or whistle Dixie?"

To read more, look for *Sha'Daa: Last Call*, available now on
Amazon.com and Createspace.com.